JANEEN WEBB is a multiple award-winning author, editor, and critic who has written or edited ten books and over a hundred essays and stories. She is a recipient of the World Fantasy Award, the Peter MacNamara SF Achievement Award, the Australian Aurealis Award, and is a three-time winner of the Ditmar Award.

Her award-winning short fiction has appeared in a wide range of magazines and anthologies, as well as a number of Best of the Year collections. Her longer fiction includes a series of novels for young adult readers, *The Sinbad Chronicles*, (HarperCollins, Australia).

She is also co-editor, with Jack Dann, of the influential Australian anthology *Dreaming Down-Under*.

Janeen has also co-authored several non-fiction works with Andrew Enstice. These include *Aliens & Savages*; *The Fantastic Self*; and an annotated new edition of Mackay's 1895 scientific romance, *The Yellow Wave*.

Janeen is internationally recognised for her critical work in speculative fiction. Her criticism has appeared in most of major journals and standard reference works, as well as in several collections of scholarly articles published in Australia, the USA, and Europe. She was co-editor of *Australian Science Fiction Review*, and reviews editor for *Eidolon*. She holds a PhD in literature from the University of Newcastle.

Janeen divides her time between Melbourne and a small farm overlooking the sea near Wilson's Promontory, Australia.

DEATH AT *The Blue Elephant*

DEATH AT *The Blue Elephant*

JANEEN WEBB

T℥
p℥
Ticonderoga
publications

Death at the Blue Elephant by Janeen Webb

Published by Ticonderoga Publications

Cover by Nick Stathopoulos

Designed and edited by Russell B. Farr
Typeset in Sabon and Japan

A Cataloging-in-Publications entry for this title is available from The National Library of Australia.

ISBN 978-1-921857-75-3 (limited hardcover)
     978-1-921857-76-8 (trade hardcover)
     978-1-921857-77-5 (trade paperback)
     978-1-921857-78-2 (ebook)

All stories are works of fiction.

Ticonderoga Publications
PO Box 29 Greenwood
Western Australia 6924

#48

www.ticonderogapublications.com

10 9 8 7 6 5 4 3 2 1

The author would like to thank the following people for their help and support:

Norman and Paddy Broberg, Ramsay Campbell, Jack Dann, Helen Doherty, Ian Drury, Andrew Enstice, Dennis Etchison, Russell B. Farr, Keith Ferrell, Martin H. Greenberg, Liz Grzyb, Louise Harris, David Hartwell, Talie Helene, John Helfers, David Marsh, Sophie Masson, Christopher Mogan, Simon Petrie, Rob Porteous, Gillian Polack, Pamela Sargent, Mark Shirrefs, John Sinisgalli, Stephanie Smith, Cat Sparks, Jonathan Strahan, Nick Stathopoulos, Anna Tambour, Dena Taylor, Louise Thurtell, Dianne Walker, George Zebrowski.

Contents

Introduction

Pamela Sargent

As both a reader and an anthologist, I've always taken a particular pleasure in reading collections of short fiction, whether by writers whose novels I've enjoyed or by authors new to me. It's especially gratifying to read a writer's first collection of short fiction, being exposed to a new writer's talents, and hearing a new and distinctive voice. If you who are reading this are anything like me, you will treasure this collection and immediately begin wishing for more such elegant fiction from Janeen Webb.

It was my good fortune as an editor to have two of my anthologies improved by both Janeen's advice and her fiction. (I should mention that she is a notable anthologist herself, having edited the Ditmar and World Fantasy Award-winning anthology *Dreaming Down-Under* with Jack Dann.) The first improvement came about when she strongly recommended that I read a short fiction collection by the Australian writer Rosaleen Love, which is why one of my 1995 *Women of Wonder* anthologies is graced with Love's fine story "Alexia and Graham Bell". The second was when I was editing an original anthology of historical fantasy and alternative history stories featuring important historical figures, *Conqueror Fantastic*, and Janeen sent me her story "The Lion Hunt". The central character of this story is Alexander the Great, and "The Lion Hunt" is one of those rare stories that captures you and then doesn't let go at the end, when the historical implications of the story's conclusion overwhelm you and you realize how much our history would have changed as a result of what befalls Alexander here.

Conqueror Fantastic was published in 2004; that same year, Janeen's story "Red City" appeared in my partner George Zebrowski's original anthology *Synergy SF: New Science Fiction* and was later reprinted by David G. Hartwell and Kathryn Cramer in their *Year's Best SF 10* in 2005. Set in India, "Red City" involves an anthropologist, his extremely irritating and very well-characterized wife, beautifully rendered historical details, a carefully worked time loop, and descriptive passages evoking the atmosphere, heat, and humidity of the setting so well that anyone reading the story is likely to swelter even in the middle of a cold winter.

Both of these stories appear in this collection, along with the delicious and creepily effective title story, "Death at the Blue Elephant," in which Death wanders into a trendy restaurant and seems like just the sort of stalker you'd expect to encounter in such a place, and "Velvet Green", where a young woman attending her cousin's somewhat tedious and annoying wedding encounters a "green man", that symbol of nature and rebirth, and follows him on a mission to rescue a careless young man who has been enraptured and imprisoned by the Queen of Elfland but seems reluctant to escape his captivity. In "Incident on Woolfe Street", the myth of the werewolf is used to depict an immigrant's dislocation and struggle to adapt to a new environment; "The Sculptor's Wife" combines elements of the Pygmalion legend, tales of the Arthurian "Lady of the Lake" Nimue, and the horror of the Prosper Mérimée story "La Vénus d'Ille" to tell the story of a monstrous creature who finds herself right at home in our celebrity-obsessed culture. The author also evokes the dangerous beauty of the Australian wilderness in "The Lady of the Swamp" and in "Manifest Destiny", a horror story rooted in the European settlement of such wildernesses and the crimes that resulted from them. And in the moving and sharply drawn "Blake's Angel", a poet seeking inspiration finds it in the form of an illegally captured and caged angel.

Janeen Webb admits to being "an inveterate traveler," and one of the delights of these stories is their varied settings—an Australian shore in "Skull Beach", the Canadian border in "Niagara Falling", Thailand in "Tigershow", and Britain in "Gawain and the Selkie's Daughter", to mention only four examples—in which the author's characters, unlike some fiction inspired by travel, manage to fully inhabit these settings rather than simply passing through them. She also brings a scholarly background in literature and a critic's eye to her stories without ever allowing her knowledge to clutter or weigh down her prose or the lens of a critic to cloud or distort her clear, disturbing, and compelling visions. There are layers in these stories that compel one to reread them and yet they also remain accessible to any reader who enjoys a well-told tale. They are so enticing, in fact, that I had to restrain myself from sitting down and reading the entire collection at one sitting. My advice, hard as it will be to follow, is to resist this temptation and allow each of these finely wrought stories to weave its spell and live within you for a time before you go on to the next one.

I read these stories under the best possible circumstances, while on a vacation in New York state's Adirondack Mountains in a cabin with few distractions, which allowed for the kind of compulsive reading and wallowing in books that I recall from childhood— the kind of reading that I suspect many people long for and find increasingly harder to experience in our age of distractions. I soon found myself in a kind of enraptured state that seemed strangely familiar but still hard to identify. It took a few days before I realized that the feeling I had had on first encountering tales of Greek and Roman mythology (some of Janeen's favorite childhood reading as well as my own) and fairy tales by the Brothers Grimm, that combination of suspenseful anticipation, nervous apprehension, and total absorption in something far removed from my own experience, had been reawakened in me by these stories. For that, and for the way in which she uses the fantastic to illuminate our past and present human lives, I admire her writing and envy you your first encounters with the imaginative journeys that lie ahead.

PAMELA SARGENT
OCTOBER 2013

Preface: What Am I Doing Writing Fiction?

The process of compiling this collection has forced me to take a long, hard look at my short stories. What do I see?

In retrospect, I can see that many of these stories are urban fantasies, and that a lot of them could be read as magical realism. I have taken ordinary experiences—a bad meal at a cafe, a nightmare, a holiday—and put them through a metaphorical blender: a process of estrangement that creates new, extraordinary situations which demand a reaction. My characters see the world through the lens of the baggage that they carry—personal, social, and ideological—so responding to strange situations, seeing the truth of what confronts them, is always a challenge.

I have always been drawn to the worlds of myth, epic, and romance; to folk and fairy tales; to the quasi-historical stories of heroes such as King Arthur, and Beowulf. I am equally fascinated by history, and by the ways in which historians construct their narratives from fragments of the past. I grew up on traditional tales. My favourite childhood book was Edith Hamilton's *Mythology*: a scholarly paperback that offered potted versions of classic tales from Greek, Roman and Norse mythology—the "Tales of Gods and Heroes"—and the stories stuck. In later years I added as many stories from other cultures as I could find into the mix.

All of these things peep in at the edges of my writing. One of the most liberating aspects of this background is that ancient stories are not constrained by concepts of age and gender: the macho heroes are there, of course, but equally a girl might rescue a prince, or an elderly lady might wield great power. So this collection contains some stories with young protagonists who face situations no less challenging than those that confront their older counterparts; it also contains tales whose protagonists are very old indeed. There are alternate histories, time-slip stories, re-workings of the "known" into the unknowable, even hard science fiction. The process of extrapolation holds steady for all these things, a storytelling tool that allows me to play with different realities to find out where they lead.

In many ways our stories cannot help but reflect our personal histories, and mine are no different in that respect. I have always been an inveterate traveller, often seeking out the physical locations of the myths and histories of my reading, often getting into dangerous situations in the process. Travelling, like storytelling, isn't always safe. So the stories in this collection have widely varied settings—some are located at home in Australia, but other settings range from the United Kingdom to India, from America to South-East Asia, from Europe to the Middle East.

It makes for an eclectic mix. What remains constant is that metaphors are actualized; creatures and characters from myth, legend, fairytale and history rub shoulders with ordinary people; and always the stories bounce off a wide range of literary sources. My protagonists come face to face with the uncanny, the supernatural, and the bizarre as they try to make sense of their mundane lives.

It seems natural enough to me: I'm still trying to make sense of my own . . .

Velvet Green

If you start looking, Green Men are everywhere—they turn up in stone statues and bas-reliefs and friezes, on pub signs and ceiling bosses, in stained glass windows, and in all manner of most unlikely places. I've always loved the Green Men that lurk under the seats in English churches, and inhabit the woodlands to bear witness to the irrepressible power of the natural world. I once dragged my friend Helen all over the UK on a personal "Green Man" tour, looking at as many variations on these wonderful carvings as I could find. The Green Man in this romance is as dangerous as any of them—like any greenworld personage he acts for his own ends, and not necessarily for the good of the humans he encounters. Here, a modern girl with attitude accidentally summons a traditional trickster, Jack-in-the-Green, who entangles her in a deadly dangerous confrontation in the world beyond the wood.

Janet shifted uneasily in her place. The wooden pew was hard, and the wedding was taking forever. It seemed such a waste of a rare sunny Saturday afternoon. The groom looked stiff as a penguin in his rented suit. And her cousin Celia reminded her of a very large meringue, standing there at the altar in her frothy white dress of tulle and satin with a wreath of pale flowers crowning her virginal white veil.

"As if," Janet muttered under her breath, "*she hasn't been living with Paul for the last two and a half years.*"

The minister droned on, mouthing the traditional platitudes about love and fidelity and sanctity.

Janet tried to shut out the ceremony by concentrating on the Abbey's famous architecture. She let her gaze linger on the ancient golden stone with its elaborate carvings, then she followed the line of the soaring gothic pillars that branched at the top into fine fan tracery. The afternoon sunlight lit up the myriad greens of the new altar window's great tree of life, making it glow: the stained-glass branches arched towards the carved roof high above her, reaching past the gilded ceiling bosses to the heavens beyond.

The minister got to the part about sex. "Marriage," he was saying, "was ordained for the procreation of children, to be brought up in the fear and nurture of the Lord, and for the praise of His holy Name. It was ordained for a remedy against sin, and to avoid fornication; that such persons as have not the gift of continency might marry, and keep themselves undefiled . . . "

"*It's a bit late for that,*" Janet thought. "*Everyone knows Celia's pregnant.*" She leaned a little forward and put her hand under the seat, tracing with her fingertips the outlines of the green man carved there. She'd admired him when she'd first come into the Abbey—the hinged seats had all been up, revealing the carvings that adorned their undersides. Janet had chosen to sit on the green man—his leering leafy face with a carved tongue sticking out suited her mood. His face said exactly what she thought about cousin Celia's wedding.

The wooden tongue curled around her questing finger, and licked her.

Janet gasped, and pulled her hand away.

"Don't fidget," her mother hissed.

"Sorry," Janet whispered. She shrugged off her mother's grasp. "Some horrible kid's left something sticky under there. It's disgusting."

"Then leave it alone."

Janet looked down at her hands in her lap. Her finger was wet. She wiped it on her green gypsy skirt, the silk skirt her mother had objected to as unsuitable for a wedding. The finger left a damp stain.

Janet sat patiently for a few minutes, but curiosity got the better of her. She couldn't remember seeing anything stuck to the green man earlier, and she couldn't leave the thought of him alone. Tentatively, she slid her hand back under the seat, gingerly touching the carving.

The green man bit her.

Janet felt his teeth pierce her skin, felt the hot drop of blood that sprang from her fingertip onto his cool carved wooden face.

Without thinking, she stuck her finger in her mouth to suck the wound. She tasted green sap, sweet in her mouth against the salt of her blood.

Everything changed.

The minister was still solemnly intoning ceremonial words over the meringue and the penguin. But there, lounging against the carved stairs that led to the pulpit, grinning broadly, as if at some private joke, was the strangest man Janet had ever seen. He was tall and lean and supple, and he seemed, at first glance, to have a face of leaves. His full green beard curled like new bracken fronds over his chest, and his long hair hung down to his elbows, coiling and twisting about him like a living cloak of vine tendrils. He wore breeches the colour of fir trees, and with them a shirt of softest green, the colour of new leaves. To this he had added a waistcoat embroidered in all the greens of a forest glade, with bright birds and butterflies picked out in golden thread. Over his shoulder he carried a long, tattered cloak of green velvet. He was barefoot, but upon his head he wore a crown of oak leaves, and in his right hand he carried a holly staff. It was as if the old forest had come into the abbey, with oak leaves tangled in its long green hair.

Janet watched in wonder as he reached a negligent green hand into his woven belt and took out a silver horn. He set it to his lips, and blew a single high, sweet note.

The minister and the congregation seemed oblivious to the intrusion. But now the stained-glass tree looked truly alive, its roots reaching down into the earth below the altar, its branches waving into the sky, so real that Janet thought she could hear its etched birds and animals chirruping and chittering. The window's green light fell across the branching roof pillars, which sprouted curling green tips. Carved acanthus leaves along the abbey columns twisted and grew, tendrils of carven eglantine writhed around their posts, and floral friezes flourished new shoots. Even the formal roof bosses burgeoned with blossom, their carved scenes suddenly animate: the pelican pierced her breast anew, the scapegoat looked nervously about him, the Hunt-of-Venus moved on.

The altar flowers opened, extending their stamens and carelessly shedding pollen on the holy embroidery. The flowers in the bride's bouquet answered, unfurling their buds and peeling back their petals in invitation. The finely chiselled saints in their wall niches grew pointed erections that tented their stony robes. Even the stony sculpted angels adjusted their feathers and looked uncomfortable. Janet could feel the carving under her wooden seat vibrating.

The strange man turned, and put a finger to his green lips. Then he winked a green eye at Janet, and beckoned her with a crooked finger.

She stood, and tiptoed towards him.

No-one noticed. The friends and relatives of the happy couple all just sat there, watching the time-old exchange of vows, oblivious to the way the lecherous carvings were behaving, unable to see the green man, or notice Janet approaching the altar.

The green man reached out and took Janet's hand. He raised it slowly to his lips, and kissed it. His mouth left a warm, sticky smudge. "You summoned me, m'lady. We have been waiting for you," he said. "Are you ready to come with me?"

"Who are you?" she whispered.

"Many are my names in many places, m'lady," said the strange man. "But you may call me Jack."

"Jack what?"

"Just Jack." He smiled. "Surely you've heard of me?"

Half a dozen possibilities sprang to Janet's mind: Jack-in-the-Green, Jack Frost, Jack-o'-Lantern . . . He could be any or all or none of them. She gave him a cautious smile. "Where are you taking me?" she asked. "And why should I go anywhere with you?"

"To the greenwood, of course," he said. "And as for the second question, that is for you to answer. You summoned me, m'lady. You mixed your blood and mine in your mouth. I am merely your guide. Come or stay, it's all one to me." He looked down, eyeing her Doc Marten boots with distaste. "If you choose to come, you'll have to get rid of those."

"Why?"

Jack looked exasperated. "None can come shod into the greenworld. Do you know nothing?" His expression became suddenly more thoughtful. "Perhaps you are not the one, after all," he said softly.

The implication stung Janet. She abandoned caution. "*Why shouldn't I be chosen?*" she thought furiously. She did not trust her voice to speak, so she said nothing. But she bent down and began determinedly removing her boots.

"I'll take that to mean you'll come then," said Jack.

Janet stood, barefoot now, and flicked her mousey-blond hair back from her face. She tried to look confident. "Since you're here," she said, "I might as well. Anything will be more interesting than this boring service."

Jack looked knowing. "Bravely said, m'lady. Come with me."

He took her by the hand once more, and stepped lightly past the wedding in progress and up to the altar window's tree of life, now swaying gently. The carved frame disappeared, and Janet found herself scrambling across a thick tree trunk where huge limbs branched in all directions. The birdsong was loud in her ears, and she was startled when a small squirrel dashed suddenly between her feet. Without warning, Jack released her hand, and she grabbed the nearest branch to keep her balance. She peered through the swaying leaves, but she could not see the ground below.

"This way, m'lady."

Janet felt herself seized firmly about the waist and whirled through the air. She heard a man's laughter as wind caught her silk skirts and blew them high above her waist. She screamed, but the scream ended in a gasp as her feet touched solid ground.

"There you are, safe and sound. Welcome to the greenwood." Jack's voice was merry.

Janet felt the blush begin, turning her neck and then her face to hot crimson. "You had no right to do that," she said. "You scared me to death!"

"And yet you still live." Jack was grinning broadly. "Fear not. Yours is not the first pair of knickers I've seen, nor will it be the last, if my luck holds true."

Janet smoothed her rumpled skirt, trying to regain some dignity. "But why do it at all?" she asked.

"Quickest way down," came the cheerful reply. "We'd have been there for hours if you had to climb down by yourself. You're not exactly skilled at woodcraft, are you?"

Janet did not reply.

Jack relented a little. "But I did not mean to frighten you. Truly, I had not thought you so timid."

"You took me by surprise, that's all. I'm not scared," she said at last.

Jack smiled at her. "So you say," he said. "I can still take you back, m'lady, if you will. This is no journey for the fainthearted."

Janet bit back an angry retort. "That won't be necessary, thank you," she said, sounding more like her mother than she would have cared to admit. "I always finish what I've started."

"In that case, we'd best be off," said Jack. "We'll say no more about it." He put his fingers to his mouth, and whistled—a piercing note that Janet thought must echo through the whole town. Then she looked about her, and realised that the town was no longer where it should be. The roads and traffic and smog that usually surrounded the raggedy square had gone, and Janet was standing on grass so thick and lush it felt like green velvet under her bare feet. The scent of pine and wild roses filled the air, and the only sounds she could hear were the rushing of water over stone where the stream cut across the valley, and the distant lowing of a single cow. The offices and shops and tea rooms were now a stand of scotch pines, and beyond them Janet could see nothing but trees— rowan, oak, and beech.

She had no time to stand wondering at the strangeness that had descended on the familiar landscape. A huge green horse came trotting into the square, whinnying loudly as if in answer to Jack's whistle. The horse was thickset and powerful. Its glossy hide was the colour of dark green holly leaves; its flowing mane and tail, and the fringes that hung to its unshod hooves, were the colour of palest cornsilk. It reminded Janet of an old-fashioned plough horse, a Clydesdale maybe, but it held its head high and moved with a heavy grace that suggested something wilder, something much less safe.

Jack hugged the horse, blew into its nostrils, and stood for a moment stroking its pale mane. He turned to Janet, grinning broadly. "Your steed awaits, m'lady. Will it please you to ride?"

Janet felt the huge horse staring down at her, waiting. It had large liquid eyes the colour of moss, and long pale lashes. She could see neither bit nor bridle nor saddle. And she couldn't see anything she could use to climb onto the creature's back. "*I'd need a ladder,*" she thought. She turned to Jack. "How . . . ?" she began.

"I'll lift you up," Jack said, "with your permission." He bowed formally, but there was laughter in his voice. "I wouldn't want to frighten the horse with your screams, would I?"

"I see," Janet replied frostily. "And how am I supposed to keep from falling off, without even a bridle?"

"You'll need no tools of coercion here, m'lady," said Jack. "Allow me to introduce you to my friend Dobbin. If he chooses to bear you, you will be safe. If not, no amount of equipment could keep you on his back."

The horse bent his neck in greeting, still eyeing Janet with ill-concealed curiosity.

"Oh," she said, "I see." She took a few hesitant paces forward, and patted the bowed green neck. "Pleased to meet you, Dobbin," she said softly. "I hope we shall be friends."

The horse whickered gently, and Janet felt a little less scared. "That's better," said Jack. He spread his tattered velvet cloak across Dobbin's broad back, and turned his attention back to Janet. "Here's velvet for your saddle, m'lady," he said. "May I?"

"I suppose so." Janet tried to look dignified as Jack lifted her high into the air and set her down on Dobbin's broad back. She straddled the horse as best she could, her skirt riding up around her knees, her legs sticking out awkwardly. She tried not to look down—the ground seemed very far away.

"You don't ride, do you," said Jack. It wasn't a question.

"I'll manage," Janet replied. "You said yourself that the horse will take care of me if he likes me."

"Yes, but that doesn't mean you can sit there like a sack of potatoes and make his job harder." Jack paused, thinking. "I'll ride with you," he said at last. He swung himself up behind Janet with a single, fluid movement, and clasped her lightly about the waist.

Janet squirmed.

"Patience," Jack said, his voice betraying his exasperation. "I'm not about to take any liberties! Just hold onto Dobbin's mane," he said, "and try not to tug at him. You won't lose your balance with me to steady you."

"Thank you," said Janet, still trying to mask her own unease. "But will Dobbin be all right with two of us to carry?"

"I'm lighter than you think," said Jack. "And he's stronger than either of us can know."

He kicked the horse's flank lightly with his bare heel, and Dobbin turned straight towards the forest. The horse snuffed the pine-scented air, and broke into a lumbering run, gaining speed as he went. Clods of green turf flew up behind him, and Janet had to duck when he plunged into a stand of pines whose low branches threatened to knock her from her precarious seat. The huge horse was swift and sure-footed, and soon Janet was clinging to his mane, head bent low to avoid overhanging boughs, knees pressed to his sides to balance herself as Dobbin sped along unseen paths beneath ancient trees.

Janet soon lost track of time. The forest light was dim, and she could not see the sun. The rushing air was cool and damp against her face, and the smell of decaying leaves was strong where Dobbin's heavy hooves kicked them up from piles that had lain undisturbed for who knew how long. There were brambles and briars blocking the way at times, and Janet caught her breath each time the great horse leapt high and sailed effortlessly over the obstacles; there were strange rustlings and scrapings in the undergrowth as small creatures scurried to make way for Dobbin and his riders. They forded streams where Janet was splashed and her green skirts muddied; they ascended sharp inclines where Dobbin's path took them through falling rocks and uneven scree and she clung to him in fear; and once, when the journey was beginning to seem as if it would never end, she smelled salt air and heard the distant roaring of the sea.

And while Janet clung and gripped the horse in fear of her very life, Jack sat lightly behind her, unconcerned, humming tunelessly to himself.

And then, abruptly as it had begun, the ride was over. Dobbin came to a thundering stop in the middle of a forest clearing, a place where warm sunlight came slanting through a circle of ancient oak trees which surrounded a patch of lush grass studded with nodding bluebells. Everything was quiet, and Dobbin's heavy breathing seemed to echo through the glade.

"Here we are, m'lady," said Jack.

He leapt lightly to the ground, and stepped around to stroke Dobbin's neck. "Well done, my friend," he said softly. "I'll give you a good rub down and sweet hay for your trouble, just as soon as I'm done with her ladyship."

The horse whickered softly. It seemed he shared the joke.

Janet heard, and felt suddenly angry. The green man and his green horse had frightened her on their wild ride, and now she found herself in the middle of nowhere with no hope of finding her way home without their help. She couldn't even get down from the horse without assistance.

"So where exactly is here?" she asked, mortified to hear the edge of tears in her voice.

The greenwood, m'lady," Jack replied casually. "You said you wanted to come. And here you are."

Janet sniffed, and wiped her sleeve across her face.

Jack relented a little. "Here, let me help you. There's few of mortal kind have ever braved this journey. You, m'lady, have ridden bravely this day. You have crossed the seven streams that guard our borders, and have come unscathed through the perilous wood. You are far beyond the human world. Do not be alarmed. You will be welcomed as our honoured guest."

Janet brightened a little at his words. "Thank you," she said. She held out her arms to him.

Jack lifted her up as if she weighed nothing at all, and set her down softly on the velvety grass.

Janet staggered, and leaned against him for support.

"Steady," said Jack. "You're not used to riding." He guided her towards a moss-covered log. "You can sit here until you feel stronger." He grinned. "Would you like me to massage your thighs for you?"

Despite his kindness, Janet heard the irrepressible impudence in his offer. "No, thank you," she said. "I'll rub them myself. I just need to get the circulation going again."

"As you please," said Jack. "Are you hungry? Shall I fetch us some refreshments?"

Janet had been too terrified to think about food, but now the suggestion filled her mind with sudden longing. "Yes please," she managed to say. "I'm famished."

Jack strolled out of the clearing, whistling happily, leaving Janet to her own devices. He was gone a long time.

Janet sat quietly, kneading her leg muscles and looking about her. All was peaceful. Dobbin began to crop the grass, and Janet found the sound of his steady munching somehow reassuring. She breathed deeply, willing the tension out of her neck and shoulders. Slowly, small woodland sounds began again as the glade's inhabitants went back about their business: Janet heard birdsong, and buzzing bees, and the rustlings of small creatures in the undergrowth. A rabbit stopped to stare at her before it bounded away into a blackberry patch, and she could just make out a pair of squirrels racing along the topmost branches of a stately oak. She began to feel a little safer.

A merry whistling broke the comfortable stillness, and Jack sauntered back into the glade. He carried his holly staff over his shoulder, now with a woven bundle knotted by its four corners to the pole. He was, as usual, grinning broadly. He laid the bundle at Janet's feet. "Are you ready to dine, m'lady?" he asked.

Janet ignored his teasing tone. "Yes," she said. "May I help you?"

"No need."

Jack untied his bundle and deftly set out a picnic on the woven cloth. He produced a large stoppered bottle, which he set beside him on the grass. Janet watched in amazement as he unpacked a plain wooden platter and two goblets. There was fresh white crusty bread, a pat of butter, and two large chunks of cheese—one a golden cheddar yellow, the other a softer, creamy white. There were salad greens, and hazelnuts and blackberries and raspberries, and honey dripping from its comb into a brown pottery bowl.

"Will this serve, m'lady?" he asked.

Janet could scarcely keep her mouth from watering at the sight of this feast. "It all looks wonderful. However did you manage it?"

Jack grinned happily. "The farmers and villagers, the wise ones, all leave their little gifts for Jack," he said. "And I do what I can for them in return—keep the butter sweet in the churn, avert the leaf blight, that sort of thing. It's *quid pro quo*. I've just been on my rounds to gather our lunch—the fruits of the fields and the woods, you might say."

"Fabulous," said Janet. "All it needs is a slice of ham and we'll have a complete ploughman's lunch."

Jack surprised her by looking swiftly over his shoulder before he spoke. His voice was low, and urgent: "If you have thoughts of meat, m'lady," he said, "you'd best keep them unspoken in this place. We do not kill for meat here in the greenwood. There are listeners everywhere, though you may not see them. And not all of them are friendly, if you take my meaning."

His nervousness was infectious.

Janet shifted uneasily in her place and peered anxiously at the trees. "I'm sorry," she said quickly. "It's a wonderful feast and it lacks for nothing. I didn't mean to give offence. I spoke without thinking."

"I know," said Jack. "And my warning is kindly meant. This is a dangerous place, for all that it is beautiful." He sighed, but brightened up again at once as he dug into his pouch for a little silver knife. "Have some cheese," he said, cutting a wedge from the cheddar.

The tense moment was soon forgotten as the two munched happily. Jack turned the conversation to other things. "You are honoured," he said, "that Dobbin likes you so much. You could have had a much rougher journey."

"He does? Really?" said Janet. "Is he a magical horse? Dobbin seems such an unlikely name for such a magnificent creature—I thought something so big would be sedate. He frightened me when he took off like that."

"I don't know about magic," said Jack. "He's as real as you or I." He gave her a significant look, then went on: "He can run swifter than the wind if he has a mind to do it. And as for his name, well, old names are best. The nursery remembers what others forget, and Dobbin is a good name for such as he."

Janet sat silent for a moment, enjoying the delicious cheese and bread, licking her fingers, soaking up the sunshine.

Jack unstoppered his flask and poured a little clear liquid into her goblet.

Janet raised it to her lips and sipped, expecting water. A delighted smile spread across her face. The drink smelled of flowers and tasted of sweet honey. It was warm on her tongue. "This," she said, "is marvellous. What is it?"

"Mead," said Jack. "You should only drink a little. It can be very potent."

"Well, thank you," said Janet. "This is the perfect end to a perfect meal." She leaned back contentedly against the mossy log. The dangers Jack had spoken of seemed remote.

"Glad to see you two taking your ease and enjoying yourselves." The voice cracked like a whip behind them. It was low and powerful, and its every syllable dripped displeasure. Overhead, the blackbirds stopped chirping. Even the bees ceased droning in the nodding bluebells. The glade fell silent.

Jack leapt to his feet. Janet sat bolt upright and dropped her goblet, letting it spill the last drops of her mead onto the cloth. Jack held out his hand and helped her to scramble to her feet. They stood together, waiting. Janet felt suddenly like a naughty schoolgirl, though she couldn't imagine what she had done wrong.

"I thought, Jack," the voice continued, "that you were to bring the girl *straight* to me. What part of that instruction didn't you understand?"

The owner of the voice strode into view, and Janet was surprised find herself facing a small woman clad in a simple long brown robe. The woman had long silver hair that hung loose to her shoulders. She wore no ornament save a girdle of green silk knotted with gold about her waist, and a small curved knife that swung glinting from the belt. But for all her plain appearance she walked like a queen, and her manner was imperious. Janet couldn't take her eyes off the crescent moon tattooed in blue ink in the centre of the woman's forehead—a dark motif etched starkly on white skin. She wondered what it could mean.

"Well?" said the woman.

"Your pardon, lady," said Jack. "Our guest was weary and hungry after her long journey, so I thought it best to feed her. We have not dallied long."

"I don't like to be kept waiting, Jack," the woman said, "and I know exactly how long you have been loitering here."

"Then you know it hasn't been long," said Jack, winking at Janet as he spoke. The irrepressible grin was back, and Janet suddenly found herself grateful for the warmth of his smile.

The haughty woman relaxed a little, and smiled back at him. "Hopelessly unreliable, as always," she said.

"Unfair, lady," Jack countered. "I am back, and I have brought the girl. Surely you don't begrudge me a little light luncheon?"

"Enough," she said. "I have no wish to be here all day. Tell me, is she the one?"

Jack looked suddenly thoughtful. "I don't know. She may be," he said at last. "She summoned me during a wedding rite, and that bodes well. And she wears our colours."

Janet shifted uneasily, listening intently as the two discussed her as if she were a pet, or an object they were thinking of buying. She did not like the direction this conversation was taking.

"Is she a virgin?" the lady asked abruptly.

Janet blushed and looked down at her bare feet. Her thighs were still aching horribly from her long bareback ride, and she felt as if she might never be able to straighten her spine again. She was conscious that she was standing bow-legged, much to the amusement of her guide. This was too much. "Why don't you ask me?" she said.

Jack cut her off smoothly. "No matter," he said airily. "There's many a bride who's gone to her nuptial bed with a little pouch of pig's blood tucked away secret, to stain the marriage sheets, if you take my meaning."

"Peace, Jack," said the lady. "We'll none of that. The girl's right. Let her answer for herself." She turned to face Janet. "And have a care you tell the truth. We have no use for liars here in the sacred grove."

"Sacred grove?" Janet stuttered. "Then you must be . . . "

"I am the high priestess. Yes. Who did you think I was?"

"I didn't know. I didn't realise. I . . . "

"Stop gibbering, girl, and answer the question. Have you lain with a man? Yes or no."

Janet was conscious of Jack's keen interest in her answer. "No," she said in a very small voice. "I am a virgin."

"Good," said the priestess. "Then you might do." She looked Janet up and down once more. "At least you have courage," she said. "Not many would dare to interrupt me here in my own place."

Despite her embarrassment, Janet had to ask. "I'm sorry," she said, "but I don't understand what this is about. What is it that you think I might do, lady?"

"The task for which you were summoned," the lady said shortly. "Did Jack tell you nothing?"

"No, lady," said Janet.

It was Jack's turn to bluster. "Well, how could I?" he asked. "I don't give away the secrets of the green world to strangers. For all I knew, you might have sent her straight back. And then I'd be in trouble for blabbing."

"Not that that ever stopped you before," said the lady. "But I take your point. You can tell her now. I have things to do. I'll leave you to it."

She did not wait for his answer, but walked, straight-backed, out of the grove.

Janet watched her go, and then collapsed onto the woven cloth still spread on the ground at her feet.

Jack groaned theatrically. "I think we could both do with a little more of that mead," he said.

Janet held out her goblet. "And then will you tell me what this is all about?"

"Yes, Janet."

This was the first time that he had used her name, and it somehow made the situation more intimate.

Jack drank deeply from his goblet before he turned to face her. His usually merry face was grave. "The tale is quick to tell," he said, "but whether you will be the one to help is yet unclear."

"Just tell me," said Janet.

Janet listened in wonder as Jack spoke of the Queen of Elfland and her young lover, of the threat to the fragile balance of the green world, of the urgent need for intervention. The shadows had lengthened a little in the glade and the mead goblets were empty again when his tale was done.

"So you see," he said at last, "it is for you to find the speck of truth in the riddle. To rescue him if you can."

Janet's face was grave. "Do *you* think I can do it?" she asked.

Jack shrugged. "You are here, Janet, for well or woe. I do not think you summoned me by chance. Would you come all this way and refuse the test?"

"No." Janet sighed. "I'm involved now. I'll go."

"Good," said Jack.

"But it worries me that you sound so fearful when you speak of the Queen of Elfland. I didn't think you were afraid of anything."

"My fear is not for myself, but for you," he replied. "Do you think the Queen is tiny and cute? Do you think she is dressed all in grasshoppers' wings and gossamer threads? Do you think she has an empty hazelnut for her carriage?"

"I don't know. I . . . "

Jack shivered. "She is tall and fair, Janet, exquisite and aloof, beautiful and dangerous. She is queen of dreams and fantasies, but she cares not for the little lives of the mortals she ensnares for her sport. All who love her know despair. All who thwart her do so at their peril."

Janet suddenly understood. "You love her, don't you?"

"It was long ago," said Jack. "And I shall never be free of the pain of it." He smiled ruefully. "There is no risk for me in this enterprise. And as for you, m'lady, if you are to venture it, we have no more time to waste."

He stood, and began deftly packing the remains of their lunch into a tidy parcel. "Now," he said briskly, "you must take my green velvet cloak. It might protect you when the time comes." He bundled it up, bowing from the waist as he handed it to her.

Janet tucked it under her arm. "But won't you need it?" she asked.

"Your need will be the greater," he replied gently. "Ask no more questions, now. Your task is set, and we must part. I'll show you the road that you must take. And later I'll stow food at the crossroads for your supper. That much I may do."

Janet stood beside him, brushing the last crumbs from her skirt. "Thank you," was all she could find to say.

They walked together to the edge of the clearing while the green man gave directions. "Go across the brook where the lilies flower and through a field of grass and on into the oak grove; at the crossroads, take the narrow trail to the right, it will lead you through briars and brambles to an ancient garden, where you will find a well. The young man is there."

Janet repeated the sequence of pathways until Jack was satisfied. "Go safely," he said. He surprised Janet by kissing her lightly on the forehead. "Our hopes go with you, m'lady."

And then he was gone.

Janet was alone in the green wood. She pulled back her hair, tucked up her green skirts and buttoned her blouse to the neck. "*Well,*" she said aloud, "*if I'm going to do this, I'd better get on with it.*" Her words sank into the silence of the wood—if there was anyone to hear, there was no reply.

She set out boldly, but the journey took longer than she had imagined it would. The way to the ford across the brook was marshy, and the dank air was clouded with little flying insects that swarmed around her and stung her skin. Janet sank to her ankles in foul black mud as she squelched unhappily past clumps of fragrant lilies, slapping at midges as she went. Then the grass in the field was tall, up to her shoulders in places, and full of burrs that stuck in her hair and clothes. She blistered her hands forcing her way through the stalks, and by the time she reached the shade of the oak grove she was sweating and miserable. The leaf mould on the forest floor cooled her abused feet, but her relief did not last long: the path beyond the marked tree took her through a tangle of thorns that scratched her legs and tore at her silken blouse. By the time she had found the garden, the sun was sinking and she was hurt and dishevelled, but still she pressed on. She crossed where a broken pathway wound between tangled weeds and overblown flowers running to seed, then she stepped warily through a break in an old stone wall.

And there, sitting carelessly in the shade by the well, book in hand, was a young man.

Janet thought he looked like a fairytale prince from a pantomime, with his coal-black hair curling to his shoulders and his slender body richly clad in a coat of gold brocade. But he was certainly not an elfin knight: no elf lord would wear a pair of ordinary blue jeans and a white T-shirt with his glittering brocade jacket. This youth must be the one she'd been sent to find. And he was gorgeous. Janet was suddenly tongue-tied. Absent-mindedly, she picked a rose, dark red and heavy with perfume, from the climbing bush that overhung the little courtyard. She turned it in her hands as she approached him.

The young man looked up from his reading. Janet noticed that his eyes were grey, and set wide over a perfect chiselled nose and generous mouth.

"Well, hello," he said languidly. "What have we here?"

"Hello," Janet said shyly.

"Is that all? Do you have a name? Mine is Thomas." His voice was alluring.

Janet's heart skipped a beat. "Pleased to meet you Thomas," she said. "I'm Janet."

"Well I'm pleased to meet you too, Janet. You look as if you've been travelling hard. What brings you here to visit me?"

Janet was uncomfortably conscious of her muddied feet and her scratched legs and the stains on her green silk skirt. She smoothed the skirt's creases as best she could, but it still looked ragged and travel-worn.

Thomas stood, dipped a small silver cup into the bucket that swung over the well, and offered the water to Janet. "Here," he said. "Would you like a drink?"

"Oh, thanks." She sipped, grateful for the diversion.

"You haven't said why you have come here, uninvited," he said. There was a slight emphasis on the last word.

Janet was instantly reminded that this was no place of safety. Blushing furiously, she looked up at him, full in the face. "I'm here to rescue you," she said.

Thomas looked astonished. "From what?"

"From the Queen, of course." Now that she came to say it out loud, the idea seemed much less plausible.

Thomas started laughing, a hysterical, high-pitched laugh that convulsed his body. He turned away from her and rested his arms against the sun-warmed garden wall, shoulders shaking with mirth.

Janet was mortified. She stood by the rose bush, twisting the stem of the double flower she'd plucked.

Finally, Thomas turned back to her, wiping his eyes on his sleeve. "Why?" he managed to say. "Look around you. Do I look like a man in need of rescue, even by a lady as fair as your good self?" He paused, and went on. "Besides, the Queen loves me. Adores me. She holds banquets in my honour and gives me all that I desire. Why ever should I want to leave? And even if I did, why should I need your help?"

Janet's mortification turned to anger. Who was he to mock her when she'd travelled all this way in such discomfort for his benefit. "A cage is a cage, no matter what the bars are made of," she retorted. "You live in luxury, but you are still in prison."

"It doesn't feel like a jail to me," said Thomas. "I'm perfectly happy. I have all I want here. Is that so bad? What's so great about your world that I should want to give up living here at my ease?"

"You don't know, do you?"

"Know what?"

"What the Queen of Elfland does with her human paramours when she tires of them."

"And I suppose you're going to tell me." Thomas' mirth had given way to sarcasm now.

Janet plunged on. "You might as well know. She sacrifices them. Every seven years she offers a human soul to the Prince of Hell. It's a kind of payment, a tithe, or maybe a tax. Whatever you call it, it's a bargain between them: she pays in souls to keep the hounds of hell away from her elfin folk. And the seven years is almost up. You haven't got much time."

"How do you know all this?"

It was Janet's turn to be wary. "I was told by those who guard the sacred grove. They sent me here in secret to rescue you if I can."

"And why would they care?"

"They have mysteries of their own to protect. All I was told is that you were not fated to die this way, and your death will upset the natural balance of things."

"Then I'm safe." Thomas sighed in smug relief. "If I'm not fated to die this way, then its obvious that I won't. I can't."

"You're not listening," Janet replied. "Fate isn't so predictable as all that. You are not safe. As things stand, you are very likely to be the next sacrifice. It would be nice if you don't die here, but the keepers of the greenworld have alternative plans to restore the balance if you do. Everyone thinks you're expendable, Thomas—especially your precious Queen."

The smile was gone from Thomas's face. "Are you sure about this?" he asked.

"Perfectly. I'm here, aren't I? Do you want to die, Thomas? If you do, just tell me, and I'll go away and leave you to it."

"Supposing I do believe you, why do I need your help? You've warned me now. Why don't I just leave?"

"Because you can't."

"Of course I can. I told you, it's not a prison."

"Prove it. Try it."

"What?"

"Take my hand. Walk out of the clearing with me. See that crooked path through the briar patch? That's the way I came. We'll go that way."

Janet reached out to Thomas, acutely aware of her attraction to him. Together they walked away from the well and stepped through the gap in the sun-warmed wall. But Thomas slipped on a loose stone and fell against Janet, clutching at her for balance—she felt his arms around her and looked up at him, her blue eyes meeting his questioning grey ones. They stood silent for a moment, embracing awkwardly. Janet tried to stop her heart from pounding at his touch. Embarrassed, she shrugged free of his grasp. "Come on," she said. "Let's go."

Thomas acquiesced, unwillingly. She noticed that he walked slower and slower as they paced through the haphazard flowers that filled the neglected garden. Together they crossed a patch of tangled grass and headed for the edge of the clearing. Then Thomas stopped abruptly, pressing his free hand to his forehead.

"My head hurts," he said. "It's a sudden migraine. I'm seeing spots and flashes. I feel sick. I'll have to lie down."

Janet turned him around. "Here," she said. "You'll feel better if you face towards the house."

"Thanks."

Thomas leaned heavily on Janet as they walked slowly back through the garden. He brightened a little as they stepped through the breach in the wall. "The headache's passing," he said. "Sorry about that: I don't know what came over me."

"I do," said Janet. "This place is spell bound. I told you, you can't leave. Do you believe me now?"

"I suppose I'll have to." Thomas still sounded weak, and Janet was worried about him.

"You'd better lie down," she said. "Where do you sleep?"

Thomas nodded in the direction of a low archway. "Through here," he said, gesturing limply. He clung to Janet's arm as they crossed the cracked flagstones that led to the chamber, but he straightened as they entered his domain. "Welcome to my bower, Janet," he said.

There was an edge in his voice, a hint of arrogance that made Janet uneasy.

The stone chamber was opulently furnished, its walls hung with richly woven tapestries depicting manticores and unicorns, its floor scattered with soft Persian carpets of red and blue and gold. There was a large silver mirror surrounded by tall, scented candles, and in the centre of the room stood a huge bed, its posts all carved with leaves and acorns and small animals. The bed canopy was swathed in a shimmering cloth of gold and crimson, and embroidered linen sheets showed beneath a coverlet of soft furs. It was luxurious, a room decorated for lovemaking, and Janet felt nervous in it.

Thomas headed straight for the bed, and sat there, swinging his legs and looking expectantly at Janet.

"There's wine in the flagon, sweetheart, " he said, gesturing towards a tray set with two goblets upon a low, finely carved table.

Janet frowned, but poured a little of the wine into a silver goblet. She crossed the room to the bed.

Thomas was recovering his self-assurance. He took the goblet, sipped a little, and then set it down beside the bed. Suddenly, he grabbed Janet's wrist, drawing her to him. "Well," he said, "if you're going to rescue me perhaps we should get to know each other better."

Janet felt strangely unsure of her feelings as he pulled her down beside him, and together they sank into the softness of the feather mattress. His left hand strayed to her breast, fondling her nipple. He bent to kiss her.

"No." She pulled away abruptly.

"What's wrong now?" He nuzzled her neck. "Aren't I good enough for you? The Queen thinks I'm good enough for her. I know the tricks that please a woman." The tone was cajoling, but the words were hard with pride and conceit.

Janet edged away. "It's not that," she said.

"What then? I know you want me. I saw the way you looked at me in the garden."

"I mustn't," she said.

"Why not? Where's the harm in a little fun?"

"I'm a virgin," said Janet, blushing once again to the roots of her hair.

Tom laughed. "That's easily remedied," he said. "I'll be gentle, I promise you."

"No." Janet snatched her hand away and retreated to the other side of the bed. "You don't understand. The high priestess said I have to be a virgin to rescue you. So I won't be so susceptible to the glamour of the spells."

"And you believed her?"

"She's been right about everything else so far. You were here where she told Jack you'd be, and you couldn't walk through the spell and out of the garden. She *knows* about these things."

"Sounds to me like she just wants to control you."

"And you don't?"

"Touché." Thomas sighed theatrically. "Then I guess I'll have to be good." His tone became wheedling. "At least until after I've been rescued. You can't blame me for trying, can you?"

"I suppose not," Janet said reluctantly.

Thomas did not reply.

Janet fidgeted in uncomfortable silence for a few minutes. At last she spoke. "So I'll just have to rescue you, won't I?"

Thomas grinned. "And then?"

"We'll see." She smiled back at him.

"It's a deal, then." Thomas took her hand again, and she did not pull away.

"So how do we do it?"

"Tonight is full moon," said Janet. "Has the Queen asked you to ride with her in the moonlight, by any chance?"

"How did you know?"

Janet just looked at him.

"Sorry," said Thomas. "Your green man told you. Yes, tonight we ride in the wild wood. How does that help?"

"It means you'll be out of this place," said Janet, "and away from its enchantment. What colour is your horse?"

"White."

"Good. It'll be easy to see in the moonlight. Make sure you ride on the left of the Queen. I'll conceal myself at the crossroads in the wood, and I'll grab you as you pass. We can hide in the bushes. With any luck, the elfin folk won't notice you're missing straight away."

"And if they do?"

"We'll have to trust each other. They'll try to recapture you, but you have to be willing if they are to succeed. And you, Thomas, are susceptible—the Queen has already imprisoned you once."

Thomas looked irritated. "So what makes you think you'll be stronger than I was?"

"I have not come here by chance," said Janet, "and I have no desire to stay here any longer than I have to." She paused, embarrassed. "I'm sorry," she said, looking up again at the scowling Thomas. "I didn't mean to sound pompous. I don't know if I will have the strength. But I'll try. Jack insisted that elfin spells are all illusion. They trick the senses and confuse the mind. Whatever happens, if we have the courage not believe what we see and feel, he says we can break free of the enchantment."

"Sounds risky."

"It is," said Janet, "but I'm game if you are."

"What can I say?" Thomas said, his self-confident grin returning.

"Then that's settled." Janet clambered down from the bed and straightened her clothing. "I'll be on my way. I mustn't be here when the Queen arrives."

"Okay," said Thomas. "I'll miss you." He blew her a kiss.

"One more thing," said Janet.

"Anything."

"Make sure you wear your green cloak."

"Why? So we'll match?"

"It's for your own protection. You don't really get this, do you?"

"Not entirely," Thomas admitted. "But I'll rely on you."

Janet picked her way back through the dishevelled garden, and took the narrow, thorny path that led back to the green wood. The sun was sinking as she made her footsore way to the crossroads, and found the ancient oak tree marked with a carved crescent moon. Jack had kept his promise: nestled in a hollow beneath the tree was a small bundle—a woven blanket tied at the corners to hold a small flask, a cup, and a parcel of bread and cheese.

Janet propped herself against the tree trunk and ate ravenously, suddenly aware that she had had nothing but a handful of nuts since her lunch with the green man in the forest glade. She wondered, briefly, how Thomas survived. The light was fading fast as she finished her meal. She sipped a little of the honey mead, and settled herself to wait. The air became colder as the darkness descended on the wild wood, and it wasn't long before Janet had wrapped herself in Jack's ragged green velvet cloak against the evening chill. The moon rose high and white in a clear black sky spangled with stars, and she heard the nocturnal animals creeping about their business. The night smells of damp pine and musty leaves grew stronger as the temperature dropped further. She draped the picnic blanket over the cloak, hugging the layers to her body in an effort to keep warm.

Alone in the dark, she waited.

Hours passed. Her muscles cramped with cold. Her teeth were beginning to chatter when she remembered Jack's mead, and sipped it gratefully, feeling the liquor warm her heart, even if the relief did not reach to her bare feet, which seemed to soak up the damp cold of the earth. Her every nerve felt stretched taught.

She jumped in fright when the sound she'd been straining to hear suddenly cut through the stillness of the night. The jingling sounds of bridle and harness and the tinkling music of the silver bells that adorned the mane of the Queen's horse were loud in Janet's ears as the elfin court rode swiftly towards her hiding place. Her mouth went dry. She felt frozen. Scared stiff.

She watched in fearful fascination as the Queen of Elfland and her court rode into sight. Tall and stately they were, their long hair flowing free and sparkling with jewels that glittered frostily, their costly cloaks of silks and satins shimmering and shining in the cold moonlight. The fair folk were beautiful, unearthly, and cold as starlight. To the left of the procession was a rider who sat uneasily in his saddle, bouncing along uncomfortably on a gleaming white stallion. The rider was smaller than his companions, and he wore a simple cloak of green velvet that streamed out behind him. It had to be Thomas.

Janet had no more time to think of the danger. The elfin court had reached the crossroads, a little open space where moonlight bathed the trees in pewter light. At the head of the cavalcade, riding straight and proud on her silver horse was the Queen—a figure so perfect that she looked as if she had been carved of ivory and moonbeams. She swept past Janet's hiding place without even glancing at the rune-carved tree.

Thomas came abreast of the tree.

Janet took her chance. She leapt out from behind the oak, and grabbed his stirrup, pulling hard. The white stallion snorted and reared, but Janet held on. Thomas fell to the ground. Janet grabbed him, trying to haul him away from the horse's hooves and into the safety of the tree roots. The horse pranced and whinnied, making a noise that echoed in the quiet wood.

The elfin court stopped, wheeled their horses, and formed a glittering circle. In the centre of the ring were Janet and Thomas, huddled together on the ground.

"What have we here?" The Queen's voice was musical, sweet and cold, a voice of honey and razor blades.

Janet struggled to her feet, feeling the hot blood rushing up to colour her chilled cheeks. She tried to remember if she was supposed to curtsy to the Queen, but she was too tangled in the cloaks and the blanket to try. Thomas finally managed to stand up beside her. Janet put a protective arm around him. "I've come to take him home, your majesty," she blurted out.

"Have you indeed?" The Queen sounded amused. "Why?"

"He doesn't belong here," said Janet.

"And you do?"

"No, your majesty: I don't. That's why I'm taking him home with me, back where we both should be."

"I'll be the judge of that," the Queen said icily. She turned her gaze to Thomas. "Are you so tired of me, fair Thomas, that you would abandon me for this impudent slip of a girl? Is your bower so wearisome? Have you forgotten the bliss we two have shared in your bed?"

Thomas said nothing. He just stood there mute, looking fixedly at the ground.

The frosty silence dragged on. Janet could hear the horses breathing, but the elfin folk made no sound at all.

"I see," the Queen said at last. "You have been taught to fear me. In that case, let the girl win you if she can. At least we'll have some sport."

Thomas disappeared.

In his place, Janet found herself holding a huge serpent whose green skin was patterned in triangles of gold. The snake writhed in her arms, hissing menacingly and coiling to strike at her face. Janet gagged on its musky smell, but she fought her terror, and held tight to its twisting body. "*Illusion*," she said to herself. The snake struck, and missed.

It changed. Janet was now clinging to the neck of a lion. Its hairy mane was in her mouth and her eyes, and the beast was roaring in anger at the intrusion. It lashed its tail and shook its body violently, trying to shake the girl loose from its back. The great jaws could not reach her, and Janet clung to its back for dear life as the lion tried rolling over onto her. Its breath reeked of rotten meat, and its fur crawled with lice. But still she held it tightly, and would not release her grip. "*Illusion*," she muttered desperately, as if the word itself had power the protect her.

The lion vanished.

Janet shrieked in terror as she found herself holding red-hot coals in her hands. The coals burned her skin. She could smell them singeing her flesh. She could see the flesh blistering. It took all her willpower not to drop the glowing coals. "*Illusion, all illusion*," she whispered through her anguish. Her mind was numb with fear. She could do nothing but hold on, and hope.

The pain ceased, as abruptly as it had begun. Janet found that she had her arms around a naked man. It was Thomas, shivering in the cold. She supported him as best she could while she snatched up Jack's cloak of velvet green from where it had fallen in the struggle. Quickly, she wrapped it about Thomas, hoping the power of the green man would protect the youth. She stepped between him and the Queen. All around her, the knights and ladies of the elfin court sat still as alabaster statues in their jewelled saddles.

The Queen applauded, a slow handclap that echoed through the wild wood. "Bravely done," she said. "We have been most entertained." She gestured at Jack's cloak. "Though I see you have had some help. Green Jack is a meddlesome man."

Janet just stood there, shaking with cold and shock. She could not reply. She did not know if she could withstand another ordeal.

The Queen turned to her courtiers. "Shall they go free?" she asked.

One by one the elven courtiers smiled gravely, and gave the thumbs up sign.

"The court has decided," said the Queen. "The boy is yours. He is easily replaced." Her clear laugh was brittle as breaking crystal. "And in token of our meeting," she went on, "I give you this gift. Fare you well."

The Queen took a red apple from her saddlebag and tossed it negligently in Janet's direction.

Janet caught it without thinking. She stood there, holding the apple, as the Queen simply turned and rode away, her bridle bells chiming, her courtiers jingling along after her. The sounds dwindled into the distance, and the moonlit glade was peaceful once more.

"That was close. Well done, m'lady." Jack dropped lightly from the branches of the oak tree. "You'd better see to your friend."

Janet gaped in astonishment. "You were there all the time," she said accusingly. "You were there and you didn't help me!"

"I did what I could," Jack replied. "But the test was yours, to pass or fail as you would. I could not have interfered without doing you greater harm." He smiled disarmingly. "Besides," he said, "you didn't need any help. You were magnificent. But I still think you should revive your young man." He poked Thomas unsympathetically with his toe. "He fainted away at the last, poor boy."

Janet vaguely remembered Thomas slipping gracelessly to the ground. She had been so utterly focussed on her contest of wills with the Queen that Thomas had become almost irrelevant—the trophy for the challenge. Yet there he was, groaning on the damp ground beside the ancient oak.

She bent down and touched his shoulder. "Thomas," she said, shaking him gently. "Wake up. It's over. You're safe."

Thomas stirred, but did not open his eyes.

"I'll grant you he's pretty," said Jack, "but he's not much use in a tight spot, is he?" He prodded him in the ribs. "Not exactly hero material, if you take my meaning."

"He's all right," Janet said. "He's had more exposure to the Queen, that's all."

Jack sniggered. "That's one way of putting it, m'lady."

Janet blushed and looked away.

The green man relented a little. "I suppose you could try this," he said, holding out a goblet of mead.

Janet knelt and raised Thomas' head so that she could trickle a little of the mead into his mouth. His grey eyes fluttered open. He began to smile up at Janet, but the smile froze into an expression of pure horror. "We lost," he whispered. "We're damned for all time."

"You're raving," Janet replied matter-of-factly. "You must have had a knock on the head. Relax. You're safe now. The Queen has gone."

"Look behind you," Thomas muttered through clenched teeth. "There's a creature made of leaves. And it's leering at me."

It was Janet's turn to laugh. "Allow me to introduce you to the man who brought me here to rescue you," she said. "Thomas, this is Jack—Jack, Thomas."

The green man bowed gracefully. "Delighted to meet you," he said. He held out a green hand to the young man. "Let me help you up."

Thomas looked unconvinced, but reached up to take the proffered hand. "Hello," was all he could manage.

Jack pulled him to his feet. The green velvet cloak slipped to the ground, leaving the skinny youth standing naked and trembling in the moonlight. Janet looked away. Jack laughed. "I think, Thomas, you'll find your clothing has survived," he said, chuckling as he pushed a tangled pile towards the young man. "You are, let me remind you, in the presence of a lady. Perhaps you should put your trousers on?"

"Excellent suggestion." The high priestess spoke sharply.

Janet turned quickly, in time to see the woman emerge from the oak tree that bore her symbol. Janet was not really surprised to see the silver-haired priestess. She now knew from experience that the shape of the green wood shifted all the time, and if the green man could appear at will, the priestess must also have her methods.

But Thomas stared at the newcomer in startled disbelief. Then he glanced down at his own nakedness. Blushing furiously, he snatched up his jeans, hopping on one foot as he tried to force the other into the cold, stiff denim. He tripped, and fell. Jack laughed uproariously as Thomas squirmed about on the ground, finally managing to pull the pants on. He scrambled to his feet once more. Jack handed him a crumpled white T-shirt, and Thomas pulled it over his head, panting with exertion.

"That's better," said the priestess, a smile tugging at the corners of her mouth. "So you're the one all the fuss is about." She gave him a long appraising look, as if she could see right through him. She shook her head, and went on: "I can't imagine why the Queen should have chosen you for her lover. Perhaps you have hidden qualities. Perhaps you were just available." She sighed. "No matter. The fair folk are capricious. Who can guess what inspires the whims of their Queen? What matters now is that you are here, and you are safe. She turned to Janet. "You have performed well, child," she said. "I knew you had courage. What will you do next?"

"I don't know," said Janet. "I hadn't really thought about it." She looked down at her torn and muddied clothes. A look of horror crossed her face. "Actually," she said, "I'm supposed to be at a wedding!"

"Well," said the priestess, "we can soon have you back there, if that's what you want."

"That's weird," Thomas broke in. "I was on my way to a wedding too! I was taking a short cut and I tripped on a tree root. Next thing I knew, I was in the Queen's bower." He blushed again. "Not that I was complaining at the time."

"Quite," said the high priestess.

Jack sniggered.

The priestess ignored the interruption. "We had hoped, Janet," she went on, "that you and Thomas here might be the next couple to grace our rites at midsummer. But now that I have met him I'm not sure he's suitable."

"He's not so bad," Janet said, feeling that she should defend him. "He did his best. He's very confused by all of this. So am I."

"Thanks, Janet," Thomas said, scuffing his bare foot on the cold ground. "I guess I disappointed everyone. I never was much of a hero. Sorry."

"That's okay," Janet said. "I was pretty scared myself." She smiled shyly at him. "I thought we did well enough, under the circumstances."

Green Jack and the high priestess exchanged significant glances.

"It seems that all may not be lost, then," said the priestess briskly. "Jack will escort you home, and we shall all, perhaps, meet again at midsummer." She turned to go. "Fare you well," she said.

"Goodbye, lady," said Janet, "and thank you." But the priestess had disappeared into the depths of the moonlit forest before the words were spoken. "How does she do that?" Janet asked the green man.

"There are some things it is better not to ask, m'lady," he replied solemnly. "But, as I value my green skin, I'm in the habit of obliging the high priestess. Her wish, you might say, is my command. So, if the two of you are ready, I'll open the way through the sacred oak and take you back to your wedding."

"It can't be the *same* wedding," said Thomas.

Jack looked smug. "Yes it can," he said.

"But I've been here for weeks. You only brought Janet into the green wood today."

Janet looked accusingly at the smirking green man. "You knew, didn't you," she said. "All the time, you knew."

Thomas felt left out of the conversation. "I don't get it," he said, interrupting them. "It doesn't make sense."

"Tell him, Janet," said Jack theatrically.

Janet sighed. "Time runs differently in the greenworld," she said. "Our clocks and calendars are of no use here. There are many doorways between our world and theirs, but they move them constantly. We can't open them without an invitation. That's the way it is. You just have to accept it."

"Nicely put," said Jack. "And now, if you will, we'll take the pathway of the tree. It's the shortest route back. Allow me, Janet. It isn't far to climb." He held out his elegant green hand to help her.

"But what about our clothes," Janet said. "I can't turn up at a wedding looking as if I've been dragged through a hedge backwards."

"No bother," Jack replied airily. "That's easily mended. You'll find there's been no damage done in your own time. You'll both be neat and tidy. And your boots, m'lady, will be right where you left them, beside the tree." He grinned merrily at them. "Shall we go?"

"Might as well," said Thomas, glad to be doing something. "I'm still cold."

"Then allow me." Jack helped them both to scramble up to the lowest fork of the oak. "This is where I leave you," he said. "Safe journey, Thomas. Fare you well, m'lady Janet. I hope we shall meet again."

Janet felt tears in her eyes. "Goodbye, Jack," she said, struggling to speak around the lump in her throat. "Thank you for everything."

"My pleasure," he said, brushing his lips gently over her cheek. "And now you must go."

Without further warning, he put a hand behind each of them, pushing them both lightly.

They fell forward into afternoon sunlight. Thomas tumbled, landing in a tangle, but Janet alighted without mishap. They were on the green, just outside the Abbey. Janet was relieved to find her Doc Martens placed neatly at the foot of the tree, and she could hear the reassuring hum of traffic around the little square. Even the untidy rows of shops had a certain charm for her at that moment.

The wedding was over, and the guests were milling about on the confetti-strewn grass, waiting while the happy couple posed for photographs on the Abbey steps.

Janet was still tying her bootlaces when her mother caught up with her.

"Where have you been, Janet?" she said anxiously. "I've been looking all over for you. And your hair's a mess. What have you been doing?" She stopped, suddenly noticing the young man at Janet's side. "Oh," she said. "I see you've met Thomas."

Janet's eyes widened in disbelief: "How do you know him, Mum?" she said.

"He's the groom's cousin. We were introduced at a family luncheon." She looked around the crowd distractedly. "And there's Celia's mother. I must just go and tell her how nice she looks in that hat. You stay here and chat to Thomas. And don't go wandering off again."

"Yes, Mum," said Janet. She looked up at Thomas, who was grinning widely.

"I think we've both had enough wandering for one day," he said.

Janet grinned back, sharing the joke. "Well, Thomas," she said, "we made it. And Jack was right—we look presentable enough."

Thomas massaged his shin. "But I'll have one or two good bruises to show for it," he said ruefully.

"Never mind," said Janet. "We're both all right. Though I have to admit I'm hungry after all we've been through."

"Me too," said Thomas. "And it'll be hours before the reception."

Janet remembered something. She reached into her skirt pocket and took out a shiny red apple, the gift of the Queen of Elfland. "Perhaps we can share this," she said. "It looks safe enough."

"Couldn't hurt," Thomas replied.

Janet bit into the fruit. "It's wonderful," she said, passing it to Thomas. "Have a bite."

The oak tree seemed to tremble.

"Thanks," said Thomas. He bit. Sweet juice ran down his chin.

The two of them stood, munching happily.

Suddenly they heard the green man laughing, his voice echoing from somewhere deep in the foliage. He was laughing so hard that the whole tree shook with his mirth. They stared upwards, and Janet thought she could just make out a green face amongst the dense leaves.

"So, you have sealed your own fates," Jack said at last. "I'll see you both on midsummer morn. And mind you come barefoot to walk on the velvet green."

Manifest Destiny

*There are two versions of this horror story: the first was
written in nineteenth century style, grammar and syntax;
the second (reproduced here) in a more modern form. The
reason for this revision was that the editor, Gillian Polack,
felt that today's readers would be uncomfortable with the
older prose style. The story was written for her anthology,*
Baggage, *for which the authors were asked to explore the
consequences of the cultural mindsets we all carry with
us: I based my story on a worrying pattern that emerged
when fellow author Andrew Enstice and I were researching
our nineteenth century cultural survey,* Aliens & Savages.
*Overwhelmingly, explorers and scientists described
Aboriginal people as either uncooperative savages, to be
exploited at will, or as "culminating apes", doomed to
extinction now that a "superior" civilization had arrived.
Both positions could be fatal for all concerned. In this
extrapolation, the two main characters each carry one of
these mindsets. The characters are fictional, but the basic
facts of the story are genuine, adapted from diary entries of
various explorers and re-located into the bush of southern
Victoria—an unforgiving environment far more frightening
than the superstitions and beliefs that the characters carry,
and far less susceptible to human control. Ultimately,
the story is about the fictional worlds that we create for
ourselves—beliefs that can be dangerously at odds with
immediate reality. Talie Helene described her experience
of reading this story as being like watching a McCubbin
painting explode—which seems to me to be exactly right.*

To see yourself as a force of history is to be absolved from both pity and guilt . . .
ROBERT HUGHES, *American Visions* (1997)

The mob had been foraging when he first caught sight of them, but they had scattered in all directions before the explorer could ride them down. He crested a rocky outcrop that gave him an unexpected view of the tangled forest, unbroken as far as the eye could see. But there was no time to contemplate the landscape, to get his bearings. He quickly crossed himself as he gave chase, trying in vain to catch one of the younger ones.

Low branches tore at him. He forced his tired horse to a last spurt of speed over steep ground dangerously full of wombat holes and slippery with leaf litter. The gap was narrowing now. Both man and horse were sweating heavily in the relentless January heat. A broad damp patch spread down the back of the explorer's shirt, almost joining with the sweat-soaked rings under his arms. He felt the perspiration trickling down, his wet collar chafing against his sunburnt neck. His trousers soaked up sweat from the horse's lathered flanks.

We both stink, he thought wryly. *This had better be worth it.* He was almost there, the rope now coiled ready in his hand. The mob was still too quick for him, zigzagging away into the densely wooded ravine, using the treacherously uneven terrain to advantage. He managed, at the last, to separate one of the older ones from the tail-end stragglers. This one was struggling to keep up with the others, but still running for its life.

"Gotcha!"

The rope snaked out, tightened.

The quarry staggered, fell to its knees.

The explorer wheeled in close, leaned down to slide the noose up the body until it was a halter about the neck.

"Up you come," he grunted, breathing hard. He pulled sharply. "Let's go."

It jerked to its feet, no longer resisting as the man tied the rope to his saddle bow. He forced the creature to move along beside, dragging it when it faltered.

It was not a long ride back to camp. The man took it slowly, resting the horse, following the trail of broken vegetation that marked his passage through the undergrowth.

In a small, trampled clearing in the midst of the dense shade of native forest the other men were going quietly about the necessary chores—mending harness, splicing rope, repairing their gear. One, a tall, fair-haired man with pale blue eyes, was bent carefully over a plant press.

The makeshift camp seemed irritatingly peaceful when the explorer rode in. Shafts of slanting sunlight lit up the massive tree trunks that surrounded the glade like the pillars of some primitive cathedral. There was distant birdsong, and the ceaseless sounds of insects grated on his senses. The whole thing annoyed the man. He swung out of the saddle, tugging the rope free. The captive sank to the ground, spent. He haltered it by its neck to the nearest tree, grimacing in distaste.

"I got one," he said.

"So I see, Richard," the naturalist replied, straightening up. "And what do you intend to do with it?"

The explorer walked across to join the other men, picked up his canteen, drank deeply. "You know what, Karl," he replied testily. He took another long swig, wiped his hand on his sleeve. "You know we're short of food, after that landslip. We lost one of our packhorses, supplies and all, all gone to the bottom of that cliff."

"That still leaves us with what the other horse is carrying. The men have repaired most of the gear, and we have our guns, and the ammunition."

"But we can't get a clear shot in this god-forsaken forest. We haven't brought down anything edible in days."

"You winged a parrot, boss," one of the others said, smiling broadly. "Karl says it was a crimson parrot—very pretty."

Richard glared at him. "As I said, Thomas: nothing edible. And so far Karl hasn't managed to hit a single thing on this whole trip. I thought Norwegians were supposed to be good hunters."

Karl shrugged. "Not all of us, alas," he said.

"Well, Thomas?" the explorer continued. "You didn't do any better than me, did you?"

"I'll take another crack at it, come dusk, boss. I've set up a hide, down there." He gestured vaguely towards a spot where the earth seemed to fold itself into a narrow slot that angled down the hill. "I found tracks."

The explorer turned away, exasperated. "I'll try my own methods," he said.

"Seriously," Karl went on, ignoring the warning signs, "do you really think you can make this one show you how to find native food?"

"It worked before."

"The last one got away, gnawed through the rope. It was quite a thick hair-rope, as I recall."

"All right, I admit that one was a failure." Richard's voice was harder, more aggressive now. "But the buck before that gave us some useful information."

"You tortured him."

"I didn't do anything we don't do to our own convicts."

"He died, Richard."

"So? You said yourself, they are scarcely human."

The naturalist shook his head. "You English," he said. "You are a cruel people."

"No more than most, Karl," Richard replied. "We do what's necessary." He stared hard at the naturalist, grey eyes at blue, daring the scientist to contradict him. "And why have you suddenly become such a great defender of savages?"

"Because I am here," Karl said mildly. "And I do not like what I see."

"Let me remind you that I am leading this expedition. I provide for all of us the best way I can. I notice you consume your share."

Karl shrugged. "You were happy enough to take my money to finance this trip."

"And you'll be taking your share of the gold when we find it."

"*If* we find it. But you always knew that my reasons for travelling with you are more scientific than mercenary."

"Well, that's as may be," the explorer went on. "I did offer you the buck's skull for your collection."

"I've told you, Richard. I no longer collect such things."

"But you did."

"Once, yes, before I realised the landholders were shooting specimens to bring to me. On this trip my specimens are strictly botanical, and entomological."

"There's no shortage of bugs, at least," said Thomas, slapping futilely at the ubiquitous bush flies.

But Richard wouldn't let the argument go. "So what exactly *did* you do, Karl? With the shot specimens, that is?" The question had a nasty edge to it.

Karl noticed that the other five men were finding reasons to be elsewhere. One got up, muttering something about taking the horse for a drink. Another, he noted with satisfaction, was sneaking water to the exhausted captive, behind the explorer's back.

"I conducted some scientific experiments, Richard," the naturalist said. "I contributed measurements to some European colleagues who were producing comparative tables of human development."

"And they found?"

"A number of indicators that Australian natives have a low plane of intellectual advancement: small development of the cranium, low receding forehead that restricts the frontal lobes, and so on."

"So they *are* no better than animals."

Karl was exasperated. "I have studied them further. They have their own languages, customs. They don't understand us, nor we them, but they are a species of human for all that."

"They can understand when they want to," Richard replied stubbornly. "No doubt about that. Uncooperative savages, that's what they are."

"That doesn't mean you can just kill them."

"Doesn't it?" he said. "Who's going to stop me?"

"It's not right, Richard. It's sad that they will inevitably die out now that a more evolved species has arrived," Karl said patiently. "It's a natural process. We should observe their ways before the end."

"In that case, they're dying anyway. I'm just helping things along a bit, and helping myself into the bargain." The explorer's thin-lipped smile was mean. "You should stick to your observations, Karl, while you can."

Karl turned to Thomas. "What do you think?" he asked.

Thomas spat. "I'm just here for the gold," he said. "I'll leave the philosophy to you."

"Very wise," said the explorer, unsheathing his hunting knife. "And leave the interrogation to me." He turned back towards the captive, knife in hand. "You don't have to watch," he said. "I can always make myself understood."

As the man took his first step towards her, the old woman started keening, a rising, high-pitched wail that cut through the summer air, a sound to set the teeth on edge. The birdsong stilled, the forest itself seemed to be leaning into the glade, listening.

Karl tried again. "Leave off, Richard. At least think of her sex. Decent people don't torture women."

"She's not a proper woman. A decent woman would at least cover her nakedness."

"It's not their way, Richard, and you know it."

"Listen to me, science man. She's a witch. Look at her. Open your eyes and look. Anyone can see she's a witch." Richard poked his knife at his captive. The old woman howled louder. She scrabbled backwards, pressing her bent back against the tree. The scent of bruised eucalyptus rose around her on the hot air.

"She's black, she's filthy, she smells bad. She's evil." The leader of the expedition was ticking off points on his fingers now. "Look again, man: bloodshot eyes, matted hair, toothless mouth, gibbering in tongues—she's a witch. And she's cursing us."

"Probably," Karl said. He sighed wearily. "She's a frightened old woman, Richard. You only caught her because she was too old to get away. The others were too quick for you, that's all. There's nothing sinister about her."

"Then what's all this then?" Richard pointed at the woven belt and dilly bag that hung awry about his captive's skinny hips. "I'll warrant those dried things are poisonous—charms and talismans. She'll put a hex on us."

"Superstitious nonsense! I had thought you a more enlightened man than that. Spells and ghost stories are entertainments for romantic women. Sensible men of the world no longer believe them."

"Where I come from," Richard said, "we don't have time for luxuries and your middle class entertainments." He fingered his crucifix on its chain in his pocket as he spoke. "Where I come from, we know what we know. And I know a witch when I see one."

Karl raised a hand, palm out, in defeat. "Then I'll leave you to your beliefs. But I will still ask you to do the honourable thing. Let her go."

"No." Richard's freckled face flamed as red as his hair. "We can't let her go," he shouted. "Don't you understand? If we let her go she'll bring back the others in the dead of night. They'll murder us in our sleep."

"They've more sense than that. They know we're armed. In my experience, they'll get as far away from us as they can," Karl said.

Richard did not reply, just stood there, radiating stubborn defiance.

Karl tried another tack. "You could at least wait until after Thomas takes a shot at the local game from his hide. If he bags any meat, you won't have to resort to torture."

"I suppose so," Richard replied, nodding to Thomas. "Do your best, Tom. We can find out what the witch knows in the morning if you have no luck with your gun." He turned back to Karl. "Will that satisfy you? The old hag gets a reprieve until tomorrow. But I'll do what I must if I have to." He shrugged. "I take no pleasure in the pain of others."

"No?"

"No!" The explorer turned on his heel. "I have better things to do than argue with you," he said as he stormed out of the clearing.

Exhausted, the explorer slept fitfully as the stifling afternoon dragged finally into dusk. The men who had remained in the camp dozed too. Even the old woman rested against her tree, eyes closed. It was too hot to do otherwise.

They woke suddenly to the sharp crack of rifle fire. There were shouts from the valley, and then the sound of snapping undergrowth as Thomas and two of his friends dragged the kill back to the campsite.

"Not a bad effort, even if I say so myself." Thomas grinned broadly, posing theatrically with one foot on the large kangaroo he had shot. "We'll dine well tonight."

"It's an eastern grey buck," said the naturalist, coming to look more closely. "It's a very fine specimen."

"It's dinner," Tom said testily. "What's the point of knowing what things are properly called if you can't make use of them? Plain kangaroo is good eating." He turned to the others. "John, Harry, come and help me butcher it. We'll sear steaks now, and cook the rest. No sense in wasting any of it."

"Right," said Richard, reasserting his authority. "Well done, Tom. The rest of you, build up the fire. Karl, you make a rack for cooking the strips."

Karl spread his hands, miming helplessness. "I'm not sure . . . " he began.

The explorer lost patience. "Never mind," he said. "Harry will do it for you. He usually does. Harry?"

"Right away, boss."

Richard turned back to the naturalist. "You wouldn't survive a day out here on your own, would you?"

Karl shrugged. "Probably not," he agreed. "I know I don't have any bushman skills. That's why I paid such a lot of money to come with you."

"Right," said Richard. "We know where we stand." He gestured at Karl's growing pile of plant specimens. "Tom's in the right of it, you know. It would make more sense to the rest of us if you could tell us which plants we could eat, instead of just collecting and naming them."

"All in due course," Karl replied equably. "It takes a lot of basic research to construct a valid taxonomy. I'm identifying small pieces of the bigger puzzle."

"Even so," Richard replied, "isn't there a way you could make your work more immediately useful?"

"I do have one helpful suggestion to make right now," Karl said.

"And what would that be?"

"I do think we should hobble the horses and make sure our gear is tied down tonight."

"Why?" said Richard. "It's totally still here. Not a breath of air anywhere."

"That's what I mean," said Karl. "It's thunderstorm weather. I've seen it before."

"Now who's jumping at shadows?" Richard said. "If there's a storm here, it will be because the witch has summoned it. And you've already told me that can't happen." He shrugged. "I don't see any need to make extra work for ourselves. We'll be leaving at first light."

"You're the leader." Karl turned away. He was quietly packing his scientific equipment into its cases and covering it in a sheltered spot beside his own carefully tethered horse when he chanced to glance across the glade at the captive.

She was alert now, and sniffing the air suspiciously.

Before long a greasy blue-grey smoke haze hung low in the still air, filling the glade with the smell of cooking meat. The men wolfed down singed steaks while the rest of the kangaroo sizzled on its rack over the fire. The light was fading fast, and the fat-splashed firelight cast flickering red shadows that glowed like stained glass between the pillars of the tall trees.

Karl made a point of sharing his meal with the captive. "There you are, grandmother," he said, holding a strip of charred meat to her mouth.

The woman nodded warily, then greedily gobbled her portion.

Karl resumed his seat by the fire. "She's as hungry as we are," he said.

"Waste of good food," Richard muttered.

"She might help us in return," Karl replied. "She certainly won't show us native supplies if she realises she won't get anything herself."

"Maybe," the explorer said. "Maybe not: who knows what a witch thinks?"

"Do you have witches in Norway, Karl?" Harry asked.

"I thought it was trolls," said Thomas. "Where did you say you came from?"

"I grew up in Bergen," Karl replied, "and of course we have such stories to frighten the children. But as I told Richard, I outgrew such fancies."

"Then I'll tell you a true story that should scare you," Thomas replied. "I was up country last year, and the squatters were all talking about it." He settled himself more comfortably. "You know that human flesh is a great delicacy for the blacks."

The other men nodded sagely.

"They call it *talgoro*. They eat the torso and the limbs, but never the head or the entrails. The most prized morsel is the fat about the kidneys—they think that by eating it they acquire the strength of the victim. It's because they believe that the kidneys are the centre of life."

"How interesting," said Karl. "For the ancient Greeks, it was the liver."

Thomas ignored the interruption. "What happened," he said, "was that a white policeman was attacked by the blacks. They beat him with clubs until he was knocked senseless, and they thought he was dead. Then they slit his skin and took out his kidneys, and ran away." He paused for effect. "But the poor fellow wasn't dead," he went on, his voice low. "His men found him, and he woke up long enough to tell them what had happened. He died properly a few hours later."

"What happened next?" Harry asked.

"Nothing," Thomas replied darkly. "They never caught the murdering blacks."

"I heard that they like the taste of Chinese best," John said. "They say that up on the Palmer gold fields they've been killed and eaten in big numbers."

Karl was sceptical. "Has anyone actually seen the natives committing these acts of cannibalism?" he asked.

"I for one never want to," Thomas replied. "Do you think your witch is a cannibal, boss?"

"She could be," the explorer replied, considering. "I wouldn't be surprised." He shrugged. "But there's nothing to worry about now. She's securely tied. She won't be eating anyone tonight."

The men laughed uneasily.

"Whites can be cannibals too," Karl said. "We've all heard about those Port Arthur escapees eating their friends."

"That's different," Richard put in. "That was a matter of survival. We'd all do it if we had to."

Karl shuddered. "I know I couldn't," he said.

"No," Richard agreed. "You'd starve defending your principles." He grinned suddenly. "We'd probably eat you."

Thomas grinned back. "Too stringy, boss," he said. "We'd choose someone with more meat on the bones."

"You're right," said Harry. "John here is much heavier."

"It's all muscle," John replied, laughing along with the others. "I'd be too tough."

"All right, all right," said the explorer. "That's enough. You're shocking our scientist." He yawned. "I'm too tired to think about anything right now. Tomorrow's another day. We'll worry about what to do with the cannibal witch then." He began settling himself by the fire. "Goodnight, lads. Goodnight, Karl. Get some rest."

"Goodnight." Karl hesitated, wanting to say more. But he resisted the impulse and moved quietly to where his gear was stowed. He laid his blanket carefully in the little hollow, making a shallow nest for himself. He stretched out, watching as the others found comfortable places. Before long, the camp was all quiet, all still. Clouds were building, and Karl lay a long time wakeful in the starless darkness before he too finally drifted into sleep.

The storm, when it came, came without warning. Lightning arced across the sullen sky and the smell of scorched ozone barely preceded the huge crack of thunder that startled the men awake. Then the sky was alive with lightning flashes and the thunder rumbled like an earthquake.

The explorer and his men woke to chaos. The horses were screaming, bucking to break their light tethers. Two had already bolted. The captive was screeching too, struggling to free herself from the strangling halter that held her in harm's way. The men ran in all directions, desperate to secure the remaining mounts, snatching up their rifles where they could, scrambling to grab their scattered gear.

"One, two . . . " Under his breath Karl began counting seconds between the flashes of forked lightning and the thunder peals. He didn't get to three. The storm front was upon them. And the wind was rising fast. The noise began as a low moaning in the tree tops. The moaning became a howling, and the howling a shriek. Tall trees whipped and bent, straining in the windstorm. Branches came crashing down. A wattle split, tore, whirled away into the darkness. The men were pelted with stinging leaves and bark and heavier gum nuts that bruised where they struck. Karl grabbed for his horse, but was driven back by the gale. He crouched in the lee of a boulder, sheltering as best he could.

Then the rain came. A few fat drops at first, then a wind-driven downpour that tore apart the forest canopy. The rain became hail, chunks of ice that bombarded the landscape, round ice balls that collected in drifts around trees and filled the cracks and crevices of the campsite. Karl watched, hunched behind his rock against the punishing onslaught. The pulsing lightning lit a madly shifting scene of flying debris and bouncing white hailstones, with a lurid red fireglow at its heart. He could no longer tell if the screams that echoed in his ears were human, animal or elemental.

"*I don't belong here*," he thought.

And suddenly he was aware that there were flitting black shadows amongst the shifting shapes of the trees, shadows that moved with purpose despite the wild storm. The tribe had come.

The naturalist stayed as still as he could, peering at the confusion of the campsite. But then the fire was smothered, the glow went out, and he had only flashes of vision when the lightning flared. He glimpsed spears, and the tall warriors who carried them. Weaponless and terrified, he shut his eyes and turned his face away.

The storm raged on, but no blow fell upon him. He lost track of the hours, wretchedly holding on for his life against the elements, until finally the rain eased a little. The thick darkness began to shade to predawn grey, and just as Karl risked movement to ease the stiffness from his limbs, the manic laughter of kookaburras pealed across the soggy sky. The dawn chorus had begun. The carolling of native magpies joining their raucous cousins to greet the day served only to remind the naturalist that he was a stranger in a frighteningly strange land.

The light grew, and Karl looked about him, badly shaken. He called, and called again, but no-one answered. He was alone. To calm his rising panic, he forced himself to take stock of his position. He was soaked to the skin, bruised and tired, but whole. His equipment was intact—though he noticed wryly that his blanket had been anchored in its hollow only by the weight of melting hail stones it contained.

The rest of the camp had not fared so well. The explorer's gear was strewn about, badly damaged, the tools scattered and ruined. Everything edible was gone, even the kangaroo meat they had left over the cooking fire. The tribe had been thorough. As Karl had expected, the captive was gone. Her rescuers had left a neatly cut halter rope dropped at the base of her tree. The naturalist stooped to retrieve a length of leather rein, realising as he did so that this too had been deftly severed. His tethered horse was missing. All of the horses had been driven off, under cover of the thunderstorm. He had to assume that they were gone for good.

The enormity of his situation was becoming horribly clear. He would, of course, wait for his companions. He hoped they lived yet, and would somehow make their way back to the campsite. He knew there was no sense in his getting himself lost searching the dense forest for them: better he should re-build the fire so that the smoke might guide them. He would not, could not think of them lying dead with their throats cut, or worse. Last night's lurid tales of native cannibalism rose unbidden in his mind. This must not be. He had refused to believe such things at the time, he would not countenance them now. No more than he would countenance the old beliefs in witchcraft—these were tales from his European childhood, not fit for a grown man of science, a logical man. Grimly, he pushed the clamouring thoughts aside and began to sift through the wreckage of the camp, setting aside anything that might be useful, salvaging anything that might be mended.

The sun was rising now, but the dark fears only grew stronger with the daylight. Hope faded to despair. The explorer would not be coming back. There would be no help, no search party, no reprieve. Without food or tools or the bush skills of his companions, the naturalist was all too aware that the chances of his retracing their path on foot, of making it back alive to the tiny Port Albert settlement were vanishingly small.

Overwhelmed, he sat by the dead ashes of the cooking fire, staring at the useless bits of cut leather that lay about him. Sunlight touched his face, and somewhere above him a native thrush trilled its liquid song into the cool morning air. The forest stirred around him, indifferent to his plight.

The scientific man put his head in his hands, and wept.

Death at the Blue Elephant

This dark urban fantasy was my first short story. After too many years writing non-fiction, it was time for a change. I had the flu, and a friend had remarked that I looked like "death warmed up"—so I was thinking about the medieval personifications of Death. And there she was, Death herself, updated to suit the present time—too tall, too thin, too rich—and absolutely amoral. She was hanging out at the Blue Elephant Café, staving off eternal boredom by offering selected clients a last, fatal fantasy—and daring me to write about her.

Death came here often.

She liked the commercial misery of the smog stained office building, a nondescript cube of sixties brutalist style, executed in particularly ugly brown brick and aluminium. The sprawling *Three Sexes Nite Club* occupied the ground floor, filling its prosaic erstwhile showroom space with throbbing musical darkness, permeating it with indelicate sounds, suggesting unspeakable acts. It sublet the only light corner to *The Blue Elephant*, a cafe whose swinging doors connected it symbiotically to its patron. The cafe never closed. It provided a convenient antechamber for *The Sexes*, a meeting place for potential revellers, a respite for tired *habitués*, a talking point for local gossip.

The cafe's street facing wall had been knocked out and replaced by trendy folding glass, the better to display its wares, and its patrons, to passers-by. Death liked the aggressively postmodern decor, a mishmash of distressed ochre paint, garish ceramics, and furniture constructed of glass and curled wrought iron whose tortured legs resembled, she supposed, the trunks of distressed elephants. It was always simultaneously breakfast time and cocktail time at the *Elephant*, where last drinks and nightcaps merged imperceptibly into first coffees and orange juices. Underneath the rich aroma emitted by its shrieking espresso machine, the *Elephant* smelled faintly of old cabbage, stale frying, dried sweat.

Death threaded her way toward her favourite table in a shadowy corner. She didn't need to advertise. She glanced at the food being deposited, with studied gracelessness, in front of a courting couple: two orders of poisonous looking *nouvelle cuisine* featuring an enormous platter of white porcelain which supported six ultra-thin smoked slivers of some unfortunate animal, curled and propped artistically against mounds of oil drizzled mesclun salad. Death never ate here. She ordered a macchiato and a brandy, leaned back at a dangerous angle and lit up an old fashioned Gitane, affecting bored indifference to the accusing glares of non-smoking customers. That was one of the things that Death liked most about this society: it gave her proper respect, worshipped at her altars. It polluted its air, adulterated its food, contaminated its water. Then it looked politely affronted at Her omnipresence. Cool.

Death would not have long to wait. Her clients inevitably found her at the appointed hour. It was traditional. The sex, of course, was optional. Tucked into her smoky corner, she set out her travelling chess set, the ebony and ivory pieces exquisitely wrought, the inlaid box intricately carved with the writhing shapes of Dante's damned, spiralling in their circles toward the central handle of Hell. A pretty thing, the gift of that old lost soul Dr Dee, a gentleman who really knew the usages of chess.

"Excuse me, may I join you? The tables are all full, and I've promised to wait here for a friend."

Death looked up through her black-lensed black Raybans into the blue eyes of a stocky, apple-cheeked young man whose short trimmed blonde curls revealed a single diamond earstud. His pleated dark blue trousers and draped linen shirt were set off by a perfectly knotted midnight velvet bow tie and a soft white leather evening jacket that suggested more than a passing interest in current fashion. Toy boy, she guessed. Well, she liked toys.

"Please, be my guest."

Death extended a thin, graceful hand, its long, pointed nails varnished dark red-black to match the deep congealed-blood shade of her lipstick. Her Oscar de la Renta ragged-cut black leather sleeve slid back to reveal a glimpse of darker silken stuff beneath. She liked the feel of dead things around her, the rasp and slide of silk and leather against her dry, bloodless-pale skin, against her jutting bones. Her wardrobe was constructed entirely of deaths in the animal world, from her Chanel tortoiseshell hair slides down to her pointed Salvatore Ferragamo handmade alligator boots. Even her Cartier nose ring was inlaid with coral. Black coral.

"Do you come here often?"

The young man smiled, briefly gripping the proffered fingertips. Death felt health in the heat of contact. A challenge, then.

"Never. My first time. I'm Jason. Pleased to meet you, Ms . . . ?"

"There's a first time for everything. You can call me Azriel."

"Greek?"

"Hebrew. Dark Angel. Do you play?"

"Play?"

"Chess." Death indicated the tiny board.

"Sorry. No. Never learned. But I'm open to experience. I enjoy games."

Not quite such a challenge after all.

"Dice, then?"

Death spilled ivory cubes onto glass. They rolled to a stop, winking ruby snakes eyes. A loaded question.

"I don't gamble."

"Never? Should you be talking to strangers?"

Jason's mouth quirked upward at the corners.

"I'll take my chances."

The real invitation, unspoken, understood, had been issued. And accepted.

Death liked this late twentieth century. Sexual entrapment and damnation through honest lust beat hands down all that tiresome dwelling with *poisons, warre and sicknesse* required of her in Dr Dee's milieu. Not that these things were at all out of fashion, of course. Never would be. But some of the plagues had been so terribly unaesthetic. Buboes. All that disgusting pus. These new designer viral mutations had real style. Invisible. Pleasurable in the transmission, and just as . . . fatal. A whole new meaning for the little death. Death and sex, sex and death, the romantic fashion.

Still, she always offered a fair contest, always offered to play by the rules. It wasn't *her* fault if nobody here seemed to know the rules of first contact anymore. At least this way the client had a good time on the road to Hell, and never mind the good intentions.

A sulky waiter materialized purposefully at their table.

"Yes, sir?"

Jason looked in vain for a menu. There was something chalked on a board on the other side of the room. Too far away to be of any use.

"Er, a glass of white wine, and, um . . . "

Death prompted. "The focaccia's good."

"And a sun-dried tomato focaccia."

"And for you, madam?"

The waiter was clearing away Death's untouched macchiato. He gestured vaguely toward the brandy balloon, but clearly thought better of attempting to remove it from her negligent grasp.

"Just wine. Red wine."

Wine, bread and salt: Death wanted to be sure she was properly invited over the threshold.

Jason was making small talk, chatting easily about his boredom with accountancy, his efforts at the local gym, his evolving interest in reiki massage, aroma therapy, Tibetan pulsing. About his attempts at getting in touch with his inner child.

He leaned forward, smiling again, his confidence growing.

"So tell me about you. What do you do? For a living?"

"I don't. I am. I be."

Death watched Jason cast an appraising eye over her outfit, saw him conclude it to be eclectic, perhaps, but pure designer Gothic chic. It certainly wasn't, by any stretch of his imagination, inexpensive.

"Sounds very existential. Does it mean unemployed?"

"No. Never."

"Independent, then?"

"Alone, certainly."

"Okay. I won't pry. I like a woman of mystery. It's romantic."

Death's eyes narrowed behind her shades as Jason switched to prudent flattery.

"Romantic. Like your hair's romantic. You've got great hair, Azriel."

He wet his lips, tasting her name.

"Gorgeous."

Death inclined her head, acknowledging. She *was* proud of her hair, of her smoke-dark cascade of spiral locks so variously crimped and curled, woven with love knots, threaded with charms, plaited with silks, tangled in elf locks, tipped in pearls, black pearls, drowned sailors"-eyes pearls. She patted her intricately snarled high topknot precariously clasped and pinned with tortoiseshell and ivory. It spoke her history, this sea wrack of tumbling artefact encrusted heavy hair that spread its riches across her narrow, bony shoulders.

"It must have taken ages to set it like that."

"Centuries."

Death sat back, chilling out while Jason talked on about his experiments with alternative cultures, about his restless search for meaning. She would give him certainty. Absolute certainty. Later. He was earnestly working the conversation around to the psychic benefits of rebirthing when the waiter reappeared, bearing their drinks and an oversized porcelain platter that he plunked down, unceremoniously, before Jason. Death conceded that the toast part with its heaped filling looked all right, if she averted her gaze from the oily green stuff wreathed around it.

"This is huge. Let me share with you."

Jason was offering to divide the food into equal parts.

Death was appalled, but gallantly mindful of convention.

"Just a tiny corner. Just to be friendly. Thanks."

She accepted a small helping on her side plate, put a morsel to her lips, washed it down with a little wine. Then she slid the plate to the very edge of the table, where a pointed snout, black and whiskery, emerged quivering from her fringed black leather bag. The nose was quickly followed by the face, paws and torso of a black-hooded rat, which was showing more than a passing interest in fragments of focaccia that Death was absently crumbling onto the glass tabletop.

Jason gasped. Death put a cold hand over one of his, forestalling his startled exclamation.

"It's only Hecate. My travelling companion. She goes everywhere with me. We've been together for ages. Pretty, isn't she?"

Jason was looking unconvinced, his gaze focused on the needle sharp teeth with which Hecate dealt with her dinner.

"They're a highly intelligent species," Death continued over Jason's obvious discomfiture. "I'm surprised more people don't carry them as pets."

She tipped a little wine into the hollow of the plate, watching fondly as Hecate slipped out a delicate pink tongue to drink.

"But they're vermin," said Jason. "They carry disease."

Death looked offended.

"Everything carries disease. It's just a matter of compatibility. But if Hecate bothers you, she can stay out of sight in the bag. She's quite comfortable."

And Hecate, right on cue, disappeared gracefully from sight.

Death settled back, toying negligently with her wine glass, enjoying Jason's sudden intense interest in his own plate. She would not have much longer to wait.

The speed at which the staff at the *Elephant* processed its customers varied, as always, in direct proportion to demand. Tonight, the crowd at the bar was growing, swelling with incoming patrons waiting in restless hope for newly vacated tables. The moment Jason finished off his focaccia, the waiter reappeared, hesitated a beat while he considered the protocol, then placed the bill carefully in the centre of the table. Death noted the practised way that Jason hesitated, delicately, just long enough for her to pick it up. He did not demur when she offered to pay.

A mistake. Death had rather old-fashioned ideas about debt and obligation.

She tried not to look too bored as he moved unsubtly into his next phase.

"Thank you, Azriel. You're a sport. My friends seem to have deserted me, and I'm all alone. Will you stay on a little? We could have a drink next door. Maybe you'd care to dance? I'd love that."

"Sure. Happy to. I like to dance. I'll just excuse myself for a moment first. I'll meet you by the swinging doors."

Death stood, noting with satisfaction Jason's surprise at her height. She towered over him. Not exactly beautiful, but striking, compelling. Definitely compelling.

Death's longish, artfully ripped silk and leather skirt rasped against her boots as she slipped out to the bathroom. It was a clinical place, with safe sex posters, a wall of mirrors, and interrogation-strength fluorescent lighting designed to encourage patrons considering dangerous liaisons to invest in the privacy of those little rooms at the back that *The Sexes* rented out, unofficially, by the hour. It didn't take Death long to vomit up the small amount of food she'd taken, for form's sake, to seal the bargain. She lingered a moment, adjusting the black on black painted Hermes scarf at her throat, applying a fresh layer of lipstick. She was cupping a little water in her hand for Hecate when they were joined at the mirror by a Goth, a serious grey-eyed girl whose uncertain smile of greeting revealed expensively capped and pointed canines. A small fortune's worth of cosmetic dentistry. Her reflection was solid enough.

Death sighed. The world was full of amateurs and wannabees.

"All these mirrors. So bright. So unkind to the undead, don't you think?"

And Death was gone. It was not this girl's time. Not yet.

She emerged, cool as ever, and there was Jason, freshly combed and eager. Death led the way, guiding him through dim alcoves that yielded fragmentary images: a hand up a skirt, a white line on a flat mirror, a flash of banknotes sliding from hand to shadowy hand. And on down to basement level, into *Damnation*, the club's cavernous dance floor. It was darkly backlit by red wall lamps and swept by occasional strobes, its low ceiling graced by an old fashioned mirrorball which reflected the dull red glow, caught the occasional lightning strobe flashes. *Manic Suede* were in good form tonight, their Morticia-thin lead singer switching effortlessly between sultry jazz based numbers and upbeat dance rhythms.

Death's dance style had an erratic, capering energy that belied her elegant appearance. It was catching: soon the *Damnation* cave was a mass of leaping, writhing shapes as *The Sexes'* patrons followed her lead. Things tended to become a bit surreal around Death. The smoke curling at the edges of the floor thickened into heated fog that coiled about the dancers as the rhythm accelerated, inexorably. Roiling shadows loomed closer, edged in the black-red glow of burning coals. Dark flames licked at keyboards, fretboards, soundboards. The band caught fire. The music came faster, faster, from scorching fingers. Tiring dancers found themselves unable to stop, found themselves capering madly, cavorting together in an antic headlong rush towards exhaustion. Death looked smug. They really were so suggestible.

Suddenly bored with the game, she took Jason's hand, now slick with perspiration. She headed for the exit. Behind her, the music limped to a last riff while the burned out band announced to the sweat-stained backs of departing dancers that they'd take a short break. They'd be back soon. Maybe.

"Let's get out of here. I'll just get my coat."

Death handed in her coat check, retrieved the thickest, blackest sable Jason had ever seen, draped it over her shoulder.

"Where to? My place is a bit of a charnel house just now. Redecorating. Perhaps we could go to yours?"

She expected Jason's hesitation. "Er, not really. I share. It would be a bit crowded. No place for a sophisticated lady."

"Moonlighting, huh? No problem."

Death stepped back to the desk. After a couple of minutes of whispered conversation, Jason saw money, and a key, change hands. Death looked complacent.

"They have a few private suites here. For parties, special occasions, that sort of thing. I've borrowed one for the evening."

She watched his Adam's apple bob as he swallowed hard. Perhaps he was accustomed to a slower pace? Well, Death didn't have all night.

The corridor at the back of the *Sexes* was a narrow, businesslike tube leading into a drab little foyer that formed a discreet hub for multiple private entrances masquerading as offices. A legal fiction, a courteous alibi to protect the privacy of clients. Death could hear clinking glasses and muffled giggles over the low hum of a jacuzzi motor as she steered Jason towards their doorway.

The suite had the gilt mirrors and upholstered ruby plush of an old-fashioned bordello, dimly lit by a glass drop chandelier with electric imitation candle bulbs that flickered irritatingly. Death cast a jaded glance over its squashy brocaded couches, its vaguely erotic framed prints, its dusty maroon velvet drapes. The centrepiece was a huge iron famed bed, swathed in crimson satin quilting, fringed and tasselled in antique gold, and connected, incongruously, to a vibrating machine. Some undergraduate interior designer's idea of amatory atmosphere, she supposed. But the suite did boast a well stocked bar fridge, and an equally well stocked bathroom whose shelves displayed a range of condoms, shrink-wrapped vibrators, dildos, Chinese balls, nipple clamps, manacles of various shapes and sizes. The bathroom smelled of bleach, and rubber. Death was amused by the padded bondage restraints, designed for tender beginners.

"Well, Jason, is this secluded enough for a sophisticated liaison?"

His only answer was a nervous smile.

She gestured towards the cold-beaded bottle in its imitation silver ice bucket. "Why don't you open the champagne? You'll feel more relaxed after a drink."

Jason obeyed, gulped down his champagne, then quickly refilled his glass. It seemed to help. He removed his tie. A muscle twitched in his smooth throat. Death could almost see the blood pumping, could smell his clean good health. She peeled him slowly out of his clothes, admiring his robust, muscled young body. So fair and full of flesh. His penis was already stirring, catching in his underpants as she stripped them from him. He reached for her Raybans.

"I want to see your face."

"Not so fast. I am not altogether pleased with you. You trod on my toe on the dance floor. Why should I pleasure you with my body?"

Death drew a thin coil of plaited black leather from her bag, unsurprised at the answering gleam in Jason's eyes.

"Ask me to punish you."

Jason slid easily, too easily, into a submissive role.

"Forgive me, Azriel. I would be grateful if you would punish my clumsiness with, um, six strokes of your lash. Or in, um . . . , whatever way would please you."

Death bent him over the edge of the bed, pleased at the way his little blonde curls stood on end as she began his punishment. Under her leather thong his full white flesh was welting nicely, raised red weals that would remind him of her in days to come. He was silent, his face buried in the scarlet coverlet, but she heard him gasp at the seventh cut. She stopped at ten. No sense overdoing it.

When she turned him over, he was afire with lust, his eyes glazed, his full erection straining hard towards her.

Death knew her customers.

She kissed him, then. A painful kiss. A kiss to pick open hell. Teeth grated against teeth as she forced his mouth open, thrust her long tongue down his throat, dripping saliva. Jason gagged, jerked his head away.

Clients always reacted to their first taste of Death. She did not try to disguise her odour of decay: up close, her body smelled musty, old, mouldering. Dead.

Death savoured these moments of recognition. She saw incipient fear behind Jason's eyes. He began to stutter something about waiting, maybe, but it was too late now for second thoughts. Much too late.

She pushed him back onto the bed, tracing a razor sharp fingernail along the length of his erection. It left a thin trail of blood and broken skin. Jason groaned, tried to push her away.

Death's answering grin was murderous.

She hoisted her skirts to mount him, exposing the papery white skin of her too thin thighs, skin that gleamed dead white, bone white. She felt his terror. She knew, now, that he struggled, willing his flesh not to respond, unable to prevent it. Death is stronger than life. She forced him down on his back, her powerful fingers talons now, raking his shoulders where they gripped. She straddled him, guiding his organ into her darkness, consuming him.

Death rode him hard, her pubic bone grinding against his pelvis, her thighbones clamping against his, grating against his soft skin, her hipbones gyrating in age-old parody of need. She felt his heat as his body betrayed him, lifted herself clean away just as his back arched and Jason was racked by painful orgasm.

Dismounting, Death idly watched a drop of spilled sperm turn pink where it mixed with his blood, blood already contaminated by her own lethal juices. It didn't take much. Not really.

Jason lay sprawled on the covers, bruised, bloodied, spent.

"You've infected me." It was a statement. "Why, Azriel?"

"It was what you wanted, Death said simply. "Don't look surprised. You came to me, invited me, submitted to me. Your choice."

She was adjusting the black on black folds of her skirt, preparing to leave. She scooped up her shoulder bag, shrugged into her coat, eased her voluminous hair over its collar.

"You can't just walk out on me. Not now."

"Stay as long as you like, Jason. The room's paid for all night. There's everything you need here. Get some rest."

"Please, Azriel. I'll do anything."

"I know."

Hecate had climbed soundlessly from the depths of the leather bag and into the satin lined pocket of the sable coat. Death absently stroked her pet's shiny fur with long bony fingers, observing Jason's hopeless struggle against the sleep she gave him. It was a two-edged gift. She knew that his nightmare was just beginning.

"Will I see you again?"

"Inevitably."

Jason was defeated. He lay back quietly, the spores of death multiplying, generating, rioting in his pulsing blood as sleep overpowered him.

Death slipped noiselessly into the corridor and let herself out through the back entrance to the street, stepping carelessly over the huddled shape of a homeless girl sleeping there. The girl radiated disease. Death's disciples were many, their numbers growing daily. She fitted in so well here, in this death driven place where the clients were so obliging.

She wrapped her coat about her against the pre-dawn chill, strolled easily towards her next appointment. She never hurried, was never late. Her Raybans reflected flickering blue neon. The *Elephant* never closed.

Death came here often.

Red City

When I spent time in India I was fascinated by Fatehpur Sikri, the Red City of the story title. The legend goes that the Emperor Akbar abandoned the city when his court astrologer predicted that the water supply would fail. But how? My explanation, of course, was that the prophet must have travelled in time to see the future. The idea simmered away until the opportunity arose to submit a story for Synergy SF, *which meant that it needed a hard theoretical base. I opted for quantum time travel, but quickly discovered that with the very knowledgeable George Zebrowski as my editor there was no chance I could fudge the science: he sent me back to the library to read articles in* Scientific American *and directed me to a swag of interviews with luminaries such as Stephen Hawking, among others, until I got the closed time curve right. (Thanks, George). It was a challenge to write the story so that every possible outcome was indeterminate. As always, I also worried about the ways in which the scientific possibilities of such a discovery would be entangled with predictably unprincipled human motivation.*

Come in under the shadow of this red rock . . .
(T.S. ELIOT: *The Wasteland*.)

Red dust devils whirled and glittered and spun in the dust wake of the only moving object on the red plain. Above, the sky was a glazed enamel blue, fired and ready to crack in the heat. Below, what scant macadam remained on the stony red road was melting, sticking, slowing the labouring car that crawled through a baking midsummer afternoon in Uttar Pradesh.

Inside the car, the heat was stifling. Everything smelled of hot dust. Lucinda Ponsonby-Smythe lolled in her corner of the back seat, her unflattering synthetic-cotton dress plastered to her body's sweaty crevices, her back sticking wetly to the imitation red leather upholstery of the straining, overheated Morris Major Deluxe. Her pale skin had taken on a yellowish waxy cast, sheened with the sweat that trickled between drooping breasts buttressed with rigid underwire that cut and clung in the heat. She was in a foul mood. Again.

"I'm suffocating," she said, irritably pushing a strand of over-dyed black hair back from her forehead as she turned to her husband sitting meekly beside her.

"You insisted on coming along on this trip, my love," he said mildly. "I did warn you it would be hot."

"You didn't say it would be *primitive*," she retorted, pointedly tapping the microcircuitry panel of her communicator wristband. "Nothing works. I can't even send a memo to my secretary." She paused for effect. "And as for this wretched translator," she went on, "it keeps making stupid mistakes."

"It's the most advanced cochlear implant there is, my darling," said Miles. "It's supposed to work even on ancient languages. It's probably just a bit literal when it comes to idiomatic constructions, that's all."

"All? No, Miles, that's not all. I don't like it. It buzzes in my ear all the time. It gives me a headache," she said.

"Relax, my love," he replied. "You'll get used to it soon enough."

Relax? How can I possibly relax in this heat? I feel frightful. I'm going to be sick. Miles, *do* something. *Make* him turn the air back on."

"Illness and my wife are old friends, I'm afraid." Miles addressed the driver *sotto voce*, hoping to save the situation. "She does understand, really."

After five days of heat soaked travel in an atmosphere saturated with Lucinda's disapproval, he feared that the long-suffering Singh was reaching the limits of his forbearance. Miles certainly was.

"I heard that." Lucinda shot her husband a poisonous look. "And I don't believe that nonsense about Indian production plants using old technology, and this thing only having a generator instead of an alternator. Singh's just incompetent. And you're encouraging him."

Irritated, Miles spoke carefully, addressing himself to the now rigid back of Singh's neck. "One more time, then. The ambient temperature is too hot for this car's small motor to run the air-conditioner. If we turn it back on, it will kill the engine. Do you seriously want to spend another four hours marooned on this god-awful road, fending off snake charmers and adolescents with dancing bears and children peddling peacock feathers?"

Miles winced at the thought, yesterday's disastrous experience all too fresh in his mind. After a morning of kamikaze driving, with Singh deftly dodging overloaded buses and trucks that vied for road space with drays drawn by camels, oxen, buffalo, even goats on the outskirts of Old Delhi, the traffic had thinned to a trickle. Around the middle of the day, when sensible people rested, the Agra road had become a deserted heat mirage shimmering into the hot distance. At Lucinda's insistence, they'd tried the air-conditioner. And the Morris had limped, spewing steam, to halt beside the only sketchy roadside shelter for miles around, where local people had materialized from nowhere to besiege the trapped tourists.

It had all been good humoured enough. The sluggish cobra and gritty peacocks were okay, but Miles was sickened by the plight of the dusty brown bears. Their teeth and claws had been pulled out, and each had a hole drilled through the bone of the snout to admit a rope that was threaded down the nasal cavity to exit at an iron ring clipped through the sensitive nostril. Rangy adolescent boys pulled on the ropes to force the bears to perform their shambling "dance" Miles most definitely did not want a repeat performance.

"You're much too soft," said Lucinda.

Miles wondered if she could read his thoughts.

Singh glanced back at his passengers. Framed in the rearview mirror, Lucinda's slack-coiled, venomous posture reminded him of yesterday's cobra in its woven basket. He contemplated the care and feeding of reptiles.

"If the Memsahib will permit the smallest of detours, I will take you to my cousin's restaurant for refreshment. He has imported beer. You will feel better if you rest in the shade."

The cousins were also traders, and she would have to buy another souvenir. A small revenge.

"Oh very well, if we must. Provided you're not taking me to another tourist trap. I do *not* want another souvenir."

"Of course not, Mem. That is why you have a private driver," Singh said smoothly.

Twenty minutes later the car shuddered to a standstill beside a hand-lettered sign proclaiming "Ice Cold Bears." Miles exchanged an amused smile with Singh, charmed by the ramshackle awning that stretched a welcome shade under dust-laden trees.

Lucinda alighted, slammed the car door, and strode into the roadside cafe. By the time the men caught up with her, she was already ordering the traders about. Her hideously expensive microtranslator implant gave her linguistic competency, but Lucinda's only verbs were in the imperative mood. "No. Take that jug away. I won't drink anything not bottled and properly sealed."

"Perhaps the Mem will take beer?" said Singh.

"Not the local muck. *Imported* beer." Unasked, she stalked to the ice chest, rummaging about until she unearthed something suitable. She turned imperiously towards her driver. "The label looks old," she said, "but Coors should be safe. Bottled in America. Still, I can't drink it out of this."

"Let me get you a *clean* glass from the kitchen." Singh whisked the bottle away behind a bead curtain, turning his back as he poured. A moment later he returned, bowing slightly as he presented the beer to Lucinda on a small tray.

She took the glass and sipped, ignoring Singh. "Miles, this tastes bitter," she said.

"It's American," Miles replied. "There's nothing wrong with it. Drink up, my love. You'll feel better. You're probably dehydrated from the heat. Here—the owners have set a comfortable chair for you. Just relax."

Singh winked at Miles, producing a bottle of Heineken lager from a private icebox behind the curtain and quickly pouring it into glasses for them both. Miles sipped gratefully, chatting amiably with the driver while the cousins spread countless carpets at his wife's hot, sticky, sandalled feet. Everyone knew she wouldn't buy. It was a custom, a diversion, something to do.

"Why do you do it, Singh?" The cold beer was a great restorative. Miles, his pale face still pink and his thinning blonde hair still slicked and sweat darkened, was beginning to recover his usual curiosity about everything. He liked people, and was genuinely interested in knowing what they thought and felt.

Singh looked startled. "Oh. You mean to ask why do I take private tours in the middle of summer?"

Miles wriggled, trying, and failing, to unstick his wrinkled linen shorts from his sweaty crotch. He wondered, fleetingly, how Singh always managed to look so fresh in his long white shirt and his immaculate white turban. "Yes. Of course."

"The university does not pay its cultural anthropologists very well, Professor Smythe. And I have family responsibilities. So I contract with the tourist board during the summer vacation to drive those who can afford a truly informed guide. Most of my clients are academics, like yourself, who find my advertisement in the small print of the on-line journals. And it gives me the chance to do a little more site research."

"Which is what I want to talk to you about. There are, shall we say, *interesting* rumours about Fatehpur Sikri. Certain, ah, unusual theories."

Singh lowered his voice. "It is a site to be approached with some caution, Professor Smythe. Your lady wife . . . "

Lucinda interrupted, right on cue: "Look, Miles. These are lovely. Come and bargain for me."

Surprised at her suddenly relaxed tone, Miles looked up to see his wife enthroned on a canvas chair amid a chaotic sea of carpets, surrounded by the gorgeous red and gold wools of Bodhoi and Mirzapur and the subtler shimmering silks of Kashmir. He thought that Lucinda looked almost regal at that moment, her dark hair pulled back from ivory skin, her mud brown eyes currently masked by startling blue contact sun-lenses. She sipped her beer, clearly enjoying being at the centre of the circle of kneeling traders. Miles went to her, brushing aside, as always, the quick thought that such pleasantness couldn't last.

Half an hour later, Queen Lucinda was yawning uncontrollably, slipping helplessly towards sleep. And Miles was shepherding her back to the car, bearing under his arm the small, rolled, string-tied parcel that contained his wife's new pastel-toned silk Tree of Life rug from Kashmir.

"You just stretch out in the back, darling. I'll ride up front with Singh, so you can take a little nap."

"I don't want to be alone."

"You won't be. I'm right here."

"I don't know why I should feel so sleepy."

"It's just the heat."

Lucinda's complaints quickly subsided into snores.

Singh mentally let fall flowers upon the shrines of his gods.

Miles slid into the front passenger's seat. "So what exactly did you slip into that beer?" he asked as the car pulled away from the little knot of waving traders.

"A thousand pardons. It was the mildest of tranquillising powders. Totally organic. Perfectly safe. The Mem was exhausted. She will wake refreshed."

"It cost me a fortune in hand-woven silk. A lovely piece, but you could have chosen a less expensive place to stop. You might at least look contrite."

"It never occurred to me that your lady wife would relax enough to buy more than a peacock fan." Singh gave a rueful smile. "But my cousins will be pleased. And besides, we must talk."

Miles nodded. "So tell me what's got everyone so excited about the Red City. Half the academic world is applying for research grants to study it, and your government can't stall all the researchers forever. Your own reasons for staying close to it aren't exactly those of a disinterested tour guide, are they?"

Singh shrugged. "Perhaps not entirely."

"I read your latest article, you know," Miles said, smiling diffidently. "That's why I asked for you specifically, *Professor* Singh. To learn more about the mystery."

"I'm honoured you have read my work," Singh replied, returning the smile. "But I am merely one researcher among many. There have always been stories about Akbar's city, Professor Smythe. It is perfectly understandable that folk stories should spring up around a rich city so suddenly abandoned by its people."

"Yes. Of course. But the folklore has always insisted that Akbar's astrologer foretold events exactly. And the recent rumours I've been hearing say why. These aren't whispered ghost stories, Singh. These sound coherent. Consistent. And in terms of quantum cosmology, they are at least theoretically not impossible."

Singh shrugged. "Akbar's astrologer was a remarkable sage, Professor Smythe. We have no evidence that he was more than that. There are other ways he could have predicted the failure of the water supply."

"But you have your reasons for investigating." Miles sighed. "You know, I've always dreamed of that astrologer's seat, perched under its stone canopy so high above the city."

Singh permitted himself a small chuckle. "Well, he'd hardly do anything really extraordinary from up there," he said. "That's a ceremonial seat, and much too exposed for serious work. The site that interests us is totally unremarkable, tucked away near the city walls. No more than a red shadow in a cleft of a red rock."

Miles leaned forward. "But a shadow that's a naturally occurring closed time curve?"

"Perhaps, though culturally it might be more appropriate to think of it as a reincarnation point. Part of the cosmogonic cycle."

Miles nodded, thinking it through. "Same concept, essentially," he said at last. "You believe the astrologer found an access point to a time loop, don't you? You think he used it. The logic of a time curve would present no problem at all to a Hindu philosopher. The implications are fascinating."

"But purely speculative."

"As you say. But fascinating all the same. Will you show me the site? Please?"

"You won't see much."

"I'll take the chance."

"Damn!" Singh swerved suddenly, barely missing a pair of peacocks taking a dust bath in the middle of the pot-holed road.

Lucinda stirred. "Are we there yet?" she asked plaintively. "Miles, I need a drink of water. It's so hot back here."

Miles bent to retrieve a bottle of mineral water from under the seat. "Normal service has been resumed," he said softly.

It was Singh who answered her question. "No, Mem," he said, "but we have not much further to travel. Tonight you will stay in the summer home of the late Maharajah. The guest wing of the palace has only recently been opened for first-class tourists. No expense has been spared to provide for your comfort. It is an accommodation fit for royalty."

"I hope it's air-conditioned," said Lucinda. "I can't bear this interminable heat."

"Of course it is. The Mem will find nothing to complain of," Singh replied, more in hope than anticipation.

He drove on in hot, uncomfortable silence for another sweltering hour, but at last he swung the car between high intricately wrought iron gates and onto a gravel drive, and the park surrounding the palace opened up before them. Gorgeous peacocks strutted through grounds that were green and lush, dropped bright feathers beneath brighter flowers. Wide garden beds surrounded leafy glades with splashing fountains, and the flowering trees that lined the long carriage way were full of chattering monkeys. At last the palace itself came into view—a long building of white colonnaded arches and domed cupolas decorated in red marble and framed by the cool gardens. Its reflection floated on the waters of a long shallow pool, disturbed only by the ripples of another cascading fountain.

Singh stopped the car at the foot of a flight of marble steps leading to the entry foyer. Half a dozen porters emerged from the shaded porch and clustered around the car. The chief doorman, immaculately attired in brocade uniform, bowed low and extended a white-gloved hand to open the car door for Lucinda, then shepherded her towards the hotel. The luggage was swiftly borne indoors. Miles paused a moment and took a deep breath, glad to be away from the dust of the road.

But Lucinda had reached the foyer, and was waiting. "Miles, do come along," she called. "I need you to register."

"Coming, my love."

"It's *Ponsonby*-Smythe," Lucinda was saying loudly as Miles reached the registration desk.

"It's all right," Miles explained to the puzzled concierge. "My wife's name is hyphenated. I'm just plain Smythe. It's the same booking."

"As you wish, sir."

The formalities were quickly completed, the luggage was delivered, and Miles found himself in a truly opulent suite where beautiful Kashmiri carpets were spread over cool marble floors. The rooms were full of antiques and artworks, and a low table had been set with a basket of fresh fruit and a brimming ice bucket offering bottles of chilled mineral water and white wine. Miles was contemplating a long cool drink when Lucinda called from the bathroom.

"Miles, do come and look. This is more like it."

The sound of splashing water was loud in his ears as he opened the door to a bathroom that was all mirrors and red marble and gold fittings. A deep bathtub was already almost full of hot water and patchouli-scented foaming bubbles, and the mirrored walls were faintly misted with steam.

"Just bring me a drink, would you darling? Champagne would be nice." She sighed and stretched languorously. "You know, I could be right at home in a harem."

"Of course you could, my love." Miles dutifully phoned room service. Half an hour later his wife was sipping her champagne in the bath, and Miles slipped outside to discuss tomorrow's plans with Singh. The two men sat comfortably on a curving garden bench beneath a spreading tree while Singh outlined his work in progress.

"It would be best if your lady wife did not accompany you," Singh said at last. "I fear she will not tolerate trailing around the site for very long."

"I know," said Miles. "I'll try to talk her out of it."

"If you'll forgive my impertinence," Singh said, "I don't understand why she wanted to come here at all. She clearly isn't enjoying it."

"My fault," Miles said ruefully. "I was excited about the Red City. I made the mistake of telling her I respect your work. Then she insisted that I shouldn't go on holiday without her, so I either had to give up the trip or bring her along. That's why we're taking the tourist route."

"But a field trip isn't exactly a holiday."

"Tell that to my wife."

"Isn't she also an academic? Surely she understands?"

"She's an academic administrator, Singh. And no, she doesn't understand. It's all budgets and committees as far as she's concerned. When it comes to research, she's only interested in the bottom line."

"Ah well," Singh said. "Perhaps tomorrow she will release you from your uxorial duties, and you can get some work done."

"I doubt it," Miles replied. "But I'll see what a good dinner can do for the cause."

The dinner was very good indeed. The Smythes dined by candlelight in a perfectly preserved banquet room, its antique details faultless from the gleaming furniture and wallpaper right down to the matching scatter cushions. A discreet plaque by the door was simply inscribed: "Wm. Morris & Co., 1898".

"This is fantastic," said Miles. "The Maharajah must have had the whole thing designed by Morris, no less, then shipped out from England and reconstructed here. I hate to think what that would have cost."

"I guess the Raj could afford it," Lucinda replied. "There's a fortune here just in silverware and crystal."

"And the food is marvellous." Miles waved his fork at the array of aromatic meats and pilafs and breads and dipping sauces spread before them in chased silver dishes. He selected another helping of chicken korma then refilled his glass with chilled Chardonnay. "The cooking here is exquisite."

"I suppose," his wife conceded. "If you like this kind of thing."

"Would you prefer something else? They have a full European menu." Miles was solicitous, trying hard to please. "Shall I call a waiter? I only ordered the deluxe banquet because I thought you'd like to try the local delicacies."

"No, thank you. I don't want another meal. This is fine. I just don't like it as much as you do."

"If you're sure, then." Miles smiled at his wife. "Have some more wine."

Lucinda smiled back grudgingly. "Very well," she said.

The evening proceeded tolerably enough. Miles ordered desserts and coffee and liqueurs, and Lucinda was smiling for real by the time they returned to their sumptuous bedroom.

"Here, let me unzip you," said Miles. "You'll be more comfortable out of those clothes."

Lucinda turned obligingly.

Miles helped her out of her dress and nuzzled her neck. "It's nice and cool in this room," he said. "For the first time on this whole trip it isn't too hot for us to enjoy ourselves. We are on holiday, after all." He took her in his arms to kiss her.

She turned her head away. "Not tonight, darling," she said. "I'm much too tired. I think I'll just turn in."

Miles was not disappointed. "As you wish, my love," he said, heading for the bathroom. Honour had been satisfied. He would sleep well tonight.

The next day began promisingly, and the Smythes were finishing breakfast in the conservatory when Miles broached the subject of their itinerary. "Why don't you relax in the palace for the day, darling," he said hopefully. "This evening, I'm taking you to see the Taj Mahal by moonlight. It's the most romantic sight in all the world. You'll love it."

"That'll be nice."

"So we'll be staying here again tonight in any case. The room's paid for. You might as well take advantage of it. And you don't really want to see Fatehpur Sikri. It's just an old abandoned city. I want Singh to show me some of the technical sites. There are archeology students working on the ruins, so there will be a lot of dust. It'll be very hot—there'll be no shade at all up there on the ridge. You'll be bored."

"I'll be just as bored if I'm stuck here. I don't want to be left alone. Anything could happen."

Miles looked around at the plush surroundings, at the opulent fittings and the extravagant displays of glistening fruit piled upon golden trays.

"Like what?"

"Anything. I don't know. I don't trust these people."

"For goodness sake. You're safer here than you would be at home. No one is going to touch you. You can sit in the garden and order cool drinks all day. Read a magazine. Get some rest. You've been complaining that you can't sleep."

"No. I don't think so. You're just trying to get rid of me. You want to go off for the day with Singh and leave me behind."

"I'm only thinking of you."

"No you're not. You want me out of the way so you can go chasing after your crackpot theories."

Miles did not reply, avoiding confrontation.

But Lucinda was warming to her theme. "I heard you two talking," she said cruelly. "I wasn't really asleep. Just dozing. But awake enough to hear all that nonsense about time loops and astrologers."

"It isn't nonsense," Miles said quietly. "The laws of quantum physics . . . "

Lucinda cut him off. "What about the laws of common sense?" she said.

"Culturally constructed," Miles replied. "What's common sense changes constantly. Common sense said humans could never fly, but airplanes are pretty common these days."

"That's different."

"How?"

"Time is a straight line, beginning to end. Airplanes included. You can't get on and off your timeline." Lucinda gave Miles a pitying look. "Besides," she added firmly, "if time travel were possible, we'd already have been overrun by hordes of tourists from the future. And we haven't, so it isn't. So there."

"Not necessarily, my dear," Miles replied, mistakenly trying to engage her in theoretical discussion. "If closed time curves do exist, they are a non-renewable resource. They'd be too strategically valuable for mere tourism."

"And you'd know, I suppose?"

Miles tried another tack. "Anyway," he said, "if future generations do figure out how to use CTCs on a large scale, visiting boring ancestors in the 21st century might not be exactly high on our descendants' priority list. We can't even get our kids to come home for the Christmas holidays!"

"*Your* kids," she retorted. A sore point, this. This was a second marriage for Miles, and Lucinda's third. "*Your* children simply refuse to spend the holidays with me. They treat me like the proverbial wicked stepmother."

Miles retreated to his theories. "Okay," he said, trying not to sound desperate. "Forget the family visits. Think about asymmetric separation. If our descendants did time travel, they would only arrive in some of the possible parallel universes. And this may not be one of them. In fact, if we haven't seen any time travellers it probably means we can assume that our universe *isn't* one of their possible destinations."

"I give up!" Lucinda turned stood, dropping her napkin and scattering breakfast crumbs in all directions. "This is total rubbish. You're delusional!"

"Probably," Miles conceded, losing patience. "So why don't you take a break and leave me to my delusions for the day?"

"No chance. I'm coming with you to this Red City of yours to make sure you don't get into any trouble. So let's get on with it, shall we?"

Miles sighed deeply. "After you, my love."

The drive to Fatehpur Sikri was hot, uncomfortable, and marred by another upset. On the outskirts of a ramshackle town an enterprising group of villagers "danced" their bears into the middle of the road, blocking the way while they demanded money. Miles scattered the few coins he had in his pockets while Singh edged the car through the crush.

"Ignore them," was Lucinda's advice.

"I can't," Miles replied. "The whole dancing bear thing upsets me."

"You're too sentimental. They're just animals."

Singh did not comment. He drove on past the villagers, and half an hour later he had parked the car outside the gates of Fatehpur Sikri. The three were walking towards the massive Gate of Victory, the entrance to the Daragh Mosque, when the clear blue sky crazed silver with lightning. The roadside peacocks squawked in protest as a sudden wind ruffled their already dusty feathers; the skeletal dogs that lived by begging scraps from the tourists barked a half-hearted challenge to the skies. Thunder cracked and boomed overhead. But there were no clouds, and there would be no rain, no damp breeze to cool this baking city of red rock and no water. Just heavier gusts of oven-fired wind from the red plain.

"Prajapati speaks," said Singh. "In the Brihadaranyaka-Upanishad Fable of the Thunder the Lord of Creation instructs us: *restrain yourselves, give, be compassionate.*"

"Really," Lucinda said, looking up at the carvings on the gate. "Does he say anything about elephants?"

"I'll collect our entry passes," Singh said tightly as he walked away in the direction of a small kiosk.

"Did you have to offend him?" said Miles.

"Have you looked at this gate?" she groaned theatrically. "As if we haven't seen enough carvings of elephants."

"Singh still hasn't forgiven you for refusing to take off your leather belt at the Temple of Ganesh."

"Superstitious nonsense!"

"Maybe. But if you didn't mind *riding* on an elephant to get to the temple, it couldn't have hurt to respect the religious custom. Singh was really upset."

"Well, it's too late now. It's not *my* problem. And here he comes."

Singh, not quite out of earshot, was reflecting that the erstwhile owner of this gate would not have tolerated her insolence. The emperor Akbar, he recalled, was in the habit of encouraging his war elephants to trample those who had displeased him. Singh could not shake a sense of foreboding that had been growing in his mind since the Ganesh incident. No good would come of it. The voice of the thunder confirmed it.

"Ready?" Singh asked as he rejoined his charges.

"Of course." Miles led the way up the impressive flight of steps to the arched entry, and paused to look at the inscription.

Singh translated: "*The world is a bridge: pass over it but build no house upon it. He who hopes for an hour may hope for eternity.*"

"A useful thought," said Miles.

"If you say so," said Lucinda.

The thunder spoke again: a long, threatening rumble followed by a loud boom as lightning forked once more across the sky. The air smelled suddenly of ozone.

Singh looked up apprehensively. "Shall we do the tour?" he said. Without waiting for an answer, he set off across the dusty, abandoned city. He ushered Miles Smythe and his ever complaining wife through the wonders of the palace of Jodh Bai, with its Temple of the Winds; the gilded Miriam's House, the Panch Mahal with its five stories of columns, then the palace of Bhirbal Bhaven, Akbar's favourite courtier. Singh had a professional guide's anecdote for each. "Bhirbal's house," he said, "was once described by Victor Hugo as either a very small palace or a very large jewellery box."

Lucinda was struggling to keep up. "Can't we rest for a while?" she said plaintively. "This place is huge."

"No, my dear," said Miles. "Not yet. I want to see the Diwan-I-Am next."

"What's that exactly?"

"The Hall of Public Audiences. Beside it is the Pachchisi courtyard, all blocked out as a game board. Akbar is famous for having played chess on it, using slave girls as the pieces."

"This Akbar seems to have been quite a character," she said. "Why exactly did he build all this then abandon it?"

"He was the greatest of all the Moghul Emperors," Singh replied in his tour-guide voice. "The legend has it that Akbar was without a male heir and he made a pilgrimage to this place to consult the saint Shaikh Salim Christi. His cave is outside the walls, near the stonecutter's mosque, which pre-dates the city. The saint foretold the birth of Akbar's heir, Jehangir, and in gratitude Akbar moved his headquarters here to Sikri and built this splendid city."

"And that's what makes him so important?"

Singh's frustration was obvious.

Miles stepped into the breach. "Actually," he said, "Akbar turned out to be very important in cultural terms. When the English envoys arrived to negotiate trading rights, it was Akbar who insisted that their influence was to be limited to commercial matters, and India's culture, beliefs and religions were to be left strictly alone."

"Which suited the English," Singh added, his tone sharp. "To them India was just a place to make money. It is said that the English didn't give a damn what religion a person held as long as he could make a good cup of tea."

"Quite right," said Lucinda. "Excellent idea. Can we get a cup of tea anywhere here?"

Singh gave up. "The archaeologists have a spirit stove," he said. "I'll take you around the walls to their dig, and I'll ask them to make tea for you. You might care to rest there while Miles visits the sites that interest him."

"Good idea," Miles said hopefully.

The pleasantries were soon over—Miles was introduced as a visiting scholar. Lucinda got her cup of tea, and one of the students set a folding chair for her beneath a canvas awning so that she could sit in a patch of shade.

"I think I will just stay here a while," she said to Miles. "But don't leave me too long, will you?"

"Of course not, darling. Singh and I are just going to see Shaikh Salim Christi's cave."

"A cave. That will be jolly."

"You'll be able to find us if you need us. Just follow the city walls."

"Thanks. I'm sure *someone* will take care of me," she said, settling irritably into the rickety chair.

Miles set off at a brisk pace, barely bothering to conceal his relief at being released from Lucinda's disapproval. Excitement was getting the better of him, despite the heat. "Can we take a quick look at the CTC site now?" he asked.

"Yes," said Singh. "While we can. It's at the cave site in any case. You might also like to see the Hathi Poi, the Elephant Gate." He smiled grimly. "I doubt that your lady wife would be amused by these particular elephants—they are very dilapidated."

Miles nodded. "I guess not," he replied. "I'm sorry she was so abrupt, Singh."

"Think nothing of it. You are not to blame. Come, let me show you the site."

The shallow cave was unprepossessing—little more than a dusty recess in the red rock of the city walls. But at the back of the cave was a cleft in the rock face, a narrow fissure no more than the height of a man. And the air around this cleft was impossibly cool, cool as the air in underground caves where water drips and chills the rock. But here there was no water.

"This is it?" said Miles.

"I'm afraid so," Singh replied. "I did warn you there is nothing much to see."

"But this is where your colleagues are conducting their tests?"

"Yes."

"Has anyone been through?"

"Not yet. It's too dangerous. The shadow field seems to flicker in and out. There is no certainty that one could return to one's own time."

"But the astrologer must have done it, if the stories are true."

"Indeed. And he may also have understood the phenomenon in ways that we do not. Sadly, there is much ancient knowledge has not survived into our own time." He sighed. "And so we must be cautious until we gather enough data."

"It must be tempting though?" Miles brushed his hand along the edge of the shadow field, feeling the texture of its cool edge.

"To see the Emperor Akbar's city as it was in all its glory? It would be an archeologist's dream, Professor Smythe. But we must yet be patient."

"There you are! We've been looking everywhere for you." Lucinda stood at the entrance to the cave, shading her eyes against the glare. "I asked Ahmed here to bring me along to find you."

A dusty archaeology student grinned sheepishly.

"Thank you, Ahmed," Singh said dryly. "That was kind."

"No problem, Professor Singh."

Lucinda stepped around Ahmed, advancing like a cross, middle-aged Alice intent on her looking glass. "So this is what you two were so secretive about," she said. "A dusty cave, and some gossip about a shadow. Is this it?"

Miles nodded warily.

Lucinda pushed her way into the space beside her husband.

"Don't get too close, darling," he said.

"Why not?" She pressed her sweaty body into the heavy air where it shimmered, coalescing in shadow around the red rock cleft. "See. It's all nonsense. I don't believe a word of all your scientific mumbo-jumbo. This is only cool air, for goodness sake. There's no mystery. I can walk right through it."

"Lucinda, *NO!*"

Lucinda ignored the warning.

Ahmed stared, open mouthed, as Lucinda simply disappeared.

Miles and Singh looked across the shadow at each other for a long moment.

"Now what do we do?" said Miles.

There was a soft, sucking sound as the air closed behind Lucinda. Abruptly, the irritating dust was gone. The cave was gone. Miles and Singh were gone. She was standing beside the red wall of the city. And then, impossibly, she heard water sounds—trickling sounds, lapping sounds. Coming from behind the rock wall.

Lucinda walked up nearby steps onto the wall and looked around. She realized that the sounds were coming from a huge cistern—part of the water supply for Akbar's city. She turned. Behind her was the city itself, drowsing in afternoon heat, but unmistakably alive. There were people everywhere: fruit and vegetable sellers trundling their delivery carts, guards in bright livery patrolling the walls, and, over by the Victory Gate, elephant handlers grooming their massive beasts.

"I don't believe it," she said aloud.

She walked as quickly as she could back down the steps and stood below the wall, looking for the sticky shadow that had transported her. But here, in the brightest of Indian summer sunshine, there was no shadow on the red rock. She was still gazing in disbelief when a tall guard accosted her.

"What are you doing here?"

Lucinda's microtranslator stuttered for a moment, but then, to her relief, unscrambled the language. Persian, she guessed. "Oh," she replied. "Sorry. I'm lost. I'm just trying to work out how to get back to my friends." She looked up at him, smiling brightly, expecting help. It usually worked.

The guard's professional curiosity gave way to an expression of pure horror as he looked down at her: his fingers flashed signs of warding and he backed away from the revelation of her blue-lensed eyes. "Demon!" he cried. He looked more closely at her sundress. "Indecent!" he added. Then, with what was clearly an effort of will, he took hold of her wrist, twisted her arm behind her back, and began to march her towards the guardhouse, keeping behind her to avoid those too-blue eyes.

Her reception by the other guards was no more encouraging. One threw a blanket at her. "Cover yourself," he said, making the sign of the evil eye and giving her a push that sent her sprawling into a dark corner of the room. "And stay there. Don't try anything."

Lucinda did as she was told, huddling under the smelly blanket despite the heat.

None of the other men would even look in her direction. A messenger was sent running, and, after what seemed like hours, a richly dressed man entered the guardroom, his gold brocade coat and matching turban almost glowing in the dim light.

The guards stood rigidly for his inspection.

"Be easy," said the newcomer.

"We are honoured by your presence, astrologer."

"You did well to send for me," the astrologer replied. "I thought it best to come myself. Demons are dangerous to deal with. Where is it?"

"Over there." A guard pointed.

The astrologer edged close to Lucinda. "Up," he ordered.

Lucinda scrambled to her feet.

The astrologer stared at her for a long moment. "Where did you say you found it?" he asked the guard.

"By the city wall, Excellency," the guard replied.

The astrologer considered for a long moment. "I'll take it," he said at last. The relief was palpable in the guardroom. "I'll need a closer inspection. My servants are trained to help in such matters. If it is a demon, I'll have it destroyed. If not, if it truly is a woman, the Emperor might be amused by such an oddity for his harem."

"But I'm not . . . "

"Silence, demon! It is not your place to speak. If you interrupt me I will order your immediate death. Do you understand?"

Lucinda subsided into shocked silence.

"Come along then. And keep yourself covered. The lewdness of your dress disgusts me." He spat expressively. Then he reached out swiftly and slipped a thin iron manacle over her wrist. He locked it, and looped its chain over his own hand.

Lucinda tried to pull away.

The astrologer yanked firmly, hurting her wrist. "They don't like iron," he said to the guards. "It binds them to the earth." He sighed deeply. "It won't be so much trouble now. But it would be as well for you to keep a sharp lookout along the walls, in case there are more of them."

The leader of the guards bowed. "It will be done, Excellency."

"Very well." The astrologer tugged on Lucinda's chain. "This way," he said, leading her from the guardroom.

They emerged into bright sunlight, Lucinda felt as though she had walked into an oven. She sagged a little, but the astrologer pulled her upright. His grip on her arm was like a vise. When they were well away from the guardhouse he leaned very close to her. "You may speak now, demon. What evil has sent you here? Where have you come from?" he hissed.

"You're the famous astrologer," she replied. "You *know* where I've come from."

"Don't play games with me," he said, his body radiating pure menace. "Who has sent you here to spy? Is it the visit of the English envoy that has brought you?"

"I'm not playing games," said Lucinda. "And I don't know anything about an envoy. But I've heard all about you. And I've seen your precious red shadow at the back of the cave. That's how I got here. So don't pretend you don't know."

The astrologer looked truly puzzled.

"What cave?" he asked.

Lucinda racked her brains. "The saint's cave," she said. "The one that predicted the Emperor's son."

"The cave of Shaikh Salim Christi?"

"That's the one." Lucinda lowered her voice. "So you do know," she said. She looked across and him and fluttered her eyelashes. "You do know about the time gate or whatever you call it: the cave where you see the future and make your prophecies. And if you'll just take me back there, I'll return immediately to my own time. And none of this need ever have happened." She caressed his hand.

The astrologer slapped her. "Do not think to defile me, demon," he said.

Lucinda paled.

They hurried on in silence for some minutes, the astrologer deep in thought. "What prophecies?" he said at last.

"The ones about what happens to this city."

"Nonsense," he replied firmly. "Do you think me simple-minded?"

"Look at the place for yourself if you don't believe me."

"I don't believe you," he said firmly. "And we have almost reached the palace. You now will desist from further comment upon such matters. Be warned. I shall order my servants to destroy you if you speak of it. They will not disobey me."

Lucinda did not reply. She was looking up in amazement as the astrologer urged her across the threshold of a sumptuously furnished building of cool marble and latticed windows– a place whose dusty ruins she had visited not two hours ago with Singh. She tried, unsuccessfully, to remember what he had said about it.

The astrologer beckoned to a waiting servant. "Find Ali," he said. "It's urgent." Then he turned to Lucinda. "Sit here." He indicated a carved chair.

Lucinda sat.

The astrologer swiftly attached his end of the iron chain to the arm of the heavy chair. "And don't move."

Alone for a moment, Lucinda tested the chain. It was too strong. She tried slipping her hand from the manacle. It was too tight.

And then the astrologer returned.

"There's no one else I can trust with this," he was saying to Ali as he handed him a small iron key.

His chief eunuch and secretary nodded sagely.

"I want you to put it in the harem, for the time being, but keep it away from the women."

"Easily done, Excellency," Ali replied.

"And I want it treated *as* a woman, just in case. It may be that the creature is just a spy—I have heard tell that such women exist in the cold climates."

Ali nodded again.

"The English envoy is to be offered a selection of women for later this evening," the astrologer continued. "So prepare this creature and put it in line with the harem women. If the envoy chooses it we will know it is a spy and he wishes to speak with it. He would hardly choose it for its looks. If not . . . "

Ali finished the thought. "If not, we will know it is certainly a demon."

"Precisely. Then I will leave you to it. I have something I must attend to."

"Yes, Excellency."

The astrologer hurried through impossibly busy streets, almost forgetting his dignity in his haste. He dashed into the guardhouse, ignoring the startled men who were scrambling to their feet. "Which guard discovered the demon?" he asked peremptorily.

The tall guard stepped forward nervously. "I did, Excellency."

"Can you tell me *exactly* which part of the wall it was near when you found it?"

"The part where the stonecutters mosque stands, Excellency," the man replied. "And the saint's cave."

The astrologer nodded his thanks. The afternoon shadows were lengthening. He strode along the parapet until he saw the mosque and the cave below. Then he descended the stone steps, and walked carefully along, looking intently at the hewn red rock. "A shadow," he muttered to himself. "A shadow among so many." As he walked he ran his hand along the surface of the wall.

And there it was. His fingers touched a patch of colder air, air that felt somehow sticky, air that was denser than it should be. He pushed. His hand met little resistance. The shocked astrologer realized that he could step right through the wall. He took a deep breath.

There was a soft, sucking sound as the air closed behind him.

"I guess I'll have to go after her," said Miles.

"Wait a minute," Singh replied. "Let's think this thing through. If you and your wife had entered the shadow space together you'd arrive together, and you'd be able to help her. But if you try to follow her now, you could end up in any of the possible parallel universes. You might never find her."

"So what should I do, then?"

"Perhaps we should wait an hour or so," Singh said. "We have no way of knowing how long the passage between one point and another on a closed time curve continuum might take. It's perfectly possible she might be in the process of stepping back through the shadow space as we speak."

"True," Miles replied uneasily. "I suppose we could give her a little time."

Once they were safely inside the confines of the harem, Ali unlocked the manacle from Lucinda's wrist. "Remember, demon," he said, "you are watched. And you have been warned." He clapped his hands.

A huge man stepped into the room, wearing nothing but loose black silk trousers tied with a scarlet sash. His muscled body glistened with oil; his shaved head gleamed.

"This is the eunuch Abdul," said Ali. "He has been specially chosen to take care of you. He knows what you are. He is not afraid."

Abdul flashed a white smile and bowed low, setting his single gold earring bobbing against his dark skin.

Lucinda just stared.

"Clean her up, Abdul," said Ali. "Have her nose and ears pierced so she can wear some respectable jewellery, then find her some decent clothes. And I want her sexually prepared. His Excellency wishes her on display with the women when the envoy from England comes to make his selection for this evening. Do you understand?"

"Perfectly," Abdul replied. "It is my pleasure to serve." He took Lucinda by the arm and led her away.

The bathhouse was a wonderful relief after the indignities of the afternoon. Lucinda was left to luxuriate for a while in rose-scented hot water, where she lay contemplating how she would get her own back. Later.

Abdul returned with two slave girls who washed her hair then dried her body with soft linen towels. Lucinda was actually beginning to relax as the girls wrapped her in a linen bath sheet and led her to a low couch. They were combing out her dyed black hair, peering in bewilderment at the gray re-growth along her scalp, when Abdul advanced with a basket of very thin sharp spikes and a little awl.

"I'll do the nose first," he said. "Hold her."

The girls deftly grabbed her and held her down.

"No!" Lucinda screamed. "You can't do this! I'm not a bear to have my nose pierced."

"Gag her," said Abdul.

The girls obliged.

One excruciatingly painful hour later, Abdul led Lucinda back to an isolated room that smelled strongly of sandalwood. "Now," he said, holding up a mirror of polished steel, "that's better, isn't it?"

Lucinda peered. Her wavery reflection showed her new diamond nose-ornament and her gold hoop earrings set with rubies. There was blood on her face.

"Here." Abdul held out a small damp cloth. "This will stop the swelling. Hold it to your nose stud while I give you your massage. You have to be ready for this evening."

"I don't want a massage."

"Do you have to be held down again?"

Lucinda scowled but did not reply.

"Good." Without further ceremony Abdul stripped her of her linen bath sheet and helped her onto a low table. He cupped scented oil in his hands, then began his work, expertly easing the tension from her shoulders, back, calves, thighs, massaging higher and higher to her crotch. It was not until he slipped an expert finger into her vagina, then withdrew it to begin masturbating her, that Lucinda realized, belatedly, what this was all about. She squirmed, trying to get away.

"Stop it," she said. "You have no right."

"I have every right." Abdul easily held her down. "Sexually prepared," Ali said. "Those are my instructions. I could have the slave girls do it. But they'd be rougher than I am. Agreed?" His oiled finger had not stopped its insistent rubbing for a moment.

Lucinda sank back, fuming. Despite herself, she could feel the tension building. She arched her back.

"There," said Abdul. "That should do nicely."

"You can't leave me like this," she gasped.

"That's the whole point," he replied indifferently. "Prepared, remember." He slapped away the hand that Lucinda had extended. "And no touching yourself," he added. He clapped his hands. The slave girls entered, carrying armfuls of silk. "She's ready," he said. "Dress her." He looked at Lucinda with ill-concealed contempt. "I need to wash."

The girls held out a selection of saris.

Lucinda felt terrible. Her sun-lenses were beginning to feel scratchy, but she dared not take them out. Her nose ached, and the other ache that Abdul had engendered in her loins was making her irritable. "I don't care," Lucinda snapped. "Anything."

They deftly slipped a red silk choli top over her head, then wound a matching gold silk sari trimmed with red about her waist, draping its final length over one shoulder. They dressed her hair, fastening it with gold pins, and gave her golden sandals for her feet. Then they stepped back to admire their handiwork.

"What now?" asked Lucinda.

The girls giggled. "The envoy will choose," one replied.

"That's enough." Abdul was back. "Come along."

Lucinda found herself propelled into a gorgeous gallery. The marble floor was patterned with shallow channels of flowing water, and the walls were draped with woven carpets dampened to provide a cool breeze. Low couches heaped with bright silk cushions were set beside carved tables bearing trays of glistening fruits and luscious sweets.

"Don't stare," said Abdul. He bustled her into the middle of a long line of women, all of whom were exquisitely groomed, perfumed, and prepared to entertain the envoy.

Lucinda did not have long to wait. The English envoy arrived, a thin, ill-looking man who stalked into the hall like a dark-garbed crow amid the peacock silks of the harem. Ali was with him, keeping a sharp eye on proceedings. The envoy moved sedately along the line of women, judiciously making his choices for the evening. He didn't even glance twice at Lucinda.

Ali glanced significantly at Abdul, who took Lucinda by the elbow and led her back to her apartment. "Is that it?" she asked.

"Yes. Later, someone will bring food. But you can be private now. I'll just leave these here with you." He held out a tray to her, silently offering her the means of sexual release.

"Don't be ridiculous." She slapped away the proffered tray, sending gilded dildoes and ivory sex toys spinning across the perfumed room. "I'm perfectly able to deal with the situation," she said.

"As you wish."

Alone on her couch, she lay amongst embroidered silks, unable to block out the soft groans of more experienced inmates in the adjacent apartments. Masturbating furiously, she plotted impossible revenge. On all of them.

The astrologer was shaken to the core. He looked ten years older as he re-entered the palace and sank heavily into a chair in the reception foyer. He waved away the servants who waited to attend him, but accepted a goblet of cold water.

Ali came running. "Is something wrong, Excellency? Shall I call for your physician?"

The astrologer shook his head. "No, my old friend," he said at last. "A shock, that's all." He drew a ragged breath. "I have seen the ruin of our great city. And now I must act to avert the evil that may befall us." He sighed heavily. "The Emperor will have to be told." He made a visible effort to restore his equilibrium. "And what of our demon?" he asked.

"The envoy ignored it," Ali replied.

"I see. It is as I thought. The demon is a danger to us all. It must die. And soon."

Ali's face did not betray his emotions. He said only: "Best not to have it done in secret. There are already rumours."

"There are always rumours."

"Fortunately," Ali went on, "the Emperor wishes to intimidate the English envoy. Tomorrow, they will play at chess in the Diwan-i-Am courtyard."

"And the pieces?"

"The Emperor has ordered the palace prison cleared. The Captain of the Guard will choose the players. Those that survive will be pardoned."

"Then the blue-eyed demon will be White Queen, I think," said the astrologer. "The Emperor will accord the envoy the courtesy of the first move."

"Excellent." Ali nodded his approval.

The astrologer was recovering his composure. "Will you see to it, Ali?"

"Consider it done."

One hour had ticked by, then two. Miles had grown weary of watching the shadow space, and still Lucinda had not reappeared.

"Well, Singh," he said at last. "What's our next best option? It does not seem that my wife has had the sense to step straight back into the CTC, does it?"

"Truly, I cannot tell," Singh replied. "We simply do not know enough about how it works. Your lady wife may have tried to return but been transported to another point in time."

"Or to this time in a parallel universe," Miles added glumly. "One in which she does not return, at least not at this moment."

"Correct," said Singh. "That's the rub. There must be an infinite number of possible temporal destinations inside the CTC. The whole thing is quite indeterminate." He shrugged. "If you had gone together," he added, "then both of you could have come back together, but still to another variant. You can't go home again, as they say, but only to something like it, but maybe to something so close that you might not even notice it isn't quite the same. Only mostly, maybe."

"True," said Miles. "But we didn't go together. And I honestly don't know what to do for the best." He sighed heavily. "I'm willing to go after her, but it would help if we could figure out where that is. Or when it is."

"Of course you are willing, Professor Smythe. And I, too, am willing to help in her rescue."

The conversation faltered into silence as both men considered their willingness.

"I have been racking my brains for a solution," Singh said at last. "But we must proceed safely. There is little point in complicating the situation by having both of you lost."

"I know."

"It seems to me," Singh said carefully, "that we should perhaps consult with the other researchers to ascertain if their findings will be of any help to us."

"But the researchers are not here today," Miles said.

"Alas, no," Singh replied. "Finding them will take a little time. Do you have a better idea?"

"No, but I'm concerned about my wife."

"I'm sure she'll be fine, wherever she is," Singh said. "She is a formidable lady."

"True." Miles managed a little smile. "Lucinda can take care of herself. I don't doubt that she'll be safe, at least for a while. Someone is probably making her a cup of tea."

"Then shall we go in search of my colleagues?" Singh said.

"What if she returns while we're away? She'll be very angry when she gets back, especially if I'm not here to meet her."

"I'll instruct Ahmed to keep watch," said Singh. "He will certainly agree. After all, it's the least he can do. He will telephone me immediately if your lady wife returns."

Miles hesitated.

His watery blue eyes met Singh's brown ones for an instant.

Miles looked quickly away. "I guess that would be okay then," he said slowly.

Singh nodded. "You have my complete sympathy, Professor Smythe."

"As long as someone is here for her."

"I understand entirely," Singh murmured.

"Do you know where we might find your colleagues today?" Miles asked.

"There is an hotel in a nearby village where they are often to be found," Singh replied. "The beer there is excellent."

"That would be most welcome," Miles said with some relief. "I'm parched."

"Then it is settled," said Singh. "I'll just go and get the boy. Do you want to write a message for your lady wife, just in case?"

"I'll leave her a note."

The next thing Lucinda knew was that Abdul was shaking her by the shoulder. "Wake up," he said. "You have been summoned."

"What?"

"No time for arguments."

Lucinda realized, belatedly, that the two slave girls were standing behind him.

"Get her dressed," he said curtly.

The girls wasted no time. Lucinda was washed, brushed, and quickly arrayed in a flowing outfit of pure white. The choli was white silk, the white sari was patterned with silver stars, and the palloo shoulder drape was exquisitely embroidered in silver thread. A long white veil covered her head and shoulders, and the veil was held in place by a crown of silver. And this time there were silver sandals for her feet.

"Good," said Abdul.

Lucinda forgot her position for a moment. "What's all this about?" she asked.

"You are to be Queen for a day," he answered, smirking. "Enjoy it."

A small bell rang.

"Your escort has arrived," said Abdul. "Come along."

Lucinda had no chance to protest as Abdul hustled her from her apartment and through a maze of corridors.

The Captain of the Guard was waiting in the entry hall.

"All yours," Ali said, pushing Lucinda forward. "Watch her. She's not to be trusted."

"I have my orders," the man replied, taking Lucinda by the arm. "As you see, I have come myself to collect her." He nodded curtly to the eunuch.

Once outside, the captain marched Lucinda through the city streets. There were people everywhere, and a feeling of carnival was in the air. Street vendors were out and about, selling sticky sweet drinks and cooking flat bread over little charcoal fires.

"What's going on?" Lucinda asked. "Where are you taking me?"

"You'll see," he replied curtly.

The Hall of Public Audiences soon came into view, but the Captain took Lucinda through a small, dark back entrance and into what looked like a holding pen where dozens of people dressed strangely in either black or white stood about dejectedly. There were guards everywhere. The place smelled of urine, and fear.

"Last one," the Captain said to his men. "Take her. And let's get this lot moving. The Emperor won't thank us for keeping him waiting."

The guards responded immediately, rounding up the people into two lines—one black, the other white.

When the group was assembled to the captain's liking, he nodded to the guards, who opened a pair of heavy brass studded doors and herded their charges outside into brilliant sunlight.

Lucinda, entering last in the white line, looked around in amazement. The scene was spectacular. The courtiers of Fatehpur Sikri were seated in shaded cloisters that surrounded the courtyard that was the Emperor's chessboard. Tall, well-muscled slaves fanned their masters with huge peacock fans set in silver, and musicians played softly in high galleries. Slaves carrying trays laden with raisins, almonds and sliced lemons threaded their way through the crowd. Other servants offered pastries and sweets, and drink servers constantly refilled the nobles' goblets from huge silver pitchers. The atmosphere was charged with excitement. Today, the game would be played in earnest.

The emperor's private enclosure stood on one side of the courtyard. A richly gilded throne had been set for him under a canopy of gold-fringed black silk. Opposite, an elaborately carved chair had been set for his opponent, the English envoy, under a canopy of white, also fringed with gold. Behind these enclosures, the banners of Emperor Akbar and of Queen Elizabeth drooped in the heat, fluttering only when the wielders of the peacock fans came close.

A hush fell upon the crowd as the Captain of the Guard arrayed his charges in their places on the board. Lucinda looked about her, beginning to understand. The people were to be players, and all had been costumed to suit their stations—the pawns wore only loincloths and carried short stabbing swords, but the major pieces had more elaborate garments and weapons. Lucinda could see that the knights wore plumes and carried spears, and the men she thought of as the bishops wore elaborately ornamented sashes and wielded curved scimitars. The black queen was dressed exactly as Lucinda herself, robed and crowned. Two courtiers, dressed to kill, played the kings.

When all was in readiness an official stood to give the signal. The music changed, and all of Akbar's court rose to its feet to welcome their Emperor and his worthy opponent. Each man took his proper seat, and the formalities began.

Lucinda tuned out as the usual speeches of welcome and reply were made and applauded. She felt hot and sweaty and uncomfortable, standing here in the summer heat, but she dared not move. Finally, a ripple of excitement in the crowd caught her attention. An official was ending his recitation of the rules for today's match: "And lastly," he said, "our merciful Emperor has decreed that the surviving players will be pardoned and set free."

The crowd applauded.

Lucinda was still trying to make sense of it when the game began.

The envoy stood to direct his first move.

The Emperor, as the astrologer had predicted, was playing the black.

The first pawn was slain, stabbed through the heart by his opponent. Two attendants quickly removed the corpse from the board.

Lucinda put her hand to her mouth, realizing, at last, the nature of the game.

The first deaths were swift and predictable as the players sacrificed pawns and set up game plans. The hot air smelled of blood and faeces, and the courtyard was already becoming slippery. Lucinda felt queasy, but she struggled to pay attention, even though attendants were there to guide her though the moves the Englishman directed.

Emperor and envoy both played with talent and confidence, and as the afternoon wore on the kills became less frequent, if not less strategic. But Lucinda slowly became aware that the envoy was losing the match. And as she watched the Emperor's knight spear the sole surviving white castle, she realized, with sudden horror, that the Englishman was playing to lose. In fact, that diplomacy demanded he should lose.

At that moment, Lucinda, the white queen, looked up obliquely. She saw the mirror of her death in the slanting path that had suddenly opened between herself and the Emperor's implacable black bishop. The man raised a bloodied scimitar in mock salute.

The endgame was upon her. Forgetting her dignity, forgetting revenge, Lucinda prayed that the envoy would concede.

Paradise Design'd

The genesis for "Paradise Design'd" was a television interview in which I saw apologists for "intelligent design" insisting that there must have been dinosaurs in the Garden of Eden. They were showing a totally unconvincing diorama depicting Adam and Eve posing in a vaguely jungle setting, complete with cycads and stylized brontosaurs. I then recalled that Milton had neglected to mention the dinosaurs when explaining the ways of God to man in Paradise Lost, and concluded that a further version was needed to remedy that lack. This story is part homage to Milton, part guide to the art of Archangel landscaping, part extrapolation of The Fall. The dinosaurs, alas, are behaving badly.

"No one must speak of this, ever."

"He'll know," Michael said glumly.

"Obviously," said Raphael. "What Gabriel means is that we don't need the news to get out elsewhere."

"And as long as we tidy up here, there's no reason it should," Uriel added. "He's very protective of His little experiment. Hardly anyone's allowed to come here."

The four archangels looked down again at the untidy pile of bloodied feathers that was all that remained of their brother, Floriel. Beside him lay the corpse of the guilty T. Rex, still smoking from the fiery sword thrust that had dispatched it.

Michael shuddered. "It's still got feathers in its teeth," he said, "and shreds of Floriel."

Gabriel winced, and readjusted his own shining wings. "We're only here because He sent us to guard His pets," he said. "So what was Floriel doing here anyway?"

"Designing flowers, he said." Raphael shrugged. "I warned him about these monsters." He gestured at the corpse. "Just look at the teeth on that thing."

"So how do those two—Uriel gestured briefly to where Adam and Eve crouched behind a huge cycad, watching wide-eyed and unafraid—manage to go about completely unscathed?"

"He forbade it. All the carnivores are blocked from attacking His pets in His Garden," Raphael replied. "It would be a different story outside the Gates."

"I guess He just forgot to include angels in the ban," Michael said. "He's not infallible."

"Don't let Him hear you say that," Gabriel said urgently. "He's a bit touchy on the subject, ever since you-know-who rebelled."

"Let's not even think about that, just in case." Uriel looked around nervously. "And what exactly are we going to do about the monster?"

Gabriel smiled his dazzling smile, and raised his flaming sword in salute. "I think a little landscaping is in order," he said.

The others smiled back.

"Molten rock? Landslide? Raging torrent?" said Raphael.

"I thought something simpler—something small enough to do the job without attracting attention."

"Well?"

"I propose that we should just slide this little bit of land and vegetation into that little hollow down there, and then apply some heat and pressure. That way we can bury the evidence and after the flames die down the pit will look like a natural pool."

"Clever," said Uriel. "I like it."

"Then let's do it," said Michael. "These things are best done quickly."

All four archangels raised their swords then brought the fiery tips down in the one place. Rock collapsed, lush jungle toppled into the hole, and the remains of the Tyrannosaurus Rex slipped down after it. After a few moments all that remained was compacted earth and a deep tar pit, black and sticky, although tell-tale red flames still licked the surface and noxious vapours swirled about the valley.

"It'll soon be still," Gabriel said. "I think it looks fine."

"But won't other animals fall in and be trapped?" Michael said, looking meaningfully to where a curious stegosaurus had already wandered perilously close to the brink.

Raphael shrugged. "He didn't forbid collateral damage," he said. "There's no shortage of wildlife here. There were lots of small things living in that bit of jungle. Maybe a few fossils will add to the charm of the Garden."

"Too late to worry about it now," Uriel said.

The stegosaur had already toppled in. Suspicious-looking bubbles were rising to the surface.

"We'd better warn the pets," Gabriel said.

"How do we warn creatures that have no knowledge of sin or death?" said Michael. "They witnessed the whole thing, and they don't even look worried."

"They're trained to obedience. We just tell them," Raphael said. "I'll do it, if you like."

"You can try," said Michael. "Maybe they can understand."

Raphael walked slowly towards the humans. "Do not be alarmed," he said. "I bring you tidings."

Adam stood to meet the angel. "Hail, thou wondrous celestial messenger," he said solemnly.

Raphael ignored the sniggering of his brother angels behind him. "I bring you warning," he said. "For your own safety, you must not go near the new pool. It is dangerous."

"Can we not drink from it?" asked Adam.

"No," said Raphael. "It is unfit for you."

Adam looked around him, hesitating until Eve came forward and took his hand. They both looked up adoringly at the angel.

Raphael tried again. "It is important that you do not go near the new pool," he said. "Can you both remember that?"

"That's three things, ethereal one," Adam said.

"What?"

"Three things we must not eat or drink: fruit from that tree, fruit from the other tree, and now water from the new pool."

"Raphael nodded, "That's right," he said. "Those three things are not fit for such as you."

"We will remember, shining one," said Adam.

"We will remember," Eve echoed.

"Then all is well," said Raphael, fervently hoping it would be.

Michael snickered. "That was convincing," he said.

"Not to worry," said Gabriel, wrinkling his perfect nose. "The smell should keep them off."

Raphael shrugged. "I tried." He glanced around hurriedly. "Any sign of trouble?"

"Nothing so far," said Uriel.

"Probably too busy laughing," said Michael.

"Wonderful!" Satan's laughter resounded from the iron Gates of Hell, echoing through the cavernous depths.

Beside him, sitting at their ease, Sin and Death were laughing with him.

"Do you still want to be bothered corrupting the pets?" Death asked.

"Oh yes," Satan replied. "The sport's too good to miss."

"Then I suggest you wait till nightfall," Sin said, still laughing. "Those angels will be tired of guarding the Gates of Paradise by then. They've had a busy day."

"Quite so," said Satan. "But they don't sleep. Any suggestions about how I should break in?"

"Mist is always good," said Death. "Anything can happen in a dense mist."

"Good idea," said Sin. "Fog and mist are such useful things."

"I'll think about it," said Satan.

"Everything seems quiet enough now," Raphael said. He was leaning against the Gate, lit only by the glow of his sword.

"True," Uriel replied from the opposite gatepost. "But the fog still seems very thick around the tar pit. We've lost a triceratops now, and few smaller creatures besides."

"Stop worrying about the dinosaurs," said Raphael. "There's nothing we can do to stop them going too near the pool. And anyway, the vapours will probably dissipate with the sunrise."

"I suppose so."

Both angels watched carelessly as a thick, long tendril of mist snaked silently towards a herd of drowsing brontosaurus.

"Our labours await, my dear," said Adam, yawning and stretching in the first rays of morning sunlight. Pterodactyls soared overhead in a perfectly blue sky, their harsh cawing echoing across the lush landscape of Eden. The air still smelled faintly noxious.

Eve looked up, all innocence. "I thought I might work alone this morning," she said. "We could achieve more if we divide the tasks between us."

"But darling Eve, we must stay together. Hast thou forgotten that an angel warned me against a malicious Enemy who envies our happiness and seeks to destroy us? Together, each can offer aid to the other and the Enemy cannot circumvent us, but each of us alone is more vulnerable. I think it best that I should guard thee."

Eve drew herself up. "All Earth's lord," she said, "dost thou doubt my firmness to God or to thee? Dost thou fear I am so weak that my love and faith can be so easily shaken? Dost thou truly think so little of me?"

"Of course not, darling Eve, daughter of light," Adam replied. "I do not doubt thee. I sought only to avoid the attempt—if the Enemy sees that we are together, he will not assault us. If we are apart, he may try, and I would not have thee in harm's way through my own neglect."

"And are we then to dwell in fear, constrained by an unseen foe? Are we to be always together because we doubt our integrity to resist the Enemy?"

"But Eve, daughter of heaven, the Enemy may be too subtle for us. I was told he has seduced angels."

"That does not mean he will seduce us," Eve said firmly. "And besides," she smiled, "what is faith, love or virtue if it is never tested?"

Adam sighed. "As God has given us free will, I will not constrain thee. But Eve, I beg thee, seek not temptation."

"I am forewarned, my lord and husband," Eve replied, already leaving.

Eve was deep in the Garden, humming to herself as she twisted tender new tendrils onto their supporting trees, when the brontosaurus spoke.

"Hail, Queen of Eden," it said.

Eve looked around, but could see no-one. "Who speaks?" she said.

"I, sovereign mistress," said the tempter through the brontosaurus that carried him. "Do not be alarmed. I have long admired and adored thee, and now I have the means to tell thee." The elongated, snaky neck bent low before her as the giant creature bowed.

"But how can this be?" said Eve. "The tongues of brutes cannot pronounce the language of man."

"Empress of Eden," the creature replied, "I shall explain all, if you command."

Eve nodded her assent.

"There is a tree," the tempter said, "whereon hangs wondrous fruit of red and gold, the fruit so high above the ground that you could not reach it, nor can other creatures. But I, with my long neck, am able to pluck the fruit and eat my fill. And so I did. And, beauteous mistress, from that very moment there was a strange alteration in me—both reason and speech, so long desired, were mine, and knowledge too, though my shape changed not."

"There are many trees that grow in Paradise, so various that many are yet unknown to us," said Eve. "Can you say where grows this tree, and how far?"

"It will be my greatest pleasure, Lady of Paradise, to conduct thee there. The way is not long."

"Then lead on," said Eve.

The tempter turned the dinosaur, and Eve followed in its swaying wake, musing on the ungainliness of the beast, until it stopped at last before one of the trees of prohibition.

"Strange creature, I fear we might have spared ourselves this journey," Eve said. "The fruit of this tree is wondrous indeed if it has caused such effects in thee, but God has commanded that of this tree we may not taste or touch. So it must be fruitless to me, though there is fruit in excess."

"How strange," the tempter replied, "that God has made you lords of all in earth or air, yet forbids you to eat certain fruit."

"We are forbidden," Eve said simply, "lest we die."

"How can you believe that," said the brontosaurus, "when I who have eaten of the fruit stand alive before you? I who have now risen above my lot by eating of the fruit tell you that it brings knowledge, not death."

Eve hesitated.

The tempter pressed on. "Would a loving God deny you knowledge that will so enhance your care of this Garden? Would He not rather applaud your enterprise? Is He not a fond parent, waiting for the day that you put off childish ignorance and, knowing good and evil, become as He is. For, celestial lady, if a brute such as I am raised to your human level through eating of the fruit, would not you, in proportion, be raised to godlike status? You are already a goddess in beauty—should you not seek to match that beauty with understanding?"

"I don't know," said Eve.

"Wherein lies the offence that you should seek to know what can be known?" said the tempter. "How could your knowledge hurt God?"

"I don't know," said Eve.

"Then look more closely the fruit," said the tempter. The brontosaurus reached out, delicately plucked a ripe fruit and dropped it at Eve's feet. "How can it do any harm?"

"I don't know," Eve said a third time.

She stooped and picked up the rosy fruit, surprised by the smooth texture of its sun-warmed skin. She caressed it, held it to her face, and then found herself inhaling its fragrance. Her mouth watered at the divine smell of it, and before she had thought further she was nuzzling it, licking it, nipping it with her white teeth. The tiniest spot of juice broke the skin, just enough for her to taste.

The world changed.

Eve bit then in earnest, burying her face in the fruit. Rich juice ran down her naked skin and fell dripping from her perfect breasts as heedless of the watching brontosaurus she engorged greedily and without restraint, hungrily eating death in her ecstasy.

The tempter had to look away.

When Eve was finally satiated, she wiped her hands on her naked thighs, leaving sticky trails there as she turned back, flushed, to the tempter. "I need another fruit," she said. "As I am your sovereign lady, I bid you fetch it for me."

"Certainly, my lady," the tempter replied. "But is it wise to eat more of the fruit before you truly learn its effects?"

"I need it for my husband," she said. "If you are right, and God is not angered, then all is well. But if He has seen, and decrees my death, then I shall be no more and Adam will be wedded to another Eve. I cannot bear that thought, and so I am resolved that he will share with me, for well or woe."

"Your wish is my command, empress," said the tempter. The brontosaurus obligingly stretched up and brought down another fruit.

☕

Adam looked up in surprise as his wife came to him, carrying a new-picked fruit that exuded ambrosial aromas.

"I am making a garland for thee, beloved," he said, offering her the armful of flowers he had been gathering against her return.

"Thank you, my lord," she said. "But I have a more important thing for thee." She held out the fruit.

Adam stared at it, wondering why she blushed so deeply to look upon it.

"I met a strange creature," she said breathlessly, "who proved to me that the tree forbidden is not a tree of danger, as we were told, but a tree of divine effect to make as gods those who taste. The brontosaurus had eaten of the fruit and was not dead, but newly endowed with human sense and speech and reason. So I also have eaten, and in growing to godhead have now understood that my future bliss will be tedious if not shared with thee." She looked at him with pleading eyes. "Fate will not now permit me to renounce Deity for thee, my lord, and so you too must eat of the fruit, that we may be again equal in love and joy."

"My wife, my darling, thou fairest of creation," Adam stammered. "What hast thou done?"

"Nothing that is not for thy benefit, my lord."

"Nothing? Thou art lost—defaced, deflowered, and now to death devoted. Did'st thou not suspect that the creature may have been the Enemy of whom we were warned?"

Eve hesitated.

Before she could frame an answer, Adam went on, talking to himself, trying to reason out his dilemma. "But how should I lose thee," he said, "and live again alone in this wilderness? How should I be parted from thee, thou who art flesh of my flesh, bone of my bone, how should I live without thee?"

"That need not be, my lord," Eve said, moving closer to him, her movements sinuous, beguiling.

Adam reached out to her, embraced her, inhaling the perfume of forbidden fruit from her hair, her skin. He breathed deeply, feeling the stirrings of lust. He nuzzled her neck, licking the residue of death's juices, and was lost.

"Give me the fruit," he said.

Taking her by the sticky hand, he raised the fruit to his mouth and bit down upon it as he led her, smiling, into the depths of their green bower.

"That was close," said Gabriel. "I've never seen Him so angry."

"Lucky for us He agreed that we could not have prevented the Enemy from entering the Garden as mist," Raphael said. "We could have been sharing the fate of the hapless brontosaurus." He shivered in sympathy.

"That is unfortunate," Michael said. "But He has a point."

"But the poor creature was innocent," said Uriel. "It was terribly confused when the Enemy stopped inhabiting it."

"But it still wanted to eat the fruit," said Michael. "And what one brontosaurus eats, so do the rest. You'd have to agree that a herd of suddenly sentient dinosaurs would create problems for Him."

"True," said Uriel. "But I still think that taking away their bodies and leaving their necks and heads to become serpents was extreme. The tallest of creatures are now the lowest, condemned forever to crawl on their stomachs and eat bitter dust."

"They'll survive better outside Eden that way," said Raphael. "They are banished too, don't forget."

"Well, He couldn't leave them here, could He?" said Gabriel. "The temptation would always be there, and serpents could still coil themselves up the Tree."

"Too late to worry about it now," said Raphael. "He has spoken."

"And the pets are condemned to make their own way in the world outside the Garden," said Uriel.

"I feel bad about that," said Michael. "We didn't protect them very well, did we?"

"We tried," said Raphael. "But we can't help them now."

"Why not?" said Gabriel.

"And disobey Him?" Michael said incredulously.

"Of course not," Gabriel replied. "But I'm thinking that we can at least atone for our part in this whole miserable episode."

"How?" Raphael asked.

"Well," said Gabriel, "He has decreed who should go from the Garden, but He hasn't said anything about who should stay."

"Good thinking," said Uriel. "Maybe we can help them survive a little longer."

"Let's do it," said Michael.

Adam and Eve walked miserably towards the Gates, downcast and uncomfortable in their awkward clothing of leaves tied on with lengths of vine.

"It's the best I could do," Eve whined.

"Obviously," said Adam. "It's your 'best' that got us into this mess."

The archangels stepped forward as the humans drew level with the gates.

"Stop bickering and listen up," said Raphael, hefting the fiery sword for emphasis.

"Greetings, thou celestial messenger," Adam began.

"Forget all that," Michael said sharply. "Are you ready to leave?"

Adam nodded dejectedly.

"Then get going," Raphael said, opening the Gates just wide enough for the two humans to pass.

"We're giving you a head start," Gabriel added in a theatrical whisper. "Make the best of it."

Puzzled, Adam and Eve stepped beyond the lush portal that had opened in the tropical wall of rainforest, and through into a harsher land. Hard at their heels a horde of serpents slithered and slipped through rising dust in a frantic rush for cover. The air was thinner, the sun hotter, the vegetation sparser. Everything was different. Eve tried to take Adam's hand, but he shrugged her away, radiating bad temper. She walked on, feeling the first prickles of sweat and sunburn. The palm-frond skirt felt scratchy, the ground was rough beneath her bare feet. The child in her belly kicked—the first murderer was restless too.

The howl of a hunting T. Rex pierced the air. Eve looked back, and felt for the first time the thrill of physical fear.

Behind the fiery swords that barred the way, velociraptors clamoured at the Gates of Eden.

The Lion Hunt

Alternate history is one of my favourite forms, so when Pamela Sargent offered me the opportunity to write a "what if" version of a conquering hero, I jumped at the chance. The decision to write about Alexander the Great began with a strange bit of serendipity: I was attending a science fiction conference at the Aristotle University in Thessaloniki, and was lucky enough to be included in a very small private tour of the burial site of King Philip of Macedon, Alexander's father. I was fascinated: the carved image of Philip that I had always imagined to be a statue turned out to be a tiny ivory tile that had not burned in the funeral pyre; the lion hunt of the story title is depicted in a surviving mosaic; and so on. The story is based on actual events: King Philip was working to unify Greece when his death (by poison) changed the course of history and Alexander took the throne. But what if the murder plot had misfired? The course of history is fragile: it could so easily have gone another way.

The wedding feast at the palace of Aegae was in full swing. King Philip looked out over his crowded hall, surveying the lavish banquet with pleasure. He could afford to be generous: this marriage of his daughter Cleopatra with the prince of Epirus was politically advantageous by anyone's reckoning. Not that he had given the happy couple any choice in the matter: matrimonial alliances were, as he had told his weeping daughter firmly, a matter of policy, not inclination. The nuptials were proceeding, as planned.

Philip appeared relaxed, sitting easily in his high-backed chair of honour, its sides elaborately carved with his emblematic lions, its seat draped with cloth of gold. Beside him was his son, Alexander, a tall and muscular young man who carried himself with the lithe grace of an athlete and the absolute assurance of one who believed in his own divinity. The two looked unmistakably alike in their ceremonial finery: the same curling hair, the same straight noses and sensual mouths, the same intense dark eyes (though Philip wore a patch to cover the empty socket of the one he had lost at Methone). Father and son were laughing together, but even at their most convivial they dominated the high-roofed feasting hall, both exuding the comfortable power of men used to iron-fisted control.

Philip's guests reclined on couches beside low tables laden with delicacies. The elaborate appetisers had been cleared away, and now there were golden platters laden with roasted meats, both flesh and fowl; and there were trays heaped high with fresh-baked breads. Soft-footed serving maids moved among the diners, pouring water from golden pitchers into silver basins so that the guests might rinse their hands, replenishing dishes and bringing ever more varieties of exquisite food. Others offered glistening fruit piled onto serving dishes and delicious pastries dripping with sweet honey on silver plates. Young men with sieves and cups filled mixing bowls to the brim with the finest Thessalian wines, and constantly refilled the golden goblets of the revellers. The aromas of spiced foods mingled with the perfumes of the company, filling the banqueting hall with a rich miasma of warm scents, the smell of indulgence.

And when, at last, it seemed the guests could eat no more, Philip called for music. The chief bard of the court took up his lyre, and the mood of the feast turned toward song and dancing. More pledges and toasts were drunk to the future of the noble couple, and the royal revellers grew increasingly raucous. It would be a long night.

The courtier Pausanias slipped unobtrusively from the room to an elegant antechamber. Away from the hubbub, he leaned against a marble pillar, savouring its smooth coolness after the stuffy heat and stifling scents of the feasting hall.

"Just look at him!" he said, gesturing in the direction of the king. "The man's a heavy drinker, even by army standards. He'll be in his cups tonight, and who knows what secrets he might betray to that sharp-eared young bridegroom he's so proud of snaring?"

"Easy, friend," said Hermias, stepping from the shadows and holding up his plump hand in greeting. "He's much more likely to bed that serving girl he's been fondling all evening. One of the privileges of rank," he added wryly. "The king is a physical man."

"Maybe," said Pausanias. "But I like it not."

Hermias considered the fastidious little courtier for a moment. He shrugged his shoulders. "There are some pretty youths here tonight, if that's your fancy," he said slyly.

Pausanias let the issue drop. "Not tonight. I have business." From the folds of his tunic he withdrew a small leather bag, a bag heavy with silver tetradrachmas. He tossed the pouch to Hermias, who caught it deftly.

"Polybus sends you greetings," said Pausanias.

Hermias tucked the bag out of sight. "The coins are good?"

"From Philip's own mines at Mount Pangaeus." Pausanias chuckled. "I tested them myself."

"Thank you, friend."

"Don't thank me yet," replied the courtier. "Polybus also reminds you that the matter we spoke of is now close at hand. Are you still with me?"

Hermias paled. "Are you set upon this course then?"

"I am. After the wedding, there is to be a royal hunt. The opportunity will serve."

"I never thought it would come to this." Hermias massaged his temples with anxious fingers, thinking hard. "A little information, here and there," he said. "That's all you asked for. A little palace intrigue. It seemed of no real consequence."

"You were willing enough," said Pausanias.

Hermias fidgeted with his tunic, smoothing the folds over his portly bulk. "Philip has always had his enemies," he said. "Everyone gossips. What harm in making a little profit from it?"

"What harm indeed," replied Pausanias dryly. "You've grown soft and fat enough serving two masters."

"Look," said Hermias, his voice edged with panic, "Philip's a man of sensual appetites, it's true: but they don't interfere with his rule. He's a magnificent leader."

"Yes, yes," said Pausanias, "nobody doubts his abilities. But his time has come. He's just announced a war against Persia, and he'll drag all Greece along with him. The confederacy has agreed to it, of course." He was beginning to pace now, moving softly in the shadowed room. "It's simple enough, my friend," he said at last. "Everyone knows that this anti-Persian crusade is Philip's way of enforcing Macedonian domination. If he controls this war effort, he controls all Greece. Polybus wants that stopped, and soon."

"But," countered Hermias, "Philip's an extraordinary general. His army would do anything for him. And he's in good shape. He'll probably pull it off."

"That, my friend," said Pausanias, his tone heavy with exasperation, "is the point. A victory for Philip would only consolidate Macedonian power. Athens and Corinth and Megara are already nervous, and the Phocians still hate him for the way he treated them after the Battle of the Crocus Field."

"Then why not kill Parmenio?" said Hermias. "He's the key to all Philip's military strategies. And he's here for the wedding feast. I saw him."

"Because Philip would just get another strategist," said Pausanias. He shook his head as if to clear away his frustration. "Don't you see?"

"No," said Hermias, nervously twisting his carnelian signet ring as he spoke. "I don't. What's so bad for *us* about another foreign conquest? It keeps the kings and generals a long way from home, and the rest of us can get on with our lives without interference. And we've done well enough from Philip's victories, you and I. Aegae prospers, and his people with it."

"Think," said Pausanias. "What happens if Philip *doesn't* win this time? What if his grandiose scheme fails, and the rest of us pay the price? Persia will take its revenge. Do you want to see Greece overrun with Persian troops? Your precious Aegae in flames?"

Hermias was silent.

Pausanias pressed his advantage. "Then spare me the hypocrisy for once, Hermias. Win or lose, one way or the other, Philip's war on Persia is a political disaster for the Greek confederacy." He paused, calculating, then went on: "And it's not as if he's an innocent in matters of intrigue. Those mines of his have financed more than one assassination in the name of diplomacy. He knows how the game is played—just look at the wedding guests in there." Pausanias jerked his thumb in the direction of the feast. "Those nobles from Epirus wouldn't dare say a word against any of it. Philip's totally and completely unscrupulous when it comes to bribery and corruption. They've all been well paid." He paused for breath. "What I'm saying, friend, is that this whole empire runs on plots and conspiracies. Philip expects it."

"And Alexander?"

"Will inherit. But he is young yet. He is strong-minded like his father, and the army will follow him, but the mourning period will give the other states some respite. Alexander will have to re-organise, and he will need to win popular consent if he is to rule. That all takes time, and time is what we need."

"I still don't like it."

"I don't see that you have a choice. You're implicated, my friend. You're bought and paid for." Pausanias casually drew a long knife, testing it against his forefinger. "You know we can't risk a security breach." His voice was low now, menacing.

Hermias sighed ruefully. "Put it away, *friend*," he said. "We both know you won't kill me here."

Pausanias nodded, letting the tension ease. "And your hand in Polybus' purse ensures your silence," he said. "You cannot betray me without implicating yourself, and Philip's justice will be swift and merciless if he scents treachery. Either way, you will die. I ask you again, Hermias: are you with me?"

Hermias sat down heavily on the nearest couch. His shoulders sagged, and he cradled his head in his hands for a few moments. When he looked up once more, his face was bleak.

"Tell me what you need," he said.

The morning of the hunt dawned fine and clear. All the palace servants had been up before sunrise, baking and packing and preparing delicacies for the hunting party. During the heat of the afternoon the king and his guests would rest in tented pavilions, and in the cool of the evening they would dine under the stars. Several heavily loaded wagons had departed yesterday, so that all might be ready for the royal party. The grooms had also been busy: the pride of Philip's stables, the glossy high-necked horses that were easily the best in all Greece had been brushed and combed and saddled for the day's work. They were led clattering into the forecourt, an extravagant gesture of generosity to those guests privileged to ride them.

Philip—dressed for the hunt in leather leggings and battle-skirt and his favourite iron corselet studded with golden lions, his sword buckled at his side—was up long before his guests, striding about the palace forecourt, giving instructions. His son joined him, arm in arm with his new brother-in-law, who seemed more than a little uneasy.

"I've never hunted a lion before," the prince of Epirus was saying.

"A noble adversary, to be sure, but no different from other beasts in the end," Alexander replied. "And this particular beast has taken one or two calves from my father's farms. It has learned to stalk its prey too close to our people. So the king wants to kill it before it ranges nearer to his horses—there are many foals this season, grazing in the high pastures." He sighed. "I sometimes think he loves those horses better than anything else in this world, including his wives."

The prince managed a smile. "I'm still nervous," he said.

"You'll be fine. Just ride with the pack, and pull back if it gets too dangerous. No one expects heroics. The more experienced hunters will corner the lion, but the kill belongs to my father today. It's the custom." Alexander grinned broadly. "Relax. Here come our guests."

The hunting procession was quickly assembled. As soon as the riders were mounted and had taken up their weapons, the party set off for the mountains. Philip rode at the head of the column, followed by his noble guests and surrounded by elite guards from the hetaerae cavalry with their distinctive long lances. General Parmenio, the strategist, was with them today: he nodded cheerfully to Alexander as he swung into his place in the line. The servants followed behind in their carts: they would travel directly to join their fellows in setting up the day camp, while the hunters ranged freely over the hills in pursuit of their quarry.

The early morning summer breeze was cool, bringing scents of wild thyme and honey as the procession followed the winding road that led to the hills above Aegae. The steep road climbed steadily, and the sun had risen high in the sky so that men and horses were all sweating freely by the time Philip halted, reigning in his mount in a space where the pass widened out onto a grassy plateau. The king sat motionless in his saddle, shading his eyes to look back over the rich patchwork of green pastures and the shimmering silver-greys of olive groves. Below him, the shining thread of a little stream cascaded over mossy rocks, on its way to join up with the wide river that snaked through the valley. He leaned forward to pat the graceful neck of his favourite horse. All peaceful, all calm.

The stillness was broken by a single shout: "Lion!"

The cry went up from Philip's left, where a line of trackers emerged into the sunlight from the shadow of the beech trees on the high ground. And the hunters were off, their tiredness forgotten, urging their horses up the rocky slope. They raced along the ridge, a curving line of superb horsemen, with Philip and Alexander riding hard on the wing with the best and boldest of the guards. Philip shouted with joy as they crested the hill and saw the quarry plunge headlong down the slope on the other side, making for the safety of a rocky outcrop that ended abruptly in a waterfall. It was a descent that would make the bravest hesitate—a sharp, uneven incline overgrown with saplings and scrubby bushes, the slope pock-marked with animal burrows that spelled death for any unlucky horse.

Many of the nobles, the bridegroom among them, hung back. But the king did not pause—he sounded his horn, and the leading hunters wheeled, giving chase under the trees. The undergrowth was thick, the ground sharper than it looked with treacherous shards and stones. The smell of leaf-mould was strong in their nostrils as they raced, ducking under overhanging branches, skittering on loosened ground. The mountain gorge echoed to the thunder of hoof beats and the din of hunting horns, and the riders' whoops of fierce joy echoed and re-echoed from the valley walls.

The hunt ran hard, and now it was Alexander in the lead, sending the stones flying as his horse cleared a fallen tree. Down and down he went, Parmenio close on his heels, and Philip rode with them, plying the whip. The horses were flecked with foam now, panting with effort. But the riders never hesitated: they ran their mounts until, in a narrow cleft where the roar of the waterfall mingled with the roaring of the lion, the quarry was brought to bay, trapped by Alexander and Parmenio against water and rock.

The lion had turned, crouched ready to spring, its back protected by an overhanging rock, and a dark cave behind. It could only be reached by way of a narrow path between the rocks and the river. Alexander shouted to Parmenio above the clashing of weapons and the yells of the hunters following in the rear. He motioned to the general to take the inner edge. He himself edged his mount beside the rushing waterfall. The sharp stink of the lion's lair made the horse skittish, shifting its feet and sending loose pebbles cascading down the rocks. Alexander steadied his mount. Parmenio was already in position.

Wordlessly, on either side of the trapped lion, the two men lowered their lances, thrusting at the beast, forcing it forward.

The animal was a huge male, powerfully muscled. It swiped at its tormentors with long curved claws that could rip a man apart. It was winded, but its snarls of defiance made it clear that it meant to fight.

Philip rode his mount straight towards the waiting beast, cheered by the shouts of his men, now arriving in the rear.

"Phil-ip, Phil-ip," they chanted. "A kill, a kill."

The king reached the clearing and leapt from his saddle, throwing off his riding cloak and brandishing his bright blade. The golden lion studs on his corselet flashed in the brilliant sunlight as Philip, the lion king of Macedon, strode forward to meet the tawny king of beasts in deadly combat.

The great lion was instantly aware of Philip: it roared a challenge, revealing sharp yellow teeth. Then it gathered its strength and sprang straight at the king. But Philip was ready for it, shouting his own battle cry: in the shock of their meeting he stuck his point straight into the beast's neck, driving the blade up to the hilt, so that the lion's heart was split in two. The beast died snarling and thrashing, and Philip was bloodied to the shoulder. He leaned against the rock for a moment, gagging on the vile, hot smell of the dying lion. Alexander and Parmenio flanked him, still wary of the great beast.

Philip straightened, and turned, triumphant, to the cheers of his followers. The blaring of hunting horns and the shouting and hallooing of men celebrating the kill made a deafening din in his ears. He did not notice the sudden clatter of hooves on the slope above him. He was holding both arms aloft, accepting the homage of his men, when a mounted guard came charging down the mountainside, his long lance spearing straight at the king where he stood, vulnerable, astride the lion.

"No!" Alexander acted instinctively, leaping from his horse and knocking his father aside. Philip rolled free, and came up quickly, sword at the ready. Alexander staggered, but stood firm, the lance quivering where it stuck in the exposed flesh of his upper arm.

A dozen swords flashed, and the assassin toppled from his horse to lie dead at the king's feet.

"Fools," said Philip. "I needed him alive. I need to know who paid him."

"You'll know soon enough, my lord," Parmenio remarked dryly. "Such things are never secret for long." He poked with his foot at the dead man. "This piece of filth is wearing a guard's uniform. You can leave me to interrogate my men," he said. "There will be no further incidents today, I guarantee it." He turned then to Alexander, his face full of concern. "You need a surgeon," he said bluntly.

"It's nothing," said Alexander. "A flesh wound. My man will see to it when we reach the pavilion."

"Even so," said Philip, "you must let us take care of it for now."

Alexander nodded, gritting his teeth against the pain as Philip himself withdrew the bloody lance-head and bound his son's wound with a strip of linen.

"This may be bad," Philip said quietly. "The tip is discoloured."

"And we have a long climb back to the day camp," said Parmenio.

"I'll be all right," said Alexander. "It will take more than a lance wound to kill the likes of me." He grinned confidently. "Don't worry. I can ride."

"You'll have to," his father replied.

There was none of the joy of the chase as the hunters picked their careful way back up the treacherous slope. Parmenio had detailed two of his men to fashion a rough sled from branches so that the slain lion could be dragged back to camp, but the king had lost interest in his trophy. He was concentrating on his son, riding slowly beside him, watching with grave concern as Alexander began to sweat and shake. By the time the party reached the top of the ridge once more, Alexander was clinging to his horse's mane, scarcely able to stay upright in the saddle.

"Shock," said Parmenio.

"I hope so," Philip replied grimly. "I hope so."

The field surgeon had been summoned, and he met the hunting party on the plateau. He had brought a wagon that would carry the wounded man to the king's pavilion.

"Gently," he said, as Philip helped his son down from his horse. Alexander pitched forward, and Parmenio had to lift him bodily onto the straw-filled wagon where he lay still, exhausted. "He'll need rest," the surgeon went on briskly. "I've brought wine to cleanse the wound, and blankets to keep him warm while his body recovers from the shock. Though I must admit I'm surprised a flesh wound has taken him like this—he's a strong young man."

"It's more than shock," said Philip, his voice pitched low. "It's poison. I'm sure of it." He held out the lance-tip, wrapped carefully in linen torn from his undershirt.

The surgeon reached for it, barehanded.

"Don't touch the point," said Philip quickly.

The surgeon faltered, then took the weapon gingerly, turning it this way and that, sighting along the edge.

"I did not wipe it," Philip said. "Do you recognise that coating on the blade? Can you tell me what it is?"

The field surgeon paled. "No, my lord," he stammered. "I can see that the edge is chipped, so it may have scraped on bone. But there is a lot of dried blood on the weapon, and I am no apothecary to tell one tincture from another." He gathered his thoughts, and added: "I do have herbs I can infuse to try to draw out poison when we reach the camp, if that is what you wish. And I can bleed the wound."

"Do it," said Philip. "And keep the business to yourself. There may be more than one traitor in this camp. I'll hold you responsible if any more harm comes to my heir. Do you understand?"

"Yes, my lord," said the surgeon, swallowing hard. "I'll do my best."

"You'll do better than that," the king said darkly. "My son must live." He turned away abruptly, striding across to where Parmenio stood, deep in conversation with his most trusted guards.

"I've already arranged an escort," the strategist said as the king approached. "No one will get near Alexander."

"Thank you, old friend," the king replied. "Will you walk with me a moment?"

"Of course."

The two moved out of earshot of the anxious guards. "My men know nothing," Parmenio said. "The assassin was a last minute replacement, when the youngest of the regular troupe was too ill to ride this morning. They say the boy was fevered and vomiting—and that they thought nothing more than that he had drunk too much wine last night. But now . . . "

"Now they are solving the riddle," said Philip.

"Now they are ashamed not to have prevented it," Parmenio finished quietly. "But with all the unfamiliar faces at the palace for the wedding, they did not think to question too closely."

"Peace, Parmenio," Philip said wearily. "I'm not blaming your men. There'll be no scape-goating or punishment in their ranks."

Parmenio breathed a sigh of relief. "A wise decision, my lord: if there's to be fighting, we'll need their goodwill."

"I know," Philip replied. "But I doubt there's an army at our gates. This smells more of petty intrigue—one of Polybus' plots, I'll wager." His voice hardened. "We'll find the men he has suborned, of course, and they will die." He stopped for a moment, tense with anger. "But Parmenio," he went on, "if he has murdered my son, I swear by Heracles my ancestor that I will raze Polybus' miserable city to the ground. And he will live to watch it burn, before I personally send his paltry soul to Hades."

"Then let us hope it will not come to that," said Parmenio. "We are already at war with Persia." He touched Philip's arm. "Come, my lord, we will watch Alexander's progress together. He's a strong man, and we must hope that it will be enough."

It was a difficult ride. Wary guards surrounded both their king and the trundling wagon where Alexander groaned in pain at every misstep that jolted him. The sun was sinking in the west by the time they had made their slow journey to the high plain where Philip's household servants had pitched the king's pavilions. Alexander was rambling incoherently, his body wracked with spasms as he struggled against the poison in his veins. He was carried gently to a couch in his father's tent, where the surgeon set to work, trembling under the king's unnerving scrutiny.

Outside, the mood of the guests was sombre. When evening came, servants washed and poured and served up laden platters for the hunters, but there was no feasting in the firelight. People talked in low whispers, eating and drinking but little. It was as if the world was holding its breath, fearful of what was to come.

Philip sat by his son's bedside, willing him to live, watching him fighting for his life. But as the night wore on, the spasms became more violent and Alexander's heart weakened. The surgeon could do nothing. Just before dawn Alexander was wracked by a last seizure, too great for even the strongest mortal heart. And the heir to the lion throne of Macedon lay dead.

The morning star shone pale in a lightening sky and the cool mountain air carried echoes of early birdsong as Philip, hard-faced, strode from the tent and ordered an immediate return to his palace. The hunting column became a slow funereal procession, with the wedding guests holding their mounts to a measured walk behind the wagon with its burden of sorrow, and the guards keeping careful watch over all. Philip rode, as was customary, at the head. He would not let them see him grieve, not his new son-in-law and these courtiers he had bought for so much silver. He would deal with his pain and loss in his own time. Would deal with that, and with his son's murderer. Vengeance—that was Philip's motto. And Philip was a patient man. He could wait.

The people of Aegae were outraged at the loss of Alexander, at the loss of so much promise, so much talent, so much spirit. They wanted blood. As Parmenio had predicted, public indignation quickly overrode paid loyalties, and the conspirators were not difficult to discover. Hermias did not resist when the guards came for him. It was whispered in palace corridors that the fat little court official seemed relieved to have been found out. He wept copious tears, and readily gave up Pausanias as the instigator of the conspiracy. And now he sat quietly in his prison cell, waiting for the day of his execution, knowing that his family would not come, that there would be no hemlock to ease his traitor's death.

The more wily Pausanias had fled from the palace on the day of the assassination. But he had not fled far enough. He too was soon exposed and dragged, bloodied but still alive, into the presence of the king. Only the intervention of Parmenio's guards had saved the man who had hired Alexander's killer from the rough justice of a jeering crowd, but it had been a violent passage, and his right arm now hung limp and useless at his side from his obviously dislocated shoulder.

Parmenio gestured to one of his men. "Fix that," he said.

The guard took hold of Pausanias' shoulder, rotated the arm, and pulled.

Pausanias fainted.

Another guard emptied a pitcher of water over him. Pausanias regained spluttering consciousness just as the king spoke to his general:

"Why?" Philip asked.

"Not for mercy," Parmenio replied. "The shoulder's a common enough injury among lance bearers. It's best to set it quickly." He looked with undisguised contempt at Pausanias, sprawled wet and bleeding on the palace floor. "We went to a lot of trouble to get that piece of filth here alive," he said, "and I assumed you'd want him coherent enough to answer a few questions. He'll stay conscious now."

"I see. Get him up, then," said Philip.

Two guards hauled Pausanias to his feet, and stood impassively, supporting him.

Philip bent forward intently. "Why?" he asked simply. "Why try to kill me?"

"For the good of Greece," Pausanias grated.

A guard struck him heavily across the mouth. Pausanias wiped away the trickle of blood with his left hand.

"Hold," said the king. "We are civilised men here, not torturers. He will tell us. He wants to tell us. He wants to justify himself. All traitors do."

Pausanias spat.

The guards looked straight ahead, impassive, unmoving.

"We know it was Polybus who paid you," said Parmenio in a matter-of-fact tone. "We have arrested the courier. He has told us a great deal. He will die with you, of course."

Pausanias sagged, but straightened his body with visible effort. "Then you don't need to ask me," he said.

"Oh but we do," said Philip coldly. "We want to hear everything you have to tell us. And you will tell us."

The questioning went on late into the night, and Pausanias, wracked by pain and venomous with anger and liberated to speak his mind by the certain knowledge of his own imminent death, told them a great deal. Told them more than he knew. By the end of that night, Philip was sure. Parmenio the strategist was already laying plans against Polybus. There would be war in Greece.

But first there would be a royal funeral. Alexander's bones would lie in his father's tomb, so many years in the making against inevitable death; against, as it turned out, the wrong death. King Philip would have to build anew—if they gave him time.

The funeral procession would begin just before sunset, but Philip had come early from the palace, to make a last inspection. He rode slowly, flanked by Parmenio's anxious guards. The road to the tombs was full of busy people, but the throng parted easily before the king's men. All along the roadside were the usual signs of a festival in the making: traders setting up their booths to sell amulets and charms and souvenir coins hurriedly cast with a rough likeness of Alexander; food vendors already turning spitted animals, starting the slow cooking process that would feed the crowds; families staking out likely picnic spots; beggars arriving. There were rich pickings at royal funerals.

"He shouldn't do this," one guard muttered to his partner. "It isn't in the plan. He has enemies everywhere."

His friend shrugged. "He's the king. He knows he is watched. What difference does it make to us?"

"The difference," hissed the first, "is that we could find ourselves fighting off assassins in the middle of all this lot." He gestured vaguely at the milling crowd.

"Not even the Athenians would try it on the day of the funeral," his friend replied. "Besides, everyone thinks the king is up at the palace, preparing to lead the procession. No one will pay us any special attention—there are royal guards riding everywhere today. Relax."

They rode on in silence.

When they reached the gates, Philip halted. He turned to the leader of his guard. "Have the courtyard cleared," he said. "I want everyone out—priests, carpenters, stonemasons, everyone."

"Sir."

The soldiers were efficient. Within minutes artisans were scurrying from their last-minute work, leaving the dusty space deserted.

"Now leave me," he said.

"But sir," the captain of the guard began, stammering. "Our orders are . . . "

"I give the orders here," said Philip. "And I want a moment alone with my son. Have your men watch the entrance. Nobody enters. Is that clear?"

"Sir."

Philip dismounted, and handed the reins to the captain. "A little space of time, that's all," he said quietly. "Then you may escort me back to the palace. Understood?"

The man nodded.

Philip entered and paced about the enclosure, noting the details, checking that his orders had been obeyed. The pyre had been built high, overlaid with sweet-smelling boughs and piled about with small offerings. The larger ones would come later, with the pomp and ceremony of the procession. Inside the palatial tomb, beyond its forecourts and antechambers, Alexander lay in the main room, ready for his last parade. The gleaming mosaics on the chamber walls were lit by bracketed lamps, which would burn untended for the correct ceremonial period. Philip noted with satisfaction that the depiction of the fateful lion hunt had been completed—though some of the shining tesserae still looked wet in their settings. The mounted figures of Alexander and Parmenio would now grace this tomb for all time, lances poised forever above the snarling lion.

In the centre of the chamber was the funeral couch, a thing of exquisite beauty, cunningly carved and decorated with beaten gold leaf and beautiful ivory miniatures of men and beasts and mythical creatures. The king smiled sadly to see a little herm from the gymnasium amongst the side-carvings, reminding him of happier times when he had brought Aristotle to Pella to educate the boy. It all seemed so long ago now, and such waste of spirit. What were all his plans to conquer Persia, to build an empire, without his son to inherit it, to carry it forward into history? Philip sighed and looked up, inspecting the accoutrements. The bed's canopy was wreathed in cloth of gold. All was as it should be—all that the trappings of wealth and power could make it.

Finally, Philip approached his son. Alexander lay in state, a crown of gold oak leaves on his brow, his body dressed in the gold-studded corselet and battle skirts of a royal warrior beneath the drape of the purple cloak so stunningly embroidered in thread of gold. His had not been an easeful death. He would burn as a soldier. Young, well muscled, dead before his time, Alexander looked every inch a king, lying there in all his majesty.

There were tears in Philip's one good eye. He reached out to touch his son, briefly, brushing his hand across the waxen cheek. "It should have been me," he said softly. "This death was planned for me. And you will be avenged, I swear it." His voice cracked. "Your assassins burn before you this day," he went on, "to make their miserable snivelling excuses to their gods. But they are only messengers. I will find their masters, and they will pay for this deed in blood and death. Polybus will pay with all that he holds dear. This I promise you." He bowed his head, and sighed deeply. "Go well, my son. Your ancestor Heracles awaits you. All is prepared for you.

He stepped back then, and walked away, straight-backed and purposeful, to where his captain stood waiting.

"I'm ready," he said simply.

"Sir."

Philip re-mounted, and rode back to the palace in brooding silence, unmoved by the noise and bustle of the crowds that parted before him.

At sunset, robed and magnificent in the trappings of his state, King Philip of Macedon rode out once more, this time at the head of the funeral procession. A huge crowd had gathered along the route, watching in respectful silence as their king came forth to preside over the pyre of his heir. Behind him, on the best of Philip's horses, rode Parmenio and the palace guards, pacing slowly—and alert, always, for any sign of disturbance. Next came black-clad women mourners, tearing their hair and strewing ashes; and then there were all the nobles of Philip's court and ambassadors from neighbouring kingdoms, richly dressed and riding in horse-drawn carriages, and bearing costly gifts for the pyre. But by far the most magnificent spectacle of all was the funeral cart that bore Alexander himself. Drawn slowly by a team of strong warriors, their muscles bunching with effort as they pulled, the richly decorated cart carried the prince of Macedon on his carven funeral bed with its trappings of gold and purple. Beside and behind him were more ranks of marching warriors, their tall lances bearing purple flags in honour of their prince.

The long procession of mourners moved with its own slow, inexorable rhythm. The outer areas of the funeral arena were already packed with jostling crowds of people anxious to witness the ritual, and attendants scurried to and fro, ordering the final arrangement of offerings. There was an expectant hush as Philip, still flanked by his guards, dismounted and climbed the stairs to his place of honour in the centre of the tiered royal stand that had been built beside the pyre. At his nod, the business of unloading the horse-drawn offerings began, and the nobles processed to their places. Finally, Alexander's cart arrived: it was drawn slowly, and with infinite care, up the ramp to its place at the very top of the pyre. The warriors withdrew. And all was ready.

Philip raised his arm in salute. His voice rang out, clear and powerful, as he spoke a eulogy for Alexander, spoke of how the world was forever diminished by this great loss. Finally, he spoke the formal words of parting, and the priests began their rituals. As the sun dipped below the horizon, the moment came: the ceremonial torch was touched to the base of the pyre, and greedy red flames crackled from it. The air was suddenly full of the smell of burning, of oil and wood and flesh.

And Philip watched, standing tall, stiff-necked, untouchable in his grief. He watched the long succession of precious offerings as they burned, and watched unmoved as the corpse of the assassin and the other still-living conspirators, staked at the four corners of the pyre, were taken ignominiously by the flames. He had had their tongues cut out, lest they defile his son's ceremony with their death cries. The fire burned greedily until, almost at the last, he witnessed, dry-eyed despite the stinging smoke, the burning of four magnificent horses in the conflagration—a last gift to his favourite son, his heir. The pyre roared and gouts of red flame leapt skywards as Alexander himself was finally consumed in all his gold and finery.

And it was over. The king turned away then, leaving the priests and the attendants to their work, to the sifting of the cooling ashes and the separation of bones and the final sealing of the tomb.

Philip would not look back. Behind him lay the smoking ruins of the future. And Alexander dead.

Incident on Woolfe Street

This story, based loosely on "Little Red Riding Hood", was my response to the hysterical reception that incoming refugees were receiving in the media at the time. I set the story in and around Melbourne's very multicultural Chapel Street precinct, where I used to live: the freezing walk through the park on a winter's night is the route I often took to my post office box in St Kilda Road—there were always rumours about what went on around there after dark. Even the friendliest place can seem dangerous at night, and the district is shown through the eyes of a protagonist who believes, against all reason, that the immigrants moving into this neighbourhood are werewolves from the old country: he sees evidence in their clothes, their food, their nightlife, everything. He has taught his daughter to fear the wolfmen, and, as a consequence, his fantasy bleeds, dangerously, into the real world.

Witold glared at the moon.

A midwinter evening: dark and clear. Barely six o'clock, and the full moon was already turning Fawkner Park to monochrome: the paths etching black lines under dim white lamps, the rising damp beneath the trees hanging in silent patches of tarnished-silver mist beneath stark black branches. All quiet, all still.

Witold turned up his collar, gripped his briefcase tight with one gloved hand, stuffed the other into his coat pocket, and strode onto the long diagonal that would take him across the park and home to Woolfe Street. He bulked large in the landscape, a great bear of a man muffled in a heavy black felted-wool overcoat. Muttering to himself, he stomped along, kicking at tree roots that fractured the dark ribbon of asphalt. He smelled mown grass and leaf mold and the sweet rot of fallen figs and, underneath it all, the animal musk of predators.

They'd be at it again tonight. He just knew it.

The rattle and hum of traffic reasserted itself as Witold neared the Woolfe Street edge of the park. An ambulance flashed by, its strobe light staining the moonlight in pulses of red, its siren piercing his thoughts. Headlights dazzled him as he reached the street. Absorbed in his anger, he did not see the old lady before he collided with her at the entrance. The impact knocked her off balance. Witold grabbed her shoulder to steady her as she staggered back.

His rough touch was not at all welcome.

"You should watch where you're going."

"Sorry. Are you okay?"

"Just winded."

"Sorry. I didn't see you."

"Obviously."

The woman with the pewter-tinted hair scowled accusingly. She was rugged up expensively in a fashionable silver quilted jacket over dark trousers and boots. A white West Highland terrier in a ridiculous tartan overcoat tugged at the leash in her right hand.

Witold didn't like small dogs.

"You shouldn't be going into the park alone on a night like this."

"Like what? It's a perfectly clear night."

"It's full moon. It's a wolf moon. There is danger tonight."

She began to back away. "Nonsense. Old wives tales. Superstition."

"You don't understand. They'll be out tonight. The wolf people. Prowling. Hunting. You shouldn't be out alone."

"Rubbish."

"I'm only trying to help. I would not let my own wife go out tonight."

"Poor woman."

Witold flushed, but kept on.

"They have no respect for age. They attack old women."

"I've been walking Hamish here in the park for years, and nobody ever bothered me. Except you." She glared at him. "I need fresh air."

Witold tried one more time. "They eat small dogs."

The woman snorted. She edged around him, letting Hamish lead her into the calm, clean air of the silent park.

Witold's face burned in the cold. He watched her go, heard a leathery rush of wings and looked up in time to see a flock of bats wheeling overhead, sketching their black-leather silhouettes across the face of the frosty moon.

The wolf people weren't the only ones out hunting tonight.

He stormed towards the intersection, grumbling. At least he could protect his own family.

Woolfe Street went on for miles. Witold's route along it would take him past the local market with its flower, fruit and vegetable stalls, its butchers and fishmongers and poulterers, its deli section where traders vied for the attention of outlandish customers by overloading their groaning shelves with gross, nameless things. Beyond the market Woolfe Street became a trendy shopping strip filled with specialty bookshops and restaurants and bars, until it came to a crossroads where, as if by common consent, fashion abruptly yielded to necessity. A block of grimy buildings housing drycleaners and boot repairers and garages formed the barrier that shielded chic society from the blank reality of the less-than-fashionable high rise public housing apartments where Melbourne stored its immigrants. Witold did not intend to live there for long.

He was still rehearsing his grievances under his breath when he reached the warm, backlit glow that announced the fashionable shopfronts of Woolfe Street's middle section. It did nothing for his mood. He hated this part of the long walk home—it reminded him of all the things he couldn't afford, reminded him of why he took a sandwich to eat at his desk, reminded him of *why* he was walking home from the St Kilda Road office-block to save the fare.

It was way too early for the clubs and discos. The brass-studded coffin doors of *The Children of the Night Club* were still firmly shut; the sign on *Vampyra's* read "First drinks 9pm"; even *Hyde's* wasn't open yet.

But the lights were all on in *Wolfie's Bar and Grill*. Always popular, it would be packed tonight, at full moon, so close to the solstice. The old culture celebrations went on for days—there would be a roaring open fire, and ribald laughter, and much smashing of glasses, and toasts in blood red wine, wine Witold suspected was laced with darker things. He'd eaten there once, before *Wolfie's* had become too fashionable, too expensive for the likes of him. The place was a carnivore's delight. Dark timber panelling, red velvet booths, heavy-scented red candles whose fat yellow flames reflected the flesh of dark-framed nudes that hung against plush red wallpaper—and over it all the juicy blood-smell of meat. The menu made no apologies: steak tartare, sausages, livers or sweetbreads for starters, followed by a main course of steak, served lightly seared—customers were offered a choice of cuts and sauces, but *Wolfie's* chef was known to have physically evicted a diner who had asked, unwisely, for his meat well done. The warm, red flesh came garnished with a grudging, limp salad. The dessert menu consisted of one red word—"strawberries".

As he passed *Wolfie's* window, Witold noted with angry satisfaction that the coat-rack in the darkly backlit entrance hall was already groaning under a burden of furs—no squeamish animal liberationists frequented this establishment. He slowed to read the chalked menu of "Solstice Specials": carpaccio, black pudding, mealy pudding (deep fried blood-and-oatmeal), blood sausage, and rare roast beef with bone-marrow jelly. Witold peered, and a pair of early diners smiled back at him from their red-curtained window booth. They were holding long glasses filled with a sticky bright red liquid. Witold hoped they were drinking Bloody Marys, but suspected they weren't. Fruit and vegetables were not welcome at *Wolfie's*. As he turned from the window he saw the waiter pause, and snicker. The couple grinned. Witold knew they were all laughing at him. He didn't care. He knew what they were.

There were more people in this part of the shopping strip, commuters on their way home crossing paths with locals on their way out for the evening. Witold could tell the wolf people at a glance. They were too neat. They tried too hard to fit in, to look respectable. They ironed their jeans, then wore them with crisp white shirts and preppy navy blazers that set off their gold watches. Their Reeboks stayed white. Their overcoats draped perfectly from their shoulders. They even carried clean white handkerchiefs. Witold saw them in the coffee shops, fastidiously wiping the wolf drool from the corners of their neat red mouths, dabbing at their meticulously combed wolf beards with starched white napkins. As if they weren't about to spend the rest of the evening howling at the moon and snacking on their neighbours' pets. Or worse. The whole thing disgusted him.

He stomped on, growling, and smiled grimly as he picked his way past the smoke-blackened barricades that protected the burnt-out shell of what was left of *Body Snatcher's Bar*. Arson, twice over: someone didn't want them re-building in a hurry. It seemed he wasn't the only one who objected to the way these perverted incomers were taking over the neighbourhood.

The crowds thinned as Witold crossed Chapel Street and walked the last couple of blocks to his high-rise home. He was unsurprised to see the flashing blue strobes and badly parked police car that announced trouble in his building. There was always trouble in his building. They were probably starting early tonight.

What did surprise him, when he had slogged his way up his five flights of unlit, piss-smelling stairs, was the small, determined crowd around his own doorway. Witold didn't trust his neighbours an inch. He elbowed and shoved his way through them, jabbed his key into the lock. But the door swung open before he could turn the handle. A very young, fresh-faced police officer was standing inside.

"Mr Jevik?"

"Yes. What's wrong?"

Witold pushed past to where Nada sat, small and pale and tearstained, her hands anxiously twisting her soggy handkerchief.

"What have you done to my wife?"

The bulge of Nada's pregnancy strained against her woollen dress as she stood to meet her husband.

Witold put a protective arm around her shoulders. "She's pregnant. You can see that. Why have you come here upsetting her? What have you done?"

"Nothing. Your wife called us, Mr Jevik. I've only been here a couple of minutes. My partner is checking the buildings. Now if you'll just calm down . . . "

Nada put a hand on his arm. "It's Katarina, Witold. She is missing."

The words were a stomach punch. Witold gasped for breath, managed to say: "When? How long?"

"A couple of hours."

"My God. Tonight of all nights." A chill feathered its way up Witold's spine. He glanced across the room to where the moon spilled cold white light through the kitchen window, adding sinister glamour to the ordinary clutter of cheap coffee mugs and draining dishes.

His nightmare came stalking into the flat with moonlight in its hair.

"Alright." Witold strained to focus his attention. The officer had re-opened his notebook. "Let's check the details, Mrs Jevik. Your daughter is five years old, shoulder length blonde hair, grey eyes. Right?"

"Yes."

"She is wearing . . . ?"

"A black tracksuit and sneakers; a red overcoat and a red knitted cap."

"Did she have anything with her?"

"A small basket."

"And you last saw her . . . ?"

"About a quarter to five. It was still light. She was doing a little errand for me. Just across the way. I told her not to leave the path."

The police officer paused, smiling: "Don't tell me: she was taking a basket of goodies to her poor sick grandmother."

Nada winced, turned away. Witold stood his ground, muscles trembling, hands clenching into fists. "Her grandmother," he grated, "was murdered. Along with her grandfather and her aunts and her uncles and her cousins. Along with her brother. In the ethnic *cleansing*." He spat the words. "You wouldn't understand."

The officer had paled.

Witold relented a little: "My daughter was ill and we had taken her to the hospital in the city. Otherwise, we also would not be here to trouble you. She's all we have. You must find her."

Nada patted his quivering hand, turned back to the officer:

"She was taking some soup to Mrs Wolan. She lives across the way. She's good with children and she sometimes babysits for me when I have to go out. She says Katie never arrived."

"Why did you send the child?"

Nada looked at him, glanced down at her bulging belly, said only: "I am having trouble with the stairs at present."

"Oh. Of course. Sorry. Do you have any idea where she might have gone? Is there anyone she usually plays with here? Anyone she might have stopped to visit?"

"No-one special. She's a good girl, always does as she's told. She wouldn't just wander off on her own. I asked all the neighbours before I called the police station."

Witold's agitation was palpable. Nada spoke quickly, forestalling her husband: "we do not want to cause any trouble. We just want to find Katie."

But Witold would not be checked. "Trouble?" His voice rose. "For God's sake, woman, it's a solstice moon, this neighbourhood is full of wolf people, our daughter is missing, and you don't want to cause trouble?" He was shouting now.

Red faced and shaking, he turned to the officer. "Start with the wolf people."

"We can't just target one ethnic group with no evidence, Mr Jevik. There are laws about . . . "

Witold cut him off. "You don't understand. You don't live next door to them like I do. The wolf people. They emigrate from the old country. They bring their abominations with them, and your government is stupid enough to let them!"

"You emigrated, Mr Jevik. Why shouldn't they?"

"You don't listen. The civil war, the *ethnic cleansing*, it is flushing out more than unfriendly neighbours, more than religious enemies. There are things they don't want to keep there. The old races are coming here as refugees. Wolf people. And worse. They bring the old ways with them. They don't want to be part of this new country. They form ghettoes. They do not assimilate."

"How do you know? They look just like everyone else to me."

Witold dropped his voice, spoke wearily: "In the old country, we have ways to know them. Wolf people are hairy on the inside. They change at full moon. Turn their skins. They have no choice. At full moon they must go hunting. They must have living meat. They prey on the unwary, on the homeless, on the defenceless—they attack small animals, old women, children." He gulped air, went on. "They smell out births—if they cannot take the newborn they eat the placenta, the afterbirth. It is a delicacy. No matter how much the rich ones try to hide it, with their special restaurants and their fancy clothes, we know the truth. If you hide their clothes, they can't turn back again: that's why they are so neat—the wolf side has to know how to find everything so it can return to human shape. And down here in the public housing they keep us awake with their howling. At full moon always some child's puppy is going missing, always someone is putting disgusting messes in the rubbish bins next morning."

The young officer flushed, embarrassed. "Too many late night horror movies, if you ask me. I suppose you want me to go back to the station for a box of silver bullets and some sharpened stakes."

He paused, visibly remembering his training. "Sorry. I shouldn't have said that. Look, Mr Jevik, this isn't helping. I know you are upset. The sooner we can conclude this interview the sooner we can do something about getting a team out searching for Katarina."

"Horror movies?" Witold was shouting again. "Do you think you'll catch them waiting at the crossroads? I am telling you the wolf people are lethal. Tonight is full moon. They have to feed."

His voice cracked. "And they have my daughter."

The search dragged on into the night. Descriptions were issued and broadcast; Katarina's smiling kindergarten photo was shown on television, news journalists with tape recorders and videocams clamoured for comment. Police public liaison officers appealed for information. Nada and Witold, tearstained and bone weary, faced the TV cameras and pleaded on the late night news with persons unknown for the safe return of their daughter. Nothing helped. Talk-show commentators discussed the icy winter weather, ran survival statistics on unprotected children exposed in similar conditions. They reminded their audiences of other disappearances, speculated on possible links to other ethnic kidnappings, wondered darkly about organized crime in the immigrant community, assumed the worst. Their ratings climbed as hope dwindled.

Nada, in no condition to walk the bitter streets, could only wait and hope that her daughter would somehow find her way home. She was taken inside, given soup, offered comfort by old Mrs Wolan, who clucked busily about the empty flat like a distracted hen in a burgled nest.

Witold insisted on scouring the neighbourhood with the official searchers, backtracking along his usual route home, holding fast to the impossibly thin hope that Katarina might somehow have been coming to meet him. Woolfe Street had moved into its night phase. It was no place for a child. Witold cursed the bitter, moonlit solstice night that had lured so many sleazy darksiders into the district. Everywhere he looked they were there, grotesque shapes outlined by moonlight and lurid neon—creatures of the night, cruising, lurking, lying in wait for unwary innocents. Hungry. He could feel their hunger.

The clubs were opening now. *Children of the Night*'s coffin doors stood ajar: a life size Bela Lugosi model spread his cape in a half-empty foyer that opened onto a cavernous dance floor where continuous-loop black-and-white horror movies flickered against empty walls. Witold peered in, shuddered to see drunken patrons jostling each other to play-act being vampire victims. He knew that others would try it for real in the club's shadowy booths where monochrome make-believe movie-light glimmered on blood spilled in earnest.

Witold stayed determinedly at the side of the officer assigned to search with him. He'd stopped shouting, stopped badgering restaurateurs, could now only nod numbly as the ritual was repeated in endless cafes and clubs and bars: Katarina's photo in a stranger's hands; the crucial question: "Have you seen this little girl?"; the shrug, the headshake, the total indifference.

The ordeal went on. Witold's boots crunched on smashed glass as he crossed the alley beside *Vampyra's*, a dark tunnel that smelled of motor fumes and cheap booze and recent vomit. His own stomach heaved as something squelched underfoot, something that reeked of blood. His scream brought his partner running. Police flashlights revealed the remains of a recently disembowelled possum. Witold fought for control, said tightly: "Wolf people. I told you."

The officer scowled. "Looks more like a dog did this."

"Same thing."

The officer pressed his lips together in meaningful silence, shrugged his collar higher around his cold-chapped ears, and resumed his patient search routine.

The moon had sunk low in a frosty sky that glimmered a cold, pre-dawn metallic grey by the time the long shift was over. Witold's anger was finally giving way to exhaustion, and the constable insisted on taking him back to the flat. They were drinking tea in the kitchen when the call came.

A cultured, European voice spoke calmly: "Mr Jevik? I have your daughter."

"What?"

"I believe I have your daughter."

"Who is this?"

"Wolfgang Sachs: I am the owner of *Wolfie's*. You came in earlier this evening with a police officer."

"And you said you'd never seen her."

"Yes. I know."

"How did you get my number?"

The voice was patient: "You insisted on leaving it with me. You wrote it on my seating plan. As you'll recall, you disrupted all my customers and insisted on checking my kitchen."

"What have you done with her?"

"I? I have done nothing."

"Then why is she with you?"

"That, Mr Jevik, is a matter for some conjecture." He paused. "But I assume you will want her back as quickly as possible. Can you come to the restaurant?"

"Yes." Witold slammed the phone down, shouted for Nada. The officer was already radioing information to headquarters. The two men raced for the stairs, heard sirens split the night as patrol cars headed for *Wolfie's* on Woolfe Street. It wasn't far. It took forever.

The squad car from the station had arrived ahead of Witold. A second car carrying Nada and Mrs Wolan pulled up behind them. Police converged on the scene from half a dozen directions. The press would not be far behind. Wolfgang Sachs stood in the entrance to his restaurant: a tall, elegant man wearing a fur-lined black leather coat over his dark evening suit. Witold stared anxiously, for the second time that night, at Wolfgang's long face. Everything about him—the high, domed forehead, the lupine eyes, the pointed beard, the sharp, gleaming teeth identified him as one of the wolf people. Everything from his carefully barbered mane of silver-tipped dark-brown hair down to the soft gleam of his Italian leather shoes spoke money and influence. He exuded charm and confidence. And he smelled of meat. Witold was afraid.

Wolfgang spoke. "Really, there is no need for all this." The sweep of his manicured hand indicated the spotlights, the weaponry, the growing number of squad cars. "The child is not a hostage." He shrugged. "More like an inconvenient guest." He turned to where Witold and Nada waited, parting his dark lips in a smile that emphasized those overlong canines: "Come in, Mr Jevik, Mrs Jevik. I won't bite."

The officer tapped his holstered weapon, nodded approval. The Jeviks stepped across *Wolfie's* red threshold. Empty of diners, the place seemed cavernous, lit mostly by dying firelight from the embers in the huge hearth. And there, tucked up safe and warm in a scarlet blanket, was Katarina.

Official procedures swung smoothly into place. The child was whisked aside, to be checked by a police doctor. Tearful reunion interviews were recorded and broadcast. The press went home. The social worker arrived. The officers got down to the business of writing up the incident for their reports.

Wolfgang Sachs obligingly recounted his story one more time: "When the restaurant closed I went out to check on Vlad"—he scratched his huge German Shepherd affectionately behind its ears. "I found the little girl curled up asleep under my dog's blanket in the back of my Range Rover. I have no idea how she came to be there." He hesitated: "She was terrified. She called me "Wolf Man". It took me half an hour to convince her I wasn't going to eat her." He looked straight at Witold. "Children get hold of some strange ideas." He paused, then said mildly: "I finally coaxed her out, moved her inside by the fire and wrapped her in a warmer blanket, persuaded her to tell me her name, then telephoned you. I gave her some hot chocolate to drink. She seems unharmed."

Katarina kept her big grey eyes fixed on her father as she answered the social worker's quiet questions. "I saw the big dog in the back of the car outside the flats. I only climbed up to pat him. He looked lonely."

Wolfgang confirmed that he had parked the Range Rover there, briefly, while he collected his dry cleaning. He'd left the back door ajar for Vlad's comfort.

"Then the Wolf Man came, and I was scared. So I hid behind the seat. I thought he'd go away again. He didn't see me. He slammed the door and drove away."

"Why didn't you say something?"

"I couldn't. Daddy made me promise never to speak to the wolf people."

Several pairs of eyes turned to Witold. He sat rigid, silent.

"What did you do next?"

"I didn't want to get eaten. I hid under the blanket. The Wolf Man let the dog out, but he still didn't see me. I stayed very quiet. I thought someone would come."

"And . . . ?"

"It was smelly in the back of the car. It got dark. I was trying to stay very still. I guess I went to sleep. Then the Wolf Man came back and found me. I screamed. But he didn't try to hurt me. He was nice." She smiled shyly. "He gave me chocolate."

Finally, the questions were over. Sunlight was touching the cold buildings as Witold carried his daughter to the waiting police car. She snuggled into his shoulder, and confided her secret:

"They didn't change, Daddy."

"Who?"

"The wolf men. The wolf dog. I watched and watched and watched. I wanted to see them turn their skins like you said they would. But they didn't do it."

Witold considered this for a moment. "Some of them," he said darkly, "the rich ones, they can afford special drugs, hormones, to stop the change."

He kissed her lightly.

"But we know what they are."

The Lady of the Swamp

This story began when the contractors who were building an extension to my house told me the local gossip about an old lady who had lived the life of a hermit in her house out by the Tarwin Swamp. They said it would make a good story. I moved the unfortunate woman into a caravan on the edge of the swamp, and wrote the original version of this as a psychological story about developers who terrorize her as she tries to protect the wildlife that she loves. The mood of the story was quiet, elegiac. And then, just as I was putting this collection together, I had an email asking for an Australian horror story in the style of Lovecraft. So I re-wrote this story, transposing the urban nightmare of Lovecraft's "The Haunter of the Dark" into an Australian wetlands setting. The lady is still there, the original theme of ecological threat is still there, but now there are much darker things out there in that swamp . . . .

Detective Inspector David Dyson shrugged into the jacket of his too-tight suit. He straightened his tie and squared his shoulders before he stepped outside to face the waiting crowd of journalists. The summer sun was high: the day was a scorcher. Dyson missed his air-conditioned city office—he was sweating before he had even made it to the end of the corridor of the country church hall he had commandeered for his search headquarters. The questions began before the heavy door had closed behind him, the reporters shouting over each other to bid for his attention. Television cameras winked on, microphones were thrust at his face.

"Come on, Dyson," one of the older men yelled. "It's hot out here. Give us a break!"

"Yeah!" said another. "The public has a right to know about this swamp massacre. How bad is it?"

Dyson held up his hand for silence.

"I know you are all anxious for answers," he said, getting a general laugh. "You all know me. I'm a cautious man. I don't jump to conclusions, no matter how tempting a quick solution might be."

"Was it wild animals?"

"There are rumours . . . "

"Patience," Dyson said. "It's early days yet. I will now read a prepared statement." He cleared his throat, his cough loud in the sudden silence.

"As you know," he said, "the remains of several bodies have been found in the swamp. At this stage, the forensics team is still working to establish the exact number: I am sure you will appreciate the delicacy of the process. DNA tests take time. My officers are checking the list of missing persons against the records of the Company concerned, in an effort to establish which unaccounted-for employees may have been in the area at the time to work on the access road. Obviously, not all of the dead are necessarily Company employees, so we are asking anyone with missing friends or relatives who may have been in the vicinity of the swamp to come forward."

He paused for breath.

"What about the old lady? What about the diaries? Why are you keeping them secret?"

Dyson shrugged. "Word travels fast," he said.

"It's a country town," one of the women said, smiling.

"All I can tell you," Dyson said firmly, "is that yesterday when we widened our search one of my officers found a cave. The only artefact in that cave was an old biscuit tin, and in that tin were a number of exercise books—the sort that kids use in school—and a bundle of loose papers. They were mostly just records of bird and animal sightings, dating back for about twenty years."

"But?"

"But the most recent notebooks contain some pretty weird stuff. I have no reason to believe they will shed any light at all on the massacre. But we are checking them out, just in case there's a speck of something useful."

"Have you found her? The old woman, I mean?"

"So far, there's no trace of her anywhere. The townsfolk here confirm that an elderly lady did have a beaten-up plywood caravan out there beside the swamp, but nobody has seen her lately. There's no caravan there now. If the journals hidden in the cave really are hers, they will almost certainly turn out to be nothing more than the ramblings of an eccentric old woman who lived rough in a swamp and spent too much time on her own. And until the forensics team is through, we can't know whether she died there—as part of the massacre or from other causes—or simply moved away."

"But . . . "

"No more questions: that's all I have for you, for now. There'll be further bulletins as and when more information becomes available."

Dyson turned to leave.

"Will you release the diaries?" one of the journalists shouted.

"All in good time, my friends," Dyson said. "I'll release them when our people are through with them."

Back in the relative coolness of the office at the rear of the hall, Dyson gulped down two painkillers with a mouthful of tepid bottled water. The very thought of releasing those journals had made his headache worse. He intended to do no such thing. He had enough trouble to contend with. He hoped—would have prayed if he'd been a religious man—the things recorded in there had not really happened. He felt in his bones that the diaries must belong to the old lady, and he'd been profoundly unsettled by what she had written. He, who prided himself on being one of the toughest in the force, had had nightmares after he'd read them. He told himself that the old biddy had probably been cooking up those magic mushrooms he'd heard grew around that particular swamp, and recording her hallucinations—that, at least would explain it. The problem was that she sounded sane enough when she wrote about verifiable events—the town meetings, the Company and so on. But then, she also recorded other things, terrifying things that could not—must not—be true.

Dyson went back to his borrowed desk. He sighed deeply as he opened the hinged lid on the big, old-fashioned tin once more, resigned to taking another look at the diaries. Some of the old schoolbooks had fallen apart when they were opened, scattering papers. Dyson decided, on reflection, that he was not being paid nearly enough for this. He settled down, unwillingly, to read, shuffling backwards and forwards through the pages of spidery handwriting, trying to figure out a plausible sequence of events.

JUNE 21ST

Today, I found a cave, a very special cave. It has been a chilly day, a day of biting winds and slippery ground. I was walking along a ridge when I skidded, lost my footing, slid down the bank. I turned my back on the wind to get my breath and wipe my muddy hands, and I was amazed to realize that I was looking at a well-preserved midden—a mound of bones and shells and debris that spoke of occupation.

I was cautious, careful not to disturb the pile. I edged my way around to see what lay behind. And I found the low entrance. I did not hesitate: I ducked my head and stepped inside, out of the wind. Everything was suddenly quiet. I fumbled in my jeans for my pencil torch, and shone a thin beam into the gloom. I couldn't see very much, but I could make out that beyond its narrow mouth the cave widened and opened into a high cavern, with clean sand on the floor. And on the sand were footprints, dozens of them, of different sizes—and all of them barefoot, except for my own tracks. I tiptoed further in, feeling like an intruder in somebody's home. I couldn't shake the sensation that the inhabitants had just stepped out for a while, that they'd be back any minute. I knew that this was not true—the first people had been cleared out long ago, hunted off their lands, never to return. And yet, I felt that I was being watched.

I explored further, and found a small, sweet-water spring that seeped through the rock at the very back. The cave had formed, I realized, when the river followed a different course. It had been left high and dry when the channel changed its path. These things happened. I tiptoed back towards the entrance and paused to sit for a while, thinking about the tribe who had used this cave. I was overwhelmed by the peacefulness of it: I knew it was a safe haven, a special place. I did not want to leave. I found it very hard to return to the swamp, but I had no camping gear with me, no food. I shall have to go back.

JUNE 26TH

Last night I found the crystal. I hesitate to write this down, but honesty is one of the privileges of age. I can at least be honest with myself, here, in my own notebook.

I couldn't stop thinking about the cave. I felt compelled to return to it—and this time I took my backpack, camping gear and bedroll. My first new discovery was a moment of pure pleasure: the lamplight revealed a whole wall of cave paintings, scenes of tribal life picked out in browns, reds, yellows and whites on the bare rock. This had been no casual camp. This was a major site for a vanished people. I wondered if it could have been a sacred place. I imagined the paintings were of a dreamtime story, but it was not a story that I recognized. I pottered around for ages, happily exploring.

But what I found next worried me. Further back in the cave, above the sooty indentation where the tribal people had kept their fire, a giant black serpent had been drawn in charcoal—it reared up, its huge maw gaping wide as if to swallow the whole world. It took my breath away. It scared the life out of me. I was shaking, and yet I couldn't bring myself to leave. And then I remembered that the giant snake must be the Rainbow Serpent. That would make sense: I knew that the mythical creation serpent was always to be found close to water—near rivers, creeks, waterfalls, lagoons—so I figured it must have been depicted here to protect the swamp. I liked that idea. I took comfort from it. I forgot that the Rainbow Serpent could also be very, very dangerous. And I stayed.

I built my fire in the ancient fireplace, and tiptoed past the enormous serpent to the very back of the cave to fetch water from the spring. And as I leaned forward to fill my billycan I reached out to the rock ledge to steady myself. My fingertips brushed against a cold, hard shape: without thinking I picked it up. I knew from the feel of the thing that I was holding a crystal—heaven knows I have collected enough of them over the years—and so I slipped it into my pocket without paying it much attention. I was too focussed on the spring's nearness to the menacing serpent: that snake's black image seemed to coil and grow in the flickering firelight.

My heart was in my mouth as I edged past it once more. I made it back to my fire, set my billycan on its tripod to boil water for my tea, and cooked my meal, such as it was. Later, I laid out my bedroll beside the fire and curled up to sleep. And when I slept, I dreamed:

it was a vivid dream of the tribe that had lived here, as if the painted fishing and hunting scenes had come to life.

In my dream I was young again. And not just young—I was young and desirable: I was kidnapped by the men from a neighbouring tribe to be the wife of a tall young man with kind brown eyes and the just-healing chest scars of recent ritual. The dream was so real I could smell the camp smoke and the body sweat when I was carried off, slung over a muscular shoulder. I knew, with the certainty of dreams, that I was happy. This was not a violent abduction—it felt stage-managed, as if the elders had orchestrated the whole thing. My handsome dream lover was everything I ever wished for: he satisfied my every desire.

But such sweet dreams do not last. Some hours later, I woke in darkness. I was cold—I needed to put more wood on the fire. I still had water in my billycan, enough to make another cup of tea. I wanted a hot drink to warm me. And as I waited for the water to boil, I glanced through the mouth of the cave, seeing the stars burning bright in a clear, black winter sky: Scorpio was climbing high into the night, blazing cold and brilliant, and the curve of its tail reminded me of the serpent on the cave wall. It was a bad thought.

A sudden gust of cold wind blew through the cave. The fire sputtered, but steadied again. Wood smoke eddied about: my eyes watered, and as I reached into my pocket for my handkerchief my fingers found the crystal once more. I took it out, seeing by re-kindled firelight that I held a fine piece of crystalline smoky quartz. I switched on my lamp, holding up the crystal for a better look.

I wish I hadn't done that.

The crystal was beautiful: it shaded from clear grey through to inky black, and it warmed quickly—too quickly—to my touch. It held me. I could not look away. I shivered, gazing into the heart of darkness. And the Darkness stared back. I felt naked, bare to the bone as a searing intelligence peered into the core of me, stripping me to my very soul. There were no words, and yet I understood that it offered knowledge, and with it power—and that it demanded sacrifice in return. It wanted blood, my blood. I did not want to know. I would not pay the price. My mind was being torn apart. I think I must have screamed before I fell senseless on the sandy floor of the cave.

I do not know how long I lay there. But I remember the dream: no matter how I try, I know I will never forget that dream.

In this second dream, my young lover was back, and I knew I should be happy. But as I offered myself to his embrace, the dream flicked into nightmare. My lover transformed into a demon, his lovemaking becoming insistent, brutal. He was hurting me, devouring me, pounding my body, bruising my bones. And then he morphed again. He turned into the great serpent itself, wrapping his shining black coils around me, crushing the life out of me. I struggled, but I could not pull away. And yet, I would not yield: the darkness that raped my body could not penetrate the core of me, could not take my mind. I absolutely refused to allow it. It was a small defiance, but it was the only answer that was mine to make. I have known despair: it cannot reach me now. I shrieked at the black, starlit sky.

I think it must have been my own cry that jolted me from fevered sleep. I woke up shaking, sweating, crying. As I struggled to sit upright, something dark and misshapen slithered away from my thighs—and my thighs felt sticky. The smell of it made me retch. I grabbed for my bedroll and wrapped the blanket around myself, desperate for cover. My breathing slowed, but I knew I couldn't stay beside the fire. The fireplace was too close to the charcoal-etched serpent. I crawled to the entrance of the cave and sat waiting for the first grey pre-dawn light, huddled into the blanket, rehearsing the nightmare. The nightmare would not leave my mind.

I tried to explain it away. Nothing made sense. All I knew was that I needed to go home. As soon as I could see the path, I gathered my stuff and scrambled down the treacherous bank. I headed back to my caravan. I was relieved to find that everything was as I had left it. The sun was rising as I lit my fire and heated water for my bath. I told myself to get a grip: I told myself that I had had a ghastly nightmare, that I had hallucinated, that I had dreamed the unspeakable incubus—that I was home safe now, and all was well.

But as I began to wash myself, the horror returned. I could see that there was blood on my thighs. I could smell a strange, musky odour on my skin. I scrubbed myself clean, remembering. I knew, then that the Darkness truly had violated me. I knew that some dark thing had used the black crystal to find me. I was very, very frightened."

It was late in the day when Detective Inspector Dyson put the journal down, massaging his temples with his fingertips. "Christ almighty," he muttered. "I can't believe I'm sitting here sifting through the sexual fantasies of an old lady." He looked at his watch. "*It's almost time for a drink*," he thought. "*I could almost risk running into the journo mob down at the pub. I'll have to see them sooner or later—there's only one hotel in this town, and we're all staying in it. God knows I need a drink.*"

On his way out he stopped by Sergeant Murphy's desk.

"Yes, sir?" she asked.

"Tell the guys in the field to keep an eye out for a crystal," he said. "A black quartz crystal."

"Sir?"

"It's evidence. If it's out there, I want it found."

Murphy looked sceptical, but did not demur. "If you say so, sir," she said.

Later that evening, duly fortified by several beers, a decent steak and a half-bottle of red wine, Dyson returned to his task. The revelations of the journal weren't any easier to stomach, but at least he felt stronger. He sighed, and went back to sorting through the pages.

JULY 17TH

For weeks, I have been afraid to sleep, afraid of what dreams might come. But the dark demon of my dream has not returned, and today I decided that I must take full control of my life once more. I decided I would not let a nightmare get the better of me. I decided that I had enough courage to go back to the cave, to face my fear.

I was shaking when I got there, but I had to do it, I had to go in. I was not surprised to find that the dark crystal was still there, where I dropped it on the scuffed sand. I am as sure as I can be that no one else knows about the cave. I would not look again into the darkness of the crystal's depths, but I put it into my jacket pocket. I will keep it safe.

I built a fire close to the mouth of the cave, and I forced myself to spend another night there, watching the winter stars wheel overhead.

I dozed, but I did not dream. There were no nightmares: I began to relax a little. I felt strangely welcome, then, as if I belonged. It seems that the danger has passed.

SEPTEMBER 25TH

I am elderly, well past childbearing age. I was not looking for the signs. My pregnancy has come as a shock.

FEBRUARY 22ND

It won't be long, now. I have known, from the moment I first felt the child kick in my belly, that I cannot call a midwife when my time comes. It would be too dangerous if word ever got out. *Devil spawn*, the locals would call it. There are superstitious souls aplenty out there. I am terrified of what my offspring, sired by the incubus, might turn out to be. I will have to give birth alone. I hope I can survive it.

MARCH 20TH

The child is mercifully small. I woke in the dead of night, my contractions upon me. I knew my time was close. I was ready: I had prepared a pile of clean rags, I had filled my water kettle and set it on my spirit stove ready to boil, I had sterilized my sharpest knife. My waters broke. I steadied myself, gripping the bar that braced my bed. I rode the waves of pain, howling at the moon.

I could sense that everything around my old caravan was still, waiting. The nocturnal animals paused in their routines, listening to my travail. I knew, in my bones, that the Dark was listening too. The Dark was waiting for its child.

It had not long to wait. The tiny dark thing slithered out easily between my thighs. I grabbed it, held it, cut and tied its cord. Its first, unearthly cry split the silence of the night. I felt the tension ease. The child lived. I placed it on my breast to suckle it. It bit. It didn't want milk, I realized. It needed blood. Instinct, and my hormones, took over. I let it feed. Whatever it was, it was mine. I knew, then, that I would care for it.

I did what I needed to do. I cleaned myself up, and when I was steady enough to walk I put the afterbirth out for the scavengers to feed on—it was the best way, the way of the natural world. I swaddled the child and held it to my body to warm it. I have raised a lot of strange creatures, orphaned creatures, out here in the swamp. I would raise this one too. Eventually, I slept.

The child's wail woke me, piercing the night, demanding its next feed. In the lamplight, the eyes that looked up at me were as blue as my own, and the tiny fingers that curled around mine were human enough. But as for the rest . . . I could not pretend, even to myself, that this alien thing could pass for human. My breast was sore where I had been bitten. I took up the sharp knife and sliced my arm, just a little, so that the blood welled up, and I held it out to the child. It sucked greedily. It was the start of a feeding routine that almost cost me my life.

JUNE 29TH

The child grows very quickly. I am weak from loss of blood. I don't know what to do to wean it.

JUNE 30TH

The Dark has provided the answer: today a freshly killed swamp rat was left on my doorstep—and the monster-child pounced. I had to turn away as it fed, gorging on sticky entrails. I couldn't watch that. I cleaned it up afterwards.

JULY 6TH

Tonight, the child left to hunt for itself. It went at dusk, and came back to me to sleep.

JULY 10TH

I was getting used to this new routine, but last night the child did not come back. I searched for it, fearing the worst. But then I heard it, and I knew it had simply moved on. It's only natural.

JULY 12TH

I know the child is still out there, somewhere in the swamp. I can feel it when it is near; I will always recognize its howl, this flesh of my flesh that haunts the night.

Dyson felt sick. He knew he could go no further with this particular line of enquiry, at least for the moment. He put it aside, and switched to safer ground. He could check the Company records that had arrived this afternoon against the old woman's diary entries: that much would be verifiable. He laid the printout of the Company's official account of its interactions with the local community on his desk, and then searched through the journals until he found a matching entry.

AUGUST 17TH

There is trouble brewing. There has been a public announcement. A coal seam gas facility has been approved in this area. My friends are indignant: they can't figure out exactly why their land should be wrecked to provide power for far-away cities.

I got a lift into town when the Company held its public meeting. I thought I might be able to help. I listened from the doorway at the back of the hall: I watched while the local mayor struggled to referee the confrontation. The community was divided. Landowners who wanted the income at any price shouted economics at conservationists who shouted back about endangering the water table and preserving wildlife habitat.

The local people know about the swamp, about what hides beneath its surface. They say the swamp is haunted. They stay well away from it at night. But nobody listens to the locals. The locals are powerless. The bulldozer men have government contracts. They have bankrolled a huge advertising campaign, extolling the public good of their depredations. I know it is all about money: what they can take, what they can make.

I had already told my friends about the environmental officers who came out to the swamp to conduct a special kind of survey. I didn't know what it was for, until now. The whole thing was a farce. Those men were public servants: they only came during office hours. I watched them crashing about in the undergrowth, putting their feet up in their hide, slurping thermos lattes and leaving behind discarded sandwich wrappers. They knew I was there. They didn't offer me so much as a packet of peanuts. They ignored me.

I did offer to help. "You might like to look at my log book," I said. "I've been recording wildlife sightings here for over twenty years. I know what lives here."

"No thanks," they replied. "We can't be sure it's accurate. The survey has to be done by accredited experts."

"Meaning yourselves?"

"You got it, lady."

So I left them to it.

The birds and animals hid until the interlopers had gone. The dark things were always asleep. And the survey men, oblivious, went home each afternoon at four o'clock. I could have warned them: I *would* have warned them, if only they had not been so busy not seeing what was there.

The Company spokesman at the meeting was a smooth, oleaginous creep. He never stopped smiling. "The government has already sold us its permission," he said. "Our fracking process has been declared safe. Any chemicals that leak into the swamp will be minimal, practically harmless."

"But you can't really know what the impact on wildlife will be, can you?" one of the conservationists asked.

"We will study the situation carefully," the man replied.

"Can you reverse it?"

"No—but we can take whatever steps become necessary," he said.

"It'll be way too late by the time you do that," another man yelled. "The damage will be permanent. You'll just be dissecting the corpses of the creatures you have destroyed."

"We've done our environmental survey," the Company man said smugly. "We didn't find anything unusual or endangered in the swamp. There's always some damage. But you will find that our projected levels are within acceptable tolerances."

"There *is* no acceptable level for mutation or death. This is a sensitive ecosystem. *Everything* that's out there will be endangered if you have your way!"

The mayor was doing his best to keep things calm. So he asked his next question: "What about the people who live here? How will your processes affect us?"

"We can't drink methane either," the first conservationist said sharply.

The Company man kept smiling. "I can assure you that contamination on that scale just won't happen," he said.

"It already has, in other places. There's a farmer up in the Valley who can light his tap water with a match. His video clip is all over the net."

The Company man ignored this. "We need to progress this industry," he said. He was good at his job: he stuck to his message. "Our development will be good for the economy. It will provide jobs for your community. We have the requisite permissions. The cheapest option is to bulldoze an access road across government land, and that means going through the swamp."

There were angry mutterings at this.

"Arrogant bastard," one of the farmers shouted. "I don't know why you bothered to come here at all. You're not listening. I tell you, that swamp isn't safe."

The Company man shrugged. "I'm a man of science," he said. "I'll leave the superstitious nonsense to you."

"Don't say we didn't warn you," the farmer said. He turned his back in disgust and strode out of the meeting.

I could see that the Company man didn't care. He had made his point. How could I speak up, after that? I know that more things will be endangered than any of them could ever guess. And it won't just be the wildlife that's at risk if they antagonize the Darkness: the Dark owns this swamp. I fear the Dark will fight back.

SEPTEMBER 28TH

Things just got worse—much, much worse. The Company is pushing ahead with its development. Today, I found out that I am personally involved. They want me out of here. Today, a Company man came to my home. He marched right up to my old caravan with its peeling ply and mouldering annexe. He didn't even knock.

"Move it or lose it," he said.

I could smell his sweat, could see the dark rings under his armpits where his shirt clung uncomfortably. He had had a long, hot walk to my campsite, and he oozed an acrid mix of perspiration and bad temper. His smile was nasty, the smug smile of a man who enjoys the pain of others, the thin smile of a small time bully. Blind Freddy could see I couldn't move it—I have nothing to pull it with, even if the tyres hadn't perished long ago and the axles rusted slowly as they settled into the soft ground of this campsite that I chose so long ago. This is my last refuge, and he can't wait to smash it down. I saw the corners of his mouth quirk again, relishing my distress.

"The access road goes right through here, lady," he said. "You'll have to be out by then."

There was a single line in the Company records: "Advised residents about route of access road through swamp."

The Inspector looked thoughtful. For the first time he felt a glimmer of sympathy for the old lady. She might have been crazy, and some of the things she'd written were truly shocking, but Dyson was beginning to suspect foul play of the more ordinary, criminal kind. He made a note to interview the Company employee who had visited the woman's campsite.

SEPTEMBER 30TH

When my friends found out, they were outraged. I told them it wouldn't help, but they called the shock jocks anyway. I listened in on my tinny little transistor radio: I couldn't help myself. It was hard to think it was really about me when the Talkback radio program buzzed with discussion about the eviction of an elderly woman from her solitary caravan on the edge of the wetlands: the morals, the ethics, the economics of it. I was bemused by the support, amazed at the vilification.

Chief Inspector Dyson paused, clicked on his email. The recording of the talkback session had arrived, as requested. He turned up the volume, listening:

"What was she doing there anyway?" a lot of callers wanted to know.

"In other cultures, hermits are respected," one woman said. "A lot of our saints chose a life of solitary contemplation. We should leave her in peace."

This, it transpired, was a minority view. The caller was howled down: the lady in the swamp was an inconvenience; she was in the way of progress; she was clearly crazy, poor thing, and should be taken somewhere institutional for my own good—perhaps a nice hostel for the homeless.

"Which is what the poor woman will be if you demolish her home," the first caller had replied tartly.

The logic of it didn't matter. The lobby groups got into the act, then the shills for the Company.

Dyson had heard it all before. He wondered how long it would be before someone accused the old lady of witchcraft, imagined her blackened billy into a spell-brewing cauldron. It was that kind of program. He turned back to the diary.

I switched off the radio, at the last. I couldn't bear it. I felt cold, numb with terror. I know how it will end: I am to be cast out once again, and this time with violence.

OCTOBER 1ST

The reporters found me, of course. I think I surprised them. I think they expected a crazed hermit, not an educated woman. They wanted to know why I was living in the swamp at all. I told them the truth, for what it's worth:

"When my husband died, I managed to keep the farm going for a while. But I missed too many payments. The bank foreclosed. They took everything. I wasn't fit for company, then. The doctor diagnosed depression: a compound of grief, loss, and humiliation. I was so ashamed. I didn't want to be in anyone's way, so I brought the old caravan here: I needed to think, to put myself back together. I found the solitude soothing, and I stayed. My husband and I used to come here, bird watching. It was always peaceful here. I didn't drop out—life dropped me."

Dyson pulled up the transcripts of the interviews. The diary account checked out. These pieces were falling into place.

He read on, still listening to the recordings, cross-checking.

It was a young cadet, clearly embarrassed, who asked the

next question. He demanded to know why the old woman was obstructing progress.

"What progress?" she said.

"We need a clean energy future," he replied. "We need new technologies."

"Who's we?" she asked.

"All of us."

"I don't use power. I don't need coal seam gas."

"Nobody should have to live like this, like you!" he said. His voice dripped contempt.

"Millions do," she said mildly.

"But not here: not in this country."

His ignorance was breath taking.

"Perhaps you should investigate some of the outlying settlements," the woman said. "Perhaps you'd like to put an access road through a humpy."

A senior reporter intervened, diverting the argument. "Let me ask you about the bigger picture," he said hurriedly. "Surely you would agree that we need better energy sources if we are to avert future disasters."

"Of course," she replied.

Dyson chuckled—the old woman was no fool—she had seen the trap.

"But saving the planet by destroying its wildlife isn't very clever," she went on. "Our beloved leaders have a lot to say about maintaining biodiversity. Surely that means the animals should survive too."

"What would *you* do then?"

"Think smaller," she said. "If every building had solar panels you wouldn't need to pollute these wetlands to feed big expensive power plants."

"Don't you think that's a bit naïve?" It was the cadet again.

She lost patience. "Naivety is believing that power brokers and energy corporations care about anything other than the bottom line," she said. "Politicians can't think small—they want the grand gesture, the big political erections, the large party donations. They want the photo op when cut they cut the ribbon on the next financial disaster."

That did it. The cadet lost it completely.

"What could you possibly know, living rough in a swamp?" he shouted. "It reeks."

"You mistake poverty for ignorance, young man. You're disappointed that I'm not dressed in rags and muttering incoherently. I'm sorry I'm not the story you expected."

"Well," said the senior reporter, wrapping it up. "Thank you so much for your time." And that was more or less it.

Dyson skipped the formalities and fast-forwarded to the coverage that had gone to air. As he had expected, there was no sympathy for the woman's plight: she was the shrill, vituperative, opinionated hag in the swamp—a self-confessed depressive, a post-menopausal neurotic who couldn't see reason. She was standing in the way of a carefully orchestrated urban dream. She'd have to go.

Dyson checked the diary again, curious to see her reaction.

"The reporters couldn't leave fast enough. I was photographed and thanked for my time. I watched them straggle back to their city-shiny four-wheel drives. I knew I'd blown it. I knew I sounded too strident, but I couldn't help myself. The words just tumbled out. These people were trespassing—they had come to my home, judging me, telling me what to think. Lord knows what they'd have said if they'd found out about the child.

OCTOBER 12TH

The Company man came back. "The press won't save you," he said. "The road still goes through here. Bulldozers don't care what rubbish they clear away." He poked a stubby finger at my plywood caravan. "This'll splinter like matchsticks."

"What happens if I don't move?"

He smiled his mean little smile. "We'll go right through you," he said.

"Murder?" The word hung in the air between us.

"Let's just say we *will* have you out of here, one way or another."

"I'm not going anywhere."

"In that case, lady," he said, "we know where you live."

There was no mistaking the threat. For the first time in all my years of solitude I feel truly afraid of other people. I am afraid of the Company men.

I was too scared to sleep in my van that night. I packed my rucksack and headed for the safety of the cave.

And now, thought Dyson, we come to the crux of it.

OCTOBER 13TH

I have never told anyone about the cave. At first, I thought that if I revealed its existence, if I told the press about its wonderful paintings, the find would be of such significance that work on the access road would stop. But now I know otherwise. Now I have seen what the press will do. Now I have decided to protect this place from a process that would surely end in its destruction. There's been enough desecration already in the wetlands. I cannot save the animals. I will shield this cave, if I can, from industry archaeologists.

The reporters think I am crazy. They won't listen to me anyhow. And after that trumped-up environmental survey, I know what will happen if I tell the Company about the cave. Carefully chosen experts will declare the cave paintings to be of no particular significance, and the bulldozer men will go right ahead. But others will know of it. There will be graffiti here within the week. The cave is almost impossible to see, even close up. And the Company men will not be looking. It will be safe enough. I think, perhaps, that I will hide here, when I am finally hunted out of my home.

Dyson picked up a folded piece of notepaper that had fluttered to the floor. He glanced at it, about to put it aside. But then he saw the date on the top of it. This note had been scrawled, hastily, and tucked inside the lid of the biscuit tin. He hoped this was what he had been looking for.

NOVEMBER 15TH

Last night was terrible. I did not dare to light my lamp. I saw flashlights splintering the darkness of the wetlands, and I did not wish to be found by the men who wielded them. I knew I wouldn't stand a chance.

Then I heard the screams. I was lying alone, awake in the darkness when the screaming started. I put my pillow over my head until it stopped, abruptly. I did not go outside to look.

I know the carnage will be terrible. I do not need to find the exact place of it to know what has happened out there. I know that the Company men have trespassed where they should not: they have been setting up their campsite, killing where they pleased, killing for sport. The Dark is angry.

And now the Dark has been hunting: I wonder if those men had a last, terrifying glimpse of fangs and claws and dark muscle before they were torn apart. I can't feel sorry for them. People tried to warn them. They wouldn't listen.

The animals will be feeding now: fresh-killed meat is always a bonanza for scavenging eagles, crows, foxes—and if there's anything in the water, the eels and fishes will be nibbling on the dead.

Dyson shuddered, but pressed on, hoping for more clues. If the note was right, some of the killings had happened a day earlier than he had thought. There was no phone signal out there—no reason that the other workers heading out to the site would have suspected that anything was wrong until they got there. And then . . . It seemed that the forensic team was right—the massacre *had* occurred over a couple of days.

NOVEMBER 16TH

Today will be my last day in my old caravan. I will sleep in my old bed for the last time tonight.

The weather is hot. I have tidied my home for the last time. Everything has been cleaned and put away. Nothing is out of place. I have put my diaries into an airtight biscuit tin, in case they may be found, in case they may be of some future use. My diaries are the record of my life in the swamp, and of the secrets I have uncovered but never told. The secrets have been safe with me. I have hidden the tin in the cave, a secret within a secret.

I have decided, now, as the last day approaches, to stay with the animals, to stay with my van. I know that if am seen near the cave, its secret will be out. I feel old, and spent, and defeated. I do not know how to start again. I feel a chill, creeping sort of horror at the thought of being stuck in an institution for the elderly and destitute. I know I cannot survive that. I cut my ties with such close-pressed humanity long ago. I cannot bear to leave the swamp, or the Dark that holds me here—my life is here, my child is here.

The day is dawning.

Today, as always, the animals come to her, drawn to the familiar cadence of her voice. Shyly, quietly, they approach her where she sits upright on her campstool on the edge of the swamp, reading. She wraps her woollen shawl tightly around her thin shoulders, breathes in the sharp air, and reads aloud in the chilly dawn mist. She is not reading a holy book—St Augustine or Lao Tze. The animals do not need improvement: lumbering wombats, elegant wallabies, shy echidnas, darting quolls, a tubby antechinus, an elderly koala in the fork of a tree—they are all listening. Where the water pools in the shallows there are lizards, frogs, and snakes.

There are other things in the swamp, things she cannot name: older things, darker things. They have had a busy night, hunting, and now they are slithering home, sliding into sleep. They will not attack by daylight—it is not their time. She knows that she is not in danger: in her left hand she holds the smoky quartz crystal that guarantees her safety—a crystal so dark it is almost black, a crystal that draws warmth from her hand, rising quickly to blood heat. She has paid her dues, has earned her place here. Her wrinkled, papery old skin is criss-crossed with scars—she has given blood, she has let her child feed. Even monsters have to feed.

As the sun rises, the air is full of the morning chorus: she hears carolling magpies, the liquid song of a native thrush, the short notes of rosellas and king parrots, the tiny chirruping of fairy wrens and thornbills and spinebills and honeyeaters, and then a raucous wattlebird, sounding like an old motor bike kick-started into morning. Further out in the swamp, black water swirls and eddies and gurgles around a rotting log where something misshapen and muddy has dived to the inky depths. Above it, she hears black swans, and the stirrings of shell duck and black duck and wood duck, even tiny grebes, and the calls of the moorhens and swamp hens and coots. She glances upwards at the piercing sound of thin cries, sees that the raptors are rising: the wedge-tailed eagles are riding the first thermals of the day. There's a peal of manic laughter from the kookaburras, and a tawny owl hoots, once, not yet abed.

Today she is reading Pride & Prejudice. *Perhaps the wombat twins will be encouraged to make good marriages, finding strong partners with glossy coats and superior burrows. She smiles at the thought, knowing that they will be as solitary as the rest. It is a sad smile. Today the bulldozers will come. Animals will die. She will not move. Perhaps she will die too. She hopes she is ready.*

As she waits, she thinks back over her life in the swamp. The animals have grown accustomed to her now. She recalls the testing, early days: the smash and grab raids by possums before she moved every scrap of food into airtight tins; the swooping attacks of territorial magpies at nesting time before her own space was firmly established; the wombat that pushed over a wooden bench every night until they reached an accommodation about its location. For the younger ones, she has always been here. They will even creep towards her fire on cold nights, sharing warmth, sheltering from the denizens of the dark.

She has helped where she could. She remembers sitting up all night with an eyedropper to trickle-feed warm milk to an orphaned baby wombat, found still alive in its road-killed mother's pouch. It lived curled up in a hand-knitted beanie until it was old enough to toddle about her camp, and it stayed with her for a while, until one day it simply left to establish a territory of its own. Since then she has raised a succession of orphans, has often had a joey sleeping snug in an old cardigan slung from a tent pole. She has waded into the swamp to rescue injured wetland wildlife, feeling vaguely responsible for the debris left by human visitors. She has removed hooks from beaks and wings, and patiently extricated tangled egrets and herons from discarded fishing line. But experience has taught her to draw the line at snarled snakes: snakes just aren't grateful.

Today, she has pinned up her long white hair and is wearing her best clothes—her dark blue pants, her cream silk blouse, clasped at the neck with her mother's pearl-and-diamante brooch, the only thing of value that she owns. Her favourite blue shawl completes her outfit—the ensemble of things that she is prepared to be seen dead in. She feels calm now. She clutches her quartz crystal as she sits, waiting for the day.

The animals are blissfully unaware of the fate that approaches them. They are busying themselves with the demands of the day— the foraging, the feeding of young, the digging of burrows. Her reading is simply another part of their routines, a gentle morning sound that is familiar, safe. The sun is shining now: the water is smooth, unruffled; there is a faint scent of gum blossom in the air, and the native bees are busy. It is a perfect blue day in the swamp.

As she closes her book and tilts her face upward to feel the warmth on her wrinkled skin, she hears a low rumbling in the distance, the thunder that presages the bulldozers. There will be no more stories for the animals. A wallaby pauses, pricks its ears forwards, bounds away from the sound. A flock of corellas rises suddenly and wheels overhead, screeching alarm to the skies. Behind them, a column of dust is rising, staining the blue to brown. Other birds take up the alarm, and the wetlands fill with warning cries. Black swans, wood ducks, water birds of all kinds take to the air, heading for safety.

The thunder grows louder: the ground is beginning to shake and the still water is rippling with shock waves. The air is sharp with the smell of crushed eucalyptus, and under it the dark stink of diesel. The animals are fleeing in panic now. Their alarm cries are lost in the deafening cacophony of grinding and cracking and tearing as virgin bushland is ripped up by the roots. She feels for the animals: she shares their terror. She wants to run too. She will not.

She bites her lips, tastes blood. She raises the crystal, smearing it with a bloody kiss, summoning the intelligence that rules beyond the Dark. She has made her decision. Now she will pay the price. She looks into the crystal, feels the vertigo as the dark mind sees her, takes her. She senses the Darkness coming. Shadows form and coalesce in the twilight under the trees, watching. She has let it in—whatever the outer Darkness brings here can be no worse than what the Company men will do. It is a choice of evils.

She stares as the scene takes on the slow horror-movie reality of nightmare. The bulldozer juggernaut is rolling towards her, destroying everything in its path. She sees a ti-tree snap and topple, revealing her first glimpse of bright yellow machinery, casting dark shadows in the swamp. Shadow rises to shadow.

The moment is upon her. She squares her shoulders, waiting.

It's a good day to die.

Detective Inspector David Dyson faced the media once more.

"I think I can be fairly confident that we have solved the mystery of the disappearance of the old lady who lived in the swamp," he said. "We have found the scattered remains of a caravan where it was bulldozed; we have found a brooch that has been identified as belonging to her; we have enough evidence to suggest that the woman's body is among the dead. This appears to have been a straightforward killing. One of the Company employees is helping us with our enquiries."

"What about the other bodies?"

"Our investigations are continuing," Dyson said. "The case is being referred to the Serious Crimes Squad." He allowed himself a tight smile. "*I never liked those smug bastards anyway,*" he thought. "*Let them make sense of it if they can.*"

"There are still some pretty dark rumours," one of the reporters said, "about what else might be out there."

"Some of the locals are still convinced the place is haunted."

"There are always rumours and superstitions around cases like these," Dyson said wearily. "I promise you, I haven't seen any ghosts."

The reporters laughed.

Dyson knew they didn't want to believe in anything other than human agency for what had happened out there, any more than he did. "There will be more updates as evidence becomes available," he said.

As he turned to leave, he slipped his hand into his coat pocket, touching the cool black crystal with his fingertips. He closed his hand over it. It warmed quickly—too quickly—to his touch.

A Faust Films Production

The first thing I learned about the film industry is that it runs on a high-octane mix of dreams, contacts and money. Mostly money. But how is an ambitious new director ever to get enough of the stuff? It seemed to me that the Devil himself would make an excellent broker, and Johnny Faust wants his dream badly enough to trade his soul for a Hollywood hit. A Faust Films Production is part homage to Marlowe's Dr Faustus and part cautionary tale—the devil, as always, is in the detail of the contract—and the Devil always wins.

Johnny Faust was sitting in *Romeo's*, sipping his usual café latte, when all hell opened up at his feet. The floor split with a hissing sound like a huge espresso machine, and the smell of sulphur leaked into the air. The woman at the next table wrinkled her nose and looked up from her magazine to stare accusingly at him. He blushed, and looked down.

The hole was getting wider, and in its depths he could see a Bosch landscape of damned souls in torment—there were crazed creatures wielding pitchforks, cauldrons suspended above licking flames, deep pits of burning brimstone, the whole nightmarish medieval scenario. He turned away politely, and went back to calling his mother on the mobile.

"Hi. Johnny here. Have you thought any more about my proposition?"

"Too expensive, darling."

"Oh come on, Mother. You know you can afford it. Look, it's a great script. I just need to be in Cannes to put the deal together. Everyone will be there."

"Can't you phone them? Fax them? Email them? Hold an online video conference? God knows there's enough technology in that apartment of yours."

"No. I told you. I need to be there in person to press the flesh, to oil the wheels. It's business."

"Okay. But I still don't understand why you need twenty thousand."

Johnny thought Mother sounded peevish. And she was being so damned unreasonable. He tried again, wheedling. "I thought I had explained. I have to go first class, have to look as if I can afford it. As if I don't need them. As if I'm doing them a favour letting them in on the deal. You know how it goes, Mother. Money makes money. If you look hungry, they'll feed you to their dogs. That's why I need the twenty gees. Think about it. There's the airfare, and the *Ritz Carlton* is expensive. And I'll need a car, a limousine, and there'll be other expenses: dinners, first nights, casinos, you know the sort of thing. I might have to make a quick trip to LA to see my agent, and if the project is as hot as I think it is, I'll need to be in London and then maybe in Brussels to broker the deal."

"So how come you didn't wrap it up when you were in London last year. That little trip cost thirty thousand, as you'll recall. And you made nothing. Zip. Zero. I had to cancel my own holiday." She paused, letting the guilt register.

It didn't work. Johnny was used to guilt. It didn't bother him.

"Listen, Mother. You know I'll pay you back when I get the film money. We're talking millions here, with a nice little percentage for me. I'll even pay you top interest. How's that?"

"Why don't you sell the Jag?"

"I need transport."

"The beach house at Sorrento then?"

"Can't. It's in Michelle's name. And she insists on keeping it for the kids."

"Mortgage the penthouse, then. Melbourne real estate is always good for a loan."

"You know it's already mortgaged. Do you think I'd be asking you if there was any other way?" Johnny was getting exasperated. "Just think about it, all right? We can both make a tidy sum, but the film business is not for the faint hearted. Dad would've understood. How do you think he made all that money you spend on clothes and lunches?"

Reverse guilt. It served only to increase his mother's sense of being unfairly used. Her son reminded her, suddenly, of her late unlamented husband in one of his less tractable moods. She hadn't liked him all that much. "Your sainted father has gone to his rest," she said tartly.

"All right, Mother. Point taken. I know you control the purse strings now." His temper was rising. "But I'll be damned if I'll let this deal go. You have to help me."

"I'll think about it, Johnny, but I'm getting tired of throwing away good money after bad on these movie schemes of yours. Why don't you go back to one of those nice television production companies that used to pay you so well? Going freelance hasn't improved your finances or your temper one little bit."

This one hit home. She knew perfectly well that his departure had been so acrimonious that he *couldn't* go back to TV production work, even if he wanted to. Which he didn't.

Johnny sighed. "Very well, Mother. We'll talk later. Kiss kiss."

He cut the connection.

And looked down again.

Now he could see into the very heart of darkness, where a huge dark angel was lying chained to the surface of a great molten lake that burned with black flames. There were muffled shrieks from tortured souls in the background. Lucifer looked straight up at him, and winked.

Johnny found himself smiling back, an easy smile of unspoken complicity.

"Excuse me, may I join you?"

The speaker was immaculately dressed. He stood by the pit, brushing tiny specks of sulphur from the shoulders of his dark Saville Row suit, checking the black flame-opal cufflinks on his snowy French cuffs.

Johnny felt suddenly underdressed in his Calvin Klein jeans and butter-yellow cashmere sweater. His Gucci loafers looked scuffed beside the polished Ferragamo leather shoes standing beside him. His navy sports jacket was draped nonchalantly over the back of his chair—he wished he'd kept it on, if only for the authority of its shoulder pads.

"Yes, of course. Please do." Johnny put down his mobile phone and held out a hand. "Faust. John B. Faust. Producer."

The man shook the hand. He looked completely relaxed. The pit began to close. "Mephistopheles. Broker. At your service."

He sat.

An aproned waiter appeared at his elbow. The broker didn't miss a beat. "Double espresso," he said. "Hot and strong." He looked at Johnny. "Another latte?"

"Sure," said Johnny. "Why not?"

The waiter disappeared once more in the direction of the groaning coffee machine, and Johnny turned back to his new companion.

"That's an unusual name," he said, twisting his napkin in his hands as he spoke. "Must be a tricky one for a broker. Mephistopheles, you said, as in Satan's envoy?"

"The same. Beelzebub, Belial, Abaddon, Asmodeus, Ehlis, Mephisto. Shall I go on? My names are many. Choose any one you fancy. You can even call me Nick, if it makes you feel more comfortable. But my role as broker is unchanged, whatever name you select. And my rates are always the same."

Johnny smiled, suddenly sure that his pals must have set him up. He decided to play along. "Then what are you doing out of hell?"

"Why this *is* hell. And I'm doing my job. I came at your summons, Mr Faust. How may I help you?"

Johnny examined his fingernails, as if he was looking for clues. "I must have overdone the dope last night. I can't be having this conversation."

"Why not?"

"You aren't real. And even if you were, I didn't call you."

The coffee arrived. Mephistopheles sipped thoughtfully. "I'm real enough to enjoy a good Colombian blend, Mr Faust. And I beg to differ. You did call me. Often. Most frequently in this past week. Just this morning you screamed at your wife that you'd be damned if you'd let her stand in the way of your future, and I just heard you tell your mother you'd prefer damnation to losing your film deal. You've shown a lot of interest in Hell lately, and I judged that you wished to summon me. So here I am. Ready to broker you the deal of a lifetime."

Johnny said nothing. He would not even look at his companion. The man's acrid cologne was starting to give him a slight headache.

Mephistopheles drained his coffee cup. "I'm a busy man, Mr Faust. If you don't want my help, I'll be on my way. I have places to go, faces to meet. But you might just ask yourself how some of your competitors are getting *their* money."

Johnny pulled his thoughts together. "Look," he said, "I don't believe in hell. Or devils."

"Fine. I'll just be on my way then, and you can pretend this conversation didn't happen." Mephistopheles gave him a knowing look. "But," he went on, "It's a great pity. My firm has a lot of money to spend, and we're looking for new film projects right now. Your agent sent us your script, and we loved it. We could be talking forty, fifty million here."

Johnny couldn't help himself. If this was a set-up, it was damned good. "How do I know you're legit?"

"You can't consult your contacts on this one. They all know me in the business, of course. And if you ask outright, they'll all deny it. The secrecy clause is part of the contract." Mephistopheles shrugged. "But you could just mention my name. If you pay attention, you'll catch them looking shifty and trying to work out whether you've signed on or not. Whether you're part of the club, whether you're on the A list or not. Because if you *are* an insider, the deals are limitless." He glanced at his Rolex. "Didn't you know?"

He stood. "I'll leave a card with you," he said. "If you change your mind, get in touch with my bankers. They'll set up an appointment."

He turned, and simply disappeared. His drained coffee cup was still warm on the table, a black calling card sitting neatly beside it.

Johnny couldn't resist taking up the card. Its expensive black matte surface was embossed in red letters: *The Broker's Group.* There was an upmarket Collins Street business address, and single telephone number.

Johnny went back to the business of the morning. But after a couple more fruitless calls to half-hearted financial backers, and a few more brush-offs by movie industry flackers, he found himself looking once more at the black card. It couldn't hurt to make an appointment. Talk to these guys. He prided himself on following every lead. If it *was* a set-up, he'd grant his pals their fun. If not . . . well, you never knew when something might turn up trumps.

He punched in the numbers. He was put on hold for a time, then a suave female voice answered his query. "I'm afraid Mr Mephistopheles is unavailable at the moment, but he is expecting you. He has a luncheon engagement, but is free later in the day. Would three-thirty this afternoon be convenient for your meeting?"

Johnny took a deep breath. "Fine," he said. "I'll look forward to meeting you, Ms . . . ?"

"Goodbye, Mr Faust. We'll have everything ready for you this afternoon." And she was gone.

Johnny paid his bill, surprised that there was no charge on it for his visitor's coffee. He shrugged, and headed for home. He spent the rest of the morning working on his pitch for the Broker's Group, setting up his presentation folder, printing up a new copy of his script, getting his figures in order. Then he made a few more calls—no one amongst his consultants and contacts would admit to having heard of the Group, but all of them hinted that it wouldn't do any harm to check them out. Everyone was always hungry in this business. He gave up on the information trail, opting instead for a chicken salad sandwich in the kitchen. Then he padded off to his bathroom for a long, hot shower and some careful personal grooming. He wouldn't be caught out again.

By three-twenty five he was being shown into the Broker's Group Building, right at the top end of town. He didn't remember it being there, but the tower of dark tinted glass and polished black granite looked very substantial. The private offices were on the top floor— the concierge had held a muted conversation before even letting the visitor across the minimalist chic foyer with its glass and steel tables and uncomfortable looking chairs. "Tight security," Johnny thought. "A good sign." He checked his appearance in the full-length elevator mirror: a handsome, blonde-haired man looked back at him. He was wearing a perfectly tailored Armani suit, crisp business shirt, Hermes silk tie with a splash of colour to remind them of his artistic credentials, shiny slip-on leather shoes and a matching Dunhill leather attaché case. The details were right, down to the Mont Blanc pens nestling in his top pocket. Now he felt like the chairman of the board, felt ready to do business, suit to suit.

The elevator chimed softly, and he stepped out onto the luxurious deep-pile black carpet of another, smaller foyer.

A black-suited secretary was waiting, her glossy dark hair pulled back severely from a plain, pale face split by a shocking gash of red lipsticked mouth. She was holding a sheaf of papers. "This way, Mr Faust," she said, gesturing towards an oak-panelled door. "Your meeting is in the boardroom."

The view was spectacular. He could see clear out to the harbour across the city. The smoky glass was obviously soundproofed: the roar of uptown traffic seemed very far away. The silence was broken only by the ticking of an ornate antique clock sitting on a black marble pedestal in one corner of the vast boardroom. The woman ushered him into a chair, laid the papers on the long oak table, and left.

Johnny was at the window looking around when Mephistopheles was suddenly simply *there*, holding out a warm hand for Johnny to shake. Johnny had not heard him approach.

"Welcome, Mr Faust," he said formally. "Do sit down. I'm so glad you've taken the time to follow up this morning's meeting."

"I'm still not sure what this is all about," said Johnny. "But I *am* looking for backers for my new movie, and to that end I'm willing to explore all propositions."

"Quite so," said Mephistopheles.

"I've prepared a proposal for you," Johnny went on. "Script, costings, market research. It's all here. I'm sure you'll find it interesting as an investment avenue."

"Thank you, Mr Faust." The broker smiled. "But you need not have gone to all that trouble." He waved dismissively at Johnny's immaculate folder. "We've checked you out already, and have deemed you a most suitable candidate for our investment product. Otherwise, I would not have contacted you."

He paused. "As I told you this morning, I can broker a deal to give you your heart's desire. That's my job. I can arrange all the money you will need for your film, and the next one too if that's what you want. I have had all the necessary paperwork drawn up already. The question is, will you agree to my terms?"

"I can't believe this," said Johnny. "How do you know what I'll need?"

Mephistopheles' voice was patient. "I told you, we've checked."

Suddenly, all Johnny's rehearsed arguments were simply irrelevant. He had to ask. "So what, exactly, are your terms?"

"They never vary. I offer your deepest wish, in your case very large amounts of money for film projects, and seven years unlimited access to our brokerage services. In exchange, at the end of that period you render up to me your mortal soul, irrevocably."

Johnny prevaricated. "I told you, I don't believe in all that religious stuff."

"And I do?"

"Yes."

Mephistopheles' eyes narrowed. "Then what's the harm in parting with something you don't believe in? Think of it as a bet where you back your beliefs against mine. If you are right, I'm offering you several million dollars for something that doesn't exist. You win. If you are wrong, you give up something you didn't want anyway."

Johnny was tempted, but still wary. It sounded too weird to be true. It couldn't be that simple. "If you really are the devil," he said, "why do you look like a merchant banker?"

"What would you prefer? A monk? An archbishop? A creature with hooves and horns? What would make you recognise me?"

"I don't know. I never paid that much attention. I never really believed in hell."

"Precisely. But you do believe in money. You believe in pieces of paper, in bonds and stocks and shares, in bank notes, in contracts. *That's* why I look like this. And I *do* have the money, Mr Faust: any amount of it. You can believe in that."

Mephistopheles picked up the sheaf of papers, selected a slim slip, and slid it across the table to Johnny.

Johnny read it, and let out a long breath. "A banker's draft," he said, "for ten million dollars."

"Development costs," said Mephistopheles. "And you'll notice it's drawn on a major city bank. I'll just step out while you phone them."

Johnny's fingers were shaking as he punched the numbers into his mobile. He was put through to the corporate finance officer. The banker confirmed that yes, the loan had been arranged for Mr Faust, and yes, he could access it immediately. Johnny was shaking even more as he slipped the phone back into its case.

"Well?" said Mephistopheles. Johnny jumped at the sudden voice behind him. "Do we have a deal?"

Johnny was hooked, already fantasising about how he would spend the money. "I guess we do," he said.

Mephistopheles smiled. "Then we just have to sign the paperwork." He walked back to the door. "Nurse," he said. "We'll need your services."

The black-suited woman appeared once more, this time carrying a metal dish that contained antiseptic, cotton swabs, a needle, and a small collecting tube. In her other hand was a tourniquet strap.

"Roll up your sleeve, Mr Faust," she said.

"What's all this?" Johnny was alarmed now.

"Indulge me, Mr Faust," said Mephistopheles. "It's traditional. To pledge your soul you have to sign in blood. Don't worry, it won't hurt."

"You really take all this religious mumbo-jumbo seriously, don't you?" said Johnny.

"Very seriously. It's your choice, Mr Faust. You can still call the deal off and tear up that cheque. You can walk away."

Johnny thought longingly of his movie. So close, he could almost taste it. And he could justify this weird set-up as pure theatre, really. "Well," he said, taking off his jacket, "it's your money."

"It is, indeed, Mr Faust."

The nurse was very efficient. She located a vein in the crook of Johnny's arm and expertly withdrew a small phial of blood. She taped a cotton pad over the puncture, and Johnny rolled down his sleeve. She handed the blood to Mephistopheles, and exited quietly, her job done. Johnny wondered, briefly, what else she did here.

The broker took out a graceful Pelican fountain pen, dipped the nib into the phial, and filled the capsule with Johnny's red blood. He screwed the top back on, and handed the pen to Johnny. "Read the document and sign here," he said. "Then we have several more pieces of paper to deal with."

Johnny shrugged, and signed. By his reckoning, ten mill was ten mill in anyone's language. The soul document of deed seemed to be old parchment, and at first the pen would not write. But Johnny shook it a few times, and the blood spurted forth, blotting the page. "No matter," said Mephistopheles. As Johnny put down the pen, his signature was already drying a crystalline red-brown. The broker took up the parchment, blew on it carefully, and whisked it away out of sight.

Then there were various other documents—bank drafts, letters of agreement and so on, which Johnny signed in turn with his more mundane black ink. The deal was done.

"A toast, I think," said Mephistopheles.

He turned to the drinks tray on the sideboard, and poured single malt scotch into two crystal glasses. "To our partnership," he said.

They clinked glasses, and drank. The scotch was very good indeed.

"Well, Johnny," said the broker, "now that you have your development money, what else would you like me to do to help you with your movie?"

"I'll need a place in LA. Something classy."

"Of course. Anything else?"

Johnny grinned, relaxing for the first time. "Oh, find me the most beautiful woman in the world to be my star. That would do to begin with," he said.

"Done," said Mephistopheles.

He was not smiling.

Next morning, Mephistopheles, immaculate as ever, walked unannounced into Johnny's South Bank city office. With him was the most beautiful woman Johnny had ever seen. She was tall and curvy. She had green eyes and perfect creamy white skin and long dark red hair that curled about her like living flame.

"This is Helena. Your new star," said Mephistopheles. It was a statement. "No doubt you'd like to see the goods?"

He signalled to the woman, who shrugged easily out of her little black Prada dress. She was wearing nothing underneath. She stood in front of Johnny's desk, a statue in scarlet stilettos. Johnny was speechless with desire as she turned a slow circle before him. He could not take his eyes off the red heart of hair between her thighs.

"Well?" said Mephistopheles.

Johnny managed a hoarse response: "She's perfect."

"Thank you," she said. Her husky voice vibrated in the room, promising forbidden fruits. She bent to retrieve her dress, and slipped it back over her head, giving Johnny a chance to recover, slightly.

Mephistopheles looked bored.

Johnny was grateful for the unstructured Gucci suit he'd worn today. He hoped the loose trousers hid the erection that was now tangled in his boxer shorts. He stood, stiffly, to kiss her lightly on the cheek. "Welcome aboard, Helena."

She nodded, and seated herself on the couch, crossing her long legs. The short skirt rode high on her creamy thighs, hiding nothing. It was an invitation Johnny could not refuse. Did not want to refuse.

Mephistopheles smiled knowingly at Johnny's discomfort. "I always deliver, Mr Faust. You requested the most beautiful woman in the world to star in your movie, and here she is. Enjoy."

He rose and left the room, soundless as ever in his polished shoes.

Johnny turned back to Helena, his usual patter forgotten. She was the object of all his desire, and he wanted her. Desperately. Still, he tried to preserve the niceties: "Perhaps you'd like me to take you to lunch, then a tour around the city?"

"Later," she said. And pulled him down onto the couch. They kissed, and Johnny felt her lips suck forth his soul. Her lovemaking was hungry, predatory. She bit his ear, and drew blood; her long red-painted nails raked his back, raising long welts. He didn't care. He was lost in an ecstasy of surrender.

They were still tangled, naked, on the couch when the office door opened soundlessly, and Mephistopheles reappeared.

He cleared his throat.

Johnny was mortified. He scrambled for his trousers, draped his crumpled shirt over Helena, who seemed unperturbed. "Christ!" he said. "I'm sorry. I forgot to lock the door!"

She slapped him.

"What was that for?"

"You must not call on Him. Not now. Not ever."

"Who?"

"She means the son-of-god," said Mephistopheles. "It's all right, Helena. He meant to blaspheme, not to sue for comfort." He turned to Johnny. "You'll need to be more careful. My people do take our beliefs very seriously."

"Your people?"

"Of course. Helena is my protégé." He grinned. "We provide for all situations." The smile vanished once more. "Well, Johnny," he said, "now that you've had your free sample, perhaps we can discuss terms."

"Assuming that I want her."

"You want her. She'll provide your every darkest fantasy."

"But can she act?"

"She *is* acting. She's playing the part you wanted, is she not?"

Johnny looked crestfallen. "I suppose so, yes."

"And she'll be perfect in the role of temptress. So, I will continue to provide her services, on condition that I remain in attendance as her manager, and that I will be present whenever you are filming."

"Why?"

"She can be, shall we say, extremely *difficult*. We don't want her running wild. She will behave if I am about. She knows her job."

Johnny wasn't sure he liked the sound of this, but he figured he could not risk having her "services' withdrawn so soon. He could always find a way of escape later, he thought.

"Okay," he said. "We'll do it your way."

"I knew you'd see reason," said Mephistopheles. "Drink?"

Johnny loved Hollywood. His old life was far away. He signed off on his divorce without a second thought. An outraged Michelle got the Melbourne penthouse, the cars, the share portfolio, everything. Johnny no longer cared. He'd even stopped calling Mother of late, since she threatened to visit him to see how he was getting along. He didn't need chicken soup and family bickering any more. It felt absolutely right to him to be cruising Santa Monica Boulevard in his Porsche, the top down and his arm around Helena. Exclusive nightclubs welcomed him—smiling, heavily-tipped doormen admitted him past the queues of wannabes and into the warm glamour of the famous and the well-to-do. He adored the Rodeo Drive boutiques, spent his Saturday afternoons spending too much money—diamond baubles, Italian leather this and that, even a vicuna-wool Emmanuel Ungaro driving coat that cost as much as his old Jag. He treasured his stuccoed mansion on its palm-lined avenue, where he had abandoned his previous taste in understated antiques in favour of the whole *nouveau riche* thing. Now he had sunken marble baths with gold dolphin taps; acres of glass and chrome arranged by Georgio, LA's hottest new designer; and even a Hearst Castle-style swimming pool surrounded by Greek statues and broken columns and potted topiary. Johnny gave lavish parties. The stars, unaccountably, attended. It was suddenly *the* place to be invited.

The gossip mills ground quickly. The casting for his movie, *Trials of Galileo*, became the subject of all the Movie News gossip columns. Major stars were signed by Hollywood's newest producer, John B. Faust. No one knew why, unless the astronomical sums he was rumoured to be paying had something to do with it. The agencies were coy about details. And then there was the question of this Helena girl, rapidly becoming a star herself, with no previous history anyone could dig up. She was, all at once, just there, looking downright predatory in her slinky evening clothes worn Rita Harlowe style, *sans* underwear. Women hated her. The media loved her. She made the cover of *Vogue*, did a centrefold for *Playboy*, gave carefully scripted press interviews. Nothing seemed to impress her at all. Johnny never expected it to.

But deals were struck, papers were signed, and filming finally began—on the lot at London's *Pinewood*, and on location in the hills of Tuscany, where Johnny's villa was as fabulous as his LA house.

He was a cool two-and-a-half million over budget, and happy as a clam.

Mephistopheles was often on the set. The crew took to calling him "Old Nick", because they had the Devil's own luck when he was about. Sequences ran to time; equipment worked without glitches; and Helena, sullen and moody and downright spiteful if unattended, suddenly remembered her lines and delivered perfect work. It was uncanny.

When he was not around things were less smooth. There was a minor *contretemps* when the assembled extras refused to recite Latin prayers in the monk's procession—Johnny eventually let them process in stately silence. There were rumours of one devil too many in the torture scenes, which were reckoned by the actors to be a touch over-realistic. There was near mutiny among the sound crew when Helena carelessly trod on the hand of a technician running cable near her feet, leaving him with a broken finger and a fierce determination never to work with her again. Nevertheless, three-and-a-half years of work proceeded, and six months after that the film was finally released.

It was, as Johnny had requested, a box office smash.

When the reviews came out Mephistopheles was kept busy with Johnny's pique at minor slights. A critic who labelled it "overly sentimental" was busted for possession; a well-known commentator had his mortgage called in; a third had his overdraft cancelled. The broker was losing patience.

"Wasting my time isn't in your contract," he said. "Petty revenge isn't worth the trouble. Think bigger."

"Okay," said Johnny. "I want an Oscar."

"Done," said Mephistopheles. "That's more like it."

And when the awards came around, there was Johnny, collecting his trophy and basking in his five minutes of fame. "It doesn't get better than this," he said, to every reporter who came near him.

He was right. It didn't. Johnny's next years were spent partying, brooding over who said what about his film career, and working intermittently on a new script, his next blockbuster. It just didn't seem to be coming together. Hollywood was as glitzy as ever, but Johnny was enjoying it less. He lost his temper more often, and was now not even speaking to Mother. No relationship was permanent, though Helena was always available on demand to stoke the fires of his lust. He slept late, gained weight, drank too much. The press lost interest, pursuing the latest hotshots, whom he envied in a half-hearted way. But underneath it all he was proud of his achievements, confident of his talents, and he knew he could be back on top anytime he wanted. He only had to ask. Finally, as he was edging up towards a full three years since the film's release, he felt ready to begin casting.

"There won't be time, Mr Faust," said Mephistopheles.

It was late evening. Johnny was driving home along the Santa Monica Freeway from yet another party when, without warning, Mephistopheles appeared at his side.

Johnny nearly jumped out of his skin. "What the hell . . . ?"

"Precisely," said Mephistopheles. He stretched his fastidiously suited legs, settled himself comfortably in the passenger seat, and said: "Well, Johnny, your time is up. I trust you've been happy with our services?"

"What?"

"This is our seventh anniversary. Your contract expires tonight. Do you have any last words?"

Johnny struggled to comprehend the implications of this. "What exactly do you mean by "last words"?"

Mephistopheles was all business now. He extracted a rolled parchment from his inner pocket. "Exactly that." He unrolled the document. "I thought you'd appreciate a spectacular death. You'll get to go out in a blaze of publicity."

Johnny baulked at the finality tone. "Death?" His voice rose. "There's nothing in the contract about my *dying*!"

"Of course there is. You agreed to render up to me your immortal soul. I have your signature on the document right here. In blood."

"Sure."

"We kept our side of the bargain. Now it's time for you to keep yours. You got your dream. In return, I get your soul. Tonight."

"But . . . "

"Did you think I could take the soul without the demise of the body?"

"Why not?"

"It doesn't work that way. I'm afraid you do have to die, Johnny. At midnight. In one minute, by my calculation. I'm never wrong about these things."

Johnny's mind refused to accept it. "This can't be happening," he said.

"It can and it is. Prepare to die."

"I'll repent."

"Indeed you will. At length."

"I mean I'll turn religious. Pray to God."

Mephistopheles was unperturbed. "You don't know how. You don't believe. But go ahead, try. You'll have to be quick."

Johnny's mind was blank. He tried, without success, to remember his childhood prayers.

Mephistopheles went on. "You know this has to be. You *do* believe in contracts, and yours is right here. Your soul is mine to take." He smiled, tightly, and went on. "Besides, if you want to be a legend in your business, you have to die young. The brightest lights burn out first. Think about it—Monroe, Dean, Holly, Joplin, Morrison . . . they all had their time."

Johnny, belatedly, realised this was serious. "I'll give you anything, everything. Please . . . "

"Everything you have is mine already. I'm just doing my job. I told you that, right at the start." He tapped the contract.

The petrol tanker loomed into sight, coming up on the outside.

"I'm afraid there is no choice, Johnny. This is what you signed up for."

A fissure opened in the road. Johnny had nowhere to go. He swerved sideways, collided with the tanker.

The blaze was spectacular. And amid the explosions, the confusion, the traffic chaos, no one noticed the sulphurous pit that opened up beneath the wreckage, or the demented creatures that carried a screaming Johnny Faust into the hotter flames below.

Gawain and the Selkie's Daughter

My interest in the Arthurian cycle goes back to childhood and continues unabated to this day, so I was delighted when Sophie Masson requested a story for her original anthology The Road to Camelot. *The contributing authors were each asked to choose an Arthurian character and to create a story that would show that character at a point of crisis in their lives—a crisis that would set them on the path to Camelot. I chose Gawain, always my favourite: he is one of the most famous of Arthur's knights, but also one of the most mysterious. Gawain has a mixed literary history, but through all the versions he remains a great fighter and a famous lover. He is a champion of women, especially where magic is concerned, so it seemed fitting that a crisis in his youth should involve a magical woman—and who could be more attractive to the young Gawain, or cause more trouble, than a Selkie princess?*

High on a rocky headland a solitary figure stood, still and silent, outlined against a pale summer sky. His cloak stirred in the light onshore breeze, moulding itself against the bulky curves of a great bear of a man, a powerful, unmoving man in a lonely landscape of stone and sea. The man stared at the shallows of a little cove, where a group of shining seals played in the dappled sunlight, slipping and diving and sliding sleek through the green water, popping up to sun themselves on warm smooth rocks, barking softly with pleasure.

The crunching sound of footsteps on loose shingle rose from below. A tall, well-muscled youth strode down the beach, a plaid blanket slung over his broad shoulder, a basket carried lightly on his arm. The breeze lifted his golden hair gently, and he laughed for the simple joy of being young and strong and alive. He laid his plaid carefully on a patch of dry soft sand above the damp of the sea wrack, then stripped off his clothes and folded them neatly beside the basket. Naked in the sunlight, he walked straight toward the lapping water and waded out a little way, close to a flat ledge of rock.

The watcher on the cliff top looked down intently as the largest of the seals swam away from the group, making for where the young man stood. It slid easily onto the warm rock platform, where it began at once to undulate in a curiously sinuous rippling motion.

The young man was waiting. Wordlessly, he reached down, and helped his lover step gracefully out of her sealskin.

They kissed as the pelt slid away, the young man's golden hair tangling with the dark honey of her long tresses. His skin was fair, lightly freckled in the manner of Orkney men, but hers was as white as any pearl, smooth and untouched by wind or rain or sun. Tall she was, and lithe, her breasts showing high and firm as she pressed against him, her limbs long and clean as she held him to her. And when, at last, the two drew apart, gasping and smiling, the young man picked up the sealskin and the couple splashed ashore. Gently, almost reverently, he helped his lady drape her pelt to dry on a smooth rock high above the waterline. Then he took her by her white hand and led her, unresisting, to where the old plaid rug lay warming in the sunlight for their delight.

High on the crag, King Lot allowed himself a little grunt of weary affirmation. He folded his massive arms across his chest, and his mottled face grew almost as red as his tangled auburn beard as he watched his son lay himself down in love with the selkie girl. Lot could see from the easy urgency of their meeting that this was not their first encounter.

He was determined that it would be their last.

The shadows had lengthened and the sea wind had turned chill by the time Gawain returned home, walking carefully along the narrow path that ran the length of the cliff beside the high salt-blackened stone walls of the castle. His brother Gareth was waiting for him, leaning casually against the heavy brass-studded oak gates that would soon swing shut against the night.

"You're in trouble," said Gareth cheerfully.

"Why?"

"You know why." Gareth smirked.

Gawain was losing patience. "I'm not that late," he said, guessing. "The gates aren't shut yet."

"It's not about being late." Gareth paused significantly. "Everyone knows how you sneak out at night. To visit a certain *lady*."

Gawain grinned at his brother. "Mind your own business."

"I would, except the whole castle's buzzing with the news of your latest conquest." Gareth lowered his voice. "This is serious, brother. I slipped out to warn you. Father saw you, on the beach, with a selkie. And he's furious."

"Oh." Gawain paused uncomfortably. "But what's it to him? He doesn't usually make a fuss about that sort of thing."

"That sort of thing doesn't usually involve the seal folk," Gareth replied darkly. "Father has been striding about the great hall all afternoon, muttering about how you've gone too far this time. Mother has been trying to calm him down. I thought I'd better tell you. Forewarned is forearmed, as they say."

"Thanks," said Gawain. He dragged his fingers through his salt-stiff hair, then straightened his shoulders and strode to meet his father in the great hall of Orkney.

Lot and Morgana sat by the hearth in high, carved chairs. A tray bearing sweetmeats, a curved flagon and wine goblets was set on a low table beside them. The food was untouched. The king and queen were talking in hushed, urgent voices. The queen looked up at the sound of her son's approach, but Lot leapt to his feet.

"It's about time, my lad," the king bellowed. "I've been waiting for you."

"So I see," said Gawain. "Is something amiss?"

"I saw you today," the king said heavily. "I saw what you did. Saw it with my own two eyes. You and that selkie girl. Don't try to deny it."

"I wouldn't dream of it, Father," Gawain replied. "What's the problem?"

"What's the problem?" King Lot was getting red-faced. "It won't do," he boomed. "My son, with a selkie! A shape-changer! I won't have it."

"It's not for you to decide."

"This is my kingdom. My word is law here," the king shouted. "And while you are under my roof, it is for me to decide."

"Enough!" Morgana's word cracked like a whip. She stood up, tall and graceful, her long red hair glinting in the firelight. She moved deftly to stand between father and son. "Stop it, both of you," she said. "This is getting us nowhere."

The two men were momentarily silent, glaring at each other.

"We do have a problem here," she continued smoothly. "And we will resolve it quietly and calmly. Agreed?"

Lot spoke first. "Agreed. Your mother is, as always, in the right of it. My hand." He held out his huge sword-callused hand to his son.

Gawain shook his father's hand. "Agreed."

"Good," said Morgana. She resumed her seat by the fire. "So tell me, Gawain," she said quietly, "how it was that you came to meet a selkie girl at all."

"It was at full moon last," her son replied. "I was walking along the shingle, coming back . . . " He faltered.

"From the fishing village, and from the bed of that pretty little dark-eyed lass who caught your fancy," King Lot finished for him.

Gawain looked down, shifting uncomfortably from foot to foot.

"No need to look so surprised, son," Lot went on. "I keep a sharp eye on my kingdom. And I paid off her father in good red gold not two weeks since. He's an understanding man where there's profit to be had. So that's settled."

"Then why . . . ?"

"Why interfere now with your love-life?" King Lot snorted in disgust. "Because today you were meddling where you should not, and no good will come of it! That's why."

"Lot, please." Morgana put a warning hand on her husband's arm. "Let our son speak." She turned her gaze back to Gawain. "You met her by moonlight, you were saying?"

"Yes, Mother," Gawain said simply. "I was walking home along the beach, and she was dancing all alone on the shore." He could not help smiling at the memory of it. "I've never seen anything so beautiful," he said softly. "Naked she was, and shimmering. She looked as lovely as a goddess, all shining silver."

Morgana quickly made the sign to avert evil. "Be careful what you invoke," she said swiftly. "Even here, with me to ward you, be careful."

"Sorry," said Gawain. "I never meant . . . "

"I know," said his mother. "Now tell me: did you hear music?"

Gawain thought for a moment. "I think there was music," he said slowly. "Singing. But I couldn't make out the tune. It was far away, out to sea maybe. As if it was meant just for her, for her pleasure."

"And then what happened?"

"She saw me. She opened her arms wide, and beckoned to me to join her."

"And you were drawn to her?"

"As if I'd waited all my life for her," Gawain said simply.

Morgana looked grave. "Enchantment," she said softly.

King Lot groaned. "That's all we need," he said. "Morgana, this is your domain. Now what do we do?"

"We?" said Gawain quickly. "I told you. I won't give her up. Not for anything."

"You will have to, my dear," Morgana said calmly. "Before you are completely under her control." She reached out and patted his hand. "I command some power, but I cannot yet know if it will be enough to break the spell that binds you to her."

Gawain pulled away abruptly. "Isn't anyone listening to me? I don't want you to break the spell, if that's what it is. I love her. I'll marry her. I'm fifteen, I'm old enough," he said defiantly. "And it's not as if she isn't a suitable match. Her lineage is every bit as good as mine."

Lot's shoulders sagged. He looked suddenly afraid. "Gawain, are you saying what I think you're saying?"

"Only that her father is the Great Selkie. The king of all the ocean realm." Gawain couldn't keep the note of pride and triumph from his voice.

"And all is well while he keeps to his kingdom and I to mine."

"Then you'll have an alliance, won't you?" said Gawain.

"Don't be a fool," said his father. "There's always more to it than that. Does her father know?"

"I doubt it," said Morgana. "The sea has been calm of late."

"We were going to tell him, to tell all of you," said Gawain.

"When?" said Lot. "When she's already pregnant?"

"That's it!" said Morgana. "I should have seen it sooner."

"Seen what?" said Gawain.

"Think," said Morgana. She spoke slowly. "Your great strength comes from sunlight and solid earth. Yet you are drawn to love a creature of moonlight and water, a creature of the shadowy sea. Think what might come of it."

Gawain and his father exchanged puzzled looks.

Morgana pressed on. "Fire, earth, air, water—all the elements together," she said. "Think what such a child could be, could become."

"Oh," said Gawain. "I see."

"I don't think you do," said his mother. "There is magic at work here, and I fear for both you and the girl. She may not have willed this union." She paused, thinking. "The question is, who has cast this spell, and why."

"The question," said Lot, "is what's to be done about it. And I think that our first plan is still the best. The boy must make the journey to his uncle, at Camelot."

"You can't just send me away," said Gawain. "I'm not a child."

"Obviously not," said Lot. "That's why you have to go."

"Peace, Lot," said Morgana. She turned gravely to her son. "You would have gone sooner or later to Arthur's court. It is your destiny. My brother will welcome you, and you will become the greatest of his knights."

"Listen to your mother," said Lot, his voice unexpectedly gruff. "She has the second sight. We have long known that this hour would come, though we did not guess the manner of its coming."

"Your fate is upon you," said Morgana, "and you must act."

"You've learned all of sword-craft and the knightly skills that we can teach you here," said Lot. "And we had planned that you should go to Arthur at your sixteenth year. Orkney is too small a place for you, for what you will be. We're bringing the plan forward a little, that's all."

"And you expect me to just leave the woman I love," said Gawain. "On your say-so."

"She's no woman, son," said Lot. "That's the problem."

"You cannot hold a selkie for long, my dear," Morgana said gently. "Even if you hide her sealskin, as some have done, she will find a way of returning to the sea. She must. It is her nature. They are shape-changers, Gawain, and they do not love as we mortals do. They cannot."

Gawain sat down heavily in the chair opposite his mother. "But I love her," he said wearily.

Morgana poured wine into one of the goblets and handed it to her son. "I know you do, dear," she said. "But this is enchantment, not a love freely chosen. And you cannot understand until you are free of it. I know. You will have to trust me in this."

Gawain looked down and swirled the wine in his goblet. "Very well, Mother," he said, sipping his drink. He would not meet her eyes. "When do I leave?"

"First thing in the morning," said Lot briskly.

Gawain drained his goblet, and stood up. "Then I'll go straight to my chamber," he said. "I'll have to pack."

"I'll send someone to help you," said Morgana.

"Don't bother," said Gawain. "I need to be alone."

"As you wish," said the king.

"Goodnight, Mother." Gawain kissed his mother on the cheek, nodded to his father, and strode from the hall.

"Gareth!" said Lot. "You can come out now. I know where you're lurking!"

Gareth stepped from behind a long tapestry. "I'm sorry, Father," he said. "I just wanted . . . "

"I know what you wanted," said the king. "But now I have a task for you. I need you to stay with your brother tonight. He won't welcome it, but I don't want him slipping out to call to the selkies. Do you understand?"

"Yes, Father."

"Good. Then be off with you."

Gareth turned to leave.

"And don't forget to kiss your lady mother goodnight."

"Sorry." Gareth pecked the cheek Morgana offered. "Goodnight Mother," he said.

"Goodnight, Gareth," she replied. "And don't fret: you too will go to Camelot, in your turn."

Gareth's face lit up with a huge smile. "Really?"

"Really."

Gareth left the hall, racing to catch up with his brother to tell him the news.

"That was too easily done," said Lot. "Gawain plans to flee. I know it."

"Gawain will not leave the castle tonight," said Morgana softly. "He will sleep." She put the stopper back firmly in the neck of the flagon, and patted a little silver vial that hung from her belt.

"What did you put in his wine?" asked Lot.

"Nothing more than an elixir of herbs," she replied. "He needs to rest."

"And we have no need for him to warn the selkie girl." The king smiled at his wife.

"Exactly," said Morgana. "And now, my lord, we have much to prepare if all is to be ready for Gawain's departure."

"Aye," said Lot. "And we'd best get on with it."

The queen rose, and took her husband's arm. The two left the hall together, deep in conversation.

Clear sunlight streaming through the chamber window awoke Gawain. He yawned and stretched and flung back the coverlets as usual, but before his feet had touched the floor he noticed his brother, still asleep, on a pallet that blocked the doorway. Memories of the night before came flooding back, and Gawain scowled, his sunny mood turning black in the space of a moment. He stood, took three paces across the room, and kicked Gareth, hard.

"Get up," he shouted. "What are you doing here? Are you supposed to be my warden, or are you just a spy? You won't stop me, you know."

"Ouch!" said Gareth, instantly awake. "That hurt."

"Not as much as it hurts to be betrayed by a brother," Gawain replied.

Gareth rubbed his injured ribs. "I was taking care of you," he said. "Father made me promise."

Gawain ignored him. "They tricked me," he said bitterly.

"It was for your own good," Gareth replied. "So you wouldn't run away to the selkies." He stood, still massaging his ribs. "And you *were* planning to go in the night, weren't you?"

Gawain turned away and stood at his window, looking out to sea. "You don't understand," he said. "You can't."

"I'm not completely stupid," said Gareth. "I know you want to be with the selkie girl. But Mother says you are enchanted. And she should know."

King Lot strode into the chamber, cutting off further conversation. "Well, son," he said. "Your men are waiting, and impatient to be off. Why aren't you dressed? Is your baggage ready?"

Gawain sighed. "As ready as it will ever be," he said. "Give me a moment to dress, and I'll be ready too."

"Good. I'll wait outside."

There was nothing for it. Gawain splashed his face with water, and struggled into his travelling clothes. It was not long before he was stomping down the stairs to the courtyard, where a dozen armed men were already assembled.

Morgana and Lot were standing by the great hall. Gawain crossed to meet them, striding across the stones with long steps. He bent to kiss his mother's cheek, observing the formalities.

She reached out and caught his hand. "Gawain," she said, "you must not part from us in anger. I know your heart is full, but we act only for the best. Destiny can be a hard master, but obey it we must." She stretched up and kissed him. "Go safely, my son," she said. "I will ward you as best I may."

"Thank you, Mother," said Gawain, touched despite himself.

"And I, too, bid you farewell," said Lot gruffly. "Make me proud, boy. I expect you to greet me as a knight when next I come to Arthur's court."

"And so I shall, Father," Gawain replied.

He turned away, to where Gareth waited, holding the reins of Gawain's horse. The brothers hugged briefly before Gawain swung up into his saddle. "Farewell, brother," he said.

"I'll be joining you soon," Gareth replied. "Farewell."

Lot gave the signal, and his men clattered out of the courtyard, Gawain in the centre of the troop.

"Will he be safe?" Lot asked Morgana.

"Safe enough on land," she replied. "Let us hope he makes the sea crossing before the Great Selkie learns the truth of this dalliance from his daughter."

The king's men rode briskly in the sunlight, arriving in good time at Orkney's little seaport. Gawain searched the horizon as he boarded the ship that would carry him far from home, but nothing broke the surface of the sparkling blue sea. Of the selkies there was no sign. His heart ached, knowing that his lover was waiting for him in their usual place, waiting and wondering, unaware she was betrayed.

The wind set fair as the ship sailed into the open ocean. The two guards who were to travel with Gawain to Arthur's court smiled for the simple pleasure of the breeze in their hair and the sun on their faces, and even Gawain's spirits lifted as his ship slipped smoothly over the shining water.

Land was in sight once more and the soft summer evening light had begun to fade from the sky when the weather suddenly changed, blowing up foul and treacherous. The ship pitched and rolled, and before the sailors could clamber aloft there came a squall so fast and strong that the sails snapped and tore, leaving shreds of canvas flapping about the mast.

The skies grew dark, and darker yet as great thunderclouds massed overhead, and the seas rose higher, mountains of green water sliding and rolling against each other as the huge wind whipped them about. Forked lightning split the louring sky and gigantic waves roared furiously as they crashed down upon the stricken ship. Men clung to the rigging, holding on for dear life as the ship bucked and plunged beneath them. The captain lashed himself to the kicking wheel, fighting to hold the ship out to sea, where she might run before the storm. Gawain made to help him but was caught by a monstrous breaker that washed him sideways in a swirling flood of salt water and broken rigging. He grasped anything he could, tumbling until he reached the mast, where he stood, bruised and spluttering and half-drowned, up to his waist in icy water. The gale shrieked in the rigging as the next wave struck, crashing onto the deck with a noise like thunder. Gawain watched in horror as the captain's rope snapped. The wheel spun free, and the ship slewed about. Gawain looked wildly about him and realised that the ship was already in the bay. He could see white fringes of breakers on either side. Then the vessel lurched sideways once more, and he understood, in terror, that although they were lying head to sea, they were moving backwards. With every wave that struck the ship, they were being sucked closer to certain wreck on the shore.

"Stay with the ship!" a voice shouted. "It's our best chance!"

Gawain looked behind him. The captain was clinging to the broken and splintered wood that once housed the wheel.

"We will founder on the shore," the captain yelled. "And then it's every man for himself. You must swim for your lives."

Gawain looked in disbelief at the stretch of broken water torn by rips and undertows that lay now between the ship and the safety of the beach.

"We'll try to turn," the captain bellowed at Gawain. "It's best if we run headlong onto the beach through the breakers."

With all his strength Gawain held the wheel against the pounding of the sea. Slowly, the torn sails shrieking their protest in the broken rigging, the ship turned. And as it turned, the waves caught it broadside, rolling it almost onto its beam ends. But at last the vessel wallowed upright, decks awash, its prow pointing towards the shore.

Gawain braced himself for the next onslaught. He could hear nothing now above the crash and boom of the surf and the howling of the wind and the awful grinding roar of the undertow sucking pebbles down from the beach. And then another giant wave struck the struggling ship with a force that tore the wheel from Gawain's grip. The ship was lifted and flung hard upon the shore with a fearful shock that shattered the decks. The crashing of splitting timber was loud in Gawain's ears as he hauled himself upright on the side nearest the shore. He looked down at the racing, seething water, a sluice of white foam and tumbling rocks that separated him from safety.

A huge roaring sound behind him announced the next wave, and again he was drenched in icy water. He readied himself as the seething water sucked away from the beach. Then he jumped. He landed heavily in turning shingle and tried to force his way up the beach. Behind him came an awful thunder, and he knew that the next monstrous wave was at his heels.

The wall of water swept him off his feet and flung him far up the beach. His eyes and mouth and nose were full of sand. He couldn't breathe. He was tumbled over and over, pummelled on pebbles as the undertow dragged him back out to sea. He tried to strike out for the surface, but the sea held him down. His lungs were burning with effort. He struck out again, only to be rolled further along the ocean floor. His vision blurred with spots of bright light; his lungs filled with cold salt water and stinging sand.

And suddenly she was there. Gawain felt warm fur beneath him and he reached for her, clinging to the selkie as her strong seal body bore him swiftly to the surface. He came up spluttering and gasping, as she held his head above the boiling foam. The pounding roar of the storm was loud in his ears as she carried him shorewards with a courage and grace that astonished the young man. Then, with one last tremendous effort, she flung him high above the line of the breaking waves.

He lay still for some moments but soon righted himself, spluttering and coughing. He sat up and stared out at the boiling sea. The selkie girl had not come ashore and Gawain could make out a sleek head bobbing just beyond the line of the breakers.

"My love," he whispered, his throat too raw for shouting. He knew she could not hear him.

"Remember me," he heard her call. And then she dived beneath the waves and was gone.

Gawain was not alone on the beach for long. Fishermen had gathered there, risking their own lives to help the shipwrecked sailors through the pounding surf, and looking, Gawain realised, for whatever booty might come their way.

They had built a fire, and there was a warm blanket and hot broth waiting for the king's son. Gawain accepted their help in sad silence, knowing, in his heart, that the wrath of the Great Selkie had sent many of his shipmates to a watery grave.

The next morning dawned clear and bright. The sea was calm, quiet after its fury of yestereve. There was bustle in the makeshift camp as the survivors searched the shore for whatever the sea had left them. The fisherfolk would stay awhile, to bury the dead and see to the wreck. But Gawain did not tarry. He used his father's silver to hire a horse, and by midmorning he had sought directions and made his farewells.

As he crested the cliff above the cove he paused, scanning the sea one last time for his selkie love. But he saw nothing save the sparkle of sunlight on water, and heard nothing but the sighing of waves on the shore. Gawain settled himself in the saddle and turned away from the sea. He would not look back again as he rode on to Camelot.

Niagara Falling

(with Jack Dann)

This story was written in collaboration with Jack Dann because Keith Ferrell, then Vice-President of Omni *magazine, thought it would be fun to see what happened if Jack and I co-wrote a story. So he commissioned this one for an original anthology he was editing with Orson Scott Card,* Black Mist and Other Japanese Futures. *The brief was to write a "Japanese Future".* Niagara Falling *was extrapolated from our own little holiday from hell at Niagara Falls: we were driving from New York to Toronto, and Jack thought that the Falls would be a romantic place to overnight for my birthday—it wasn't. After various trials and tribulations we fetched up in a hotel which was completely unprepared for English-speaking guests: the reception staff spoke only Japanese, the signage was in Japanese, the lobby shops displayed their prices in yen, the other guests were all Japanese tourists. Given that this was a Canadian hotel, the experience was beyond weird. We finally managed to find our room, and things were looking up until we made the mistake of having dinner in the highly recommended award-winning "Italian" restaurant—where we both got food poisoning. When we were well enough to travel, we left. The problems encountered by our fictional characters in this future version of the strange hotel are even weirder than our own.*

The wedding was the best that money could buy. A wooden platform was built right in the middle of Melbourne's Royal Botanical Gardens; it overlooked the swan lake that was surrounded by a blaze of yellow and orange and pink flowers specially lit for the evening party. Under a chandeliered tent, five hundred people dined at cosy tables aglitter with glassware and vintage bottles of Möet and danced to a full orchestra.

Helen Donoussa née Nisyros sat sweating in her gown at the head table beside her husband of exactly four hours and twenty-five minutes. It was unseasonably hot for April. "Kostas, you're not supposed to look bored, this is supposed to be the most exciting night of your life." Helen had a way of pulling away and looking down her nose when speaking, which had always mesmerized suitors, admirers, and acquaintances. Although, feature for feature, she was rather plain (except for her thick, golden blond hair), she looked regal; and everyone imagined her as being beautiful. Kostas, however, *was* beautiful: black, curly hair, square face, deep brown eyes, and a dimple in his right cheek, which made him look off-balance and vulnerable. He was twenty-five years old, had already tried seventeen cases before juries, and had won them all. But he didn't earn nearly as much money as Helen, who was a designer. She could turn an apartment into a virtual Georgian mansion.

"This is interminable," he said. "No one looks like themselves. Everyone's ugly. It's—"

"It's business," she said.

"I thought we were doing this for your family."

"Same thing," she said. "But it's really for you . . . for us." She extended her hand to an elderly man, one of her father's law partners, who had worked his way down the table, shaking hands and offering hearty congratulations. Kostas greeted Mr Spiriounis, whose business he would eventually inherit, and then stood awkwardly before him while the old man chatted up the bride.

"You know, your father loves you very much," Mr Spiriounis said.

"Why of course he does, Uncle Dimi," Helen said, gazing up at him, as if she was the one standing.

"No, no, no, I mean if he just loved you as fathers just love daughters, he would have given you a lovely wedding at Arbeena Court or Ballara or Ascot House, and everything would have been a virt: the flowers, the starry night. But this"—he motioned with his arms, gaining everyone's attention, and spoke loudly, playing to Helen's father—"this is *real*."

"Yes, Uncle Dimi, and it's hot, too," Helen said, as if she were complimenting her father for her discomfort.

"But this is wonderful. This is how it used to be, for everyone, not just for those who have achieved the success your father has." Uncle Dimi looked toward Helen's father, for whom he was talking loudly, but Mr Nisyros was preoccupied with important Japanese clients who were bowing and presenting him with gifts. "Well, will you excuse me?"

Helen blew him a kiss and Kostas sat down as Uncle Dimi backtracked to glad-hand the clients still talking to Helen's father.

"Why is he always kissing your father's ass?" Kostas asked. "He's the principal partner."

"He thinks Daddy can help him stay in the firm, but he's already out."

"What do you mean, already out? There would need to be a vote by all the senior partners. I would have heard something."

"Daddy told me he's out, and when has he ever been wrong?" Helen asked.

"Maybe he should have taken *you* into the firm."

"He couldn't afford me, and now you're acting insecure and nasty. You don't have to stay. You could open up your own practice and make a fortune. Or you could ask me to dance."

Everyone stepped back to watch the bride and groom, who were not in the least self-conscious as they danced a perfect box step to a Strauss waltz. "You see, this is our perfect moment," Helen whispered into Kostas's ear. "You, my darling, are like a jet plane. When you stand still, you're awkward, but adorable. But when you're moving, you're like the music itself. You're beautiful. You're perfect."

Regaining his self-esteem, Kostas danced even better. He dipped her and twirled her and stood razor straight, cutting a fine figure.

"I wonder if Niagara Falls is a virt," Helen said.

"I'm sure the Falls are real."

Helen pulled back and looked at him contemptuously.

"What does it matter, anyway?"

"Professional curiosity."

"Well, we'll probably be the only professionals in Australia who've ever seen it," Kostas said. "Except for the guy who was bowing to your father and his family, friends, and associates."

Pleased, Helen giggled; and they left in the middle of the next dance, when everyone had crowded onto the floor. Daddy would be angry for a few minutes, and then he'd laugh that they'd "eloped."

By 3:00 AM Helen and Kostas were seated comfortably in Connoisseur Class on a 999 Qantas suborbital.

"I think we should put in an appearance at David's party," Helen said, as she gazed out the porthole window at the tarmac and the green runway lights. They were both seasoned travellers, resigned to spending as much time on runways as in the air.

"Well, it's too late now," Kostas said. The vibration of the engine was comforting and made him sleepy. He activated a privacy guard and the aisle and cruising automated stewards disappeared behind gray vibrating walls. "You didn't want to go, remember?"

"I was hungry."

Kostas didn't turn to look at her, but he could imagine her lips pursing into a pout. "Well, forget the party." He waited a beat and continued. "We did act like shits. The party was in our honour, after all."

"What you mean is that I'm a shit," Helen said.

"I didn't say that. I didn't want to go to a party either. I'll make up excuses when we get back."

"I'm sure the party is a bore and a half, and I'm tired, but we should put in an appearance," Helen said. "Come on, we'll virt in, apologize—you can make up one of your good excuses—and honour will be satisfied."

"We were specifically invited in person, remember?" Kostas said. "It's very bad form, especially for the guests of honour. I'll think of something when we get back."

"Well, *I'm* going to peep in," Helen said.

"You won't even get in."

Helen activated her privacy guard, walling herself away from Kostas. "*Oh, yes I will . . . .*"

Defeated, Kostas acquiesced; and Helen showed good form for their arrival. The guests at the party—if, indeed they would permit them to attend *en virt*—would see Kostas and Helen as Jan Van Eyck's "Giovanni Arnolfini and his Bride." Helen created their virtual images, her hands making tight motions on her lap, as if she were surreptitiously trying to conduct a symphony rather than manipulate data. She used an ancient geofiguration operating system, for she had trained with an old Mac designer, who died last year at 122, God rest his irritable soul.

Kostas lost his face to Van Eyck's financier Giovanni Arnolfini. His features became pale and sharp and thin, aristocratic, a spoiled little boy who had grown into selfish ennui. He wore an ermine cape and a large, velvet hat with a wide brim. But Helen retained her own features, now framed in a white lace shawl from which protruded two devil's horns of twisted blond hair. Her green dress, outlined with rabbit fur, cascaded to the floor in delightful folds.

"Come on, Kostas, stand up," Helen said, and she took his hand. "Stand up straight, there's enough room. There, that's close to the original painting. I just made us a bit better, that's all. What do you think?"

Kostas laughed. "You're beautiful, but are you sure you want to look pregnant?"

"I'm just being true to the painting. Let everyone think what they like." She giggled.

"You're not pregnant, are you?"

She shrugged. "Think whatever you like. Now what do you think of . . . you?"

"I can't see myself, but the frock feels nice and soft." Kostas said.

Kostas and Helen, like everyone else, wore self-cleaning virt body webs that were the texture of ancient nylon stockings.

"Well, you look very nice. Do you want a mirror?" She grinned at him, as she did when she was being provocative, when she was goading him.

"I'll trust you, but we don't have much room to move here."

"Stop being a baby," Helen said. "Once we're in, we'll sit," and she rang them into the party, leaving Kostas to make all the excuses while she waved hello to all their friends. They stood in a large living room that opened onto a pond and garden in the oriental style. Some of the guests were still dressed in the formal eveningware that had changed so little since the nineteenth century; most of the others were naked.

"Why, you didn't have to be embarrassed," said David, the host of the party. "This party was for you. We could have made it virtual, if that would have been easier."

"When we get back, we'll have to have a party for all of you," Helen said. "Our way of doing penance."

"Well, we can do it right now," one of the other guests said, and in a trice the room dissolved, giving way after a few long moments to endless veldt at twilight. The sky was blood red, darkening into clotted purple only at the horizon. The guests reappeared as golden pelted lions and padded around the Van Eyckian Kostas and Helen, who both seemed to be sitting on a cloud floating but a foot above the veldt.

Helen squealed with surprise. The rank smell of wet animal fur was overpowering. "You planned this all along."

"Well, we *were* getting a tad bored just standing about," David confessed, "so Ellen started working up a story we could play." Host and guests could only be distinguished by their voices now.

"It was interesting to get on for a while *au fond*," another said. "Somehow, though, it feels . . . naughty."

"Well, we're not being naughty now," said another.

"Tell us about the story," Helen asked.

"First tell us if you're pregnant," said Ellen, who settled back on her haunches before the newlyweds. "Your virt's pregnant, anyway." Everyone laughed, and she continued: "And where are you going on honeymoon. It seems that none of those who love you know. Now isn't that just a little bit odd?"

"I'll tell you exactly what I told my husband," Helen said. "Think whatever you like."

"About which, your pregnancy or the honeymoon?"

Helen laughed. "Both." After a beat, she said, "Now let me guess the game. It shouldn't be too difficult." Her friends circled them, and the scene took on a decidedly deadly cast. As it became darker, the other guests padded around Helen and Kostas in ever diminishing circles, feral eyes glowing.

Suddenly one of the guests leaped at Kostas, tearing at his legs, biting, ripping through to the virtual bone.

Kostas screamed in pain, and Helen said, "Okay, I'll give up . . . a little. I'm pregnant. Now, you see, you've spoiled it for Kostas. And I'll never really find out whether he's excited or upset."

"Well, tell her." The guests stopped pacing, all now watching Kostas, who was bleeding quite realistically, and was, indeed, in realistic pain.

"Oh, he won't reveal his true feelings in front of anyone," Helen said. "Not even me."

"You are pregnant?" Kostas said, angry and in pain.

"Would you like me to make the baby go away?" Helen asked. "Is that what you want?"

"No, of course not, but—"

"You see, I'm now married to this man, and I don't know him at all." With that, Helen transformed herself into an unpregnant bride. "And I'll tell you where we're going on our honeymoon. America!"

There was a gasp from the guests, and Helen disappeared, leaving her bleeding husband to the uncomprehending lions.

"Why did you lie about going to America?" Kostas asked Helen, who sat beside him sipping a champagne cocktail and reading *The Vision of God* by Nicholas of Cusa. As she was of a flamboyant nature, she read publicly, and the text, set in flames, hung in the air before her like the tablets of Moses. Nicholas was her saint, the saint of VR designers; he had dreamed of creating an image so potent as to be "omnivoyant"—all seeing. An icon of God.

Helen shrugged. "Give them something to talk about. And maybe I was angry with them for biting you. After all, you are the groom. And we'll practically be in America, so I didn't lie very much."

"Are you angry at me?" Kostas asked.

"Did you really think I might be pregnant?"

"For a second, maybe."

"You really didn't think I'd tell them before I told you," Helen said.

Kostas shrugged. "I asked you before, remember, and you wouldn't tell me. Who can know what you think?"

That pleased her, and she smiled. "I worried that if I was pregnant . . . that you wouldn't be pleased."

"Of course I'd be pleased."

"Well, good. I assumed that you really truly loved me, so I took revenge on the party guests for you."

"What did you do?" Kostas asked.

"I drowned them. They stank from dampness anyway. That's what gave me the idea. They won't be able to turn off their game until they're all practically choking to death."

"Christ, they were giving us a wedding party."

"One that they'll never forget," Helen said.

"They'll hate us."

"They'll love us."

An hour later they landed at the Tad Wink International Airport, which was less than an hour from Niagara via the underground magnetic.

They were in the Confederacy of Canada.

And in love.

"Are you sure you want to go through with this?" Kostas asked, uneasy with the third world presence of human functionaries, each of whom was almost certainly carrying a cocktail of disgusting, transmittable diseases. He tried not to breathe too deeply.

"We've had all our shots," Helen said. "Stop obsessing about your health. Do you remember the survival rules? Never eat anything uncooked or anything that might have been left standing. Never eat fruit that you don't peel yourself. Never drink the water. But don't worry," she said unctuously. "This is supposed to be a bath house. I'm sure it's clean."

Irritated and humiliated, Kostas turned to the interpreter, who, though obviously a male, wore a black veil; he also wore traditional western clothes: suit, tie, and sneakers. The interpreter stammered a rehearsed apology: the lifts had failed. Again. As usual. They'd be working tomorrow. Maybe. But it wouldn't be so bad: only ten flights to climb. Helen just shrugged and watched a lime-green turtle struggle with her luggage. The glittering Regency foyer with its Corinthian doorways, black marble insetting, and domed alcoves was serviced by bears and seals and all manner of aquatic and terrestrial creatures. But for all the expensive touches, everything looked dusty and soiled. Even the light streaming in through the windows seemed gray.

"You see," Kostas said to Helen, "it's just as I thought. All the porters and clerks are virts."

Helen giggled. "No they're *not*. They're all wearing costumes. Can't you tell? It's just like America."

Kostas understood. She was right, damn her.

He watched the cartoonesque turtle pushing their suitcases on a trolley across the huge marbled lobby to the ornamented stairway. Something about the comfortable angle of the turtle's carapace betrayed the deformity beneath: A hunched back, maybe, or a twisted spine.

Yes, it was just as he had heard.

All the natives suffered some form of genetic damage.

And now that he knew what to look for, he could well imagine some subtle deformity covered by the translator's veil.

Their suite was shabby, the wallpaper aged a nondescript brown, the curtains faded, the obligatory Edo *ukiyo-e* prints of courtesans and erotica clung tiredly to the walls, a relief of form and figure fading one into the other. The traditional curtain-dais, latticed shutters, sliding doors, and screens seemed out of place in what would have passed for a cheap-jack motel room in any civilized country on the Pacific Rim. But these amenities were costing $12,000 a night, not including tax.

Kostas checked the bathroom and was relieved to find that the plumbing worked after a fashion. Everything smelled of a recent application of disinfectant. But he was not pleased to see a hinged basket under the toilet paper dispenser and a metal sign screwed into the wall that read in Japanese, Arabic, and English: Dispose of Paper in Basket, Not Toilet. He was, however, fascinated by the slightly out of focus moving figures and the ranked characters of the sexual services menu, printed on rather grubby paper that had slid into the porcelain bathtub. He hadn't had it in his hand a second when he heard Helen gasp and call his name.

He stepped back into the bedroom, where Helen stood staring at a wall of water. The Falls. The exhausted turtle had brought in all the luggage and had depolarised the far wall to reveal the great horseshoe of foaming water that threatened to crash into their suite. Dismissed, the turtle was now bowing out of the room, and Kostas saw a clutch of real money in its bony hand. He remembered uncle Dimi slipping Helen a Japanese envelope at the wedding, and wondered if she had told the truth of their destination. He doubted it. The family was still traditional enough to disapprove of purchasing sexual games, no matter how fascinating and foreign, for its women. It wouldn't approve of his complicity, either.

"You called me in for *this?*" Kostas asked.

"Can't you hear it? Can't you feel it?"

The ancient waters roared their indifference, muted only by the heavy glass.

"Before the turtle turned off the wall, I just thought I was hearing the air-conditioning," Kostas said. "But I'm surprised that you're so taken with it all. Don't you think it's just a bit tacky?"

Helen pulled him toward a balcony. The doors sighed open, and the Falls sounded like constant thunder. "There. Can you feel it? Can you smell the ozone?"

"I smell *something*," Kostas said.

Helen embraced him. "It's supposed to act like an aphrodisiac. That's why it's so popular."

"Do you believe that?" Kostas felt dizzy looking out at the Falls and down at the Japanese gardens below. From this vantage, everything below looked small and perfect and at rest . . . and about to be overwhelmed by the Falls.

"No, but this is all real. I can tell the difference."

"No you *can't*," Kostas said.

"You're being very unromantic," Helen said. "This was a sacred place. You can still feel it."

"You're being very silly."

"And you're acting like a lawyer." Helen pulled away from him and went back inside.

Kostas followed. "I *am* a lawyer." The balcony shut out the noise behind them.

"I can see that. Here we are on our honeymoon and you're still clutching paperwork." She gestured at the sexual services menu that he was still holding.

"I found it in the bathroom, but I can't make out a damn thing . . . except for a few of the pictures, and they're fuzzy."

She took the menu.

"Could your Mac scan something that wrinkled?"

"No," she said, sitting down on the bed, her head propped on the large, hard pillows.

"There should be some clean copies in the desk," Kostas said.

"Uh, huh, I already looked. No computer, no postcards, not even a pencil. And no screen. Can't call out, can't see in."

"It's probably just a style thing. The stuff is there somewhere, just opaqued."

"Uh, huh," Helen said. "You could run downstairs and find out."

"I'm not—"

"Or you could just tick a box, any box, from each section. It's like those "authentic" oriental restaurants . . . half a dozen basic items, with hundreds of minor variations. Look at the back page to see if there's a banquet." There wasn't. "So, here, let me surprise you."

Helen thumbed some of the items at random, and pink circles appeared around the Japanese ideographs. "There. This is supposed to be an adventure. Now . . . don't you feel adventurous?"

As if responding to Helen, the room replied, in English, "Please forgive the inexcusable lapse of hospitality, Mrs Donoussa. Hotel Niagara is undergoing complete renovation. All hospitalities are being upgraded. It was most unfortunate that the hospitalities on this wing were down when you arrived. To make up for any inconvenience, we'll provide a special supper for you on the private roof garden and free run of all our bath and pink facilities. To answer your questions, you need not fill out any paperwork to use our facilities. Just tell us and all will be arranged. Postcards will soon be delivered and the room properly cleaned. If you need to make any calls, you need just ask."

"So where did *this* come from?" Kostas asked, waving the wrinkled services menu in the air.

"Our apologies, sir. The brochures for our pink salon do not usually find their way upstairs. But all your preferences have been noted."

"What is your pink salon?" Kostas asked.

"We're very proud of it, Mr Donoussa. It is an exact reproduction of the famous *Futago no Kyabetsu*, which thrived in Osaka before the Millennium. But unlike the ancient Osaka club, we offer intercourse as well as massage and violence service. It's very authentic and down-market. We had a customer murdered just this week. That caused quite a sensation."

"How do we turn you off?" Helen asked.

"Would you prefer privacy?"

"Yes," Helen said. "Immediately, if you please."

The room was silent, but this place definitely did not feel private.

Helen's belle epoch high heels clacked against the marble floor of the lobby as she and Kostas left the hotel to have dinner in the fabled streets of Niagara Falls. Perhaps they would dine in the private roof garden tomorrow. Tonight they wanted privacy. They wanted to explore. In her crimson striped jacket and her gown that pushed her rouged bosom up and out like a pouter pigeon, Helen looked like a main character in a costume drama taking place in the mock period style of the hotel lobby. She was tall and confident and full of herself, in marked contrast to the groups of pin-neat Japanese businessmen hurrying through the lobby with their tour handlers like multi-legged beasts scurrying out of the way of predators. Kostas wore pegged trousers and an apricot yellow ascot ruffled in his shirt. It would be sticky out in the streets, so he dressed casually. But the thrill for Helen was to be seen, discussed, and complimented.

As she and Kostas reached the door, they had to step back, for a Muslim potentate entered with his entourage of bodyguards, servants, wild noisy children, and wives and concubines wearing silk headdresses and ornamented veils. The potentate was turbaned and dressed in white; he had a handsome, pockmarked face, shaven cheeks, and a black mustache and beard. He stopped when he saw Helen, as if he recognized her; and he nodded to her as she and Kostas stepped past.

"Do you know him?" Kostas asked.

"No, I never saw him before," Helen said. "Why do you ask?"

"Because he looked at you as if he recognized you."

Helen took his arm, obviously pleased, and they made their first foray out of the hotel. They walked down Bender Street to Falls Avenue, through the checkpoint guards and into the formal gardens of combed sand where pumice white rocks seemed to float like islands in a stationary gray sea, past the European gardens with turf walks bordered by strawberry beds, through copses of elm, chestnut, and fir that hid the sight but not the sound of the Falls. They walked beside the long wall that overlooked the crashing, steaming waterfall. Mist rose into the sky, creating soft clouds that turned to neon as the kliegs came on to illuminate the Falls. It became dark very quickly, and the damp, chilly air smelled of ozone and chestnuts and grilling soymeat. Vendors called out to Helen and Kostas as they passed. "American hot-dogs, California hamburgers, real-authentic." Children played tag and ate real-authentic soy and vermiform dogs and burgers. Lovers leaned against the stone wall and necked or made love in the open. Natural Canadians strolled past, many veiled or masked or costumed in cloaks or coats too warm for the cool evening. The Confederacy had declared this perimeter by the Falls public land, and the Japanese Trade Corporation had not been allowed to purchase it.

Around the horseshoe of the Falls, neon beckoned: geometrical lines and clouds of suffusing light rising into columns, cliffs, and spires. Along the narrow public streets money and organs were gambled for a burst of white ecstasy; telefac booths took junkies through their personal and prerecorded stations of the cross, while five and dime virts provided empty dinners for those who had never seen or smelled real meat and dreamland sex for those who could only imagine the pleasures to be had beyond the public perimeter.

But Kostas and Helen were anxious to see the *real* Niagara Falls. They could come down to the strip to slum later in the week. After all, there wouldn't be anything much here that they couldn't see for a dime in Sydney or Melbourne or Adelaide . . . except for the Falls. At the checkpoint beyond the Japanese gardens Kostas asked a guard dressed in an olive drab uniform where the best restaurants could be found. The guard pointed his Ouzi 5000 riot rifle at the ground and indicated that he did not speak English.

"Even if he did speak English, you can't ask someone like that to recommend a good restaurant," Helen said. "He'd just send you to the Japanese equivalent of a greasy spoon." Kostas didn't argue, although he'd always found the best food in foreign towns by asking the advice of policemen and outworkers. They walked hand in hand past the neat grounds of hotels and the much more grand corporate lodgings. But beyond the hotels were winding, narrow streets chockablock with blinking billboards, holos, videotects, and neon signs, an entire city turned into a twentieth century amusement park: Ferris wheels, parachute rides, the original steel-reinforced Cyclone roller coaster lifted right out of Coney Island, tunnels of love and death. And there were, of course, the dioramas that Niagara Falls was famous for: American city streets that were cracked and overgrown with the brown fronds of fleshweed were resurrected here in all their glory. There were the original Golden Gate Bridge (or rather one quarter of it; the rest had been moved to New Japan near Chile) and Lombard Street and an exact recreation of Washington Square Park and ancient Japanese red lamp districts such as 1950s Koganecho and Shiroganecho and Osaka's Tobita district, circa 1911. Beyond were the sandy beaches of 17th Century Watakano Island with its welcoming *funajoro* and *sentakunin*—ship whores and washer women. And on every street corner were holos blinking ketchup red and whispering in the three major languages: THE JAPANESE TRADE CORPORATION WELCOMES YOU. EVERYTHING YOU SEE IS REAL. THE NEW NIAGARA FALLS IS A VIRT FREE ZONE. ENJOY IT BUT BE CAREFUL! BE REMINDED: YOU HAVE SIGNED A DEATH WAIVER. WE HAVE PROVIDED DANGEROUS SITUATIONS ESPECIALLY TO MAXIMIZE YOUR ENJOYMENT. ALL CHILDREN UNDER SEVENTEEN MUST BE BRANDED.

As danger simply was not on for the first night of their honeymoon, they decided to try a famous Philadelphia restaurant called Locanda Veneta for a quiet supper and spend the rest of the night inhaling ozone from the Falls and making love: Kostas, after all, came from a traditional family. The ambiance of Locanda Veneta was a kitschy interpretation of late twentieth century Italian (red velvet chairs and red felt on the walls and well-lit but poorly executed oil paintings). The lasagna della casa and the spinach and ricotta cannelloni were execrable, as were the roasted quail and the calf's liver with polenta. To add insult to injury, the food was tremendously overpriced.

Helen credited the bill and Kostas suggested a safe cab to the hotel and a judicious dose of mebeverine hydrochloride to eliminate any possible irritable bowel syndrome that might have been touched off by Locanda Veneta's poisonous cuisine. "Now I understand why they have danger signs at every corner," Kostas said, once they were on the street.

Helen had decided they would walk. They had come here for excitement. And anyway she had a special surprise waiting for Kostas.

"What?"

"Don't worry. It's right at the hotel. We're going to take it easy tonight." With that she grinned and stepped off into the crowds of tourists and paid pickpockets, rapists, whores, and murderers.

Helen led Kostas across the hotel's lobby, past the banks of elevators, to Shinmachi Soaplands, the hotel's Bath House. The entrance—antique temple doors that reached almost to the ceiling—was behind a display of huge fans and screens, and a grandmotherly old lady dressed in tenth century full court costume was waiting for him. She shooed Helen away and said, "*Wasure nai,*" which meant "Don't forget."

"What?" Kostas asked, pulling away from the grandmother, but Helen simply blew him a kiss and left him there.

"I thought we were going to spend the night together," Kostas shouted, immediately embarrassing himself, for everyone nearby suddenly stopped talking.

Helen turned and said, "We will . . . now let the old lady do her job." With that she disappeared behind a tour group of new arrivals who had enough baggage to move house. And Kostas slipped through the doorway to the pink salon with the old lady who introduced herself with a bow and a faint smile as Sei Shonagon, the boss and bitch of this court. Indeed, the spacious room resembled a royal court; no expense had been spared. Grandmother Bitch led him through indoor gardens under high, timbered roofs. They passed an old man playing a thirteen-pipe flute. Beside him was a naked woman playing a zither; she must have weighed at least three hundred pounds.

One by one Grandmother's nieces appeared with their enamelled fans and hair ornaments and formal long-trained skirts. Kostas found himself smiling nervously as any bridegroom, as he was introduced to these shy women, several of whom looked prepubescent, all of whom had Canadian Confederacy Department of Agriculture and Health facial implants that glowed with a soft, green light: official proof that their blood was at this very minute clear of all communicable infections. Grandmother introduced each niece by her proper name, and Kostas would say, by rote, "*Taihen utsukushii desu*, or *yubi na*," telling each woman, or girl—it was difficult to determine their ages—that she was very beautiful or very graceful. One of the nieces wore horn-rimmed eyeglasses. Whether it was an affectation or a foil for some minor degenerescence, Kostas couldn't tell. He called her *riko na*, the last of the three compliments he could remember, and she beamed at him, for being called intelligent was the highest compliment one could receive in Japanese soiree society. Although unintentional, he had just made his selection. Grandmother's other nieces, looking properly crestfallen, excused themselves, and Grandmother recounted Pretty Girl's virtues and specialties. She was expert at pretend games such as pervert in the park and had invented and perfected *ososhiki supesharu*, which was now popular all over Japan: the funeral special. She could provide him with all the delicacies on the pink menu, from a simple bath to *ippo tsuko* (one-way street), *name-name pure* (lick-lick play), *paizure* (breast-urbation), or *sakasa tsubo hoshi* (upside-down pot service).

Grandmother bowed and excused herself.

Pretty Girl, although blushing, led Kostas through the gardens to a wonderfully hot and steamy bath, a huge improvement on the tepid water of his suite. Before she undressed him, he asked, "Why do you wear eyeglasses, Pretty Girl?" Kostas felt awkward, felt a need to communicate before being "served."

She kneeled before him, settling back comfortably on her haunches. She had very delicate features, except for her mouth, which was full. An application of lipstick would have made her look voluptuous, but she blurred her lip line with white face powder. Her hair was very long and lustrous; black, with brown highlights. "I'm blind, Mr Donoussa."

"Kostas."

"Kostas." She said the word as if she were tasting it. "I like it very much."

"Do the glasses allow you to see?"

"No, they are for the comfort of others. They are like clothes to cover me. If you wish, you can see me without them?"

Kostas nodded, then realized she couldn't see him and said, "Yes." But he looked away when she took the glasses off and laid them carefully beside her. Her eye sockets were empty, brown hollows, dark gouges in her powered-white face.

"There are many who find my blindness attractive. If you find it repellent, I can put my glasses back on. Or perhaps you would rather one of my cousins instead?" She bowed her head.

"No, I wish to be with you," Kostas said, feeling an exotic rush of both attraction and repulsion as she undressed before him . . . as she bathed him and soaped him and efficiently fellated him. She was shy, yet able, and as he watched her serve him everything he had ordered on the menu, he dreamed of an eyeless, delicate Helen who would cater to his every wish. He dreamed of Helen as Pretty Girl performed *kuchu kimmu*, aerial service, which required that he only lie on his back while she climbed astride him. He dreamed of Helen as Pretty Girl led him back to the bath for a full body massage and pubic hair "brush wash" on a tatami mat. After a moment of ecstasy, his gaze drifted back to Pretty Girl's glasses, which rested neatly folded on the floor where she had left them.

Her lost, brown Bette Davis eyes gazed intently at him through tinted windows.

But Kostas was shocked out of his reverie by a glimpse of shiny black, nine-inch stiletto heels. Suddenly, his wrists were seized and handcuffed behind him, his ankles bound, and his knees pushed forward, so that Kostas found himself with his chest on the mat and his buttocks raised, pink and exposed. He glimpsed someone the size of a sumo wrestler moving gracefully toward the door. As he shouted for help, the diminutive Pretty Girl merely consulted the menu, then produced a gag, which she tied very carefully, so as not to bruise his gums. She brushed her hands across his face, as if seeing him with her caress.

There was nothing Kostas could do but resign himself to his fate.

After all, there's always *something* you don't like on the menu. And at least Pretty Girl was small.

He ground his teeth as she lashed his buttocks, carefully pressing down the ends of the whip so as not to leave welts on his soft, white skin. The whipping was mercifully short. When she teetered back into his line of vision to offer him his choice of authentic antique MADE IN TAIWAN battery operated dildoes for *anaru zeme*—anal attack, Kostas shook his head. He felt a cold blob of KY jelly followed by the tip of a boot heel as Pretty Girl gave him full measure, pumping, rotating her ankle, gradually working deeper inside him.

He was mortified to find his erection hardening as she increased the pressure. Then another woman wriggled onto the mat, sliding beneath his belly to take his penis in her mouth. Her technique was familiar, and Kostas's mortification turned to true humiliation as Helen sucked the juices from him in an explosive orgasm.

He stared at Pretty Girl's glasses, as if he could focus himself into one small object. He felt soiled, defiled. Sex was private. That's what they'd agreed. That was to be the only rule.

The image of Pretty Girl's brown eyes stared back at him.

And suddenly Kostas felt a shiver fan down his back.

Someone was watching them . . . and it wasn't Pretty Girl.

When Kostas woke up, he was alone in his suite. His head ached and there was a metallic taste in his mouth, as if he'd been drugged. He told the room to turn off the wall, and morning sunlight blazed through the window plate. Niagara Falls was a dull roar, a vibration that could be sensed rather than felt. From his bed he could only glimpse blue sky threaded with sheet white cirrus. He listened for bath noises; there were none.

"Where's my wife?"

"There was no message left for you, Mr Donoussa," the room said.

"When did she leave?"

"She was previously in the room from 3:36 PM to 5:17 PM yesterday, Mr Donoussa."

"Yes, go on."

"She has not returned, Mr Donoussa."

Kostas was now sitting on the side of the bed, his hands shaking, his voice gravelly. Something had gone terribly wrong. He knew it. He could feel it. As he blinked, he imagined Pretty Girl's glasses staring at him. He tried to remember. He remembered calling to Helen, then . . . waking up here.

"When did *I* return?"

The room didn't answer.

"When did I return?"

Again, no answer.

The room was dead.

Kostas went down to the old Niagara Falls strip, which was already crowded with penny ante gamblers and the skinny junkies out for a small, cheap shot to their pleasure centres. The day-shift whores had been out since dawn, calling and revealing and heckling. Most were occidental and thick-featured, illegals from the US side and Canadians who couldn't qualify for the dole. One tried to hard-sell herself to a middle-aged, balding man who was with another woman and four children. The man ignored her, even as she danced in front of him; he put his arms around two of the children and looked straight ahead, as if the casinos, virt parlours, and pink palaces were gold-steepled cathedrals. Kostas noticed that the children were dressed in identical, garish-red outfits. They would certainly be easy to find. And just then Kostas felt suddenly homesick. He heard the internal thunder that always preceded tears and focused on the task at hand, as if he were in court.

He found a plastic booth near the toilets in the seediest looking casino on the strip. The sliding doors kept opening and closing until he hit the control panel hard with his fist, then the booth darkened. Activating his office's privacy code, he waited until sufficient phantom circuits were created and the image of his father-in-law resolved a few feet away from him. He wore a well-pressed suit and looked morning fresh, although he had probably already been in the office for fourteen hours. Mr Nisyros was compulsive about shaving and washing, which he did every few hours.

"Christ, what kind of a hole are you calling from?" Mr Nisyros asked. "I'm surprised the bugs managed to secure a line. Is everything all right?" He paused for a beat, then said, "I can see that it's not."

"Helen's missing."

"Then find her."

"I tried. I did everything—"

"You mean you reported it to the hotel and the corporation, don't you?"

"Yes," Kostas said. "What else would you have me do?"

"I would have had you call me and not alert the Yakuza mob."

"I most certainly did not—" Kostas controlled himself. "Do you have any suggestions?"

"Yes, go to the hotel and wait in your room."

"Don't you want to know the details of what happened?"

"Wait in your room, send for room service. Stay away from entertainments."

And Mr Nisyros faded into the fetid, smeary darkness of the booth, leaving Kostas to wonder why he wouldn't talk on a secure line.

Kostas did as he was told. Actually, there was no choice, for if Helen's father was correct and the Yakuza mob was involved, he would be at risk. But if Angelos Maitland Nisyros told him to stay in his room, then there he would be safe.

But what about Helen?

If Kostas thought about her, if he imagined all the terrible possibilities, he would go mad. He paced the room—twenty-two steps from the door to the balcony, thirteen steps wide. Angelos had warned him to stay away from virts. No, he told himself, the old man told him to stay away from everything but food. At least the amenities were working. He ordered a BLT and hot sake. The plate was brought by one of the hotel officers, an occidental who wore a red, paisley tie and a blue uniform. The officer explained that the hotel provided authentic American-style bacon, then whispered out of the room as quickly and quietly as a robot . . . or a trained valet.

Kostas sat well away from the balcony, sipped the warm sake and watched the Falls. It was as if the air itself was vibrating; and as he gazed at the natural wonder, he felt himself falling as so many had done before him, sliding through the thundering storm of water and steam and foam, crashing onto the rocks below, to disappear. The day passed in increments of agony, for he could not escape memory and could not quiet his mind. He imagined all the possibilities, all the myriad deaths and tortures that Helen might be suffering right now as he drank and ate and remembered.

Yet she had manipulated him.

And he was helpless. He had tried to find her, and failed. Now her father was in control. As if in defiance, he opened the balcony doors and stepped out into the sunlight. He looked at the gardens below, perfectly laid out, as if he were an impotent god; and he felt a great surge of anger, of rage.

Helen was probably somewhere enjoying herself. And Kostas was being played the fool.

"Mr Donoussa, would you kindly step back inside," the room said.

"Why?"

"It is the wish of your father-in-law, Mr Donoussa."

Dawn.

Kostas sat in the back seat of an antique Rolls-Royce Silver Steamer and gazed out the bullet-proof window. The chauffeur wore a traditional *keffiyeh* head dress and *abayeh* and barely spoke, except when Kostas asked him a direct question. His cologne—oil of roses and sandalwood musk—permeated the cabin, overwhelming any lingering odors of strong tobacco, old leather, and sweat. There was no one else on the road. Empty tenements had given way to rocky scrub, and then the scrub and scrabble had disappeared; not even such hardy flora could grow in stone. Kostas was being driven across a stone desert. Gray escarpments rose in the distance, but the fused land was flat and pocked and utterly devoid of life. It was hard to believe that three hundred miles behind them was a living wall of water. And gardens of flowers and leaf wet to the touch.

But now he was in the *real* Canada, which wasn't very different from the arid lands of America.

Kostas thought he saw forest, but he had mistaken the grotesque stands of rock cones for trees. Yet this was still temperate climate; *something* should grow here. The pot-holed, broken roadway suddenly ended, but the driver only slowed down a little as the rubber-padded crawler tracks eased the Rolls over rocks and ridges. As rough as the ground was, there were only a few bone-shaking jolts. Although Kostas was worn out, he couldn't sleep; and the day seemed an eternity. Finally the noxious atmosphere deepened into sunset, which had become a crimson swirling of oil in a sea of turquoise. In the distance was a mirage of green, a forest of imported eucalyptus that could endure here better than the firs and deciduous oak and pine that had thriven for millennia.

And above the forest, on top of a smooth butte, was a fortress of polished, white marble burning in the last rays of the sun.

"Sheik Mohammed bin Dakhil-Allah el Faud awaits you in the gazebo," the chauffeur said as he hurried Kostas through formal avenues of green, where lush, scented foliage and splashing fountains bespoke a fortune vast enough to lavish water upon this parched earth. In the centre of the gardens, the huge, stained-glass tent that roofed the gazebo glowed like a mosaic of jewels. Over the damp exhalations of plants and the evening smells of cooling stone came the rose perfumes of Arabia, and the unmistakable aroma of freshly ground coffee.

Once inside the gazebo, Kostas—nervous and exhausted—felt that he had somehow fallen into a kaleidoscope. Soft lighting revealed a floor strewn with gorgeous carpets: silk Herekes tossed over Bokharas and piled with plush, tasseled cushions. The finest weaving, achieved by master craftsmen calling patterns to swift-fingered children soon blinded by the task. Panels of gold filigree supported the netted glass and woven draperies on the walls, framing a profusion of shimmering reds, golds, and indigoes that shifted patterns and confused the eye.

The sheik waved the chauffeur away, then rose to meet Kostas.

"*Masalama*, Mr Donoussa. My home is your home. The gazebo is at its best at moonrise, wouldn't you agree? A fitting welcome for an honoured guest." Mohammed bin Dakhil-Allah el Faud looked to be in his mid-forties and moved with the assurance of one used to exercising the power conferred by wealth, and willing to be seduced by its luxuries. His immaculate white thobe revealed the rounded contours of a body overfond of the sweetmeats that glistened in their golden dishes at his feet. His heavy black mustache drooped over full lips, which parted in a smile of greeting to reveal teeth stained by a lifetime of betel and coffee. He extended pudgy, ringed fingers to Kostas, who was momentarily surprised by the strength he found there.

"Blessings upon you and your household, your Excellency," Kostas said. He knew how to respond, as he had escorted many of his father-in-law's powerful Arab clients around Melbourne.

After an obligatory exchange of pleasantries, Kostas was invited to be seated on the carpets opposite his graceful host. The sheik poured coffee into tiny, exquisite cups.

Kostas sipped, and could not suppress a smile of pure delight. "This is wonderful, your Excellency." He looked at the stained-glass tent above. "This . . . is truly magical."

"And it also has the virtue of being real, Mr Donoussa. I leave virts to the infidel. In Islam, we do not reproduce images of the body, not even in art. And all my food, including the coffee, is hand-grown in safe soil. This is my personal blend. I have made it myself for you, to the traditional recipe: black as night, sweet as love, and hot as hell. It is a metaphor for your current situation, is it not?"

The coffee was like a jolt of amphetamine, clearing Kostas's head and sharpening his senses, which had been dulled by fatigue, grief, and frustration. He felt as if he were just coming out of a trance . . . .

The sheik continued to speak, his plump fingers now interlaced with the silken, black-tasseled cord of priceless, pure amber worry beads; their soft clicking punctuated his sentences.

"Your father-in-law has explained your situation to me, and here in my home you will be safe from the Yakuza." The sheik made a clucking noise of disapproval. "In Niagara, you would have disappeared just like your wife. As if you had never been."

"What do you know of my wife?" Kostas asked reflexively, realizing only after he spoke that he had broached courtesy, that the sheik would tell him in his own time.

Or perhaps would decide not to tell him anything.

"The Yakuza do not like bad publicity," the sheik continued, as if uninterrupted, "and news of an international abduction would be very bad for the tourist business. By now, the incident will not have happened. But they cannot come here. You are safe, *Inshallah*." The sheik nodded to Kostas, giving him permission to speak.

"I appreciate your concern, your Excellency. Yet I must confess that I had expected to meet my father-in law here with you. I am a lawyer, and I wish only to negotiate the release of my wife."

"That would be unwise, my son. Your laws are of no consequence here. Your father-in-law, however, is a respected man of business. He has property rights to the abducted woman and can speak as an equal with Sheik Fauzin el Harith. The sheik is a reasonable man, a traditional man. Your wife will be safe under his protection."

Kostas remembered meeting the Muslim potentate and his retinue of slaves, wives, and concubines in the lobby of the hotel, remembered how he had looked at Helen . . . with recognition. Kostas felt soiled, for no doubt the man had watched everything, had watched Kostas and Helen making love in their room . . . had watched them later in the pink salon *à trois* with Pretty Girl. It was Fauzin el Harith's eyes that had been staring out at him from Pretty Girl's glasses. "Protection? He has kidnapped—"

"You are young, and emotional, as befits a bridegroom, but this is now a business matter for your elders. Sheik Fauzin el Harith has simply employed the means at his disposal to procure a woman who captured his fancy." Mohammed bin Dakhil-Allah el Faud shrugged, then continued. "He was of course not quite within the law, but he is a powerful man. And powerful men—such as your father-in-law and perhaps myself—are not within the law." He smiled, as if enjoying the idea. "It may be that the matter of your wife can be resolved with a negotiated ransom. Maybe yes, maybe no. Certainly Sheik Fauzin el Harith could be an important business ally for your father-in-law. Pain is often the messenger of joy . . . and wealth. But I will take care of you, as I promised your father-in-law. I would do the same for my own sons. But it is better that you should remain here where you are safe. It is important that you are secure and available when the need arises. So you will be my guest. I am honoured to have Mr Nisyros's adopted heir under my protection. I have many children, praise be to Allah, and I will introduce you to my family. But perhaps not just now. You will feel much better after some rest."

The gentle tone admitted no argument.

Kostas realized that he was now, like Helen, a prisoner.

An honoured prisoner in a cage of gold.

He could do nothing but wait.

The days passed like the long hours in the Rolls.

Servants attended Kostas at all times, and from them he learned that it was an honour that Sheik Mohammed bin Dakhil-Allah el Faud had received him privately and served him with his own hands. It was an especial honour that he even allowed Kostas to speak to his daughters, who were always dressed, or rather hidden, in virgin-white gowns, headdresses, and veils. He thought it odd that he had not met any of the sheik's sons, but would not broach etiquette and ask.

Kostas waited for another audience with the sheik. When that was not forthcoming, he became more insistent. The guards told him that the sheik was busy.

The sheik was always busy.

Kostas kept to himself and waited for the all-important call from his father-in-law or a summons from the sheik. Wrestling with the dead weight of memory, he relived every moment of his last night with Helen. Indeed, it was as if Helen were already dead and he was in mourning. Then almost against his will, he began to come back to life. He read in the sheik's library; rode the sheik's horses in the scrub below the butte while a Sikorsky gunship helicopter flew overhead; walked every inch of compound in the polite and distant company of his guards; and found himself spending more and more time with the sheik's eldest daughter Sagan. She was as tall as Kostas, and was named after a man who had saved her father's life. Although she, too, was always attended by servants and would not remove her veil, she claimed to have visited the ruins of Manhattan and to have lived on her own in Toronto.

"Tell me about the man you are named after," Kostas asked as they sat in a long, lush garden. Beside them goldfish as large as trout swam back and forth along the edges of a brackish pond, as if waiting to be fed. Beyond—and white as Sagan's gown—were huge marble buildings built in the shape of tents: the soldiers' barracks. The architecture was as striking as the winged opera house in Sydney, Australia.

"I've already told you," Sagan said, her beautiful, dark eyes gazing out at him, as if from silken prisons.

"Was he an infidel?"

She laughed, and the guards standing a discreet distance away from them came to the alert, as if Kostas were about to do something untoward. "Do you think my father would name me after an infidel?"

Kostas shrugged.

"No, he is not an infidel. You won't find many infidels in Kentucky." She looked into the distance. "Have you been to America?"

"No."

She shook her head. "Better here."

"In the desert?"

"Better here."

"Didn't your father worry that you would be in the company of infidels when you lived in Toronto?" Kostas said.

"Why are you obsessed with infidels?" She smiled. "Are you asking if he would let me marry one?"

"Would he?"

"He allows you to keep me company."

Shocked, Kostas realized that he had been leading the conversation back to that, for if he lost Helen, he wanted Sagan. He wanted everything to end with physical intimacy, for then he could not be hurt. If language separated him from this veiled stranger, that would have been even better.

But what did he have with Helen? Emotional connection? Pain? Understanding? All of that, and he wallowed in the pain, yet he knew Helen little better than he knew this veiled princess, this outlander who was slumming with the infidel.

"I'm sorry, Kostas." That was the first time she had called him by his given name. "I was taking advantage of you, playing with you. You must be in great pain over your wife."

She watched him, waiting for him to speak; he had to say something. "I feel better when we're together."

"We can be together as much as you like."

Kostas nodded, thinking about Helen, wondering what she was doing while he was having this conversation. He felt no anxiety now. He was empty, and content.

And as he sat there, holding Sagan's hand while the guards purposely looked the other way, he realized that he had been trapped once again. By Helen. By his father-in-law. By her father.

There was nothing to be done but relax and accept it.

An arrangement had been made.

In time, Sagan would remove her veil . . .

The Fire-Eater's Tale

(with Jack Dann)

This second collaboration with Jack Dann was commissioned for Strange Attraction, *an original anthology based on a kinetic sculpture by Lisa Snellings. The sculpture depicts a crowded Ferris wheel sited in a midnight carnival, and the humanity of the demented creatures riding the wheel is very much open to question. For the twenty-five stories and poems in the volume, the authors were each given a photograph of one of the creatures and asked to put this character into a story based on their interpretation of the sculpture. To complete the circle, Lisa then illustrated the stories based on her visualization of the fiction. The result is a truly bizarre collection of dark imaginings. The Fire-Eater's Tale literally plays with fire in a fantasmagorical tale of pain and revenge.*

Fire. It was always fire . . . .

Gron was almost an elemental himself, slipping between the worlds at will.

They'd been afraid of his deformity, the filthy, stinking raiders who had swept down from the mountains to rape and murder his miserable family, to gorge on the meagre food of his pitiful village. Their superstition had saved his life, if not his body. "*Demon*", they had called him, passing him back and forth between them as they abused him. It amused them that the demon-child wept and screamed at their torture, these men more hideous than any demon of the priest's imagining. But they dared not kill him outright. So they hurt him past his enduring, then left him, unconscious, face down and naked and bleeding in the smouldering ashes of his home. And they moved on.

But still he did not die. The fire that melted his face and smeared his skin across his misshapen bones showed its secrets to the dying child. Halfway between this world and the next, Gron had seen them—the salamanders, the firedrakes, the elementals. And, fleeing from his pain, his spirit had loved them, loved them with his child's simplicity, for their wildness and their fierce joy, for themselves. And so they touched him, marked him for their own.

When the circus folk found him, this charred phoenix-child annealed in the ashes, they felt the luck on him. Adopted him. And Gron was home. In the weird family of the sideshow troupe, he fit right in. A freak among freaks, his vestigial extra head was of no particular consequence. Nestled in the hairy bosom of his bearded adoptive mother, his sobs subsided. His healing was slow, but safe. Cocooned from the prying eyes of the world, Gron lived.

Now, when he swallowed the fire and spat it back into the night, the elementals danced for him. And those with eyes to see watched in wonder.

The show was about to begin in Madison Square Garden.

"*This Show of Shows*," this *Olympiad* of circuses, this *city* of carnivals included troupes from all over Europe and Asia and South America—over a thousand circuses and sideshows had been brought together to perform in and around New York's concrete version of the Crystal Palace. But Gron and his company were nowhere near the glittering centre rings inside the protected walls of the Garden. Like hundreds of other troupes and companies, they were relegated to the parks and streets that had been cordoned off from traffic. Gron's troupe had been cast from the light, thrown almost into the sea, for they were to perform on the grounds of the 79th Street Boat Basin. The park seemed to glow in the night, fairy lights netted over trees, lamps casting baleful yellow-eyed illumination and deep, stationary shadows; and gimcracked arc lamps burned into the very sky itself, announcing that even here in this little park by the river, the circus would play, clowns would dance, horses would prance, acrobats would build fleshy, almost geometric forms and then collapse, tumbling past gleeful children and their watchful parents, a Ferris Wheel would revolve, arcade hucksters would

shout at passers-by in Bosnian and broken English, and black hide
tents would hide the traditional and universal grotesqueries, which
sometimes included Gron, the two-headed boy, the demon who
could also eat coals, inhale fire, and exhale the spirits of the dark
like fine streamers.

"Precious boy, come out," Drakulic—the owner of the circus—
cried into a microphone; and his high-pitched voice boomed through
the sound system provided by the City of New York. Drakulic, who
was tall and broad-shouldered, stood on the matted, muddied grass
that functioned as the centre ring. High above him a huge canvas
blotted out the moon and dim stars like a ceiling.

Gron was in one of the small tents beside Slavenka, who had
become his mother after his family had been killed. She, not
Drakulic, had found him, and he was no more than a little child
then, and he had cried at the sight of her; he had thought she was
some sort of an animal, or a werewolf, or a man who looked like a
woman; but she wasn't a spirit, or a ghost of the dead, as perhaps
he was; she was human and fleshy and smelled of sweat and animal.
Now, sitting beside her in the cage that protected them from the
onlookers who shouted and laughed and joked and tried to get their
attention, Gron could imagine that he was back home. Anything
would be better than this place they had come to. He inhaled
Slavenka's odour and glanced at her: she was beautiful—tall, thin,
and her eyes were deep and piercing. She could kill you with her
look Drakulic would say. She was beautiful; her face was delicate
and high-boned, but you had to see through the curly black hair
that grew on her cheeks and neck and chin . . . on her arms, and her
breasts, which Drakulic said were God's perfect shapes. Young men
who had paid their five dollars to see her said things Gron could not
understand, but he knew they were bad; just as he knew that they
hated him for the vestigial head that grew out of the hollow of his
neck like a fat radish out of dirt.

"Go now," Slavenka said to him as she stared grimly at those
who watched her. "Do as your father asks." She stood up and
danced flirtatiously and stuck her tongue out at the men making
obscene gestures at her.

"I could kill them," Gron said.

Slavenka rolled her hips and laughed. "They are only boys and
men. If they can break the bars, they can have me. But they can't.
They do not have gifts as you do. But you cannot have me because

I am your mother." She laughed, her voice like bells and paper rattling. "Now go to your father." Just as Slavenka had become his mother, so Drakulic called himself his father.

"I am afraid."

She turned away from their audience. "Afraid of the fire?"

Gron nodded.

"Then you must not eat it. But *you* must tell your father."

"And here he is, ladies and men, my son, who has been burned and befriended by the fire."

As Drakulic spoke into the microphone, so did a small, dark-haired woman, translating his words into English. It sounded to Gron like an echo, or like the terrible sounds one remembers from dreams. Gron stood before Drakulic, head bowed, waiting for the proper moment to speak. Drakulic went on, telling Gron's story, but out of respect, he did not mention the small head, which was nothing more than a lump of scar tissue, a sort of goitre, cracked and blackened, as if by fire. Those who had seats close to the grassy ring could see Gron's scarred lump, but those higher and farther away could not.

"Ladies and men," shouted Drakulic, "if you watch carefully, you will see something you have never seen before. You will see the demons of fire, you will see them wrap themselves around my son like snakes, you will see . . . ."

And then Gron was alone, surrounded by the crowds.

It was too late to be afraid of the fire.

The salamanders came at his call, and they danced for him when he spoke to them, here in this strange, raw country across the ocean. But their game was rough, dangerous, menacing. Here, they were not used to being summoned, and they took it ill that he could command them at all. They challenged him, running with their sinuous lizard forms along the length of his body, their claws catching in his circus finery that was designed to expose his chest and shoulders, their small, sharp teeth seeking purchase on his ears, his nose, his fingers—on every inch of exposed skin. Gron felt the tiny trickles of his blood, but, in the throes of his fire-ecstasy, it was of no matter. He filled his lungs, took the flames into his throat, and exhaled them high into the night. He became the creature of fire that the crowds had come to see, blazing like a human bonfire in the dark centre of the ring. The salamanders covered him, their long tails whipping through the blaze of his hair, their fiery lizard tongues darting, licking his blood and sweat, tasting him, taking his measure. They felt his love for them, and they fed from it. Gron staggered in their embrace, and still they sucked at him.

The show went on, the onlookers unaware of the struggle they were witnessing. Gron almost made it through his routine. On his last, spectacular fiery exhalation, his control slipped, just for an instant. It was enough: the crowd gasped as a huge lizard-shape, gorged on Gron's life, escaped shining and glowing into the night, swimming with a peculiar crocodile-gait into the darkness, disappearing into the parkland and streets beyond. The applause was rapturous, unafraid.

Gron's father helped him from the ring, hoping the audience would mistake his son's limpness for a deep bow, bowing and smiling himself.

The torches guttered.

The show was over.

And in the trailer, Gron lay like the dead and dreamed with the eyes of fire.

He rode the fire-lizard that was gaining its life from him, that was growing stronger while Gron grew weaker. Gron felt himself slipping inside the fire-lizard, becoming the testing, inconstant shape of fire, and he crawled along the pavement of Riverside Drive, spun through the air on Amsterdam Avenue as he licked and tasted this world of cement and dirt, this world of endless flesh and scurrying insects. He was fire swirling through the streets and buildings until they exploded into flames . . . into searing heat and fiery light . . . into life, his life; but it was the fire-lizard, not Gron.

Not Gron.

For Gron was lying cold and shivering in dream-sweat in Slavenka and Drakulic's trailer.

It was late next day when the trance left him.

He awoke from his nightmares of conflagration to find his body criss-crossed with razor fine cuts, bruised with the love-bites of lizards. These things he could understand. But his muscles were inexplicably sore from running, and the sweat of his exertions was dried and stinking in the armpits of his nightshirt. And more alarming than any of these things, his vestigial head had grown. Gron touched it as one would touch a newly-discovered boil or tumour. It felt larger indeed, no longer cracked and rubbery. There would be the eye hollows, and the bridge of a nose, and the high ridge of cheekbone and—he pulled his hand away reflexively, as if he had been suddenly bitten, or burned; and he heard, or thought he heard, a voice that was not his own.

It spoke to him alone with the terrible sound of dreams.

"What it is, my precious boy?" Slavenka asked. She sat beside him on her bed, tending and nursing him, just as she had all night. She dipped a rag into a basin of water and herbs, then rolled the rag between her hands and placed it over his forehead. "Your body has been marked. It is a miracle. You, my son, are a miracle. Jesus' miracle. His own. You will rest until your skin is smooth." She touched his vestigial head, as if with longing, as if she were adoring it and not him, talking to it . . . not him.

Praying to him, as if he was the Saviour himself.

Gron, for his part, couldn't speak; yet he heard a voice that was his.

"No, my darling son," Slavenka said, "you are far too weak to get up. Your fever will break soon, and then I will feed you."

And indeed Gron's fever did break.

He shivered and drank some of Slavenka's medicine, even while his head-shaped goitre burned with the heat of a firedrake's birthing; and while he shivered and drank and burned, fires burned all over New York.

It was as if arsonists had been working in concert.

The first floor of the Empire State Building was blackened, yet unharmed, but one block away Macy's and the A&S Plaza had become six-alarm fires. The Whitney Museum had caught fire, curiously, impossibly, for the exterior was unharmed; but the fire destroyed everything inside, including Alexander Calder's magnificent circus sculpture in the lobby. A hundred years of art turned to charcoal and ashes.

At 200th Street and Southern Boulevard, the forty-five acre forest in the Botanical Gardens was in flames, and thousands of butterflies took to the air like bats, escaping, as if they were the firedrakes transformed.

Gron felt a little stronger as the day wore on and the nighmares receded, but there was no escaping the insistent heat emanating from his neck. Necks. He yearned to be alone. And in the peace of the twilight, in the little space when the daylight had died and the fairy-lights were not yet lit, when the fairground was not yet open for business, Gron crept away from the caravan and went where he always went when he wanted to be alone. The Ferris Wheel turned slowly for its solitary rider, its lamps unlit, its music-box silent. He swung high into the purple air, the garish little metal car creaking in the soft, damp breeze that tasted of salt from the ocean, air that was cold against his burning skin. At the top of the arc, Gron could see the reddish glow of spot-fires still smouldering in the distance, could identify the bitter back-taste of smoke in the salty air. The old Gron was afraid, afraid for himself, afraid for his family.

The new Gron-head exhalted.

That night Gron performed for a huge audience that had spread throughout the grounds surrounding the main tent—word had spread of his "trick" of turning fire into a great golden lizard that ran into the night, flaming like a fireworks display. Although Slavenka was worried and begged him to rest, Drakulic thought the enormous crowds more of a miracle than the miraculous marks on Gron's body. Or the disturbing changes in Gron's vestigial head.

Slavenka worshipped it.

Drakulic ignored it.

And Gron . . . he was being choked by it. It had grown larger, defining itself in the exact image of Gron—a perfect likeness that was the size of a canteloupe. It had taken Gron's voice and his will. It had taken *him*. Now *he* was the shrunken, lumpish head that had no will or desire. He could but watch and listen and think his thoughts, which were nightmares, as if he had dreamed his life and this head with its white teeth and smooth skin and phlegm-yellow eyes . . . as if he had dreamed his mother and father and the men who had killed them—who had raped his mother and forced him and his father to watch before they killed his father, and then raped and tortured Gron himself—it was all dreams, dreams, dreams, only the firedrakes had seemed real; and now, they, too, were dreams, even as Gron watched himself perform, as he . . .

Ate a coil of burning, tar-dipped "link"

Devoured a plate of lit sulphur with a fork

Then burning wax

and exploding gunpowder, all the traditional feats that had been passed from fire-eater to fire-eater through the generations.

Gron felt dead as he watched, but then he—his other self who was in control—poured lighter-fluid over himself and danced in the flames, and suddenly the salamanders, the firedrakes, the elementals were dancing all over him, pricking, stabbing with clawed feet, with flashing yellow mouths distorted by the heat from their fiery bodies, and he could hear the audience shriek and shout and cheer as his clothes burned away from his body, revealing his other head, this one now alert and exultant, the grinning phoenix aflame—ah, what a good trick, what a perfect trick; and the elementals wreathed the small head aborning, burned it into spirit, into essence, into themselves; and Gron was on fire, in agony, dying now, dying as he should have years ago when the raiders murdered his family—and murdered him; but the pain was so great, so overwhelming that it became ecstasy, even as his father and other men in the troupe were pouring water over him, trying to douse the elemental fire, trying to save his flesh. But he was no longer flesh, and he performed his last trick, the trick the audience had come to see: he turned into a great golden lizard that ran into the night, flaming, burning, illuminating; and now, now he was free, he could move, he could shout, and the nightmare that was his voice

Was the crackling and hissing of fire.

He took the shape of the boy with two heads, but he was of one mind.

One mind . . .

Now he could look through the eyes of fire, though the eyes of dream; and he could see Drakulic and Slavenka standing over the remains of his flesh. Slavenka was screaming, as if at Gron, as if he had deceived her, which he had. She touched the place where his vestigial head had been. It had been burned away, all burned away, and she kneeled, praying and mumbling, "My son, the fire will save you, but do not let it take you . . . do not let it take you." Her palms were black, burned from touching Gron . . . what had once been Gron.

Drakulic pulled her away, and then he beat his chest and his face, for he had brought Gron back to the fire, had asked him to perform, had begged him.

But all that was dream.

There was a new, burning world before him.

A city . . . .

The great fire of New York had begun. The greatest city on earth was burning, burning as Carthage burned, as Rome burned, as London had burned before it. The city was aflame, a conflagration, a pyre of souls burning into the dead, flat sky; and Gron was the sweeping fire, the pneuma, the very soul of the eternally changing devouring element. He was the fire-maker and the fire; he was the lambent flame, the sleeping fire, the cheerful fire, the cosy fire, the raging, killing fire. His hot soul coursed through the elementals. He was death's bright angel, and with every inhalation and exhalation, he burned the city, wreathing Manhattan and Harlem and Brooklyn and Queens in white heat, melting skyscrapers and boiling the ocean; and he could see . . . he could see without pain, without memory—which were one and the same. The world had turned red and white, the mandrakes and creatures of high temperature danced and made love, changing, interposing, breathing in all the oxygen, boiling, scourging. And Gron drifted in the flames, slept in the fire, awoke recreated in his own incandescent image--

to behold, through the knives of fire and veils of smoke, a vision beautiful and terrible, terrible and eternal. The Ferris Wheel, rotating in the char and dust that had been the park on 79th Street, told his story. Outlined against a molten sky, the great wheel of fire revolved, its spokes and tower smoke and heat; and there were Slavenka and Drakulic in their fiery gondola seats, and the men who had killed his mother and father in the swinging gondolas above them; and as the wheel slowly turned, he could see his life turning, rolling before him, and he wished it gone.

Wished it into the white-hot flames of dreams and death.

And still the city burned.

Skull Beach

This story began with a nightmare—one of those vivid, wide-screen Technicolor nightmares that are more real than real life. I saw a seawall of bones heaving up from the depths of the ocean to create a shallow lagoon: I had to write the story to find out why. The setting is a typical summer holiday beach, and the action combines the folklore of Davey Jones' locker with the sexual fantasies of two adolescent boys: the problem is that nothing is as it seems, and the Skull King has never played fair. As always, interaction with mythic creatures is fraught with danger: it's a rite of passage story, with the usual caveat—"be careful what you wish for."

When the first skull came rolling up the beach, it was a curiosity.

Jason and Jeremy clambered down from their fishing spot to stare at the grinning intruder where it lay in the sunlight, gleaming white and sparkling with salt crystals. Swimmers waded ashore, calling to their friends. Before long, a small crowd of campers from the nearby coastal reserve had converged upon the spot, standing about in the sun, chatting and speculating—a shipwreck, a gangland murder, a suicide. The beach patrol arrived. They called the local police, the police called city headquarters, headquarters called forensics. A team was sent to investigate.

But before the police had even left the city, before the helicopter loads of chattering news crews had taken off, the skull was followed by another wave of bones. The ocean heaved up a jumble of femurs and tibias and ribs and notched vertebrae, dumping them on the sandbar and leaving them to wash up the beach, tumbled by hissing foam and tangled with stranded seaweed.

At first the beach-goers thought—hoped—it was the rest of the body that belonged to the skull. But soon it was clear even to the most amateur anatomist that these bones had come from a multitude of bodies. The king tide rolled in, and with it more skulls, more broken bones to lie bleaching on the little beach, dead white under the hot summer sun. The day wore on, and still the relics kept coming, wave after wave of grinding bones—as if the sea had grown weary of its burden of dead, as if it was spewing up a whole holocaust of scattered bodies and giving them back to the land.

The big waves pounded on through the night, depositing their burden of bones. By morning, when the forensic team finally arrived, the ocean had built a new reef. There, at the high water mark, was a perfect sea wall of packed bones, a new barricade between the surf and the wet, low tide sand. The local wildlife was already moving in—seaweed draped the jutting edges, sand crabs scuttled under settling bones, molluscs suckered into place, sand flies crawled into crevices.

Now the news teams swooped and screamed, squabbling like seagulls over information scraps. The beach was soon littered with cables and canisters and pump-top water bottles; technical crews worried about sand and salt; newscasters posed and postured and theorised. Someone found an old professor who droned on and on about king tides and oceanography and shifting sands and the secrets of the sea. Everyone enjoyed the sensation. No one had a clue what caused it.

Within a few days the lower skulls had grown a slime of green hair. Water backed up behind the new barrier, brackish and swampy. At low tide, the wall of bones began to stink. The media lost interest; the sensation-seekers went home; the forensic team finally got down to some serious study; the campers went back to their sandcastles and sunburn, to their dripping ice cream cones and charcoal-burnt sausages.

Jason and Jeremy didn't care about the swamp smell. They explored anyway, crunching over bones that shifted under their weight, slipping and skittering their way out to the point where they usually fished.

It was Jeremy who hooked the big skull and dragged it to the surface.

"Just another old head bone," he said. He clambered down closer to the water to release his hook. He hefted the skull. "I'll throw it back."

"Don't do that," said the skull.

Jeremy froze, staring at his catch.

The skull had a tongue. "I'll make it worth your while," it said.

The words reverberated in Jeremy's head. He hesitated, looking across to Jason for support. "This can't be happening," he said at last.

Jason shrugged. "Why not? I heard it too."

"Why not indeed," said the skull. "Allow me to introduce myself. I am the King of Skulls. But you can call me Davey."

"Davey?" said Jeremy.

"As in Davey Jones," said the skull.

"Yeah. Right," said Jason. "Sure you are."

"I have many names," the skull said impatiently. "Would you prefer to call me Guardian of the Cavern of the Seas? Lord of the Drowned?"

Jeremy shrugged.

"The point is," said the skull, "that I can grant your heart's desire." It waited a moment, then added: "if I choose, that is."

"What do you want," said Jason tentatively.

"The rest of my skeleton," the skull replied. "I want my bones. You help me, I'll help you."

"You're kidding. How exactly are we supposed to recognise *your* bones in all this lot?" Jeremy spread his hands wide. "There are thousands of old bones here." He raised his arm, ready to throw.

"I didn't say it would be easy," the skull said urgently. "But if you stop waving me about and put me on top of the pile, I'll give directions. *I'll* know."

"I don't think so," said Jeremy. "We'd be here forever."

The skull's voice became wily. "Would you like a down payment? To prove I can deliver?"

"Sure," Jason cut in quickly. "Prove you can deliver our desires."

The skull smirked. "Too easy," it said. "No problem: meet your new girlfriends."

The boys stared. Two girls came walking out of the waves, tall and tanned and blonde and looking like the winners of a wet T-shirt contest. They made straight for Jason and Jeremy.

"Well don't just stand there," said the skull.

Jeremy lowered his arm and put the skull down on top of the nearest pile. Jason was scrambling over the bone wall, clambering his way towards the girls. He was already on the beach and close to them by the time Jeremy had caught up, red-faced and panting.

"Well hello," said one of the identical blondes. "I'm Laura. This is Linda."

"Hello yourself," said Jason. "I'm Jason. This is Jeremy."

All four nodded.

"Are you twins?" said Jeremy.

"Not exactly," Laura replied. She looked sidelong at Linda. "More like sisters."

Laura smoothed back her long hair, then stepped a little closer to Jason. "I think," she said, "that Linda and I should get out of these wet things." She tugged at her dripping T-shirt, pulling it tighter against her erect nipples.

Jason stared, swallowing hard.

"You could help me, if you like," said Laura. "Come on." She took his hand, pulling him with her towards the sand dunes.

"You too," said Linda, reaching for Jeremy.

"Okay," was all he could manage to say. Somewhere, far away beneath the buzz of his hormones, his mind registered that despite their wet clothes the girls' hair wasn't even damp. He suppressed the thought.

The four moved toward the dunes, grasping and groping. By the time they reached a secluded spot the girls were clinging like limpets, and the fondling was getting serious.

Laura kissed Jason long and hard, biting him with small sharp teeth.

Jason tasted blood. He didn't care. He pressed himself against her, trying to ease her back onto the sand.

She pulled away. "We'll need a place," she said. "I'm not doing it out here in the open."

"Why not?" Jason was desperate. "There's nobody around."

"There might be."

"Me neither," said Linda. She had slipped her hand down the front of Jeremy's shorts.

He was finding it hard to breathe. "But there's no place we could use for miles," he said hoarsely. "It's a national park. No buildings."

Linda shrugged. "Ask the king."

"What?"

"The Skull King. Tell him we need a place."

"I knew there'd be a catch," Jeremy muttered.

"We'll wait here," said Laura. "With Jason."

Jason grinned at his friend. "Yeah," he said. "Good idea. You go. You caught him. You ask him."

Jeremy carefully disengaged himself from Linda. "All right," he said huskily. "If I have to."

"And tell him nothing too small," said Laura. "Tell him we want comfortable beds."

"And proper baths," Linda added. "And . . . "

"I get the picture," said Jeremy. "See you."

His shoulders slumped as he turned away to trudge dejectedly back across the hot sand. He retraced his steps and began to climb the wall of bones. He was sweating again by the time he reached the top. The skull was where he had left it, looking out to sea.

"Problem?" said the skull. "Already?"

"It's the girls," said Jeremy.

"You don't like them?"

"It's not that. They want a beach house. They won't have sex with us if they can't do it in a proper place, with beds and everything. They said you'll provide one."

The skull laughed. "Did they now? Greedy things."

"Well," said Jeremy. "Can you?"

"That depends," said the skull. "It's not part of the free sample. You'll have to use up one of your wishes."

"What wishes?"

"Oh come now. It's the usual deal. Haven't you read any stories?" The skull sounded exasperated. "I have certain powers. You perform a service for me, and I give you three wishes in return. Everyone knows how it works."

"I guess so," said Jeremy.

"So, what's it to be? Do you want a beach house or not?"

"I guess so."

"Done. Look back across the dunes."

Jeremy looked. There, where he had left Jason, was a large, open house.

"Thanks," said Jeremy. He turned to leave.

"Take with me with you," said the skull.

"Why?"

"I like to watch."

Jeremy stared with revulsion at the salt-rimed pearls that were the skull's eyes. "Another catch," he said.

"You might need me," the skull countered.

Jeremy sighed. He picked up the skull and carried it with him to the house. The place was magnificent—a cool, inviting structure of marble columns and tall arches hung with filmy drapes that sighed in the sea breeze. Jeremy walked cautiously through tiled corridors, following the sound of giggles until he found a shallow indoor pool where Jason and the girls were laughing and splashing. The girls were naked. So was Jason.

"Come on in," said Jason. He blushed. "We started without you. Sorry."

Jeremy looked down, marvelling at how sleek the girls looked in the water.

"Aren't you forgetting something?" said the skull.

Jeremy jumped.

"You can put me down over there," it said.

Jeremy parked it on a low coffee table and deliberately turned its face to the wall.

"Hey," it said. "I said I like to watch."

"So watch the wall," said Linda. "Dirty old man." She giggled, and turned her attention back to Jeremy. "Don't mind him," she added. "He's just jealous. Why don't you slip out of those sweaty shorts?" She leaned back on her elbows against the shallow steps, arching her back so that her breasts broke the surface of the water.

It was too much. Jeremy forgot to be cautious. He peeled himself out of his shorts and stepped eagerly into the warm waters, slipping willingly into sins of the flesh.

The sex was frenzied. If the boys were innocent, the girls from the sea were not. They slithered and slid, touching and teasing, scratching and biting. And if some things they did didn't seem quite right, Jeremy was too far gone to care. He was drowning in sensual pleasures, sinking into erotic depths he'd never dared to imagine.

At one point Linda slipped from the pool, wrapping a soft towel around herself. "Let's try the bed," she said.

Jeremy followed eagerly. The sex began again. He was vaguely aware that Jason was there too, rutting wildly in the next bedroom. Jeremy lost track of time, lost himself in a miasma of pleasure until, exhausted, he fell asleep. And through the fog of his jumbled, tumbled dreams he heard an argument.

"You promised," a female voice hissed. "You said this time we could keep them."

"They're such nice pets," said a second. "Young and juicy. You promised."

"Patience," said the skull king. "All in good time. They haven't found my bones yet."

"I don't care about your old bones," said Laura.

"Me neither," said Linda. "You don't need them."

"That's not the point," said the skull. "I want them."

"It's your own fault anyway," said Laura. "You ordered your people to clean out the cavern."

"Yeah," said Linda. "You should have put your stupid bones somewhere safe if you didn't want them thrown out with the rest."

"Enough!" the skull's tone was menacing. "What's done is done. And if you want to keep your toy boys, you'll do as I say."

"Maybe," said Laura.

"We'll see," said Linda. She poked at Jeremy with her toe. "Wake up, you. I'm bored. I want to play."

Jeremy desperately wanted not to be awake. His body hurt. He felt sore and chafed. "Let me sleep," he said blearily. "Just for a while."

"No chance," said Linda. "We're not here so you can snore at us. We deserve better than that."

"You bet," said Laura. She was shaking Jason by the shoulder. "You're turning out to be a disappointment."

Jason mumbled something unintelligible.

"In that case," said Linda, "we'll have to amuse ourselves." She pulled Jeremy's hair, hard. "We want clothes," she said. "Gorgeous ones. And jewellery. Lots of jewellery. Tell the Skull."

"That hurts," said Jeremy, awake now. He sat up, rubbing his head.

"Well?" she said.

"Okay. Okay. Skull, give them what they want."

"And is that your true wish?" the skull said wearily. "You've only got three."

"Yeah," said Jeremy. "Anything they want."

The skull king sighed. "Waste of a good wish," he muttered.

A huge, dripping sea chest appeared beside the pool in the marble hall. The girls made a beeline for it, jostling each other in their eagerness. The chest's rusted hinges creaked as Laura and Linda forced it open and began pulling out lengths of filmy silk and handfuls of gold bracelets and necklaces and finger-rings set with emeralds and rubies and sapphires and diamonds.

"This is more like it," said Laura, hauling out long ropes of pearls and slipping them over her head.

"Oh yes," said Linda. She sauntered to the mirror, draping her body in long swathes of priceless silk brocade. "This is more my style." She reached for a long strand of black pearls with a diamond clasp. "These will do for my hair, I think."

"No you don't." Laura snatched back the pearls. "The pearls are mine. You know I always have the pearls." She rummaged in the trunk, came up with a glittering tiara. "Here, have some diamonds."

"I'm so *over* diamonds," said Linda. "And I don't see why you should always have the pearls." She grabbed at them.

Laura held them just out of reach.

Linda dropped her brocade and lunged at Laura. She slipped on the wet floor, clutching at her friend.

Laura swung a punch.

Both girls went down in a tangle of glittering baubles, fists flailing. They fought dirty, raking at each other with their long fingernails, grabbing handfuls of hair, trying to get close enough to bite.

Their screams woke Jason. He scrambled to his feet, and came into the room at a run. "That's enough!" he shouted. Without thinking he waded into the fight, bending down to pull the girls apart.

They turned on him, clawing and kicking and biting. Laura grabbed his genitals and squeezed hard.

Jason gasped in pain, stepping back instinctively.

Linda caught him with a flying blow behind the knees. He overbalanced, slipped, and fell heavily. There was a loud crack as his head hit the tiled corner of the pool. And then there was silence.

"Oh well," said Laura. She shrugged.

"Boring," said Linda.

Both girls turned their attention back to the finery in the sea chest. Jason lay still as a stone beside the pool.

Jeremy staggered into the room, bleary-eyed. It took him a moment to make sense of what he saw. Then he dropped to his knees, desperately checking for signs of life. There was an ugly cut on Jason's temple, and his breathing was shallow, ragged. Jeremy splashed his friend's face with water, trying to help him back into consciousness. "What happened?" he asked the skull.

"A minor misunderstanding," the skull replied.

"I wish none of this had ever happened," Jeremy muttered.

"None of it?" said the skull.

"None of it," Jeremy said vehemently.

"And it that your final wish?" said the skull. "To wish it all undone?"

"Yeah. I should have thrown you back. I knew you'd be trouble." He paused, thinking. "I guess I can still do that."

"Not so fast, my friend." The skull's tone was hard as old bone. "You've taken my down payment. The girls gave you a good time, didn't they?"

Jeremy nodded miserably.

"So now it's your turn to pay up. I want my bones. And you're going to search for me."

"I can't leave Jason like this."

"Why not? He's out cold anyway. He'll come around eventually— probably. No one will ever know."

"I'll know." Jason looked at the skull with loathing. "How could I live with myself if I left my best friend?"

"Touching." The skull yawned. "But you still owe me."

Jeremy was thinking hard. "What if I wish Jason back to health? Can you do that?"

"Maybe," said the skull.

"Didn't think so," said Jeremy. "You can't do anything real, can you?" He gestured wildly at the beach house, at the giggling girls. "This is all lies and illusion, isn't it?"

"Bravo," the skull sneered. "If I had my hand bones I'd applaud you."

"So get rid of it. My final wish is to put everything back as it was."

The skull sighed. "And then you'll reunite me with my bones?"

"If I can."

"Very well." The beach house simply vanished, and with it all the treasures and finery. All that remained was a flattened patch of sand, two outraged naked girls, and Jason, who moaned as he opened his eyes.

"Hey!" said Laura.

"Why did you have to go and do that?" said Linda.

"Oh shut up," said the skull. "You were too greedy. The game's over. Go."

Before the girls could reply they began to change. Their torsos stretched, their arms shrivelled, their legs fused. Finally they lay in the sand at Jeremy's feet, two sleek, shining eels with female faces, faces with sharp, pearly teeth and wide blue eyes framed by long blonde hair. They paused for a moment, then slithered away, side by side, heading back into the ocean.

Jeremy felt sick.

"Satisfied?" the skull asked.

Jeremy nodded, watching in horror as his lover wriggled towards the water. "What are they?" he managed at last.

"Lamias," the skull replied matter-of-factly.

"Huh?"

"Snake women. These ones are related to certain water faeries," said the skull. "Pretty things, but unreliable, like all of them." He paused. "But they have their uses," he added. "You enjoyed them."

Jeremy deliberately turned his back on the water, focussing instead on his friend.

"What happened?" said Jason, standing up at last. "I feel terrible."

"You don't want to know," Jeremy replied.

"And now," said the skull, its tone businesslike. "Your friend has recovered. And if you'll be so good as to take me back to the point, we'll just call it a day. No hard feelings, I hope."

Jeremy picked up the skull. "Jason," he said, "are you okay? "Can you walk?"

"Sure," said Jason.

"Then we'll just do this one last thing."

The boys made their way back across the sand dunes until they came to the water's edge. Jeremy looked at the bone wall, noticed two other boys farther out, fishing off the point. He hesitated.

"Why should I put you back?" he said to the skull. "So you can do this to the next person?"

Skull chuckled. "You said you'd help me."

"And I will," Jeremy said grimly. "I know now where *your* bones must be. If you're Davey Jones, your bones are still at the bottom of the ocean, in your locker. I'm going to reunite you with them." He didn't wait to talk about it. He hefted the skull and threw as hard as he could throw.

The skull splashed into the sea and sank into the ocean. It was laughing as it went under, sinking down and down and down to its home in the Cavern of the Seas, where the dead men lost their bones.

Tigershow

This magical-realist story is based on hallucinations reported by returned servicemen suffering post-traumatic stress disorder. The protagonist endures constant migraines. In his mind, he inhabits the "forests of the night" of Blake's poem Tyger Tyger, conflated with flashbacks to the real jungles of his military service. When his present domestic reality blurs into outraged memory of the live sex "Tiger Shows' of the title, he is stalked by the tigers of his nightmares: and something has to give.

Robert had another one of his headaches. They'd been with him since his stint as peacekeeper up on the Thai border. Nothing helped. He drove in a red haze, the pain at his temples blurring his vision, cruelly sharpening his other faculties. He gripped the wheel tight, too tight, straining white knuckled against sensory overload. He could hear the deep resonant purring, a rumbling basso underneath the steady thrum of his engine. He could smell the musky cat smell, the feral taint underlying the hot macadam, the diesel fumes, the gritty smog.

The tigers were everywhere. Stalking, always stalking. If he let his eyes unfocus, very slightly, the predators were there: he glimpsed the outline of a stripy haunch in the stark barred shade of a railing fence, saw the edge of a twitching tail almost concealed in the palm fronds of a roadside planter box, recognised the yellow reflection of tiger eyes in a plate glass shopfront window.

Robert concentrated, conscious of his own sweaty flesh smell close about him. He narrowed his gaze, tried to blend with the moving herd. But he knew in his heart, in his guts, in his bones, that he was tiger meat. Today's special, *Robert tartare.*

Adrenalin pumping, he accelerated sharply. And as he drove, he cursed: raging at the traffic, the noise, and the summer heat. All he wanted was to get home, out of the stuffy car, out of his scratchy, stifling suit. He needed to get away from the glaring sunlight, away from tiger country. He needed to be quiet, to be safe. The old Bar Beach house might belong to Adele's family, but it was his only refuge. Mercifully near the sea, it offered respite, offered hope. There would be an evening breeze. Maybe at dusk he would take a walk on the beach, clear his head. Let the boom and crash and roar of the surf drown out the threat reverberating in the hunters' incessant purring.

But tigers were patient. They didn't mind the heat. They would wait.

Stalking, waiting, stalking.

Burning.

Robert caught a glimpse of receding orange taillights as another car pulled away from his house. Untrimmed yellow bougainvillea whipped across his windscreen as he turned into his driveway. Bright birds flew up, shrieking cries of alarm. He sensed the tigers, here ahead of him. Violating his sanctuary. His lawngrass was summer dry, tawny, striped with long afternoon shadow. Dangerous.

The moment the creaking garage door announced him, his daughters came running across the yard, oblivious to the threat. Red haired and freckled like their father, they were both brimming with news, vying with each other to tell it first.

"Daddy. Daddy. Guess what?"

Robert squared his shoulders, composed his face, tried to look fatherly.

"What, sweetheart?"

"Uncle George had a heart attack. He's in the hospital. There was an ambulance with lights and sirens and everything."

"And Grandma and Aunty Beryl and Aunty Val were here with Mummy."

"They just left."

"And Aunty Maggie has come to live with us."

Robert's fatherly facade cracked.

"Christ almighty!"

He strode up the path, flanked by anxious children.

"Adele!"

"Don't shout, I'm right here. In the kitchen."

The bamboo blinds were rolled down against the gold-black heat of the setting sun. Robert told himself the purring undertone was just the refrigerator. Adele sat at the scrubbed table, looking tired and worried. She was wearing a dress that Robert hated, a loose Community Aid handcrafted cotton sundress in a muddy yellow woodblock print that drained her skin of life. She had pulled her mouse blonde hair straight back into a ponytail, exposing a pale freckled face so innocent of cosmetics that her untinted eyelashes almost disappeared against her wan complexion. Her upper lip was sheened by perspiration in the close atmosphere of late afternoon. She looked young, and vulnerable.

She turned to face the storm.

Robert's face was livid, his words almost a snarl. "Do we *have* to have *that* woman in the house? Maggie never lifts a finger unless its around a glass—spends half her life in the Beauty parlour and the other half in bed. She'll wear you out fetching and carrying for her. It's a wonder George hasn't had his heart attack before now."

"Sssh. She'll hear you. It's only for a couple of days. She doesn't drive, and we live closest to the hospital. She's family, Rob. It's the least we can do."

"And we'll never hear the end of it from your mother if we don't. Right?"

"Don't be nasty. Aunt Margaret is Mother's sister. Of course she's concerned."

"Then let *her* put her up. I don't like you rushing around playing taxi whenever there's another crisis in that interminable family of yours. Your place is here. With me. You have more than enough to do with two small daughters. That's why you quit teaching, remember? And your mother thinks . . . "

"Don't start that again. You know Mother's too ill for houseguests."

"So what about the others, then? You had the female mafia round here drinking cups of tea and calling the shots, making decisions affecting *my* family. Without consulting me!"

"You were at work, Rob. You know how you hate to be disturbed there. Uncle George's collapse was very sudden. I did the best I could."

"Our house stinks already."

Adele swiftly removed an ashtray overflowing with lipstick stained butts.

"Look, Rob, Aunty is old and she's terribly upset. I've put her upstairs in the spare room. She'll be company for me, and she's very good with the girls. Try to be nice. For my sake."

The stairs creaked. Aunt Margaret—"Maggie to my friends"—was nervously dressed to the nines in an overtight red silk suit with *faux* tigerskin trim and shoes to match. As usual, she had overdone it: too much rouge, too much lipstick, too much jewellery. She descended at full sail, corsets straining. In her perfumed wake trailed her roly-poly pedigreed Pekinese, Soo Tze Wong, an overfed untidy little bundle of yapping yellow-brown hair.

"Bobbie, darling! How lovely to see you. It's been simply ages. Come and give your poor old aunty a kiss."

Robert found himself crushed against an overlarge bosom, trying not to gag in its Crabtree & Evelyn miasma of musky rose. He glowered at Adele over her aunt's shoulder, grimaced as his captor smeared a bright red lipstick kiss across his cheek before releasing him. His headache throbbed.

"It's *very* kind of you to let me stay over, Bobbie. I'm worried sick about George, and I just couldn't bear to be alone in that big old house without him. His heart, you know. Just like a man, not to let on there's anything wrong until he keels over in the street. Right outside the cake shop. Lucky Mrs Rowan was looking out at the time. Well, she'll certainly have something to tell her customers. It's a hotbed of gossip, that cake shop. Still, he's in good hands at the hospital, and all we can do now is wait and hope. I must say I could do with a drink. Scotch would be fine, dear. I'll just sit over here, out of everyone's way."

She stopped to draw breath. Robert seized the moment:

"We don't allow dogs in the house, Margaret. They shed hair; they make me sneeze. I'll just put yours outside with our Butch. The girls can feed them both later."

Maggie looked horrified.

"You can't put my poor little Soozy outside in the dark with that big black Butch monster of yours. Anything could happen. He'd be all over her." She waggled a coquettish finger: "We don't want any hanky-panky of that sort, do we dear."

Robert's face darkened.

"Of course not, Aunty." Adele was solicitous, anxious in the glare of her husband's outrage.

"It'll be all right, Rob, just this once. I'll see to it. Soo Tze will be fine in the laundry. She can curl up safe and warm in the cane basket."

Adele sighed, visibly wishing she too could curl up somewhere safe.

"Now why don't both of you have a quiet drink in the lounge while I finish cooking dinner?"

The uneasy truce lasted through a strained and awkward meal. Robert ate methodically, keeping his eyes on his plate. His roast chicken tasted of ashes. The children were subdued, eating their vegetables without protest, knowing better than to interrupt one of his moods. As the dishes were cleared and conversation limped into uncomfortable silence, Adele declined her aunt's perfunctory offer of help in the kitchen.

"Why don't you take Emma and Amy upstairs, Aunty? They'd love a story before bedtime."

"And no spoiling their teeth with sweets."

"Why Bobbie, I wouldn't dream of it. Not after all the fuss you made about those Christmas chocolates. I've brought fruit this time. Cherries."

The children looked crestfallen.

Safely upstairs, she put a warning finger to her lips then fished in her handbag to produce a ribboned package of glacé cherries sparkling with sugar crystals. Robert listened to the stifled giggles with suspicion, but forbore immediate investigation.

"She doesn't mean any harm, Rob. Let it be."

But Robert was irritable, restless. He couldn't relax. His head hurt. In the soft quiet of the evening air he could just hear a low, faint growling that was not quite the usual background roar of the sea. Something moved against the softly shadowed light of the yellow midsummer moon that hung heavy in the heavens. Night prowlers.

"It's too quiet up there. They're up to something."

"Probably falling asleep over the story. I'll take a look."

"No, you watch your movie. Relax. I'll go."

Robert's first explosive shout brought Adele running up the stairs. Frozen in tableau before the hall mirror were Emma and Amy, their nightgowns festooned with Aunty's beads, their lips pouting red in Aunty's pillarbox lipstick, their expressions bewildered by the force of their father's wrath.

"Get that muck off your faces. Now. This minute. Before I tan your hides for you!"

The girls fled to the bathroom.

Adele, shielding the children, coaxed the combatants back downstairs.

Robert was still shouting. "I won't have my daughters tricked out like painted whores."

Aunt looked fazed. "Really, Bobbie, calm down. It was just a bit of fun. Dress ups. That's all. A little sparkle never hurt anyone."

She swayed slightly.

Robert caught a hint of whisky.

"I *know* what you get up to, on all those long afternoons. You and George. And at your age! Well, not in my house you don't."

Ignoring Adele's frantic signals, Aunty tried again to mollify him. "Don't be so uptight, Bobbie. There's no harm done." She giggled. "Like they say in the song: *Little bits of powder, little bits of paint, makes a lady seem like, what she really ain't.* They're little girls. They deserve some glamour once in a while."

Robert felt the tightening at his temples. The red haze was back. The low, throaty growling was drawing closer. His voice rose above it.

"Well I won't have it. I won't have my children corrupted. You're a guest here, Margaret. Do what you like in your own house, but not in mine."

"It's not *your* house."

"Bloody family! Always rubbing it in that it's your money. Always trying to take control. Well they're *my* children, and what I say goes!"

"I won't stay where I'm not welcome."

"Suit yourself."

The sound of tearing fabric interrupted the argument. The girls had crept halfway downstairs to eavesdrop, and Emma had trodden on her sister's trailing hemline.

Robert looked up . . .

There were two young girls on the rickety bamboo staircase. They were much too young, with painted red lips and red fingernails and a price on their services. Out too late, touting for custom in the noisy bar.

He tasted the bitter Mekong whisky burning in his throat, twisting his guts, found himself pushed close to the stage in the crush of soldiers. Too close. A rank sweet smell of sex and sweat surged through the haze of cheap dope and cheaper Camel smoke that thickened what was left of the air in the room. The egg lady had finished her act. Two naked prepubescent girls now dripped candlewax onto the heaving shoulders of a spotlit woman efficiently fellating a grinning corporal. Cheers and whoops announced his orgasm, and as the woman rose to bow, dripping wax and sperm, Robert's stomach heaved. He turned his burning face away. And found himself eye to eye with a teenager patiently arousing a large yellow dog, in readiness for the next act.

A drunken chorus began its chanting, beating time with bottles and glasses:

"Old Mother Hubbard, she went to the cupboard, to get her poor doggie a bone . . . ."

Girl and dog ascended the smoky stage.

Stiff backed and stiff groined, Robert fought his way out, his tented trousers drawing wolf whistles from his mates and lewd offers from the girls. His flaming cheeks matched his carroty hair.

"Hey, Aussie boy, let me make you a man."

"Hey, Robbo, give her one for me."

"For you, discount, big boy."

"Show us what you've got, mate."

"Pussy pie, sugar?"

"Come on, your turn next on stage—looks like parts of you are ready . . . "

"You can try before you buy, guy."

"Don't be a wimp—you might be dead tomorrow."

"You maybe want Greek, mister?"

The dog was barking now. The chanting got louder: *"And when she bent over, Rover drove her, 'cause he had a bone of his own."*

Unsure of whether the applause was for the dog or the recitation, Robert refused to look back. His anger pushed him free of the crush of bodies. His breath came in ragged gulps. And there, in the marginally cooler air of the doorway, was the Madam herself. She loomed, overweight and overblown in a too tight red silk *cheong san*, fanning her bulk with a draggled peacock fan, grinning at his discomfiture.

"Wassamatta, soldier? You no like Tigershow? You want maybe something little bit more special?"

She winked conspiratorially.

"I have clean girls, virgins. Clean boys too. Very young. Little bit extra . . . ."

She didn't finish the sentence. Robert lunged, caught at the silk, dragged her off her feet. He felt bones crack as his fist collided with her jaw, heard the shrieks of women, and heard someone crying his name, pleading with him to stop. Small hands were pulling him away, tugging at his clothing. Cold water hit his face. He came up spluttering . . .

Adele was sobbing as she hauled desperately at his bunched fist.

Aunty Maggie was slumped in a chair, silent, her neck twisted at an unnatural angle. Her cheek was a swollen lump of bruise purple, her lipsticked mouth drooled a trail of blood and splintered tooth.

Adele dropped Robert's bloodstained arm. Felt frantically for her aunt's pulse. Ran for the phone.

And there, on the staircase, were his terrified daughters. Two silent, roundeyed ghosts. They peered through the bannisters at the wreckage of their livingroom, at broken flower stems and fragments of shattered crystal, at the ruin of their family.

In the sudden stillness, the purring was unbearably loud, a monstrous animal engine reverberating through the forests of the night, echoing against the stars.

Tigershapes were everywhere, looming larger, closer, as amber strobes approached the house, throwing the foliage into sharp-striped relief, revealing predators crouched in every shadow.

Robert turned, slowly, ignoring the pain in his throbbing head, pulling the shreds of his courage about himself, willing his flesh and bones to obey.

Smearing aside his hot, slow tears, he stepped out into the sultry moonlight to meet his tigers.

Burning.

Locked in the laundry, Soo Tze was yapping furiously.

Hell is Where the Heart Is

This is my Valentine's Day story. The plethora of hearts and flowers and sentimental overkill in the media got me thinking about phrases like "I give you my heart," which led inexorably to an image of surgical heart transplant and the obvious question: what would happen to a transplant recipient if the donor's one true love really was embedded in the heart muscle? In matters of the heart, we are all at risk.

Tell me who invented the human heart. Tell me, and show me where he was hanged.

LAWRENCE DURRELL

The man in the immaculate Saville Row suit was talking at her, his words spilling across his polished desk in her direction. Each phrase held some new horror, the deep-down visceral gut-wrenching *personal* horror of words like terminal, and transplant, and urgent. She felt paralysed, trying desperately to focus through the shock. His lips moved again: "Mrs Hardcastle, Penelope, would you like someone with you through the rest of this consultation. It often helps. Is that your husband in the waiting room?"

Penny nodded, numbly. The surgeon patted her shoulder encouragingly as he stood, moving past her to speak softly to his secretary. Penny was not encouraged. She stared through the window at the park below, where other people were going about their lives. She barely noticed when John, his face frowning deep with concern, eased into the seat beside her and took her cold hand in his.

The surgeon went on, his composed, professional voice grating on her nerves. "I believe in being honest upfront about these things.

In the long run, false hope is much more damaging than plain truth. And I believe these final tests I'm ordering will confirm my opinion that Penelope's situation is dangerous. All the indicators tell me she will almost certainly need a heart transplant in the very near future if she is to survive."

"How soon," said John. His voice was hoarse with worry. "How long have we got?"

"There's never an exact answer. But we are talking weeks, not months. I want to re-admit Penelope into the hospital as quickly as possible. It is absolutely essential that the heart is monitored constantly, and that the patient is rested and fully prepared for the procedure as soon as a suitable donor organ becomes available."

The conversation went on, the surgeon drawing diagrams and explaining procedures, roughly sketching out incision lines and insertion points on office notepaper. The consulting room smelled of disinfectant, and soap. Penny was trying hard to concentrate. She felt as though the men were discussing a technical problem, a problem in pipes and valves that happened to need replacing. Not Penny. Not her body.

Her husband was speaking again: "Forgive my asking, but how many of these transplants have you done?"

The surgeon spread his hands wide. "You don't want to know how many," he said wearily. "I lost count a long while back. By all means seek a third opinion. All I can do is assure you that this is routine surgery for me. There are never any guarantees."

John shrugged. "For you, this happens every day. For us, it's new territory. It's traumatic. We need to understand what is happening here."

"Of course. And there will be a whole support team looking after Penelope. I'm just the first step in the process. I'll give you some literature, put you in contact with our special psychologist, make sure you both have a chance to meet the rest of the surgical team. The safety net is there for you both, and for your family, John. You won't be alone."

They rose, shook hands. The surgeon said: "Let me know what you decide. If there's something you want to go over, any point you need clarified, just call."

He walked them to the door.

Despite John's comforting arm about her shoulders, as they left the consulting suite Penny felt very, very alone.

When she awoke in her narrow hospital bed, the world seemed far away. She seemed to have been transformed into some strange fleshly machine, a machine whose purpose was unclear. There were wiggly green lines on a monitor screen whose pulsing lights confirmed her existence. The machine hummed gently, its needs fed by the tubes that snaked in and out of her body at various points, monitoring vital signs, carrying blood and saline and God-knew-what else.

A tired-looking man came softly into the room, sat himself down wearily beside her bed, gently took her cold fingers in his warm hand, careful not to disturb the taped needle that dripped measured painkillers into her veins. His creased face looked slept-in, as rumpled as his suit. With him were two pale children, radiating anxiety. The girl clutched a drooping bunch of flowers from the downstairs charity shop.

"It's me, Penny. John. Your husband. Will and Emma are here. Your children. Can you hear me?"

She nodded, lifting her head a fraction from the pillow.

He squeezed her fingers. "Look. Emma has brought you flowers. She'll pop them into a vase for you."

Emma fiddled with the blooms, obviously glad of something to do.

"Mother sends her love." John turned away briefly, depositing a plastic bag in the closet. "Your clean pyjamas are in there, if the nurse asks."

His monologue dragged to a halt when Penny did not respond. John's need of her was clear as he gently buried his face in her dark hair, hiding his tears from his children. He sniffed, blew his nose, then kissed her lightly on the forehead.

Penny managed a weak smile. "Don't worry," she said. "I'll be alright."

She lapsed back into her drugged doze after the effort of acknowledging her visitors. She knew them, of course, but it didn't feel right.

The feeling still wasn't right when she finally returned home.

The new heart did not make that little skip the old one always had when John took her in his arms.

She wept her frustration, feeling miserable and disconnected.

John was patient. "You've been through a huge trauma, love," he would say. "Let's just give it time."

So she let him love her, feeling warmth, appreciation, sympathy, and companionship when he was with her, sometimes even desire. But not love. The new heart did not love him, no matter how much she willed it.

It was months before she realized it loved someone else. Someone she didn't know. Someone she'd never even met.

And it meant to have him back.

After a dreary convalescence, the day came when Penny returned, thankfully, to her job at the bank. The tedium of customers worrying about their small holdings seemed like bliss after her boredom at home.

On Friday afternoon her friend Cassie caught up with her in the tea room. "Come on Penny. Let me take you for drink. We'll celebrate your release back into the world. Everyone shows up on Friday, and they'll all want to catch up with you."

Penny hesitated, twisting her scarf in her fingers. "I don't know that I'm ready for crowds."

"Nonsense. We'll just go for one drink. The *Heartache*'s just next door, after all. It's not as if you have to go out of your way or anything."

"John will worry if I'm late."

"So phone him. Leave a message. He'll understand."

"Okay. But just one drink."

"Great. I'll meet you in the foyer at five."

They rode up in the elevator with a chattering group of colleagues to the top floor of the plush *Intercontinental Hotel*, where the *Heartache* bar was popular with city employees. Throughout the week the sleek cocktail lounge furnishings and spectacular view over the city made it a favourite pickup spot for the well-heeled and terminally single. But on Friday nights Happy Hour was thronged with black-suited bankers and insurance executives swapping stories of this week's ups and downs, exchanging hot tips and office gossip. The five o'clock rush to nowhere.

Penny was enjoying herself. She was the centre of curious attention. She was ordering her second glass of Riesling when Cassie tapped her on the arm.

"Don't look now," said Cassie, "but we're being stalked by the head-office wolf."

"Who?"

"Grant Simpson. Hot-shot broker. Corporate Accounts. Private clients. Thinks he's God's to gift women." She giggled. "The women he dates mostly want to give him back! A new girl for every party—no-one sticks around long enough to go out with him twice."

"Is he really that awful?"

"Worse, now that his wife died. Poor Anne, she adored him. God knows why. He cheated on her every chance he got. He was always on the prowl. She didn't deserve to be treated like that, and now she's dead. And," she added significantly, "he was driving."

"Car accident?"

"Intersection smash. The passenger side was hit. Anne was killed outright. Broken neck. He walked away without a scratch. There's no justice in the world."

"You'd think he'd die of guilt."

"Fat chance. Brace yourself, Penny, here he comes."

The man closing in on them was stylishly, fastidiously turned out. A wolf in wolf's clothing: suit by Armani, hand-made snowy fine linen shirt set off by a Hermes dark patterned silk tie, shoes by Gucci. He was a real fashion plate. His thinning, sandy-blonde hair was cut boyishly short, parted on one side so that its ends flopped deliberately over his forehead to set off his ice-blue eyes. He should have been handsome, but the effect was too calculated to be convincing. His open features were overlaid with complacency, a sneering self-regard that Penny loathed at first sight.

The heart skipped a beat.

His advance was downright predatory. Penny felt frozen, trapped in the headlights of his intense regard as he moved in on her.

The heart was beating faster.

"Hi Cassie. How's business with the middle classes? Who's your lovely friend?"

Penny tucked her corporate-logo scarf tighter about her neck, suddenly self-conscious about her surgical scars.

"Hello Grant. This is Penny. She's married."

Penny smiled weakly.

"Grant Simpson. Pleased to meet you." He was standing too close, his Poison after-shave using up all the oxygen. He held out his hand, shook hers for a beat longer than protocol permitted, smiling engagingly.

Penny looked down, flushing slightly. She noticed the engraved initials on the stylish Dunhill cigarette case and lighter he'd placed carefully on the bar.

"That's nice. What's the U stand for? Unusual?"

He sighed, dramatically. "Everyone asks that. Might as well get it over. My father was a Civil War buff, and with Simpson for a surname, he just couldn't resist naming his son for his hero. Read it with an imaginary comma: Grant, Ulysses S. It was hell at school, but I learned to fight real quick. Respect through skinned knuckles, grudge matches, and long hours in the gym." He posed for her. "Anyway, I think of myself as more the original Ulysses type, always up for a new adventure." He leaned closer. "And my best friends call me Gus."

Penny smiled again, finding it suddenly difficult to breathe in the thickening atmosphere.

"Gus. We had a tomcat called Gus once—short for Asparagus. The most exotic name the kids could think of at the time."

He swallowed hard at the implied comparison, recovered immediately to say: "You have children then?"

"Two. A boy and a girl. Teenagers now."

"Charming." He lowered his voice. "You look like you could use some air. What say we go somewhere quieter . . . "

Penny looked around quickly for her friend. "Sorry, Gus. Cassie, we have to run. I promised I'd be back by seven," she said brightly. She took Cassie by the arm and steered her firmly in the direction of the door. "I can't believe I was flirting with that creep!" she said.

"How much wine have you had?"

"Just the one glass." Penny blushed. The heart was still racing. "Is he really as bad as the gossips say?"

"He's worse. Heartless. I used to find Anne sobbing her heart out in the Ladies. She really loved the bastard, and he treated her like dirt."

Penny sighed, willing her heartbeat to slow to a calmer rate.

The ride home was uneventful.

Next Monday morning when she arrived at the office there was a single red rose on her desk, with a card bearing one word—Friday.

Penny spent the rest of the week in an agony of indecision, listening to the argument between her head and her heart. Her mind rehearsed the overwhelming evidence against anything so foolish as a comfortably married woman getting involved with another man, especially one who was everything she despised, especially one who was already the mainstay of city gossip. The heart did not listen. It just felt warm at the thought of him.

The heart won.

Next Friday, she was in the *Heartache* bar at five past five. He was totally self-possessed as he strolled over to where she sat fiddling with her drink, took her hand, and bent to whisper: "Let's get out of here."

She did not resist.

His apartment was close by, one of those new inner-city warehouse conversions where mellow old timbers clashed horribly with brushed stainless steel fittings and too-bright feature walls. Very trendy. Everything was in its place, neat and cold and closed up tight.

"Come in," he said. "Champagne's on ice."

His arrogance was breathtaking in its casual presumption. He moved to kiss her, and Penny felt suddenly like meat being steered towards a marble slab.

The heart skipped a beat.

"I can't," she said.

"Of course you can. That's why you're here."

Her throat constricted. She could only nod her assent.

He peeled away her clothing, obviously fascinated by her scars. He ran his tongue down the purplish-red length of the long gash that started at her breastbone, tracing the slightly raised welt of the healing tissue. "It's weird, this transplant stuff. How does it feel, having part of someone else inside you?" He grinned at his rehearsed *double entendre*. "Apart from the usual, of course."

"It's just a muscle, Gus. Nothing more. The surgeons are wonderful technicians, but that's all it is. A spare parts replacement service."

He reached for her, pulling her down upon the bed.

Penny closed her eyes, her heart beating wildly at his embrace.

He was an expert lover, though what surfaced of Penny's mind regarded him as a bit too clinical. He focussed on his technique, turning her this way and that, putting himself through his paces, bringing her to an aching climax beneath him. It was soon finished.

They sprawled in the rumpled sheets, sated. His pillow talk was desultory, almost bored. Penny caught him sneaking a look at his watch.

She rose, collected her clothes, headed for the bathroom. There were fresh towels laid out. Confident bastard.

When she returned, he had dressed in jeans and a fresh shirt, ready to go.

He grinned at her. "Well, that was fun. Where would you like me to drop you? Home? Back at the bar?"

"No thanks. I'll make my own way home from here. It will look less obvious."

He laughed. "Maybe."

She moved closer to him, reached to kiss him. "Until next Friday, then?"

His smiled vanished. "No. Of course not. You can't imagine we'd want some kind of involvement, Penny. One to a customer, that's me. It's not as if we were in love or anything. We're just two consenting adults, having a bit of mutual fun. End of story."

He paused, considering. "Truth is, I just wanted to try it with a transplant person, that's all. I'm sorry if you imagined it was something more. I thought you'd feel the same about me—novelty value."

Penny could not prevent the tears that welled up, reddening her dark eyes. She fished a crumpled tissue out of her blazer pocket and dabbed at her nose. The heart was beating wildly.

"No," she said. "I didn't realize. I should have."

His eyes were colder now. "Oh stop it, for godsakes," he said. "You're not hurt. You remind me of my wife. She was one of your bleeding-heart organ donor types—always going on about the greater good and social responsibility and all that. There must still be bits of her around everywhere—cornea, kidneys, lungs, heart . . . "

Penny felt a chill feather up her spine.

"When did she die," she said.

"Last April. Why?"

"What date, Gus?" Penny's mouth was dry, the words an effort.

"What does it matter?"

"It matters. What *date*?"

"April 9th. Why? What's so important?"

"The date of my transplant, that's what."

The heart was beating erratically now.

Incredibly, Gus was laughing. "Well I'll be damned. This is great. Two women at once." He tapped her chest. "Hello in there, Annie. Did you miss me?"

Penny pulled away, appalled. "We don't know for certain, Gus. It could just be coincidence. It just freaked me out, you know?"

"Well, coincidence or not it's a hell of a trip!"

Penny grabbed her bag, bolted for the door, slammed it after her. She hailed the first cab she could find, and collapsed into the back seat, crying hysterically, her heart beating a-rhythmically now.

"You alright, love?" The taxi driver sounded concerned.

Penny managed a strangled answer: "Fine, really. Just had a bit of a shock. I'll be alright soon."

By the time she reached home she'd dried her tears, but the heart still hurt, and there was an ominous tightening in her chest. She paid the driver, walked unsteadily to her front door. Emma opened it.

"Mum, you look awful!"

"Thanks. I'll just lie down for a while. I'll be okay. A difficult day, that's all."

Emma looked doubtful, but left to make her a cup of tea. When she returned, Penny was curled up in pain, clutching her chest.

"I've taken my pills," she said. "They don't help. Call the emergency contact number for me, Emma. I think I'm going to need the hospital."

Emma dashed for the phone.

Penny was much worse by the time she was wheeled into the hospital. Her surgeon was there, his expression concerned. His diagnosis was instant.

"Rejection. Let's move, everyone—she hasn't got much time."

Rejection. The word resonated in Penny's mind as a needle slid into a vein, and she lost her last, tenuous hold on consciousness.

She did not re-awaken. Ever.

Upstairs, in Recovery, Calypso Jones was drifting into post-operative awareness.

Her new heart felt all wrong, somehow.

Full Moon in Virgo

This is a ghost story, and a love story. It began with a drive with friends over the spectacular Hill Fort of Eggardon Heath, a drive that became seriously dangerous when the mist rolled in and we could no longer see the track. Eggardon is an ancient place, and there are ghost stories aplenty associated with it. I had read reports about people who swear that they have seen a Roman cohort marching along a road that is no longer there. For this story I chose a single Roman soldier, a guard assigned to the temple of the Goddess, and aligned him with a modern woman whose needs are strangely similar to his own. On the night of Beltane, the doors between one world and the next are open, and if the Goddess permits . . .

Fifteen minutes after Martin's unexpected arrival at Selena's isolated cottage in Kings Farm Lane, the argument had begun again.

The two of them had made it through the pleasantries: the cups and cakes were set out by the fireplace in the front room, the tea was poured, they'd settled into armchairs, chatting amicably about the relative health of family and friends. It couldn't last.

Martin's timing was instinctively bad, as usual. Tonight was Beltane, and Selena's tiny New Age shop in Bridport would be busy this afternoon, dispensing crystals and incense and amulets to clients who observed the pagan rites, selling Selena's gorgeous hand-painted silk scarves and deep-fringed shawls to the growing number of patrons who appreciated original design-work.

"Look, Martin," she said. "I really don't need this today. Can't we just have a reasonable cup of tea together and try to be friends? I have to leave soon to open up in town. Business will be hectic later."

"Your *little* shop." The words were a snarl. "All that mumbo-jumbo: mantras and incense and healing crystals, self-help books for the terminally bored. Zodiac signs and tarot readings." His voice was getting louder, harsher. "Not to mention all that pagan chanting that you peddle, and your rituals for that goddess creature! Fat middle-aged women dancing about naked at full moon! It's too disgusting to think about! You can't possibly *believe* in any of it."

He stopped, redfaced, to catch his breath.

She shrugged, hunched her shoulders slightly, preparing to weather his storm.

He was pacing the room now, kicking at her exquisite Turkestan rugs. "You can't live like this forever!" He waved his arms about vaguely, his gestures taking in the clutter of silks and baubles on the dining table, the litter of papers she'd planned to sort that morning. "Come back to London with me, Selena. Come back to the real world."

"This looks real enough to me. I like it here. It's beautiful. It's quiet. I can be myself here: I can walk in the bluebell wood, I can listen to the birds. I can work here."

"You call this work?" He picked up a handful of newly screened silk scarves, and then let them fall fluttering to the floor in bright confusion. "You call this art? Mucking some paint onto bits of cloth? Stringing a few beads onto leather thongs and flogging them off to gullible tourists?" His voice cracked with contempt. "It's downright embarrassing!"

"It's what I do, Martin, and I like it."

He snorted. "You're away with the fairies if you ask me!"

"Nobody asked you!"

He looked her up and down, taking in her shining long red-gold hair, the flowing white cheesecloth blouse, the full, multicoloured silk skirt that swirled above her soft calfskin boots, the heavy silver Virgo pendant that hung between her breasts. "Just look at you," he said. "Dressed up like some fairground Gypsy fortune-teller." His every movement broadcast hostility.

She took a deep breath, gripped the tapestried arms of her chair. "I'm not married to you anymore, Martin, and I'll do as I please. So you can stop shouting. I honestly don't know why you bother to drive all the way down here just to bully me. You won't change my mind."

He stopped pacing, moved to stand beside her, and tried another tack. "Selena. Listen to me. I love you. I know you're still grieving over the baby business. You're not yourself. I'm disappointed too. But running away isn't the answer." He put a hand on her shoulder. "Come back with me. We'll try again."

"Don't." She cringed away from him. "Don't touch me." Her voice was hard with unshed tears. "You know it's useless. Your sperm count's too low. The IVF didn't work. All those months of discomfort: hospitals, procedures, hormone injections, and still nothing!" She pushed on, hating herself for the sob rising uncontrolled in her voice. "And then the miscarriage. They told us, Martin." She wept openly now. "They told us it was time to stop trying. Time to get on and build our lives some other way."

"I know, darling," he said. "But . . . "

"But you blamed me. You told everyone it was all *my* fault. Maybe it was. But you pushed all your frustrations onto me, buried yourself in that precious legal practice of yours. Left me to cope with the pain and the loss of it any way I could." She looked up at him, the tears sliding unchecked down her cheeks. "And I'll never forgive you for that. Never."

She rose shakily, found the tissues, and blew her nose loudly. Then she turned her tear-smudged face back to his mottled red one. Her words were bleak: "Just go away, Martin. Go back to the city. Find someone else, someone who likes the money you make, likes the way you live. I've had it."

"Selena, darling. Listen to me. I don't want anyone else. I only want you. Please."

Her despair took refuge in irritation. She snapped: "And for goodness sakes don't grovel, Martin. I know you don't mean it. We'd be back to our old routines in no time at all, and I'd be lonely and isolated and miserable again. No thank you."

She crossed purposefully to the hallway, held out his coat. "Drive safely, Martin. I have enough to feel bad about already."

He took the tailored camel hair driving-coat in silence.

She suffered his perfunctory peck on her cheek, closed the door behind him in silent gratitude as he strode back up the path, let out a long sigh of relief as she heard the black BMW roadster roar into life, scattering birds in the lane as it sped away. He was heading back to London. Back where she no longer belonged.

☕

She was late now. She scooped her silks and beads into a carton, slipped a light topcoat over her blouse, snatched up her keys. Her elderly muddy-white Mazda spluttered and coughed, but the engine caught and she was off, the open box slipping and spilling its contents across the back seat as she chugged up Bell Stone hill.

When she finally arrived, out of breath after the steep walk from the back lane because parking spaces were tight by now, her shop was already open. The brass bells over the door chimed their welcome as she pushed inside, her arms full.

"Be with you in just a moment." The cheerful voice issuing from the back room belonged to Julia, the silversmith from Shipton Gorge who sub-let display space and helped out when she felt like it. "Is that you, Selena?"

"Yes. Take your time."

"I was just about to make coffee." Julia bustled into the room, stopped short. "And you look as though you need it. Here, let me take those. You sit down."

Selena sat, sniffing miserably into a damply crumpled tissue. "I'm all right. Really. Just give me a minute to collect myself."

Julia disappeared in the direction of the tiny kitchen, reappeared quickly with two steaming mugs. "Here. Drink this. The kettle was already on the boil." She busied herself arranging the new stock, draping the gorgeous silks so that Selena's trademark—a naked maiden clutching a wheat sheaf—was clearly on display.

"These are really beautiful. They'll sell out in no time." Julia's clear grey eyes were dark with concern as she turned back to her friend. "There's no need to explain. I can see from your face that that horrible ex-husband of yours has been harassing you again. Nothing else upsets you so much."

"I'm not going back."

"Of course you're not. How could you? Why don't we talk about more important things."

"Like what?"

"I don't know. You could start by telling me about your trademark. A customer was asking before you came in."

"It's simple enough. Virgo's my star sign. You know that." Selena hesitated. Then the words came tumbling out in a rush.

"And the logo is a tiny revenge on Martin. He always called me a "typical Virgo', meaning the finicky, obsessive, *tidy* earth-sign type in the Sunday Paper horoscopes, a good little housewife. But she's so much more than that. She's a paradox, purity and fertility together. And she was in the sky when I moved down here a year ago. So when I learned she was also the Saxon spring goddess, Eostre, for renewal, she seemed a proper symbol for my new life. You can see her constellation now, if you look, all through Easter, at Beltane . . . "

She stopped, embarrassed. "Sorry. I didn't mean to run on like that. I've never really tried to explain it to anyone before. Just tell them it's the major female zodiac sign and leave it at that."

"Of course. It's interesting, though, the way you thought it all out like that. It's always the quiet ones you have to watch. You're full of surprises." Julia's look was suddenly sly. "Speaking of which, how's that ghost of yours? Is he still up there on Eggardon?"

"I wish I'd never told you. People will think I'm fey. Martin already does!" Selena smiled wanly.

"That's better. A little smile can't hurt. And stop worrying about Martin. Martin doesn't count. And I haven't breathed a word, honestly. Cross my heart and hope to die. So tell me."

"I see him," Selena said, "but only in the evenings. He's always in the same place, just beyond the gate that leads into the fort. He looks Roman, stands very still, almost as if he's guarding the ruin of that old temple under the ramparts."

"Oh well, that's alright then, if he's a *Roman* guard." Julia laughed. "Plenty of Roman ghosts around here. There's folk that swear they've seen a whole cohort of them, soldiers marching up to the hill fort, marching up to their knees in dirt and grass in some places because their *feet* are striding down where the Roman road *used* to be."

Selena did not hear the mockery in Julia's voice. She went on: "I've become quite used to him. I always take that road home when the weather isn't too bad. It's lovely, soothing. And I like him being there. The first time I wasn't sure I was seeing anything, thought I was imagining him. But he seems to be getting more substantial, more *real* somehow." Her voice was dreamy now. "Maybe one night I'll stop and speak to him."

"Careful, Selena," said Julia. "You'll talk yourself into it. I know Martin is a beast, but don't you think you could find someone a little more . . . well . . . *alive* than a Roman *ghost* for your next time around?"

Selena laughed, guarding her thoughts now. "You're right, of course. And thank you for jollying me out of my blues. No more ghosts today. Martin's gone back to London, the sun is shining, and," she looked out at the woman browsing intently before her display window, "the Saturday crowd will be on us any moment."

The rest of the day passed busily in village gossip and intermittent sales, and by closing time both women were tired, glad to get away.

"Well, it's been a good day," said Julia. "I'll be able to afford to make more pieces after today's trade. Do you fancy a quick drink? A pint of Palmer's Best to celebrate?"

"No thanks. Not tonight. I'm all in. I'll just lock up and head home. You go on." Selena was much happier now. "And Julia," she said, "thanks again, for this morning."

"Not at all. Don't you go picking up any strangers on your way home, now."

"The chance would be a fine thing, don't you think?"

Julia grinned. "See you next week then?"

"Of course. Business as usual."

"Goodnight."

"Goodnight."

The light was fading fast, but Selena still decided to take her favourite route, by Spyway, up across Eggardon, and down the steep slope of Kings Farm Lane. She hoped, in her heart, that her Roman would be there, that she would see him.

But she was not prepared for the way it happened. Not at all.

The dense cloud rolled in from nowhere. One minute Selena was enjoying the view to Powerstock Common, the next the road was shrouded in heavy mist and she was driving dead slow, navigating by feel and instinct, the pale yellow glow of her headlights serving only to show up the occasional fuzzy tree-shape on the verge. She ground the gears. As she neared the gate across the unsealed track, the engine sputtered, and died. Selena was alone, alone in the muffled, eerie silence of the thickest mist she had ever seen. She could no longer see the steep drop she knew was there on either side of the rampart. She was too afraid to drive further, and too afraid to stay there.

On impulse, she eased herself out of the car. The mist seemed a little thinner without the haze of her headlights, but it was cold, clammy against her skin. Her hair was soon curling about her in damp tendrils, her clothing clinging moistly to her body, draining it of warmth, her lightweight boots soaking up water from the ground. Hugging her arms about her, she walked slowly up to the gate. She told herself that maybe she could see the extent of the mist if she climbed a little higher, that maybe it was just a freak patch and she could nerve herself to drive through it if she could see where it ended. It was still thick at the gate, so she walked on across the slight dip and up onto the main rampart.

When she saw the strange, looming shape of a horsehair crest in the fog, she imagined it might be her Roman ghost, thought she might get a closer look at him. The form outlined in the peculiar misty light seemed friendly, a familiar presence. Selena felt detached, unafraid. She drew closer, close enough to make out the face-flanges of the helmet, the moulded leather breastplate shaped to the outline of his body, the leather straps hanging over his short tunic, the high leather boots with their front lacings, and over it all the heavy dark red cloak.

She stopped, two paces from the figure, reaching out tentatively, dreamily, towards it. Her hand jerked back, convulsively, as she heard the first sound of a deep voice in the mist:

"Be welcome, lady," he said.

Selena felt frozen, unable to move, unable to speak for pure fright.

He held out his hand to her. "Do not be afraid. Come with me, lady, let me take you where it is dry and warm." His calm voice radiated reassurance.

Her cold hand seemed again to move of its own accord, stretching across her fear to meet him. The fingers that gripped hers were surprisingly firm, and warm.

Selena felt her anxiety melting at his touch. She nodded assent, allowed him to lead her, unprotesting, into the ruins.

She had visited the remains of the ancient temple that lay tucked in under the ramparts once before, picnicking on a bright summer's day, but then it had seemed lifeless, a tumble of fallen masonry beside a dew pond. Now, she saw that its pillars framed an open space against a rock wall, a space in which a small brazier burned with a tiny, welcome flame, its warmth keeping out the chill of the mist.

She tried not to think too hard about how this might be, reminded herself to live in the moment.

He helped her out of her sodden topcoat, and spread it out to dry. He put aside his helmet. He turned back to her, his brown eyes regarding her gravely in the dim light.

"I am called Gaius Quintus," he said.

"Selena. Pleased to meet you."

"Ah. You are named for the Goddess. Of course. I have hoped that you would come. I have watched you passing to and fro over the long months, and I have longed to be with you. And now you are here."

Selena knew she should say something, didn't quite know what it might be. She settled for the safety of the commonplace. "The mist, you see. My car stopped. I'm on my way home. I live down there, off Kings Lane." She gestured awkwardly, trailed off into silence.

His easy questions seemed harmless enough. "You are married?"

"No."

"Yet the house is yours?"

"Yes. Of course. I bought it when I moved to Dorset."

His smile broadened. "And you honour the Goddess. You wear her sign." He reached gently between her breasts to touch her pendant, the naked woman with the wheat sheaf that Julia had worked for her in heavy silver.

"Oh yes. I have always felt an affinity with the Goddess."

"It is well. You are of the *heterae*, then."

"The who?" Selena searched her memory for the term, came up with only the prim schoolgirl phrase, "temple prostitute", knew it wasn't right. She decided to let it pass.

"A free woman," he said.

"Oh, yes, I am certainly that." She laughed ruefully. "And what about you? Are you a free man? How on earth did you come to be here?"

Gaius looked grave. "I was stationed here with my legion. When the attackers came, it was my lot to defend this temple of the Goddess, to protect her women. I swore to guard it with my life." He paused, then said simply: "I have kept my oath."

Selena's blue eyes were wide. "What happened?"

"I remember the battle, the fighting, the confusion, the pain. And then: nothing. Until I awoke to find myself here, alone."

"And you didn't leave?"

"Lady, I could not. My oath has held me."

"All this time?"

He sighed, sounding suddenly weary. "Lady, I have been true to the Goddess. Through all the changes, through all the tribes and battles, through all the brigands and treasure seekers, I have stayed in this place. Always I have watched, have listened, have learned the tongues of those who come here, that I might speak with them at need." He drew a deep breath. "And now you are here. Look, lady, the moon is smiling for us."

The cloud-wrack had parted, its silver rags spread now across a clearing sky. Slowly, silently, the moon had climbed into the house of Virgo, resting there awhile to bless those who beheld her. Below, in the darkened valley, Selena saw where moonbeams spilled across fields and orchards, striping the land in silver light. The wind turned back leaves that glowed pale underneath, and she smiled to see the silver fruit upon silver trees promised in the poetry of her childhood.

Gaius took her arm, her white sleeve as luminous as mothwing in the silvery light. She looked up at the sky where he pointed through the handle of the Plough at the bright star Spica, the Virgin's spike. "See, lady," he said, his finger tracing out the constellation, "there is Carmenta, goddess of prophecy, and Vindematrix, the virgin grape-gatherer."

"An unfortunate star," said Selena, under her breath.

If he heard, he did not respond. "Tonight, lady, the Goddess is at home. Tonight, the Goddess permits."

He knelt before her then, his leather breastplate sheened pewter in the moonlight, his hand about her ankle. Selena felt the heat of it through her thin boot, warm against her cool flesh.

"The Goddess permits," he said again, and bowed his head.

Selena felt she was missing something important.

His grip was more insistent now, his voice more strained. He tried again: "Lady, will you have me?"

"Oh," she said. "I see. I don't . . . " She stopped. "This can't be happening." She stroked his dark brown hair, searching her mind for a gentle refusal. But the words, when they came, were not her own: "I will," she said, "for the Goddess."

She felt his smile in the darkness. His warm hand slid higher, caressing her thigh, moving higher, more confidently beneath her silken skirts until it found the soft, secret places it sought. The fingers were expert, deft. And when he led her back to the warmth of the brazier, spread his heavy red cloak on the ground for her, helped her gently from her clothes, Selena's need was as urgent as his own.

It was a rhapsody in moonlight and mercury. Long, lingering moments of touch and taste and tenderness sliding into urgency as their bodies strained together, pulling moonwise. Their little cries fluttered like silver moths into the night, until, at their bodies' climax, Selena felt the hot spurt of his white seed and held him close as a great cry of pain, of joy, burst from him to split the night. Then Gaius was weeping. And still she held him to her.

Sated, they lay together, bathed in quicksilver sweat and the moon's luminescence, looking at the stars. The ground was growing colder under her back, but Selena did not want to move. Not yet. She snuggled closer under his muscled arm.

"Where did you learn to do . . . " she hesitated " . . . those things? You know."

"The *heterae* were willing teachers." He smiled at the recollection. "Especially in the long cold nights when there were none but favoured officers of their guards for company." The smiled widened to a grin. "And I have been ever willing to serve the needs of the Goddess. As you see."

She laughed, contented. "Then I am glad she chose me."

"And I too." His voice was more serious now. "The Goddess has at last heard my prayer," he said. "In you, I am rewarded." He paused, his fingertips tracing lazy whorls upon her pearl-white belly. "Lady, you have released me. You have released me into life, and into death. And I thank you."

"That sounds so very formal. Like goodbye. But surely I can come to you again, now that we . . . " Her voice trailed away.

"Nay, lady: I will be . . . gone."

She sat up. "Gone? Where?"

"To my rest. The Goddess has released me. My soul is in my seed. My life now lives in you." He cupped her belly, tenderly. "And I may go."

"You mean the third face of the Goddess, don't you? Maiden, Mother, and . . . "

He stopped her mouth with a kiss. " . . . And the one we do not name. Yes. I have done my duty through these long years, guarding this sacred place. But the world is changing once more, and others will come. The Goddess has, at last, let me go in peace."

The moon was riding higher now.

He reached deep into a crevice in the stone, and pulled out a little leather pouch. "These," he said, "are for you." He took her hand, and pressed two perfect silver Roman coins into it: they gleamed lustrous, cold in the pale moonlight. "I have kept them safe, against this hour, that I might pay the price of my need."

Selena looked affronted. "I'm not . . ." she said. "You don't have to *pay* me."

"The Goddess demands this token," he said simply. "You must not deny my gift of love." He went on. "And this," he said, "is for our son, when he is old enough." The great gold arm ring he slipped over her wrist was cold to the touch, heavy with the weight of centuries.

"Our *what?*"

"Son. Your son. Me." He looked perplexed. "My son, Gaius Sextus, that is to be."

Selena's eyes widened in disbelief. "How can you be so sure? I don't understand," she said.

"But you must. It is the will of the Goddess. My life will be reborn, that my bones may be at peace."

Selena shivered in a sudden gust of wind. The sky was clouding in again. The storm had circled around the hills. There was fine rain in the air. She knew she should go, before it came back to embrace Eggardon in its thick mist once more.

Gaius cast his cloak about her shoulders, the cloak that smelled of sex and moonlight. "This will keep you warm. I need it no longer, lady," he said.

He was walking her, firmly, in the direction of her car. At the gate, he stopped, his arm about her shoulders. "I can come no further, lady," he said. "My time ends here." He kissed her, tenderly. "And now you must go."

"But . . ."

"Go. You must. When the time comes, you will remember me."

Selena could have sworn he was fading now, his words more distant. She turned, walked the last yards to the moth-white bubble that was her car, clambered inside. Everything was as before, the smell of incense, the litter of silks and wrapping papers, the bright baubles in their boxes strewn across the back seat.

Selena was not reassured.

She looked back, her gaze seeking the place where the ghost should be.

Gaius Quintus was gone.

The car started, as she had known it would. She drove in silence, her tears making silver snail-trails down her cheeks.

Back in her cottage, Selena made hot chocolate for herself, and then lit the fire set ready in the grate, though the room was not cold. She needed the comfort.

The coins, under her magnifying glass, were in mint condition, the profile of the Emperor stamped clear, the edges sharp. And the thick gold Roman arm-ring, with its heavy engraving, was worth a collector's fortune. She turned it this way and that, making out the marks scratched deep into its inner surface. Gauis Quintus was there, and a sketchy eagle. And beside it, the sigil Virgo, sign of the Goddess.

Selena sat staring at these things until the fire burned low in the grate. She went late to her bed, exhausted.

She slept well. It was mid- morning when she finally awoke to birdsong and bright sunlight filtering through her curtains. She got up, stiff from the night's events, wandered to the bathroom. Wrapped in her thoughts, she stepped lightly over yesterday's clothes, discarded in a damp muddy heap on the floor. She smiled to herself as she ran a hot, scented bath to soak the coldness from her bones, to wash the dried whorls from her skin. She emerged fresh and pink, and singing.

Pregnant or not, Selena felt just fine.

Over her tea and toast, she contemplated the silent truth that spoke in two silver coins, a gold arm-ring, and an ancient red cloak of Roman cut hanging behind the kitchen door. She knew, instinctively, that she could tell nobody, not even Julia.

A little later, in her workroom, she lit an incense stick, sandalwood for the Goddess, then turned to mix her dyes for the new silk designs she would make today—designs of whorling silver moths, spiralling for joy in a midnight sky.

Blake's Angel

This story had its origins in my experience of walking the strange and wonderful Angel Project, staged for the Perth Writer's Festival. Each participant had to go alone, and was directed to a sequence of installations in various locations around the city. Some of these featured actors costumed as angels who appeared in incongruous situations—a warehouse, a multi-storey carpark, a display home, even a church. The original angel of my story was a handsome young man trapped inside a huge wire cage outside a supermarket—he was clinging to the mesh, wearing nothing but shorts, combat boots, and a pair of feathery wings. His blonde hair somehow reminded me of William Blake's angel etchings, so I put this image together with newspaper reports about bird smuggling, and came up with the horrors of the illegal angel trade.

Then cherish pity, lest you drive an angel from your door.
— WM. BLAKE, Holy Thursday

Inside the iron mesh cage, the angel was shaking.

A fine drizzle had begun falling from a steely-grey sky, and a sharp wind had sprung up, whirling grit and candy wrappers and greasy food scraps along the grimy alley. The angel shivered. His wings ached where they had been clipped, and he shuddered again at the remembrance of dirty secateurs and the foul breath of the men who had pushed his face into the filthy ground to stifle his screams. He hoped his wounds were not infected. Another bout of trembling took him, a rush of heat and a cold sweat that told him he was hoping against the odds. He tried not to radiate his distress, determined not to call for help. That was how they'd caught him, dropping their rank net as he struggled with the lock to release Alisha. God only knew what they'd done with her now.

The angel-seller's booth was at the far end of a ragged line of street traders, obscured by a tangle of ducts and pipes, beside heaps of empty cardboard boxes and wooden shipping pallets, well away from prying eyes. The alley stank of slops from the food vendors' stalls—the reek of rotting cabbage and congealing chicken blood mixing with the pungent smells of heavy spices, of curry leaves and fenugreek and cumin. A tomcat had pissed at one corner of the angel cage, marking territory and adding to the stink of the neighbouring medicine stall with its stands of tiger balm and antler velvet and rhinoceros horn and bull's pizzles for virility, with its ginseng roots and mounds of bark and leaves and its strange homunculi floating in specimen jars.

At the front of his booth the trader lounged, smoking a roll-your-own and pausing occasionally to spit through yellowed teeth. Once in a while he swiped a damp rag across the grubby glass-topped counter displaying angel-wares: feathered earrings, necklaces and bracelets of beads and angel feathers, woven angel headbands. A revolving stand offered key rings, bookmarks, pens, and little terracotta angel statues with glued-on feathers. From the grimy striped awning dangled clusters of charms and amulets made of genuine angel products—feathers, hair, skin. There were long single feathers bound with red and gold thread, for luck; round wheels of shorter feathers radiating from bunches of herbs, for healing the sick; silver pendants with a lock of angel hair inside, for courtship. And at the back, carefully wrapped against the dirt, there were pure white angel-feather bridal fans, for marital harmony. On an upturned crate behind the stall, a wrinkled old lady sat, sipping tea and muttering to herself, rocking to and fro while she stitched the recent clippings from the angel's wings into such a fan, a special wedding order.

The angel felt sick.

A sudden flurry of activity announced that someone, a tourist, a prospective customer, had blundered into the alley. The traders swooped, crying their wares, offering remedies, bric-a-brac, heart's desire. A pimp in a grubby T-shirt and even grubbier jeans sidled out of a doorway, said something: the newcomer blushed, shook his head, kept walking.

The angel locked his fingers through the wire mesh, climbed a little way up the rocking cage to watch the man's progress, glad of any distraction. There were rumours, he knew, of a man who frequented the markets and bought caged creatures just to watch them fly free. One glance told him this was not the man.

This man was short, stocky, and round in the belly. His crumpled white cotton shirt was stained dark at the armpits; his baggy khaki trousers were shiny at the seat and knees. He looked embarrassed as he waved aside the importuning traders, but he made his way steadily toward the back of the alley, towards the angel-seller's booth.

The angel-seller affected to look bored, flicking his rag about, miming disinterest as the man approached.

The customer stopped at the angel-wares counter, looking furtively about him. His domed forehead was beaded with perspiration, and he smelled of sweat and cheap white wine. He put down the scratched leather briefcase he was carrying, tucking it safely between his scuffed loafers.

The trader slouched, elbows on the glass countertop. "You want to look, mister?" He pointed at the cabinet. "Plenty pretty things. All authentic. He held out one of the amulets. "Look at this. All real angel feathers. Guaranteed. I can give you certificate."

The customer cleared his throat. "No. Thank you. I'm not looking for trinkets or artefacts." He leaned towards the trader, said softly: "I heard, that is I was told, that you might have, you know, *live* specimens?"

The angel's heart sank.

"Who told you?"

"A friend. At a writers' workshop. I've come a long way." The man mopped his mottled face with a once-white handkerchief.

The trader looked the customer up and down, evaluating. "It'll cost you," he said.

"I know. I can pay." He squirmed around, pulled a worn leather wallet from his frayed hip pocket.

The trader leaned further forward, conspiratorially. "Maybe I can help you. You come around the back." He edged out from behind the counter, unlatched the side gate, gestured towards the grimy cages obscured from public view by the canvas of the stall.

The customer put away his wallet, picked up his briefcase, squeezed his bulk through the little gateway. He took a few steps in the direction of the cage. The angel hung there on the wire, eyes averted.

The customer stared. Despite his recent rough handling, the angel's beauty was breathtaking. He shone like a gilded icon in the greasy light of the alley. The skimpy white robe that the trappers had draped about him when they stole his clothes hid nothing of his perfectly muscled form, and his darkening blue-black bruises served only to accentuate his flawless creamy-white skin. He had a mop of shining golden curls that rippled to his broad shoulders, and his averted gaze showed the customer a faultless profile that seemed carved from alabaster.

The man looked abashed. He simply stood and gaped, absently pushing grubby, nicotine-stained fingers through his thinning white hair. "My God," he said at last, "it really looks like an angel."

The trader grinned, exposing his yellowed teeth. "Genuine angel," he agreed.

The customer paused, peered, adjusted his rimless spectacles. He stroked his little white goatee beard, looked nervously around him. The alley was quiet, except for the low mumbling of the old lady, who had deliberately turned her back.

The angel could smell the little man's need, could taste his hunger, and his fear. He fought down his own nausea, and turned his head. He raised his impossibly blue angel-eyes to meet the watery pale blue human ones that observed him.

It was the customer who first lowered his gaze. He fidgeted, jingling his keys in his trouser pocket. The lonely sound echoed in the alley.

"OK?" said the trader. "We have tea now."

The customer said nothing as he was shepherded back towards the front of the booth. Right on cue, the old crone hobbled up to the counter with a tray, which held a chipped teapot and two little round cups. She backed away again, and the trader poured. Jasmine-scented steam wafted upwards, and the customer took the proffered cup, relieved to have something to hold in his hand. He sipped in silence for a moment.

"Genuine angel, very beautiful," the trader began again, nodding judiciously. "You have questions?"

The customer cleared his throat. "I'm a poet," he said. "I'm looking for inspiration. Is this angel inspirational?"

"Ah," said the trader. "I thought you looked like a sensitive man. We get a lot of artistic buyers." He smiled his crooked smile. "Yes, he's one hundred percent inspirational. It's what they do best. Just look at him."

The poet glanced back toward the cage, the longing plain in his worried face.

"And the women," the trader said, leering. "The women are drawn to them. You'll be a very popular man with the women." He winked.

The poet swallowed uncomfortably, ignoring this direction. "Does he sing?" he asked.

"Oh yes, but he won't do it here in the cage. He is just captured. When he is recovered, he will sing for you. Celestial music." The smile was back. "Ask anyone."

"You know I can't do that. The angel trade isn't exactly legal, is it?"

The trader shrugged. "If you want the angel, you buy him. No one will stop you. It's up to you."

The customer seemed nervous again, twisting the cup in his hands. He looked about him, obviously weighing his options. He took a deep breath. "How much?" he asked.

The trader wrote a figure on a scrap of paper, pushed it across the counter to the rotund little man.

"You're joking," the poet said.

The trader spat deliberately into the gutter. "Very rare specimen," he replied. "Tall, well muscled, pure white wings. You've seen for yourself."

The poet named a lower price.

"For that," said the trader, "it would be more profitable to break him up for parts." He swept a hand across his display case.

The poet paled. "You wouldn't," he said.

The trader shrugged. "These are all genuine." He patted the glass, then took up his pencil stub once more to write another figure. He smiled as he slid it across the counter. "I have overheads," he said. "If he doesn't sell . . . " He let the implication hang in the fetid alley air.

The poet swallowed hard, countered once again, a higher bid this time.

The trader shook his head, then produced a grubby calculator from beneath the counter. "I tell you what I'll do. You seem like a genuine buyer," he said. "For you, special price. I work out my margin."

He tapped away, then held out the calculator for the poet to see.

The poet's shoulders sagged. "You guarantee he's inspirational?" he asked.

"Absolutely. One hundred percent," the trader replied. "You can't go wrong with this one."

The poet was sweating now. He typed in a slightly lower figure. "That's my final offer. It's all I've got."

The trader spat again. "My children will not eat tonight. Make me a little bit better offer."

"Sorry. That's that then." The poet sighed, picked up his badly scuffed briefcase, preparing to depart. "As I said, it's all I've got. Take it or leave it."

The trader held out a dirt-streaked hand. "OK," he said. "Deal."

The poet took the hand gingerly. "Deal," he replied.

The trader pulled a dog-eared receipt book from under the counter. "What name do you want on the delivery docket?"

"What? Oh, sorry. Williams. Blake Williams." The poet inspected his fingernails. "And I'm not local. I'll want him shipped."

"That'll cost extra."

"How much?"

The haggling process began again.

In the cage, the angel listened, aching with disease and despair.

Night fell. The angel could sense his brethren loitering nearby, drawn by his anguish. Strange shapes in lumpy overcoats that concealed the telltale wings, they waited, poised and light-footed, to see if they could help. He tried again to damp down his pain, to deny his captors their lure. "_Wait_," he sent. "_This is a trap._" It was hard, so hard, for them to see a fellow creature suffer, to go against their very nature, to turn away. But tonight they managed it.

The angel-cage was hoisted into darkness, and the nightmare journey began. Ten days later, the angel sat hunched in a corner, heartbreakingly beautiful, tethered by an iron chain to an iron bedpost. The ankle-cuff chafed his smooth white skin, raising ugly red welts. The fever had passed, but he was still weak. He needed to rest. He shuddered to remember the crate, the stinking livestock lorries, the jolting darkness, the motion sickness. Passed from one smuggler to the next along the angel network, he'd finally been delivered to the poet's grotty attic apartment in its seedy downtown neighbourhood. Now his new owner was showing off his purchase to his closest friends.

George and Katrina lived in the ground floor apartment of Blake's building, and they'd seen the packing crate arrive at the end of the day, watched it hauled ungently up the narrow stairs. They'd immediately dropped by, agog with neighbourly curiosity. Now they stood, holding freshly filled wine glasses, staring in astonishment at the exquisite winged creature shackled to the bed. The angel glowed golden in the grey city light, the richness of his presence making the poet's modest apartment seem even shabbier.

"So the rumours we've been hearing are true, Blake," said George. "You've actually bought a real live angel."

"As you see."

George peered at the quivering angel from a respectful distance, but Katrina stalked right up to him. She slid a crimson-painted fingernail down his bare arm. The angel flinched. His blue eyes blazed. "He's absolutely gorgeous," she said.

"Don't, Kat," said George. "You'll frighten him."

"Nonsense, darling," she purred, reaching up to stroke a shining, white-feathered wing. "He knows I like him." Her red, lipsticked mouth widened into a dreamy smile. "Maybe I can help you clean him up, Blake. Give him a nice hot soapy bath, or something?" The way she eyed the bulge in the angel's loincloth was downright predatory.

Blake cleared his throat. "That won't be necessary, thank you." The words sounded more formal than he had meant them to. George looked uncomfortable.

"Suit yourself," said Katrina. "I'm only trying to help." She sauntered back to stand beside George, still gazing longingly at the angel.

There was an awkward silence, in which all three regarded the dejected acquisition. It was George who broke the impasse. "He doesn't look very well," he ventured.

"I reckon it was a pretty tough trip," said Blake, relieved to steer the conversation back into safer waters. "And I'm not sure what to feed him. I should have asked. I tried fruit, but he hasn't touched the apple. He's had a little water."

"I heard they don't survive well in captivity."

"He'll be alright. He just needs time to get used to a new environment, that's all. He's probably pining."

"Pining?"

"They're social creatures. He's lonely because he's separated from his flock." The poet poured out more wine for his friends.

"Well," said Katrina, her voice low and throaty, "he won't be lonely with *me* around. I'll always be happy to keep him company."

A fleeting expression of appalled understanding crossed the angel's perfect face. He huddled closer to the bedpost.

Again it was George who spoke. "So why the chain?" he asked. "His wings are clipped. He can't fly out of the window." George appeared genuinely distressed. "He looks so miserable. It can't be right to keep him chained up like that."

"It's the iron," Blake replied. "It keeps them grounded to the earth. They can't escape while they're bound with iron."

"Is that how they capture them, then?"

"Sort of. They lure them close to an iron cage, then they net them. They use pain for bait. It's the empathy. They're drawn to suffering. They can't stop themselves. They have to try to help. It's their nature." He grinned. "So I reckon he'll respond to my misery and help me over my writer's block." The smile vanished. "He'd better. He cost me my life savings."

"I'm sure he'll be just wonderful," said Katrina. She tucked her free hand under Blake's arm, snuggling close, conspiratorial. "And I'll visit him everyday while you're working, so he won't be lonely."

"Well I still think it's wrong to cage something so magnificent, so . . . pure," said George. "You can see he doesn't belong here. Show some pity, Blake. Let him go."

"No." Blake's jaw stiffened. "Not till I get my inspiration. Then I'll think about it. Maybe."

George looked down at his glass, fiddled with the stem. He could not bear meet the angel's blue gaze. "Well, let's hope that's sooner rather than later, then," he said.

"Don't be so grumpy, darling," said Katrina. "Blake's just told us how valuable the angel is. You can't expect him to pay all that money then just set the creature free. He might as well throw his money away."

"Would it make any difference if I offered to buy him from you?"

"No. He's my angel and he's not for sale." Blake forced a smile. "Give it a rest, George. I thought you'd be pleased for me. It'll all work out, you'll see."

George drained his glass, suddenly aware that he needed to be away from the sight of the chained angel. "Well, thanks for the drink, Blake," he said. "I'll see you around. Are you ready, Kat?"

"Not yet, darling, I'll just stay and finish my wine. I'll be down in a little while." She kissed him lightly on the cheek as he turned to leave.

Blake topped up her glass, and Katrina draped herself languorously across the end of the bed, almost touching the angel. Teasing. The angel shrank from her, furling his injured wings more tightly about himself. Blake swallowed hard, but did not comment. The bottle was emptied, and the talk turned to other things.

Weeks stretched into months. Living in the same room as an unhappy angel had not improved the poet's temper. Neither had Katrina's constant visits. She just couldn't leave him alone, always popping in with this or that transparent excuse. She knew Blake worked naked, but she didn't care. She barged in whenever she felt like it, which was all the time. She'd even insisted on afternoon tea, complete with angel cake, for God's sake. Blake's patience was wearing very thin. He was still blocked, and drinking heavily. He sat at the table, staring balefully at a silent keyboard. Once again he addressed his captive, continuing his drink-sodden monologue. "So you still refuse to help me, then? You know you'll never get out of here unless you do, don't you?"

The angel remained hunched, silent. He touched the tin water dish with a wary toe. His wings drooped in defeat.

"What sort of angel are you, anyway? They promised me you could sing. *Celestial music*, that's what the trader said. That's what I paid for."

A faint smile sketched itself across the angel's pallid face. He shook his head, miming: "*No*'.

"No? You mean you can't or you won't?"

The angel shook his head again.

The poet hurled a bottle at him, missing by a wide margin. The angel shrugged, spread his hands in a universal gesture: "*Please, no.*"

The poet raised an unsteady hand, menacing. "Well," he said, "you're bought and paid for." His face took on a look of drunken cunning. "If you don't inspire me *very* soon I can always sell you back for spare parts."

The angel's sigh was almost audible.

He lifted his head, straightened his stooped shoulders, smoothed his wings. Decision shone plain in his beautiful, pale face.

He cleared his throat.

And he began to sing.

The first pure notes, high and sweet, dropped like clear honey into the dank air of the attic apartment. The hum of the traffic receded.

The poet peered blearily over the rim of his wineglass, and smiled. "That's more like it," he said.

The sound swelled, wordless, clean and sad, filling all the building's space with its aching melancholy, growing in magnitude until it seemed the walls trembled.

Downstairs, George and Katrina stopped to listen as the unearthly music flowed through their apartment and out to the street.

"It's wonderful," said Katrina. "I knew he'd sing eventually. I'm going right up to see."

"Maybe you were right," said George. "Maybe it was just a question of time. I've never heard anything so beautiful." Tears were starting in his eyes.

"You're such an old softie," said Katrina. She gave him a quick hug. "Are you coming up to Blake's with me?"

"No, not yet. I don't want to intrude. I'll listen from outside for a while."

"Suit yourself." She was already out of their apartment, taking the stairs to Blake's attic two at a time.

George headed for the street, where a curious crowd was gathering.

The volume of the angel's lament increased: he sang of his shame, of his sorrow, of his longing. He sang of torture, and of death.

The poet was weeping now. It was not gentle. Great wracking sobs convulsed his chest. Hot tears ran unheeded down his red-veined nose. He gulped for air. "Stop it," he cried. "For pity's sake stop it."

The angel sang on, unheeding. Window glass shattered.

Katrina dashed into the room. "The door was open," she began.

Blake cut her off with a gesture. "Not now," he moaned. "Not now."

She stopped, open mouthed, in the middle of the room. The angel towered over her. He stood erect, his ankle-chain stretched taut. His feathers had re-grown, and he held his huge, shining wings outspread, filling the tiny apartment. He seemed totally unaware of her intrusion.

The sound soared.

The apartment walls began to crumble, wide cracks spidering up the bricks and mortar, plaster fracturing, timbers snapping and splintering. A fissure opened in the pavement below. A fire hydrant burst, sending plumes of frothing water high into the air.

And still the angel sang. The barrier was broken. From all over the city, other angels joined their brother in his chorus of grief. His solo voice swelled into a choir.

The roof caved in. Katrina shrieked, unheard, as a roof-beam crashed down upon her. The poet was buried were he sat, sobbing, head in hands. Golden light poured from the ruined building, illuminating the cloud of plaster dust that rose into the night sky. Somewhere in the distance, sirens wailed.

The music changed. The lament became a hymn of praise, spiralling upwards to the heavens. The chains of iron snapped.

Draggled and dust streaked in the wreckage, the angel wept.

And flew free.

The Sculptor's Wife

This story began, oddly enough, with an episode of Kevin McCloud's Grand Designs, *the inspirational architecture/ building television series. I was in the process of adding an extension to my house as an owner-builder, and was, of course, very involved in the minutiae of the project and paying close attention to the details. But as I was watching enormous excavations being carried out for a large house in the English countryside, I found myself wondering just what else might have been dug up in the course of so much building work in such a history-rich location. The thought led to excavations of the archaeological kind, by way of another television program—*Time Team. *Somehow I got from Roman foundations and medieval remains to the legend of Merlin, trapped in his cave by the enchantress Nimue. And I extrapolated from there.*

What is it men in women do require? : The lineaments of gratified desire.

WILLIAM BLAKE

The first time the sculptor saw the tall, lichen-covered boulder, he knew *she* was in there. Something about the slightly crooked plane of the stone drew him to it. Half buried in landslip on the very edge of the woodland, the sunlit rock seemed somehow to radiate warm promise. He had to have it. He had to have her.

The negotiations were easy enough. The wealthy couple building their stylish, green-oak framed house were happy for him to take the big rock. They had no use for it. The excavations for their basement had collapsed a sort of ancient cave, they said, and this odd stone had emerged when they tipped the rubble. They wished him well and hoped to see the sculpture, in due course.

He promised them an invitation to the opening of his wholly imaginary next exhibition.

Moving the stone was harder. He used up a lot of favours from friends and acquaintances in getting it levered out of the bank and lifted with chains onto a cart and hauled up the narrow, muddy track to his studio deep the woods—a tiny, isolated holiday cottage that his mother let him use, rent free. The cottage stood in a little clearing beside a lake, hidden from the outside world by thickets of oak and ash and rowan. The sculptor loved this place: loved it for its serenity, for its slanting sunlight and its shy woodland animals, for its birdsong, and the droning of its bees.

Finally, the rock took its place at the centre of his studio, at the centre of his life. Alone with the stone at last, the sculptor caressed it. It warmed to his touch, and he felt his fingers tingle in anticipation. The stone seemed almost to vibrate: he could feel *her* reaching out to him, wanting him, waiting for him to set her free.

He had made his preparations. The cottage smelled sweet, perfumed by bunches of strange herbs that his mother had collected throughout the summer and hung to dry on the unlined wooden walls. The stone floor had been swept clean; there was a stack of firewood beside the stove, a supply of tallow candles on the rustic dresser, an assortment of canned and bottled foodstuffs in the larder. The sculptor felt ready.

Slowly, with infinite care, he began to craft the image of his desire. He worked each day until the light failed and his fingers bled. He forgot to eat, forgot to sleep, forgot to do the little ordinary things that everyone ought to do. He was unshaven and haggard. He smelled bad. But his focus was absolute. He was driven: his only waking thought was to create the perfect woman to be his perfect bride; and if he slept, he dreamed only of her.

Weeks dragged into months, but finally the day came when his masterwork was complete. Summer sunlight shone through his open window as he washed her, carefully cleaning away the last of the chisel dust with water he had taken from the Glastonbury Well, the well at the world's end, famous for its magical properties. As he towelled her dry, it seemed to him that the pinkish stone took on a warmer, fleshly hue. At the last, he moistened her full lips with

Glastonbury water and fancied that those lips parted a little. He stepped back, hardly daring to breathe as he beheld the bride he had always longed for, stone-flesh perfect.

They stood awhile in silent tableau, flesh regarding stone regarding flesh.

She opened her eyes.

Her eyes were as blue as cornflowers, as he had known they would be. He took her outstretched hand to help her from the pedestal, and the exquisite fingers were warm, as he had known they would be. He led her, newborn, unresisting to the alcove where he kept his bed. Wordlessly she lay down in love with him, as he had known she would.

Later, lying heavily in the crook of his arm, she pushed back her long black curls and spoke her first words.

"My name," she said, "is Nimue."

The sculptor sat bolt upright in surprise. He hadn't known about that.

"Nimue?"

"The very same: you've heard of me, of course. The damosel of the lake, the famous enchantress: yes? You may consider yourself enchanted."

"But . . . "

Nimue yawned, showing pearly teeth and a tongue as pink as any cat's. "Come along now. You will, of course, be obedient to my wishes. That's how it goes. I'll need rather a lot of things. I'll dictate, and you can make a list. I take it you can write?"

"But I created you," he protested. "I made you to be my fair lady, my perfect bride. *You* are supposed to obey *me*."

"What an interesting delusion, my dear." Nimue stretched, and the sculptor couldn't help admiring anew her wondrous curves, her flawless skin. "The fact of the matter is," she said, "I called you from within the stone to release me, and you obeyed. You've been eager enough until now—obsessed, even. I expect your obedience to continue." She smiled. "You should know that even master magician Merlin was no match for me. I trapped him in a cave: he'll never escape." There was more than a trace of smugness in her husky voice. "So I'm not expecting any trouble from you. Besides," she added with a chillingly transparent attempt at coquetry, "there are some obvious advantages for you. I will, after all, be your wife." She lay back. "I'm all yours, my dear."

The sculptor shrivelled, his erstwhile ardent flesh no longer willing.

She peered down her perfectly chiselled nose. "That's not very impressive," she sniffed. "You'll have to do better than that." She reached down and took his shrinking flesh in her stone-strong fingers. "Here," she said, "let me help you." She began kneading him purposefully. "I have needs too, you know. It's been a long time. It was no fun at all being stuck inside that stone."

The sculptor watched in disbelief as his recalcitrant erection grew under her insistent fingers. "But I don't . . . " he began.

"Of course you do," she replied. "I want you rock hard, and you will not disappoint me. Do you understand?"

He could only nod, his mind fogged by the hopeless desire that now overwhelmed rational thought.

She mounted him, relentlessly grinding against him, stone against bone. The weight of her almost crushed the life out of him. He found himself fighting for breath. At last she fell back, sighing. "Better," she said. "I'm sure you will learn to please me, in time."

The sculptor rolled away from her, his abused flesh red and sore. His chest hurt, and his mouth was dry. "I'll just go and clean up," he croaked. "Shall I bring you some water?"

"Later," she replied. "I'm not done with you yet." She reached for him, casually draping one heavy, sculpted arm across his torso, pinning his bruised ribs to the sweat-soaked sheets. "Here," she said, "let me help you."

The nightmare began, in earnest.

Next morning, Nimue sat up suddenly in the tangled mess that was all that now remained of the sculptor's bed. "I'll need clothes," she said. "I'm bored. I want you to take me out."

The sculptor groaned and turned away. Everything hurt. "There's some old stuff of my mother's in the dresser," he said. "Help yourself."

She slapped him.

The sculptor felt his cheekbone bruise.

"Pay attention, husband," she said. "I'll need proper gowns, velvet, adorned with pearls, and gold embroidery. And jewels: I must have decent jewellery."

"I don't have any money," the sculptor replied, cringing away from her. "I can't buy you clothes, or jewels—or anything else."

"Then what use are you?"

"I was good enough to release you." He sighed sulkily. "I wish I'd never found that stone."

"But you did. And here I am. And believe me, husband, you are bound to me, for weal or woe. Don't think to escape me."

"I wouldn't dream of it," he said, thinking furiously about his masonry tools, about the sharp edge of his chisel, knowing all the while that he couldn't bring himself to mar the terrible beauty he had created.

Nimue relented a little. "I won't really need your money," she said. "I usually find that people are most generous. Just take me to the market and I shall choose what I need."

The sculptor was wary, but thought it best to humour her. "I'll lend you one of Mother's dresses," he said. "And when you are ready, I'll take you into town." He rummaged about in the dresser and came up with a long dark blue caftan with wide, cord-edged sleeves. "Here," he said.

"I can't wear this," Nimue said. "It looks like a bag. It will be far too big for me."

"Then I can't take you shopping," the sculptor replied. He took down one of his mother's silk scarves from where it hung on a peg by the door. "You can use this for a belt if the dress is too large."

Nimue scowled at him, but snatched the dress and scarf from his hands. She dropped the garment over her head and tied the scarf as a sash. "Very well," she said. "I'm ready. Let's go."

"You look lovely," the sculptor said, marvelling at the way the old blue dress clung to his stone bride's curves—it had never looked like this on Mother.

The enchantress was unworried by her first ride in a car, and when they arrived in the market town the sculptor watched in disbelief as she alighted, slammed the door, and sashayed across the street into the most expensive clothing store she could see. She walked in as if she owned the place, demanding immediate attention.

Nobody demurred. The assistants had a slightly dreamy, unfocused look as they ignored their other customers to dance attendance upon Nimue. The enchantress smiled happily as she tried on this and that, primping and twirling before the long mirror as she acquired dresses, coats, even hats.

"I'll take these," she said at last, gesturing vaguely toward the rather large pile of accoutrements. "And I'll wear this."

"Certainly, madam: I'll have the rest boxed, shall I?"

"My man here will take them," she said.

"But . . . " the sculptor began to speak.

She silenced him with a look.

"And you can burn this old thing," she added, kicking the offending caftan into a corner.

"I'll take it," the sculptor said, snatching it up and hastily bundling it under his jacket. "Mother is fond of this dress."

Nimue shrugged. "As you wish, husband," she said.

The shop assistants wrapped her selections and simply handed the packages and bags to the sculptor. The assistants seemed perplexed, but did not ask for payment.

"Thank you all so very much," Nimue cooed as she made for the exit. "You have been so very helpful."

"What happened in there?" the sculptor asked as he followed his bride up the High Street, laden with her shopping.

"What usually happens: when I want something, people give it to me. You should know that." Nimue smiled. "Shoes next, I think," she said. "You may take those things to the car. I'll be over there." She pointed to an elegant outfitters emporium whose window displayed an assortment of shoes, handbags, and accessories.

Shoes, it transpired, were a problem: she was too heavy for high heels. After several attempts, crumpled footwear lay scattered on the carpet of the store and the worried assistant was at a loss as to what to offer next.

"Perhaps you should try flats," the sculptor said, watching in dismay as the heels of a pretty pair of red leather stilettos folded up like a concertina under Nimue's weight.

"Perhaps," the enchantress replied.

Half and hour later, a relieved shop assistant handed over several packages and turned back to deal with the debris as the sculptor took his wife's arm and guided her out into the street.

"That should satisfy you," he said. "You've had quite a shopping spree. The car's full of stuff."

"I still need some jewellery," Nimue replied. "Then you can take me to lunch."

The sculptor sighed heavily as he obeyed, carefully opening the door to the jeweller's establishment and following his wife into a sparkling interior of polished brass and mirrors and bright down-lights.

The beautiful Nimue, now stylishly clad and shod, lavished her attention upon the astonished proprietor. "That looks nice," she said, unerringly choosing the most expensive item from the display—a sapphire and diamond necklace.

"Allow me," the jeweller said.

Nimue obligingly swept her dark curls aside as the man fastened the necklace for her.

"I can offer you earrings to match," he said, "and a ring." He slipped a large sapphire ring onto her slender finger and stood back to appreciate the effect. "It's perfect for you," he said.

Nimue put on the earrings and admired her reflection in the mirror, turning this way and that. "Yes," she said. "These jewels will do."

The strange compulsion happened again. Beads of sweat formed on the jeweller's brow and the man tried desperately to resist Nimue's charm. "Those pieces were made for you," the jeweller heard himself say. "They match your eyes, my dear." He fought the words as they were forced from him, but the enchantress was too strong. "They are my gift to you. You must take them. I insist."

Nimue smiled, accepting the king's ransom in sapphires and diamonds as no more than her due. "I shall think of you whenever I wear them," she said. "Thank you so very much."

The couple's first attempt at lunch together was not a success. The sculptor chose a modest café and steered Nimue to a table for two by the window. He ordered tea and sandwiches, but when the food came, his bride was far from satisfied.

"What's this?" she said, curiously lifting the white bread to reveal a thin slice of ham smeared with avocado paste. "I want a hot meal. I want wine."

"We're not licensed, and we don't do meals," the waitress replied sullenly. "Only cakes and sandwiches."

"That's not good enough," Nimue began, clearly getting ready to cause a scene. "And I don't like your tone."

The waitress shrugged. "So?"

The sculptor stood hurriedly. "We'll try the pub," he said. "Sorry." He reached into his jacket for his wallet. "What do I owe you?"

"Nothing," Nimue said. "We haven't eaten anything."

"You ordered the sandwiches," the waitress countered. "It's no concern of mine whether you eat them or not. I just work here. You have to pay." She held out her hand.

Nimue grabbed it, and squeezed.

The sculptor heard bones snap.

"I think not," Nimue said, releasing the hand.

The waitress turned pale with shock, looking down in disbelief at her broken fingers. She tried to speak, but found that she could not.

"Come along, husband," Nimue said. "This insolent girl won't bother us any more." She stood, and led the way from the teashop.

The sculptor followed at her heels, shuddering at the casual violence, realizing just how easily his own bruised ribs could have been broken bones. "I'll take you somewhere nicer," he said quickly. "I know a country pub. It's down by the river, and it has a charming garden. I'm sure they serve a decent steak there. I'm sure you'll like it."

"Very well," she said. "I do hope the servants there will have better manners."

"Of course, my dear," he replied, thinking only to get her away from the town before someone called the police and he was asked to explain the events of the morning. Nobody would believe him—he didn't believe it himself.

Later that afternoon, the sculptor had just managed to coax his recalcitrant bride back to the safety of the cottage when he heard the deep rumbling of an engine in the narrow laneway. He peeped out of the kitchen window, confirming that the Morgan sports car that was his mother's namesake, the car she adored more than any of her other possessions, was bearing down upon him. The top was down. Above the immaculate cream-and-chrome bodywork and wire wheels he could see his mother at the polished-wood steering wheel. She was fashionably kitted out in headscarf, wrap-around sunglasses, leather driving gloves and jacket. She looked supremely confident, capable of anything.

The sculptor pulled back from the window in alarm.

"What is it? What on earth is that growling noise?" Nimue asked. "It sounds dangerous."

"It is dangerous," the sculptor replied. "It's Mother—she's obviously decided to visit me."

"Well she needn't bother," Nimue replied. "She can turn right around and go away again." She raised her arm, preparing to speak an incantation.

The sculptor blocked her, stepping in front of her and knocking her arm aside. "Don't," he said. "It's her cottage."

"So?"

"So you are my wife. You're family now. You'll have to meet my mother sooner or later. You should at least be civil to her in her own house."

"I'll see. It depends how civil she is to me," said Nimue. "She will have to understand that *I* am here now. As your wife, I take precedence."

The sculptor headed for the door, anxious to forewarn his mother. He was too late. His mother had already alighted and reached the cottage.

"Hello, dear," she began cheerfully as she opened the door, bringing with her the familiar scent of apple blossom—the only perfume she ever wore. "I came to see how you are getting on with that statue of yours." She stopped dead in the doorway at the sight of Nimue. "Oh," she said, quickly making a complicated warding gesture with her fingers. "What have you let into my house?" She stared at the enchantress.

Nimue was the living image of the sculptor's desire, and his mother hated her from the moment she saw her.

"Mother," said the sculptor, "this is Nimue. Nimue, this is my mother, Morgan."

"Morgan!" said the enchantress. "I might have known." She turned back to the sculptor. "You never said your mother was a sorceress."

"A what?" The sculptor shook his head in bewilderment. "She's a real estate agent."

"Is that another name for witch?"

"Certainly not."

"Enchantress, then: she knows how to exercise coercion. I can feel it."

"And I can feel your attempts to confuse me, dear," Morgan said acidly. "The glamour won't work on me: I'm immune."

"As am I," Nimue shot back.

"So I see," said Morgan, methodically easing off her driving gloves and placing them on the table with her sunglasses. She took off her headscarf and shook out her fashionably cut red hair, deliberately making herself at home, reclaiming her space, marking her territory.

Nimue glared at her.

The sculptor felt the full force of the compulsion that his bride levelled at his mother. He felt the hairs on the back of his neck stand up. He wanted to run.

Morgan didn't even blink. She affected not to notice the spell. "If that's the best you can do," she said, "I'd suggest we call a temporary halt to hostilities." She turned to her son. "Put the kettle on, would you dear? Your *wife* and I have things to discuss."

The sculptor watched helplessly as his mother and his bride sat down at opposite sides of the old oak kitchen table, waiting for him to bring the tea. He could practically see the battle lines that had been drawn between the two of them.

As he waited for the water to boil, the artist in him couldn't help noticing that the two stylishly dressed women made a striking picture in the shabby old cottage: his mother in tight-fitting black leather that set off her cropped red hair and grey eyes; his bride in a flowing soft blue summer dress that accentuated her beautiful curves and highlighted the deep blue of her eyes and her long blue-black curls. He suppressed the urge to set up his easel to paint the scene, or at least to photograph the women where they sat, upright on straight-backed antique wooden chairs, each planning her next move in a power play in which he himself was the only prize.

He made the tea, set out a plate of custard creams, found milk, sugar and clean cups. His hands shook, making the cups rattle in their saucers as he set the tray down between the adversaries. "Shall I be "mother"?" he asked nervously, offering to pour.

Morgan gave him a stern look. "I think not, dear," she said, "not while I'm here." She grasped the handle of the teapot before Nimue could pre-empt her. "This is still my house. I'll do the honours."

She poured the tea.

Nimue sniffed suspiciously.

"You haven't poisoned it with weed killer, have you, dear?" Morgan asked sweetly.

The sculptor shook his head, wondering how she had read his thoughts so easily. He watched as his mother sipped, then his bride.

Both nibbled at the sugary cookies, smiling guardedly as they ate the custard creams—which both of them loathed—neither prepared to give the other the satisfaction of a missed bite.

"I think you should leave," Morgan said at last. "You know you don't belong here."

"Not a chance," Nimue replied. "I'm just getting comfortable. Your son set me free. He'll do anything for me."

"And for me," said Morgan. "He always has done."

"Don't I get a say in this?" the sculptor asked, trying not to sound plaintive.

"No, dear," both women responded in unison.

"The conflict could prove too much for him," Morgan said. "It could tear him apart."

Nimue shrugged. "Do you care? I know I don't."

Morgan's face mottled red with anger. "How dare you," she said. "You don't really want him, but you won't let him go."

"The red-faced look doesn't suit you, *mother*," Nimue said coolly. "It clashes with your hair. If you are so concerned about your son, you'd best leave him to me. That way he won't have to deal with the stress of being pulled this way and that between us."

"Nice try," Morgan retorted. "You'll tire of him soon enough. And I'll be there for him when you do."

"How touching."

Morgan ignored the interruption. "In the meantime," she continued, "I have a better idea."

"Oh?"

"I suggest we join forces, at least for now, in the interests of domestic harmony."

"And how do we achieve that?"

"As I said, we declare a truce."

"How quaint."

"You'll enjoy it," Morgan said. "I can offer you much more entertainment than my poor son can."

"Such as?"

"I'm on my way to meet a client," Morgan said. "I'm taking him to view a castle. I had thought my son might like to join us for a picnic tea. You could come along too, if you are interested in such things."

"A castle?" Nimue said. "That sounds more like it. I'll just get my new coat."

Nimue took the passenger seat in the Morgan sports car, leaving the sculptor to squeeze into the tiny space behind the seats. The drive was mercifully short, and before long the three of them were strolling towards the castle gate—the sculptor laden with a wicker picnic basket, wine cooler, and plaid rug.

A pale, black-clad man with spiked hair and too many piercings—his nose, his ears, even his eyebrows sported an assortment of silver rings—was lounging by the gate.

"You're late," he said, by way of greeting.

"An organisational misunderstanding," Morgan said airily. "The important thing is, I'm here now. And I have the keys to the castle. Shall we proceed?"

"Who are these?" the man asked, pointing a black-lacquered fingernail at the sculptor and his wife. He turned up the high collar on his long black coat and leaned back arrogantly against the wrought iron gate.

"Allow me to introduce my son, Cedric, and his bride."

"Nimue," said the enchantress. She held out her perfumed hand and stepped forward, radiating charm.

The effect was almost comical. The man straightened up, bowed, and kissed the proffered hand. "Divine," he said. "Simply divine: You, my dear, are the most perfect creature I have ever seen."

"This is Mr Rupert Bailey," Morgan said.

"Pleased to meet you," said the sculptor.

Bailey ignored him.

"Mr Bailey manages *Pink Diamond*," Morgan added.

Nimue looked blank.

"The girl band," Morgan said quickly. "They're huge."

Nimue frowned. "Monsters?"

"Where have you *been* all these years?" Bailey asked.

"Trapped inside a rock, if you must know," Nimue replied. She pouted prettily.

Bailey roared with laughter. "Good answer, my dear. You'd have to be walled up not to have heard of my girls. They're sensational. They've made me a very rich man. But you—you are beautiful, and witty into the bargain—I can see we'll get along famously." He took her arm. "Will you walk with me. Are you at all interested in castles?"

"Of course," said Nimue. "I was once married to a king. Pellinore, his name was. He had a rather fine castle, though I must admit it was terribly chilly in winter."

The man grinned. "Perhaps I shall buy this one. Would you like that?" He licked his lips, flashing his silver tongue stud.

"Perhaps." Nimue smiled dazzlingly.

Morgan hurriedly unlocked the gates.

Nimue swept through the entrance like a queen, leaning on the arm of the client, leaving her mother-in-law to follow as best she could and her husband to bring up the rear of the procession bearing his unwieldy burden of picnic paraphernalia.

Morgan caught up with Rupert Bailey where he had, perforce, to wait for her at the front door. As she bent to unlock it, she tried to warn him. She really did. "I don't think it's a good idea for you to take up with my son's wife," she whispered.

"Don't be such a prude," he replied. "Nimue and I are getting along famously. I'm thinking of making her a star. I'm sure your son won't object to that."

"Object to what?" said the sculptor, joining them at last. He was breathing heavily from the brisk walk. He dropped his burden of picnic things, which fell rattling onto the uneven flagstones.

"I was just telling your mother that your wife has star potential."

"Oh," said the sculptor. "In that case, who am I to stand in her way?"

Bailey beamed. "Good man," he said. "Ah, here she is now."

"I was just looking at the defences," Nimue said brightly. "They'll need repair."

"I'll bear that in mind when we come to talk terms," Bailey answered. He took her hand. "Come on, let's look inside."

"We'll meet you on the roof terrace," Morgan said. "The view from the battlements is magnificent. I've brought a picnic for afternoon tea. I'll set it out ready for you."

"With champagne, I hope?" Bailey said.

"Of course," Morgan replied. "Nothing's too much trouble for such a valuable client."

"Good." He turned back to Nimue. "Let's go, princess," he said.

Up on the roof terrace, the sculptor helped his mother to set out the picnic.

"Surely you aren't thinking you can just unload her onto someone else," Morgan was saying.

"Why not? She's beautiful and captivating—she's certainly got your client wrapped around her little finger." He stopped, recalling the broken fingers of the hapless waitress. He brushed the recollection aside. "As far as I'm concerned, he can keep her. He can probably afford her. I feel much better now that she is concentrating on him. It's as if she drains all my energy from me."

"That's exactly what she does do," his mother replied. "She is animated by the energy of those around her. Without that, she would revert to a stone statue."

"Can we lock her away, then? Till she winds down, so to speak?"

"Difficult," Morgan replied. "She is very strong. She would simply rise up again when the next power source came along. She would call, and somebody would find her. She summoned you, after all. She's been feeding on your life force while you worked to free her. And now you have given her back her true form. It'll be easier for her now."

"What, then?"

"I don't know. I'll think of something." She smiled at him. "Maybe she *could* become some sort of star—at least in Bailey's business there's a chance that nobody would notice that she isn't actually human."

"Until she drains someone completely," the sculptor said darkly.

"We don't know that that would happen."

"Don't we? She's greedy. She'll go too far: she has no limits, no self control, and no conscience at all."

"Then we'll have to find a way to restrain her."

"Good luck with that," the sculptor said sourly. "She's beyond me."

There was a clattering on the stairs, and a tall, leggy blonde wearing a skin-tight silver top, a short red leather skirt and very high stiletto heels strutted across the gallery and stepped out onto the stone terrace.

"Thought I'd find you up here," she said. "The real estate office told me their agent was planning a roof picnic." She looked out at the sweeping panorama of the castle's manicured grounds and the dark green of its surrounding forest. "I can totally see why," she added. "The view is stunning." She shook hands with Morgan. "I'm Skye," she said. "You must be Morgan."

"Pleased to meet you," Morgan replied. "Would you care for champagne?"

"I don't see why not," Skye replied, accepting the proffered glass. "Where's Rupert?"

"Right here, my darling girl," Rupert Bailey said, emerging onto the terrace. His coat was rumpled, his gelled hair was messy, and his lips looked bruised and swollen: when Nimue kissed a man, he stayed kissed. "I could do with a drink," he croaked.

Morgan handed him glass of champagne, which he gulped down.

"Thanks," he said, holding out the glass for Morgan to refill. "I needed that."

Nimue appeared right behind him. She looked perfect—not a hair out of place. "Aren't you going to introduce me?" she asked.

"This is Skye," Morgan said quickly. "Skye is the lead singer of *Pink Diamond*. Skye, this is Nimue."

"Sure." Skye frowned. "No need to ask what you've been up to, Bailey," she said.

"Rupert is going to make me a rock star," Nimue breathed. "Isn't that thrilling?"

"I wouldn't get too excited," Skye replied, giving the enchantress a thin smile. "Mr Bailey says that to all the girls. It gets him laid, more often than not. You've been had, honey—in more ways than one by the look of it."

Nimue's eyes narrowed. "Are you saying he lied to me?"

"Of course he lied to you. It's what he does best."

Nimue turned to face Rupert Bailey, suspiciously narrowing her eyes. "Can you make me a star or can't you?" she demanded.

He spread his hands wide. "I could . . . " he began.

"Except he's contracted to me, and to *Pink Diamond*," Skye finished for him. "So he can't take on any new clients just at the moment." She put down her glass and turned back to the sculptor's mother. "I'm really sorry, Morgan," she said. "I didn't mean to spoil your picnic. The castle is lovely, but Mr Bailey here seems to have over stepped the mark. Perhaps we can do this again another day?"

"Of course," Morgan said smoothly. "Just call my office when you're ready to take another look."

"I won't be made a fool of," Nimue said quietly.

The sculptor heard the menace in her words. He rose to take her by the arm, hoping to soothe her.

"Let it go, Nimue dear," Morgan said softly. "These things happen."

"Not to me they don't." Nimue shook herself free of her anxious husband. "If I understand aright," she said to Skye, "the only reason that Rupert can't make me a star is that he is bound to you."

"Correct," Skye replied. "I'm sorry, but that's the way it is."

"Then that's easily taken care of," Nimue said, frowning in concentration.

The tension in the air was palpable. The sculptor watched in horror as Skye suddenly walked over to the battlements, teetering unsteadily on her high heels. Her eyes were unfocused. Her muscles quivered visibly as she tried desperately to change direction. The sculptor recognised her bewildered expression: it matched the ones he had seen this morning during his bride's shopping expedition.

Skye was dangerously close to the edge, but she was somehow resisting the compulsion to jump.

"Mother!" the sculptor shouted. "Do something!"

His shout broke Morgan's counter-spell, the spell that was shielding Skye, holding her back from the brink. It was only for a second, but that split second was enough. Skye toppled over the parapet, screaming as she fell to her death.

Nimue strolled to the edge and glanced casually at the body that lay sprawled on the stones below. "You'll need a new lead singer, Rupert," she said. "Now you can make me a rock star after all."

Rupert Bailey was suddenly sober. He stared at Nimue, his bruised face a mask of horror. "You killed her," he said, his voice flat with the effort of getting the words out past the beguilement that still held him in thrall to the enchantress.

"I never touched her," Nimue replied. "She fell. We all saw it."

"You made her jump," he said stubbornly.

"Prove it."

"You know I can't."

"Exactly."

"But I know it. In my heart, I know it."

"Then you also know I did it for you, only for you, my prince," Nimue said. She reached out to take his hand.

Bailey backed away from her, momentarily forgetting the sheer drop behind him.

"Careful," Morgan said. She reached out and touched his arm to steady him.

He stopped stock still, shuddering.

"You wanted me to do it," Nimue went on, relentlessly sweet. "You said yourself that you wanted me. She was the only obstacle. She was in our way."

"I never said I wanted to be rid of her. I never said I wanted her dead. I loved her."

"Then you should have been more specific." Nimue shrugged. "Anyway, she's gone now. So you can make good on your promise. I'm ready to take over as lead singer. I'm ready to be a star."

Bailey prevaricated. "The other girls won't like it."

"Of course they'll like it," Nimue replied. "People always want what I want."

"But you won't sound like Skye," Bailey said.

"Of course I will. I can sound any way I want to."

"But all the girls in *Pink Diamond* are natural blondes," Bailey said, clutching at straws now. "It's their key look."

"Too easy," Nimue replied. Her dark curls lightened as she spoke, shading from black to ash brown through honey to pale Nordic blonde. "Like this?" she asked, twisting a perfect lock of blonde hair in her fingers.

"How is that even possible?" Rupert gasped.

"She's changing her appearance from my son's sexual fantasy to yours," Morgan said matter-of-factly. "She's seeing into your desires, right down to your dreams. You might as well accept it, Bailey: you invited her across the threshold and into your life, you offered her stardom, and then you had sex with her. As far as she's concerned, that sealed the bargain. She's your problem now. Enjoy."

Bailey shook his head, trying to clear his thoughts. "What is she?" he asked.

"An old fashioned enchantress," the sculptor replied. "Straight out of *King Arthur and his Knights of the Round Table*."

"Yeah, right," said Bailey. "Thanks for the heads up on that!"

"No," said Morgan. "It's true."

"It can't be."

"Of course it can, my prince," said Nimue. She smiled radiantly, her pearly white skin and deep blue eyes now framed by long silver-blonde hair. She was beautiful, and cold, and deadly as any ice queen. She ramped up the compulsion that enthralled her new manager. "You may consider yourself enchanted, Rupert Bailey," she said. "I'll need clothes. And jewels—I must have decent diamonds."

Bailey could only nod.

"That's better," she said, taking his hand in her bone-crushing grip as she gazed into his unfocused eyes. "I'm ready."

This time, he didn't have the strength to resist. He was already planning her rise to stardom.

"Aren't you forgetting something?" the sculptor asked.

"What, ex-husband?" Nimue replied.

"There's a body down there: the body of a very famous singer. We'll have to call the police. The media will have a field day when word of this gets out."

Morgan laid a hand on her son's shoulder. "It's all right, dear," she said. "Mr Bailey is an important client. He knows I'll take care of it."

"Thank you," Bailey said.

"I think you should take Nimue away now, Rupert, out of harm's way," Morgan continued. "You *really* don't want her to meet the press just yet, if you take my meaning. She doesn't officially exist: nobody need ever know she was here."

"Good thinking," said Bailey, recovering a little of his composure. "What will you say?"

"Nothing but the truth," Morgan replied. "The truth is always safest. I shall say that I was preparing a picnic tea up here for you while you toured the castle. My son and I were alone here when Skye arrived. My office will confirm that she was coming here to join us. I shall say that she was drinking champagne when she wandered too close to the edge in those very high heels she was wearing. I shall say that we were all terribly shocked when she overbalanced and fell to her tragic, untimely death."

"The police will know I was here."

"Certainly: I shall tell them that you arrived up here on the battlements just after Skye fell, and that you were so overcome by grief that you simply couldn't stay here with the body. You did not actually witness the accident, so it seemed to me it would be all right for you to leave. I shall be terribly contrite if that proves not to be the case. The police will contact you, and you will corroborate my story."

"Someone is bound to see Nimue leaving," the sculptor said. "Whatever she's done, she's still gorgeous—she's not exactly invisible."

Nimue smirked. "Nobody will see me," she said. "I can be invisible if I choose."

"Of course you can," Rupert Bailey said wearily.

It took only a few short weeks for the public outpouring of grief at Skye's untimely death to subside. The heaped bouquets withered on the castle's wrought iron gates; the autopsy confirmed the alcohol in the singer's blood; the judge at the inquest ruled death by misadventure. Life in the music industry returned to something that approximated normality. Almost.

Nimue made her debut at Skye's memorial concert. The other girls—Amber and Jade on guitars, Crystal on drums—were obviously struggling. Bailey passed it off as grief, even when Crystal's drum solo reached a frenzied crescendo that ended only when she broke her sticks. Nimue's likeness to her predecessor was uncanny, but the old harmony wasn't there. The girls were resisting. The enchantress didn't care: from the moment she stepped onto the stage and felt the focus of thousands of fans upon her, felt the love, she was exultant: so much energy to draw upon, so much available power. She knew she could rule them all. She knew she had been re-born for this, only for this.

She reached out—beguiling, coercing, compelling. Her fame grew. She was soon the darling of the media, beloved of talk show hosts, adored by her fans. The press was ecstatic. Rupert Bailey was constantly at her side, protecting her, promoting her. Amber and Jade and Crystal, their resistance crushed, were constrained to declare themselves overwhelmed by her talent. They dared not leave the band. *Pink Diamond* was re-named *Heart of Stone*. Their new album rocketed up the charts. Nimue was triumphant.

The sculptor was horrified. As he sat watching the huge television screen in his mother's London flat, he tuned in to yet another of his stone bride's media appearances. He noticed that Rupert Bailey had aged considerably, and had developed an annoying facial tic. He felt a pang of sympathy watching the way the agent kept looking nervously over his shoulder, wincing if he was accidentally touched. The presenter mentioned that Bailey's ribs were broken, and strapped tight under his gothic garb. The sculptor knew why.

"Well, what are you going to do about *her*?" his mother asked, setting down two steaming mugs on the low glass table. The room filled with the aroma of freshly brewed coffee.

"It's not all my fault," the sculptor said, picking up his mug and inhaling deeply.

"Of course it is, dear," Morgan replied. "Would you like a biscuit?" She placed a plate of chocolate biscuits in front of him. "These are your favourites," she added.

"You can't blame me for everything that's happened: that's not fair. I had less than twenty-four hours with her."

"But *you* let her out of the stone. You handed her over to poor Bailey. So yes, it is your fault that we now have a sociopathic statue controlling a large chunk of the media: Nimue has a huge following. She's feeding on it, growing stronger all the time. Now she's talking about going into politics. She must be stopped before she causes real harm."

"I never imagined she would get this far."

"I know, dear." Morgan sighed. "But the fact remains, you are responsible. It's up to you to do something."

"How can I? Look at her!"

He gestured at the screen, which showed Nimue being interviewed for a lifestyle program. She was at home in her castle—now billed as the perfect rock star's retreat. She sat before the cameras in a burnished chair, carefully positioned beside a blazing fire in the great hall, looking every inch a queen. The sculptor saw that she was dressed in the tight, figure-hugging black leathers that the *Heart of Stone* girls now all affected, set off by her shining blonde hair and heavy, diamond-encrusted jewellery that sparkled under the spotlight. She was even wearing long black boots with high heels. She looked powerful, and very, very expensive.

"Tell us about your amazing boot heels," the presenter said, right on cue. " Our fashion-conscious viewers are dying to know."

"I had the heels specially crafted from polished black granite," she replied. "They are very strong. They go with my *Heart of Stone* image. Pretty, aren't they?" She stretched out an ankle for the viewers to admire.

"Very pretty," the interviewer agreed.

"She tells the truth, and nobody sees it for what it is," Morgan remarked. "It's a great technique."

"I know what you mean," the sculptor said glumly. He turned up the sound. "The interviewer just asked about her background. Listen to this!"

"We didn't have central heating in Camelot," Nimue saying brightly. "It's a great improvement."

The presenter laughed. "And I suppose you knew King Arthur?"

"Of course." Nimue lowered her voice conspiratorially. "And I hate to say it, but the rumours about his incest with his half-sister are almost certainly true."

"How dare she!" Morgan said indignantly.

The sculptor looked up in surprise.

"Really?" the interviewer asked. "Are you sure?"

Nimue nodded. "But then," she added darkly, "his sister was always trouble. And his wife, Guinevere, was not the innocent she made herself out to be. She and Lancelot were lovers: they denied it, of course, but they weren't fooling anyone, if you ask me. I'm sure Arthur knew."

"But wasn't Lancelot involved with Elaine?"

"I felt sorry for her," Nimue replied. " She tricked Lancelot into bed with the help of that interfering old busybody Merlin. That's how Galahad was conceived, you know."

The interviewer lapped it up, and the producer let it run, thinking it was great shtick for a rock star who owned a castle. He knew that Nimue's fans loved the fantasy: they wanted the fairy tale to be true, and to hell with reality. Reality was dull. Nimue was glamorous, exciting. She was good for ratings.

Unwisely, the interviewer changed tack, trying for a different angle. "Let's come back to the present," he said. "Let me ask you about the rumours that there were rather a lot of unfortunate mishaps on your last tour. Is it true that a technician who criticised you was electrocuted while he was wiring the set?"

Nimue shrugged. "Accidents happen," she said.

"What about the cartoonist who caricatured you?"

"What about him?"

"He was killed in a road accident on his way home from your concert."

"That's just karma," Nimue replied. "If you go around making fun of people you have to expect payback."

The presenter missed the warning signs—the narrowed eyes, the impatient tapping of the fingers on the arms of the chair.

Rupert Bailey didn't. He tried to intervene. "I think that's enough," he said. "Nimue is tired. She needs to rest now. Let's wind this up."

She waved his objections aside. "I'm fine," she said, turning back to concentrate on the interviewer. "What exactly are you suggesting?" she asked.

"Only that trouble seems to follow you," he said lightly. "There are those who would say that anyone who crosses you is in mortal danger."

"You can't help bad luck," she said.

"Of course not: it's just that bad luck for others always seems to be good luck for you. After all, you did get your first big break when *Pink Diamond*'s original lead singer died in a horrific fall, from the battlements of this very castle. It all seems terribly dramatic, terribly dark and gothic. Do these things haunt you?"

He was half joking.

She wasn't. She was focussing her full attention on the man confronting her, this man who dared to question the legitimacy of her meteoric rise to stardom. She was the very queen of celebrities. She would have to silence him.

The sculptor saw the shadows change as the lighting rig began to topple. Along with thousands of viewers, he watched in dismay as a metal spar came loose and poleaxed the interviewer where he sat, killing him instantly. There was blood everywhere.

Nimue rushed to the waiting arms of Bailey, turning her pretty blonde head away from the grisly scene.

The sculptor caught a last, fleeting glimpse of the agent's despairing face before the live feed was cut.

"That'll make the evening news," Morgan said drily.

"Bailey will spin it," the sculptor replied. "You know he will. You know how it will go: poor Nimue couldn't possibly have been responsible—she herself has had a very lucky escape, and she's just devastated about what happened. She feels deeply for the poor man's family. She hopes that viewers will respect her privacy."

"True," said Morgan. "As I said before, she's more dangerous than she ever was. You have to do something to stop her."

"I still don't see how," he replied. "She'd destroy me as soon as look at me."

A split second before the doorbell rang, Morgan spoke again. "As it happens," she said, "I've arranged for someone to help you."

Before he could ask, she rose to answer the door, and the sculptor was astonished to see that his usually middle-aged mother was suddenly transformed: she was younger, slimmer, and most definitely beautiful. The fine wrinkles had vanished from her pale skin, and when she ran her fingers through her glossy red hair the scent of her warm, apple-blossom perfume filled the room.

"Close your mouth, dear," she said. "Don't gape like that: it makes you look stupid."

The sculptor complied, shutting his mouth with an audible snap. He was learning a lot about his mother. There were things that, on the whole, he'd rather not have known. He sighed.

Morgan opened the door to a youngish, athletic man with wavy chestnut-coloured hair and wide grey eyes that matched her own. "Merlin, darling," she said. "I'm so glad you could make it. Do come in."

"Morgan, my love—it's been a long time. You haven't changed a bit," he replied. "You never change."

"No more than do you," she laughed.

As the door closed behind him, Merlin swept her into his arms and kissed her, deeply.

The sculptor, embarrassed, affected not to notice.

After a long moment, Morgan pulled away. "Let me introduce my son," she breathed, straightening her clothing. "Cedric, this is Merlin."

"Pleased to meet you," Merlin said, not in the least abashed.

The sculptor was dumbfounded. "Not *the* Merlin," he stuttered. "Not the magician?"

"The very same," Merlin replied. He grinned, a grin that made his handsome face seem even more boyish. "I can see why you might be surprised."

"Surprised?" said the sculptor. "That doesn't even begin to cover it!"

"Manners!" Morgan said sharply.

"It's all right, Morgan," said Merlin. "It's a bit much for him to take in."

"Sorry," the sculptor said shortly. "It's just that Nimue—the enchantress—bragged that she had walled you up in an enchanted cave, from which you could never escape."

Merlin grinned again. "The first part is true: she did. I admit I allowed it."

"But?"

"I taught Nimue all the magic she knows," Merlin said. "But not all the magic that *I* know: I had good reason to want to disappear for a while. Her treachery made a good cover story."

"And let Merlin go about his business unimpeded," Morgan added.

"But you must have loved her," the sculptor said.

"Briefly," Merlin said. "But part of my curse is that I see true: her glamour could not last for long."

The sculptor nodded. "It wore off for me pretty fast," he said.

"She let you go, dear," Morgan said. "You were just a means to an end for her: a handy man with a chisel."

The sculptor swallowed back his rising bile. "That's hard to take, Mother," he said.

"Sorry, dear," she replied. "But under such circumstances as these it's as well to face facts."

The sculptor was needled. "Then let me ask *you* for some facts," he said. "I never met my father, and you two seem pretty well acquainted. Was it Merlin here?"

"I'm afraid not, dear," Morgan answered cheerfully.

"You mother and I go back a long way," Merlin said, putting his arm around her shoulders. "But I do not, alas, have the honour of being your father."

"He was an ordinary mortal," Morgan said." And before you ask the obvious next question, I'll tell you straight that the magic in my family only manifests in the female line. I'm sorry to say that you're plain mortal too."

"But he has serious talent, all the same," Merlin said. "He responded to Nimue's call, so he must have inherited some residual power."

"Alas, yes," said Morgan. "Enough that he was able to recreate her true form for her—which is why we're in such a mess."

"Don't reproach him too much," Merlin said. "He was following his art, his dream: he couldn't have known what she is."

The sculptor smiled gratefully. "Thanks," he said. "That's the first kind word I've had on the subject."

Merlin was thoughtful. "You gave her back her form," he said slowly, "but you are not a sorcerer. You could not alter her substance."

"Meaning?"

"She's still stone: we can work with that."

The sculptor hesitated. "Does that mean you know how to undo her enchantments?" he asked.

"Perhaps."

"She killed again today, and this time on national television," Morgan added. "We have to stop her. We need your help."

"Of course," Merlin said. "You had only ever to ask, my love."

The two shared another long, romantic look.

The sculptor cleared his throat. "Do you have a plan?" he asked.

"Nimue was turned to stone a long time ago, when she double-crossed a sorcerer whose powers far exceeded her own," Merlin said. "That has not been undone: stone is still her element, no matter how animated she has become."

"Hell, yes," the sculptor said. "She weighs a ton."

"So we treat her as stone," said Merlin. "Stone is hard and cold and strong, but it can be cracked, and broken. It can be confined."

Morgan nodded. "We'll have to get close enough," she said.

"That's easily done," Merlin said. "She'll react to me."

"Whatever makes you think she'll do that?" the sculptor asked.

"You said that Nimue still thinks I am safely entombed. If she learns that I am free, she'll want to destroy me. She knows full well that I'm her most dangerous adversary."

"Right now she feels safe, and in control: that's always a dangerous illusion. She won't want Merlin to challenge that position."

"Exactly, my love," Merlin said. "That's what all these killings are about: she craves total control." He grinned mischievously. "I think it's time we went to a *Heart of Stone* concert, don't you?"

Morgan grinned back. "I'll call Rupert Bailey. We'll need VIP seats, so she'll be sure to see us."

"My thoughts precisely," Merlin answered. He pulled her closer. "And in the meantime, you and I have some catching up to do."

"You're reading my mind," Morgan answered. The apple-blossom scented air in the apartment positively crackled with sexual tension.

The sculptor stood. "I'll just get my coat," he said hurriedly. "I've suddenly remembered I have an appointment in Bloomsbury this afternoon, at the Museum."

"See you later then, dear," his mother said absently, gazing into Merlin's eyes.

The sculptor all but ran from the Barbican flat: he did *not* want to know what happened next—he really did not.

Daylight had all but faded from the London sky when the sculptor returned to his mother's flat. He opened the door cautiously, only to find Morgan and Merlin curled up together on the couch watching the evening news. The pair looked very pleased with themselves.

"We've got front row tickets," Morgan said. "Do you want to come along?"

"I don't think so, Mother," the sculptor replied. "I don't want to be anywhere near *her*. Not unless I absolutely have to."

"Perfectly understandable," Merlin said. "We're just going along to reconnoitre." He smiled at the sculptor. "We'll be off, then."

"There's dinner in the fridge, if you want it, dear," Morgan said. "We'll just get changed." She headed to the bedroom, with Merlin at her heels.

Minutes later, the sculptor stared in disbelief as the pair re-emerged, ready to leave. They both appeared even younger, and were now dressed alike in black jeans and shirts, with matching black leather jackets and boots. He realised, belatedly, that his mother was wearing a nose ring. "Have fun," he said, not knowing what else to offer them.

Morgan laughed. "We will, dear," she said. "It'll be a good show."

Merlin took her by the hand and the pair scampered off to the concert, giggling like a couple of teenagers.

The sculptor sat back on the couch, looking down at his hands, the hands that had started all of this. His head ached. He felt bone weary, confused, and very, very alone.

By the time Merlin and Morgan arrived, the concert was well underway. Nimue swaggered, centre stage, gorging on the energy of the crowd as she sang what had become her signature song, *Love Hurts*. Her fans were with her all the way: they moved with the music, giving her their vital essence, giving her their love. She revelled in the power of it. She strutted her stuff. She was in control. She was queen.

Then it happened. She felt the atmosphere change, felt a chill blast of indifference as a young couple slipped into the VIP seats in the front row. As they settled themselves, Nimue saw them link hands. And everything changed. Some sort of shield spread out around them, blocking the energy transfer. At first it was just the front rows, but then it grew, spreading until it encompassed the whole stadium. The fans didn't notice: they were still enjoying the show, still radiating energy. Nimue could see it, could smell it, could feel it pulsating through the venue. But she was being denied: try as she might, she could find no access to absorb the life energies she required.

She stamped her foot in frustration.

The stage cracked with the force of it. The girls looked startled, but kept playing, covering Nimue's faltering performance.

But then her voice cracked. She lost it. She raised both arms and hurled a bolt of pure energy at the shield, at the couple sitting calmly behind it.

The shield held. Silver-blue lightning arced back at the stage. The lights shorted out. The power failed. The air filled with the smell of burnt ozone. The music stopped.

The crowd stampeded for the exits, fearing fire.

Rupert Bailey stepped hurriedly onto the stage. "Ladies and Gentlemen," he shouted, "please be calm. Please stay in your seats. We have a technical fault. Our people are working on it now. Normal service will be resumed as soon as possible."

"I don't think so," Merlin said softly.

"Come on," Morgan said: "it's time for you to meet the band."

The pair headed backstage, still holding hands.

The scene that greeted them was chaotic. Nimue was in a towering rage, ranting and cursing and throwing anything that came to hand. Everyone—except for the hapless Rupert Bailey—was staying out of her way: technicians scurried about, repairing the still-smoking wiring; a makeup artist cowered in a corner; Amber, Jade and

Crystal were resignedly drinking thermos coffee while they waited to go back onstage.

Bailey was trying to calm his star. "Nimue, princess," he was saying. "You were doing great: I don't understand what's spooked you. Can you tell me what happened?"

Nimue simply pointed to where Merlin and Morgan were picking their way through tangled wires and cables and lighting paraphernalia, making for the crowded backstage area.

"*He* happened," she said darkly.

"Hi Rupert, hi everyone," Morgan said brightly. "I've brought a friend: Merlin, meet the girls."

The atmosphere altered once again. The gloom lightened perceptibly as Merlin entered the room. Amber, Jade and Crystal smiled, their smiles becoming genuine as they were suddenly set free from Nimue's compulsion. They rushed to thank him.

"Wow," Jade said. "Whatever you just did, please keep doing it."

"Yeah," said Amber. "I feel years younger."

Crystal clasped Merlin's hand. "Where have you been all my life?" she giggled.

Rupert Bailey shook his head in bewilderment. "What's happening?" he asked.

"We're blocking her control," Morgan murmured, miming air kisses as she hugged him. "But we can't keep it up indefinitely. We're here to help you, but you'll have to play along. Can you do that?"

Bailey nodded.

"Get *him* out of here," Nimue said. She turned to face Merlin, her whole body tensed, poised to strike.

"Nimue, darling," Merlin drawled, grinning boyishly. He disentangled himself from the musicians. "I thought you'd be pleased to see me. It's been such a long time."

"You're supposed to be dead," she said flatly.

"As, my darling, are you," he countered. "At least I have a pulse."

"I'll kill you."

"You already tried."

"Then I'll try again. You're no match for me, Merlin. You know that. I outwitted you last time."

"Ah, but my powers have grown since then, my sweet," he said. "I'm much younger now, and much stronger." His demeanour hardened. "I know what you are. I know your true essence. I can break you."

"I'd like to see you try."

"You've just had a little demonstration. Look around you: your fans have gone, and you no longer control your band." He gestured to where the girls were packing up their instruments.

"See you," Amber waved. "I'm out of here."

"Me too," said Jade. "I reckon we're done for tonight."

"You can't just leave," Nimue said.

"Watch us," said Crystal. She turned to the makeup artist. "Want a lift?"

"That'd the great," the girl replied, still giving Nimue a wide berth. "I'll get my stuff."

Nimue struggled to coerce them back. Nothing happened. She was trapped inside her own aura. "What do you want, Merlin?" she asked at last.

"You know what I want," he said softly. "You took something from me. I want it back."

"It's not here."

"I know."

"What are we looking for?" Morgan asked.

"It's just an amulet," Merlin said. "But it is important to me."

"My guess, then, is that it'll be in the woods, in the broken cave where my son found her stone," Morgan said. "If it's an object of power, Nimue would have kept it close—she would have had it with her."

Nimue shot her a look of pure venom.

Morgan smiled back. "That hit the mark," she said. "You've never been a threat to me, dear," she added sweetly. "Just an inconvenience: as I told you right back at the start, I'll be there to pick up the pieces when you are done."

"So," said Merlin, "shall we meet tomorrow at Morgan's cottage? There's no point in wasting time."

"I'll arrange it," Rupert Bailey said hastily. "Shall we say around noon?"

"In that case, I'll organise a picnic lunch," Morgan added. "We might as well keep this civilized."

"Thank you," Rupert said. "I'd appreciate that."

"No," said Nimue. "I won't do it."

"I don't see how you can refuse, princess," he said. "We'll just give Mr Merlin back whatever it is you owe him . . . "

"Stole from me," Merlin interjected.

"Took," Bailey amended, "and then I'll get your career right back on track. Nobody will remember tonight: it'll be just a minor hiccup, you'll see."

"What if I don't agree?" Nimue said.

"I'll be there at every concert," Merlin replied. "I'll be running interference: your fans will see you stripped of your magic. I will be the end of your career."

Nimue scowled. "Very well," she said. "You can have your stupid amulet back, for all the good it will do you. It never worked anyway."

"Not for you, no," said Merlin. "It takes more power than you ever had to wield it."

"If you say so." Nimue sulked.

"We'll see you tomorrow then," Morgan said.

"Tomorrow," Bailey echoed. "We'll be there."

"Why are we bothering with a picnic?" the sculptor asked. Once again he had squeezed into the tiny space behind the Morgan's seats, and his muscles were cramping with strain.

"It's just for the look of the thing," his mother replied. She put her foot down, accelerating around a truck. Morgan never used the slow lane. "It's for Rupert, really," she added. "Everyone knows he is fond of champagne picnics. It'll make it plausible that he should insist on joining us for lunch."

"We need to manoeuvre Nimue close to the lake," Merlin said, shouting to be heard above the growling engine. "We'll set up the picnic on the shore, so we have a reason to go there after I retrieve my property."

"Why the lake?"

"Ah," said Merlin. "That remains to be seen. It all rather depends on my being reunited with my amulet."

The sculptor gave up any further attempt at conversation. He leaned back, the wind whipping his hair around his face. He closed his eyes as his mother pulled out to overtake another car: as with so many things Morgan did, he preferred not to look.

Rupert Bailey's car was already parked outside Morgan's cottage when the trio arrived. Morgan parked behind it, blocking the lane.

"Just in case," she muttered.

"It won't be a problem, my love," Merlin replied, stretching as he stepped from the car.

The sculptor crawled from his cramped spot behind the seats, massaging his thigh muscles as he stood waiting for his circulation to return.

Rupert was waiting nervously by the door. "I've made a cup of tea for Nimue," he said. "I didn't think you'd mind."

"Of course not," Morgan said brusquely. "You can bring her along when she's finished it. We'll be a few minutes setting up for the picnic lunch, in any case. We'll be in our usual spot, down by lake. There's a table and some benches near the old jetty. It's a pretty place, shaded by oak trees. You'll have no trouble finding it—just follow the path."

The picnic things were quickly arranged, and the group was soon ready for the walk to the site where the sculptor had first found his bride.

"It's not far," he said.

"I should think not," Nimue replied. "You can't seriously expect me to go traipsing about the countryside in *these* shoes."

"We wouldn't dream of it, dear," Morgan said tartly.

"Don't let's bicker, princess," Rupert said. "It's a lovely day for a walk. We'll be back in no time for lunch. Let's just do it, shall we?"

"Very well," said Nimue. "Though I don't really see why I have to come at all."

"Stop prevaricating," Merlin said testily. "Let's go."

Nimue's beautiful face creased into a frown, but she forbore to reply.

The stroll through the picturesque woodland was uneventful, and the party reached the spoil heap without mishap.

"Here," the sculptor said. "The stone was tipped with this lot."

Merlin was dismayed. "I was expecting a cave," he said.

"The cave was all broken up," Nimue said smugly. "I could have told you. You'll never find your stupid old amulet in this lot. Can we have lunch now?"

"Wait!" Merlin was concentrating hard. "It's here. I can feel it." He reached out for Morgan. "Can you join with me?" he asked.

"Of course, my love," she said. She took his hand, adding her power to his.

The air around them vibrated with energy. Power spoke to power. Merlin found the spot.

"Here," he said, scrabbling among the loose stones. "It's under here."

Morgan bent to help him.

They both forgot about Nimue. They turned their backs on her. Merlin's blocking spell slipped.

The enchantress took her chance. Rupert Bailey staggered as she fed on him, brutally sucking out his energy. She had no time for finesse. Bailey was failing, struggling to stay alive. Nimue concentrated, channelling his dwindling life force into her fingertips. She raised her arms, willing a landslip, ready to hurl the bolt of energy that would bring the overhanging rocks crashing down on her enemies as they dug for Merlin's amulet.

The sculptor saw her. He ran, knocking her to the ground in a flying tackle that left him gasping for breath. She went down heavily.

"I'll kill you," she said. She smashed her arm down on him.

He felt his collarbone snap.

She hit him again.

Pain blossomed into bright spots before his eyes. He lost consciousness.

Morgan felt her son's distress. She turned. "No!" she shouted. She did not hesitate: the spell she hurled at Nimue immobilised the enchantress where she knelt, her arm raised for a killing blow.

Merlin rose from the rubble, triumphantly clutching a mouldy leather thong from which dangled a small, leaf-shaped object. "Got it!" He glanced up from his prize, only to see Morgan fiercely holding Nimue captive, while both the sculptor and Rupert Bailey lay, unconscious, in the dust.

"I'll take Nimue," Merlin said. "You tend to your son."

"Thanks." Morgan strode across the uneven scree and took her son in her arms, scanning him for wounds. She breathed gently into his open mouth.

The sculptor opened his eyes.

"Easy," Morgan said. "You did well, my dear."

The sculptor smiled up at her. "What about Bailey?" he asked.

"He'll be fine," Merlin said, joining them. "Nimue is contained," he said. "Thanks, Cedric." He turned to Morgan. "I told you your son had talent," he added.

"Did you find it? The amulet, I mean," the sculptor asked.

"Yes," Merlin said. "It's whole, but it looks rather the worse for wear."

The sculptor sat up, gasping in pain as his broken collarbone moved.

"Easy," Morgan said.

"I brought this," the sculptor said, pulling a silver flask from his inside coat pocket. "I thought we might need it."

"What is it?"

"Water from the Glastonbury well," the sculptor said. "I had it at the cottage, for . . . for her," he said.

"Brilliant," Merlin said. "That's exactly what we need." He unscrewed the cap and tipped a little of the precious water onto his handkerchief, carefully cleaning away the dust and grime.

"There's a pattern," the sculptor said. "I can see it coming through."

"Runes," Morgan corrected.

"Runes of great power," Merlin said happily. "Can you feel it, Cedric?"

The sculptor reached out to touch the amulet. He could indeed sense it vibrating under his fingers. "I feel it," he said. "It's warm."

Merlin shared a look with Morgan. "When this is all over," he said, "I think perhaps I had better offer your son some training in the arts: no ordinary mortal could sense this."

Morgan smiled. "But first things first," she said. She laid her hand upon Rupert's chest.

Bailey coughed, his whole body shuddering. "What happened?" he managed to ask.

"Nimue was draining energy from you," Morgan said matter-of-factly. "My son saved you. You need to rest, but you'll be fine."

"What about her?" Bailey pointed at Nimue, still frozen in place.

Merlin made a complicated gesture.

Nimue was re-animated. As control returned to her limbs she completed the blow she had aimed at the sculptor, driving her fist into the ground where he had lain.

The sculptor shivered: "I'm so glad that didn't connect with me," he said.

"Come along, Nimue," Merlin said. His voice was hard, commanding. "It's time for lunch."

"Yes," said Morgan. "We could all do with a drink."

Nimue scowled, but acquiesced: she was in no position to argue.

Rupert Bailey was devouring his third piece of chicken when he heard Nimue gasp. He smelled musk and sweet lilies on the sudden breeze that ruffled his hair, and he looked up to see the enchantress staring in alarm at the suddenly rippling waters of the lake.

The sculptor could only gape in astonishment as the Lady of the Lake, clad all in shining white samite, emerged from the waters and glided to the end of the jetty. She was radiant: the sculptor, tongue-tied, could only long to speak with her, to touch her. He knew in that instant that he would ache for her for the rest of his life.

Morgan gently put her hand on his arm. "No, dear," she said softly. "It cannot be."

The Lady overheard. She smiled at him and shook her head.

The sculptor felt as if his heart would break. He felt the tears start. He drank deeply from his champagne, hoping to hide his pain.

Merlin's glance was all sympathy.

Nimue was scornful. "You're pitiful, ex-husband," she said. She turned her attention to the Lady, regaining her composure. "What're you doing here, anyway?"

"Is that any way to greet your family?" Morgan chided.

"Merlin summoned me," the Lady said, ignoring the interruption. "So here I am. It has been a great many years since last he last used the amulet to call my name."

"Lady." Merlin bowed. "You honour us with your presence."

She smiled. "Yes, yes," she said. "But what is it you desire of me? Are you checking on the Sword? I assure you it is safe."

"I know, Lady," Merlin replied. "I have called you today to ask if you will consent to take your sister, Nimue, into your care."

"And why should I do that?"

"She is doing great damage among the mortals of this time. She has killed when she should not. She has brought danger to herself, and to those around her. It would be best for all concerned if you will take her—for her safety, and for ours."

The Lady sighed. "Very well," she said. "I see the responsibility is to be mine once again." She beckoned. "Come along, Nimue."

"No." Nimue's voice was a flat denial. "You can't do this."

"I think you'll find we can," Merlin said mildly.

Nimue tried desperately to re-connect with Rupert Bailey, trying to gather his energy to her once more as she cast about for enough power to make her escape.

Merlin shook his head. "No," he said. "Bailey is protected. You must yield."

"Nimue," the Lady said gently, "this is not your time. Better you should take your ease with your family than that you should remain here and perish from the world."

"What do you mean?" Nimue asked.

"She means," Merlin said, "that now that I have regained my amulet"—he touched it briefly where it hung at his throat—"I have recovered the power to break you and scatter your stone atoms to the four winds. I'm offering you an alternative."

"You lie," Nimue said.

"No, dear," Morgan said. "He does not. The decision is yours—choose swiftly."

Nimue shook her head. "I don't believe you. Merlin never commanded such magic."

Merlin sighed. "Once upon a time I poured a large measure of my personal power into this amulet, for safekeeping," he said. "And now, I am restored. Choose."

The Lady held out her hands. "Come along, my dear," she said.

The sculptor felt the compulsion: his body vibrated with it.

Rupert Bailey simply stared as the drama played out around him.

Nimue could not, in the end, resist. Her lovely face set in an anguished, tortured expression as she took one forced, hesitant step towards the Lady, then another, compelled to move forward along the jetty until, at the very edge, the two women clasped hands. The water was deep here, glittering in the sunlight where the lily-scented breeze ruffled its surface.

"I'll bid you all farewell," the Lady said. "You and I, Merlin will meet again: of that I am certain."

Merlin bowed. "I shall await the day, Lady," he said.

"And I, Lady," Morgan said.

The Lady nodded her acknowledgement before she focussed her gaze upon the sculptor. "And I shall watch your progress with interest, young man," she said. "Great things await you."

The sculptor, still speechless, could only bow, copying Merlin.

The Lady smiled at him—a benediction.

The sculptor felt his collarbone knit: in that split-second he knew that he was healed, and heart-whole. "Farewell, Lady," he managed, at last.

The Lady took a last step towards the lake, pulling Nimue after her.

"You haven't seen the last of me," Nimue shouted, struggling. "I'll be back. Another will come to rescue me. I *will* have my revenge!" She toppled forward into the icy water.

The sculptor felt one last twinge of regret as he watched a burst of bubbles rise to the surface.

The enchantress sank like a stone.

Story Acknowledgements

"Velvet Green" by Janeen Webb, Copyright © 2014 by Janeen Webb. Original for this Collection.

"Manifest Destiny" by Janeen Webb, Copyright © 2010 by Janeen Webb. First published in *Baggage*, edited by Gillian Polack. (Eneit Press, NSW, 2010). Reprinted by permission of the author.

"Death at the Blue Elephant" by Janeen Webb, Copyright © 1997 by Janeen Webb, First published in *Enter...* , edited by Louise Thurtell (HarperCollins Flamingo, Sydney, 1997) and *HQ Magazine*, November/December, 1997. Reprinted by permission of the author.

"Red City" by Janeen Webb, Copyright © 2004 by Janeen Webb. First published in *Synergy SF: New Science Fiction*, edited by George Zebrowski (Five Star Press, Maine, USA, 2004). Reprinted by permission of the author.

"Paradise Design'd" by Janeen Webb, Copyright © 2008 by Janeen Webb. First published in *Dreaming Again*, edited by Jack Dann. (HarperCollins, Sydney, 2008, and Harper EOS, New York, 2008). Reprinted by permission of the authors.

"The Lion Hunt" by Janeen Webb, Copyright © 2004 by Janeen Webb. First published in *Conqueror Fantastic*, edited by Pamela Sargent (DAW Books, New York, 2004). Reprinted by permission of the author.

"Incident On Woolfe Street" by Janeen Webb, Copyright © 2000 by Janeen Webb. First published in *HQ Magazine* #68, January/Februrary, 2000 (HarperCollins, Sydney, 2000). Reprinted by permission of the author.

"The Lady of the Swamp" by Janeen Webb, Copyright © 2014 by Janeen Webb. Original for this Collection. Forthcoming reprint in *Cthulhu Deep Down Under*, edited by Steve Proposch, Christopher Sequiera and Bryce Stevens.

"A Faust Films Production" by Janeen Webb, Copyright © 2004 by Janeen Webb. First published in *Little Red Riding Hood in New York*, edited by Martin H. Greenberg and John Helfers (DAW Books, USA, 2004). Reprinted by permission of the author.

PAMELA SARGENT is the editor of several anthologies, among them the Women of Wonder series, and the author of many short stories. Her novels include *The Shore of Women*, *Venus of Dreams*, *Earthseed*, *Climb the Wind*, and *Ruler of the Sky*. She has won a Nebula Award, a Locus Award, and in 2012 was honored with the Pilgrim Award, given by the Science Fiction Research Association for lifetime contributions to science fiction and fantasy scholarship.

AVAILABLE FROM TICONDEROGA PUBLICATIONS

978-0-9586856-6-5	Troy by Simon Brown (tpb)
978-0-9586856-7-2	The Workers' Paradise eds Farr & Evans (tpb)
978-0-9586856-8-9	Fantastic Wonder Stories ed Russell B. Farr (tpb)
978-0-9803531-0-5	Love in Vain by Lewis Shiner (tpb)
978-0-9803531-2-9	Belong ed Russell B. Farr (tpb)
978-0-9803531-4-3	Ghost Seas by Steven Utley (tpb)
978-0-9803531-6-7	Magic Dirt: the best of Sean Williams (tpb)
978-0-9803531-8-1	The Lady of Situations by Stephen Dedman (tpb)
978-0-9806288-2-1	Basic Black by Terry Dowling (tpb)
978-0-9806288-3-8	Make Believe by Terry Dowling (tpb)
978-0-9806288-4-5	Scary Kisses ed Liz Grzyb (tpb)
978-0-9806288-6-9	Dead Sea Fruit by Kaaron Warren (tpb)
978-0-9806288-8-3	The Girl With No Hands by Angela Slatter (tpb)
978-0-9807813-1-1	Dead Red Heart ed Russell B. Farr (tpb)
978-0-9807813-2-8	More Scary Kisses ed Liz Grzyb (tpb)
978-0-9807813-4-2	Heliotrope by Justina Robson (tpb)
978-0-9807813-7-3	Matilda Told Such Dreadful Lies by Lucy Sussex (tpb)
978-1-921857-01-0	Bluegrass Symphony by Lisa L. Hannett (tpb)
978-1-921857-06-5	The Hall of Lost Footsteps by Sara Douglass (tpb)
978-1-921857-03-4	Damnation and Dames eds Liz Grzyb & Amanda Pillar (tpb)
978-1-921857-08-9	Bread and Circuses by Felicity Dowker (tpb)
978-1-921857-17-1	The 400-Million-Year Itch by Steven Utley (tpb)
978-1-921857-24-9	Wild Chrome by Greg Mellor (tpb)
978-1-921857-27-0	Bloodstones ed Amanda Pillar (tpb)
978-1-921857-30-0	Midnight and Moonshine by Lisa L. Hannett & Angela Slatter (tpb)
978-1-921857-65-2	Mage Heart by Jane Routley (tpb)
978-1-921857-66-9	Fire Angels by Jane Routley (tpb)
978-1-921857-67-6	Aramaya by Jane Routley (tpb)
978-1-921857-35-5	Dreaming of Djinn ed Liz Grzyb (tpb)
978-1-921857-38-6	Prickle Moon by Juliet Marillier (tpb)
978-1-921857-43-0	The Bride Price by Cat Sparks (tpb)
978-1-921857-46-1	The Year of Ancient Ghosts by Kim Wilkins (tpb)
978-1-921857-33-1	Invisible Kingdoms by Steven Utley (tpb)
978-1-921857-70-6	Havenstar by Glenda Larke (tpb)
978-1-921857-59-1	Everything is a Graveyard by Jason Fischer (tpb)
978-1-921857-53-9	Ambassador by Patty Jansen (tpb)
978-1-921857-59-1	Kisses by Clockwork ed Liz Grzyb (tpb)

TICONDEROGA PUBLICATIONS LIMITED HARDCOVER EDITIONS

978-0-9586856-9-6   Love in Vain BY Lewis Shiner
978-0-9803531-1-2   Belong ED Russell B. Farr
978-0-9803531-9-8   Basic Black BY Terry Dowling
978-0-9806288-0-7   Make Believe BY Terry Dowling
978-0-9806288-1-4   The Infernal BY Kim Wilkins
978-0-9806288-5-2   Dead Sea Fruit BY Kaaron Warren
978-0-9806288-7-6   The Girl With No Hands BY Angela Slatter
978-0-9807813-0-4   Dead Red Heart ED Russell B. Farr
978-0-9807813-3-5   Heliotrope BY Justina Robson
978-0-9807813-6-6   Matilda Told Such Dreadful Lies BY Lucy Sussex
978-1-921857-00-3   Bluegrass Symphony BY Lisa L. Hannett
978-1-921857-07-2   Bread and Circuses BY Felicity Dowker
978-1-921857-23-2   Wild Chrome BY Greg Mellor
978-1-921857-27-0   Midnight and Moonshine BY Lisa L. Hannett & Angela Slatter
978-1-921857-37-9   Prickle Moon BY Juliet Marillier
978-1-921857-41-6   The Bride Price BY Cat Sparks
978-1-921857-45-4   The Year of Ancient Ghosts BY Kim Wilkins
978-1-921857-68-3   Havenstar BY Glenda Larke
978-1-921857-58-4   Everything is a Graveyard BY Jason Fischer

TICONDEROGA PUBLICATIONS EBOOKS

978-0-9803531-5-0   Ghost Seas BY Steven Utley
978-1-921857-93-5   The Girl With No Hands BY Angela Slatter
978-1-921857-99-7   Dead Red Heart ED Russell B. Farr
978-1-921857-94-2   More Scary Kisses ED Liz Grzyb
978-0-9807813-5-9   Heliotrope BY Justina Robson
978-1-921857-98-0   Year's Best Australian F&H EDS Grzyb & Helene
978-1-921857-36-2   Dreaming of Djinn ED Liz Grzyb
978-1-921857-40-9   Prickle Moon BY Juliet Marillier
978-1-921857-92-8   The Year of Ancient Ghosts BY Kim Wilkins
978-1-921857-28-7   Bloodstones ED Amanda Pillar (tpb)

THE YEAR'S BEST AUSTRALIAN FANTASY & HORROR SERIES
EDITED BY LIZ GRZYB & TALIE HELENE

978-0-9807813-8-0   Year's Best Australian Fantasy & Horror 2010 (hc)
978-0-9807813-9-7   Year's Best Australian Fantasy & Horror 2010 (tpb)
978-0-921057-13-3   Year's Best Australian Fantasy & Horror 2011 (hc)
978-0-921057-14-0   Year's Best Australian Fantasy & Horror 2011 (tpb)
978-0-921057-48-5   Year's Best Australian Fantasy & Horror 2012 (hc)
978-0-921057-49-2   Year's Best Australian Fantasy & Horror 2012 (tpb)

WWW.TICONDEROGAPUBLICATIONS.COM

THANK YOU

The publisher would sincerely like to thank:

Elizabeth Grzyb, Janeen Webb, Pamela Sargent, Nick
Stathopoulos, Jack Dann, Jason Fischer, Jason Paulos, Robert
Hood, Jonathan Strahan, Peter McNamara, Ellen Datlow,
Grant Stone, Sean Williams, Simon Brown, Garth Nix,
David Cake, Simon Oxwell, Grant Watson, Sue Manning, Steven
Utley, Lewis Shiner, Lezli Robyn, Talie Helene, Isobelle Carmody,
Stephen Dedman, Felicity Dowker, Terry Dowling, Dirk Flinthart,
Lisa L. Hannett, Kathleen Jennings, Martin Livings, Penelope
Love, Jason Nahrung, Angela Slatter, Anna Tambour, Kaaron
Warren, Cat Sparks, Donna Maree Hanson, Pete Kempshall,
Karen Brooks, Jeremy G. Byrne, Kim Wilkins, Marianne de
Pierres, Bill Congreve, Lucy Sussex, the Mt Lawley Mafia,
the Nedlands Yakuza, Shane Jiraiya Cummings, Angela Challis,
Kate Williams, Andrew Williams, Kathryn Linge, Al Chan, Alisa
and Tehani, Mel & Phil, Jennifer Sudbury, Paul Pryztula, Helen
Grzyb, Hayley Lane, Georgina Walpole, Rushelle Lister, Nerida
Fearnley-Gill, everyone we've missed . . .

. . . and you.

IN MEMORY OF
Eve Johnson (1945–2011)
Sara Douglass (1957–2011)
Steven Utley (1948–2013)